RAINY FACES

by
ERALIDES E. CABRERA

Gotham Books

30 N Gould St.
Ste. 20820, Sheridan, WY 82801
https://gothambooksinc.com/

Phone: 1 (307) 464-7800

© 2025 *Eralides E. Cabrera*. All rights reserved.

No part of this book may be reproduced, stored in a retrieval system, or transmitted by any means without the written permission of the author.

Published by Gotham Books (May 31, 2025)

ISBN: 979-8-3493-8551-3 (P)
ISBN: 979-8-3493-8552-0 (E)

Because of the dynamic nature of the Internet, any web addresses or links contained in this book may have changed since publication and may no longer be valid.

The views expressed in this work are solely those of the author and do not necessarily reflect the views of the publisher, and the publisher hereby disclaims any responsibility for them.

I can't imagine the horror of that tragic day.
Souls suddenly being ripped out of their
Physical bodies.
For each soul I pray,
That their spirit enters the next plain
With ease.
Not staying attached to this earth,
Because of this tragedy.
All mankind is able to see,
The cost we've paid to be free.

Lost Souls, Dioris L. Arlequin, 2005.

To my friends, Karl Cramer and
Ines de la Flor Cramer

Table of Contents

Chapter 1 1
Chapter 2 36
Chapter 3 73
Chapter 4 108
Chapter 5 139
Chapter 6 175
Chapter 7 208
Chapter 8 238
Chapter 9 292

Chapter 1

"Ride along," Margaret said. "Fear is for the old. It's rife among the weak. But not in us. We live and die in danger. As they say, those who live by the sword will die by the sword." Robin nodded.

"Well, that's us. We will die by the sword because we sure live by it."

She gleamed with a smile, short and thin-lipped.

"Where are we going?" Robin said.

"Just ride along. Morning will be coming soon. We need to find shelter."

She chuckled and turned away, throttling up her bike's engine. The thundering sound sent vibrations to the windows of the Cape Cod house behind them. Margaret was riding a maroon Harley, model FLSTF Fat Boy and Robin; behind her, a happy blue customized Sportster.

"Don't fall back too far, girl. Stay on course."

Robin slowly got her left foot on the foot rest. She released the clutch and her bike rolled down the driveway, following Margaret's. Margaret's engine roared and she was off like a dart out of the sloping driveway and into the street. She bent her upper body sideways, as she turned left, picking up speed. She rode to the end of the block and braked at the stop sign.

Robin came not as fast and stopped behind her, waiting to make the turn.

"Pretty manta, what do you see? A little mermaid in the sea. Well, that could be me, just really, silly old me."

Margaret sang into the wind. Her voice carried over the sound of the engines.

"Poetic," Robin yelled from behind.

"No, prophetic."

Her black hair hung loosely over her shoulders almost covering her breasts. She wore a tight black blouse and black pants that cuffed over her high black leather boots. She took a left at the intersection and sped uphill on the road, her engine roaring with fury again. Robin rode close behind, trying to keep up. The autumn wind was chilly at this time of night and it seemed to cut razor sharp through the women's cheeks.

"Ohoooo!" Margaret hollered, her voice now barely audible to Robin.

The two bikes rolled up the road, one shortly after the other. Margaret's black attire and black helmet made her hardly visible in the darkness. The potent Harley seemed to be missing a driver with its silver-colored double wall back exhaust pipes and its twin white engines. A cool breeze swept from the east. The two headlights of an upcoming vehicle flashed its high beams as it got close to them.

"Can't you see we're coming?" Margaret yelled. "What are you, blind?"

The vehicle's horn echoed ahead of them, then at their sides and finally to their rear as it passed them.

"What's he beeping at?" Robin asked.

"Who knows? Jerk! Just follow me."

They went up about another mile on the road, now leveled, before Margaret slowed down. She turned left into a side street without making a full stop. Robin yanked her right foot on the brake but couldn't make it on time. She went past the intersection. She stopped for a moment. She could hear the sound of Margaret's engine gradually dying in the distance.

She dragged her bike back with her feet and checked her rear and then ahead before making a U-turn. She throttled up her engine and turned right at the intersection. The street she was on was short. It connected to a major local highway. She was moving slowly at a walking pace, looking for any sign of Margaret's bike. She reached the end of the street. The traversing highway seemed busy tonight with lots of cars zooming by. Robin stopped at the corner. The lampposts at each side of the intersection flooded the area with light. The town had them installed at the insistence of Tarzan Motors, a used car dealer located at the southeastern corner. The dealer wanted the area well-lit to keep teenagers from roaming around the car lot. Robin rolled up slowly into the lot, her feet dangling free from the footrests and stomping the ground to brake the bike. She stood up above the seat and perked her head to glance through the rows of neatly polished Hondas and Toyotas. She moved sideways trying to get a glimpse but saw nothing. She stopped at the last row and got ready to turn back into the street but first looked at the corner across. There was a Jiffy-Lube on that spot. Robin accelerated slightly and swiveled the front of her bike's wheel to turn it around. She gave the engine some thrust and rolled back down. She hadn't gone more than ten feet when out of the darkness Margaret's bike sprung out down the south side of the street, its engine thundering. She came up unexpectedly and carelessly, oblivious as to any traffic. Robin quickly jammed her brakes to avoid a collision. Margaret passed near her front wheel and then arched a turn to stop almost at a parallel position to Robin. Robin was taken aback. Margaret's face was white as snow and blood was dripping down from her lips. A dark leather object was hanging from her neck.

"What happened?" Robin asked, alarmed.

"Ride along," Margaret said, laughing, as if Robin's question had been a joke.

Margaret's engine roared. Her rear tire grazed the pavement and she was off again. Robin turned to follow her. Something on the side of the road, where Margaret had emerged from, got her attention. The dark empty stretch next to the car lot was eerily silent. Two bizarre figures dangled loosely from the open doors of a convertible, their heads thrown back against the doors, oozing blood that dripped into the pavement.

"Margaret!" Robin called, "Margaret!"

But Margaret was way ahead. She had turned into the highway and Robin could hear her engine going in the distance. Robin made the turn into the highway gracefully, probably as gracefully as she had never before. She felt agitated and anxious to catch up to her friend. She worked her bike's engine to a fury. She saw the amber light at the first intersection on the highway and sped to beat it but could not make it. She stepped on the brake pedal, coming to a dry halt, almost under the light. She looked ahead and saw Margaret crossing the highway from the intersection's jug handle. She was going south, in the opposite direction. Seeing no traffic, Robin quickly turned left, around the divider, and then sped in a southerly direction to catch up. She came alongside Margaret at the next light. Margaret was sitting calmly on her seat, singing out loud with her very raspy voice.

"Faces come out of the rain, when you're strange. When you're strange. When you're strange. Da, da, da, da."

"Margaret! Margaret! Those people back there! Did you see them?"

"Let go, Robin. Let go."

"What happened back there?"

Just then the light went green and Margaret's engine roared. This time Robin kept up, riding right alongside of her on the next lane.

"Margaret! Margaret! They're dead!"

"That all depends on what you call dead, Robin. Dead giving life to the living is not dead."

Her face was clear now and that made Robin look again. Margaret had a smirk on her face as she looked ahead under the black helmet.

"Margaret, did you . . .?"

Robin's words were drowned under the sound of Margaret's engine, which stormed loudly as she sped away. Robin found herself struggling to catch up. She came across a slow-moving car in her lane and she switched to the left. They came to another red light and

Robin tried to get close but as soon as she came beside her the green switched on and Margaret was off again like a bat out of hell. They did not run into any more lights. Gradually, the highway stretched out into a country area where the penumbras of the dying night engulfed the road making it seem like a dark tunnel. Robin was now riding parallel to Margaret. She saw her begin to merge into the exit to the left of the highway and she followed instinctively. They were entering Route 9 and ran into a red light about two miles down.

"Margaret!"

"Robin, we're almost there. Just follow me. Next exit we take the jug handle."

"But Margaret . . ."

The roar of Margaret's engine drowned her words. Robin was following her a short distance behind. They seemed to be going on a slight downward slope and Robin imagined that the scenery would be magnificent if it was only daylight.

Margaret's bike swayed sideways with grace as she got off on an exit, then came around to cross the highway, and then went straight. The road was a single lane and Robin had to keep pace behind her. Robin could see nothing on the sides. Every now and then she ran across the silhouette of a house, standing lonely and quiet in the meadows of this New Jersey dawn. She began noticing the first signs of dew when suddenly Margaret's bike slowed down and her brake lights came on. Robin slowed almost to a stop and followed her. They went on a short dirt road and Margaret rode her bike under a tree. Robin stopped behind her.

"What are we doing?"

"Look behind you," Margaret said. "Here's home."

Robin turned to gaze at the bulky shadow behind them. It was a house with the trace of a faint light at a window.

"Park your bike," Margaret said. "It needs the rest."

Robin saw her take her helmet off and dismount. She gently brought her bike into one of the motorcycle stands lined up in a row under a large tree, getting both tires into the groove and locking the bike on the swivel caster. Robin counted six other bikes parked in other stands.

"Margaret, those people out there . . ."

"Come inside," she said. "Follow me."

Margaret hung her helmet on the tip of one of her handlebars and walked casually towards the house. It was still dark but Robin could see her long hair, black or brown, parting at the back of the neck. Robin followed her. They reached the door at the end of a stone walkway with high ferns on both sides. Margaret was opening the front door as Robin looked up. It was a big house, large and high, with long rectangular windows, a long balcony on the second floor and a gambrel roof. It was like the old north eastern houses built with finesse, under the guidance of Dutch or Scandinavian workers who had immigrated to America in the late nineteenth century and whose culture had somehow prevailed in these prairies. Robin felt it was different. It was unlike any other house she had seen before.

"You're not just going to stand there and look at the roof, are you? Come on in."

"No, of course not," Robin said, finally taking a step forward and coming inside. The house had no foyer and one walked straight into a spacious living room furnished with an upholstered green love seat and three armchairs also green. A tall shade lamp by a window had been left on. There was a bookshelf to the right side of the room that occupied the entire wall. It was replete with books. To the left was a long wooden stairway that went into the upper floor. Margaret walked confidently across the room through an open door at the end. Robin followed her. A short hallway connected the dining room and kitchen. Margaret went into the kitchen, also a large room equipped with beautiful oak cabinets. She opened one of the cabinet doors and took out a can of coffee.

"How do you like your coffee, Robin?"

Robin was still looking around the room and not hearing her.

"Robin, how do you like your coffee?"

"Oh, I don't. . . I don't drink coffee," she said, looking startled.

"So what shall you have? Nothing?"

"Chocolate?"

"Hot chocolate, right?"

"Yes. Actually, I can make it myself."

"No, sit down. Rest. I'll do it."

She set a strainer on top of the electric coffee pot and poured a teaspoonful of coffee inside. She added water and let it brew. She opened two cabinet doors at the same time, spreading her arms wide, and began fidgeting through the contents until she found a pack of chocolate powder. Robin had retreated into a small kitchenette table and sat in one of the white cushioned chairs. She gazed around the olive wallpapered room. She still felt agitated.

"Margaret, those people out there. I . . ."

They heard the clamor of several footsteps rushing downstairs and walking towards the kitchen. The first one to enter the room was a tall, slim young girl with shaggy, jet- black hair. The other two, dressed in black, like the first one, were older, probably in their thirties, and wore their long hair loose and frizzed.

"Margaret, what do we have here?" the first girl said.

All three had come to stand around the kitchen table and smiled furtively at Robin. What Robin found most noticeable was their very white faces, looking as if white powder had been meticulously sprayed on them.

"That's Robin," Margaret said, turning around. Robin noted their similar complexion.

"Robin, that is Linda," she said, pointing to the tall girl who had been first to enter the room. "That one there is Donna and that one is Flora. All virgins of the night," she said and laughed.

"Nice meeting you," Robin said grimly.

"There are some men around," the girl named Linda said. "They'll be down in a minute."

She said it as if in answer to a question and Robin nodded as Linda reached out and grabbed her hand to shake it.

"They're about to go to sleep but you'll get to meet them," Flora said, taking Robin's hand from Linda's. Then Donna grabbed it.

"Men are an important part of our lives here. We couldn't live without them."

"I'm not really sure Robin is interested in your men craving," Margaret said quickly. "Girls, any coffee?"

"Smells too good to say no," Flora said, and reached for four mugs from inside one of the cabinets.

"I have Robin already," Margaret said, smiling. "We only need three."

Flora reached back with one of her long arms and returned one of the mugs into the cabinet.

"How do you have her?" she asked, smiling back.

Her face was long, with bony features and reddish skin that seemed to glow under the oval light of the ceiling fan. She had freckles on her exposed shoulders.

"With chocolate," she said. "Hot chocolate. She prefers that over coffee."

"Really, Robin?" Donna said behind Flora, as if the conversation had been between them all along.

"What does that tell you about a person?" Linda said before Robin could answer.

"She's savvy," Donna quickly said.

She probably could have passed for Flora's sister. Her face was freckled and had long wavy hair with touches of blonde.

"Right," Linda said. "She knows not to drink coffee at this hour."

"She wants to sleep peacefully throughout the day," Donna added almost simultaneously.

"There's caffeine in chocolate too," Flora said.

"Not as much," Linda retorted.

"It's the best of the two choices," Donna said.

"Did Margaret give her a choice?" Flora asked.

She stood next to Margaret, her back against the counter. Margaret turned and placed a steaming mug of hot chocolate on the kitchen table by Robin.

"Of course, I gave her a choice. I always do."

The other three looked at each other with an expression of awe. They heard rushed footsteps coming down the stairway.

"The men are coming," Linda said.

"They're here," Donna rectified.

The three young men were of the same height, with straight brown hair and very white skin like the women's.

"John, Zeke and Randall, Margaret said, introducing them.

All three walked directly towards Robin and took turns shaking her hand.

"A little crowded in here," John said.

He led the other two into the room in a row. He had black eyes and an energetic-looking face. The second one, Zeke, had square shoulders and a pleasant smile that showed itself from the moment he walked into the room. Randall, the last one, seemed older, with some streaks of gray in his brown hair. His face had been scarred on the left cheek.

"Let's move into the living room," Margaret said and grabbed her coffee mug. She had served the other girls. "You guys want coffee?"

"At this hour?" The one named Zeke said.

"Want it or not?"

"We'll take it," John said.

"Go to the living room," Margaret said again.

"How's your chocolate?" she asked Robin who was still sitting at the kitchen table.

"Nice and warm," she said looking up.

"Go ahead and join them. You're not really thinking of staying here by yourself, are you?"

Robin was sipping chocolate from her mug. She looked up at Margaret.

"No, I guess not."

"Go ahead. I'm bringing cups for these guys."

She got up slowly from the table with some hesitation.

"Margaret . . . I . . ."

"Go ahead, Robin. I'll be there in a minute."

"Robin, come on," Linda said, peeking into the room from the door.

Robin pushed her chair in and walked out of the kitchen.

The others were sitting in the center of the room, on the carpeted floor, with legs crossed, the three women holding their mugs. Linda sat in between Flora and Donna, leaving space for Robin.

"Sit down," she said and tapped the floor next to her. "Relax."

"It's urgent that you do," Flora said.

"It could be life saving," Donna said and laughed.

Robin remained standing for just a moment longer while the men who were sitting across from the women egged her on.

"You need to get loose," John said. "We can see the stress on your face."

She came down clumsily and bent her knees upward as she sat down.

"Let go," Randall said, grabbing her legs and crossing them. Robin looked at him and smiled faintly. She took a sip from her mug.

"Where's home for you?" Flora asked, moving her head forward.

"Cape May."

"Long way," Donna said.

"It's so serene there. I like it," Linda said.

"You rode your bike all the way up here?" John asked casually.

"Yes."

Margaret walked into the room carrying a tray. She handed each of the men a cup of coffee. Robin took the time to survey the room. There was a large screen TV against the wall behind the men. On top of it hung a tapestry in gray and black colors depicting a wolf posed for howling. His nose pointed towards the silver clouds and his mouth showed a row of shiny-looking teeth. Robin kept her eyes on the image. The others noticed it.

"You like our wolf?" Flora said.

"Does he scare you?" Donna said.

"Don't be scared," Zeke said. "He never hurt anyone."

They all laughed except Linda.

"Margaret," she called, "it's time."

Margaret had retreated from the group as she drank her coffee and observed them. Her face looked windswept.

The group gazed up at her. Robin was still lost on the wall tapestry. Margaret went towards them holding her coffee cup in her hand. She came to the middle of Zeke and Randall and then sat down on the floor, cross-legged.

"We want to thank you for this evening, Margaret. We all do," Linda said.

"It was a great night," Margaret said. "We've found a novelty."

"Have we?" Linda asked.

"Don't you see her? She's beautiful. She's a fine specimen, tall with silky brown hair that flies in the wind. Imagine that."

They knew she was describing Robin. Linda kept on.

"Do you trust her, Margaret? Does she know?"

"She'll know soon enough."

Robin froze. Her cup was on her lips as she was about to take a sip.

"What's this all about?" she said. "What are you people into? Some kind of sect?"

"You can call it by any name you like, Robin. We'd just rather be thought of as friends, survivors."

Margaret took a drink from her cup and then turned her back to Robin. Robin got up and walked around the circle to face Margaret. She was wearing her black boots over her pants, which made her look taller than she was. As she stood a few feet away from Margaret and over the backs of Flora and Donna, she seemed quite an imposing figure.

"Tell me something, Margaret. Did you kill those people out there? Did you do it?"

"It's none of your business if she did," Linda replied curtly.

"Wait a minute," John said, intervening. "Let her ask whatever she wants."

"That's right," Margaret said. "Let her ask. Let her ask all she wants. Tell me, Robin, what do you want to know? What exactly do you want to know? I'll give you all the answers you want. Just shoot."

"I wanna know who killed those people at the car dealer lot.

Their heads were hanging from the car windows, nearly decapitated. I saw blood in your lips."

"You're a very observant," Margaret said. "I like observant people. They're not just crowd followers. They watch, take interest, and ask. That's good.

Kill? You mentioned the word kill. That I can't answer. I just don't know what that means and neither does anyone else in this room. You can have a nice life, Robin, wear whatever clothes you like, look sexy or dull, ride your bike in the middle of a storm. Nobody is gonna care. It makes no difference to anyone. But you just have to take care of the bare necessities. You must feed to survive."

Robin had a look of disbelief. Her right arm holding the mug seemed to have frozen in midair. She stared blankly at their faces. Slowly she began to sense danger. She found herself a stranger in a house of people she did not know. She considered herself a resilient person, not afraid. She was a young woman in her mid-twenties who loved adventure and bikes. She had learned to decode and look beyond stereotypes. Women who rode bikes were not necessarily lesbians. They could be ladies like anyone else. Bikers did not have to be tattooed or take drugs to ride. They could just do it for sports or for freedom, as she did. She rode for freedom because she loved life and what it had to offer. But she had never before encountered such a situation. There was a certain aura of darkness about these people. There was something lifeless about them, something that had to do with death. She didn't like it. She didn't like what she was hearing and up to now she had been willing to pass up the others as plain horseplay.

People who got caught up in a certain style of living and hung on to it desperately, as drunks hang on to alcohol. But she couldn't pass up Margaret. She was not a joke. Robin kept seeing her face in her mind, smiling with glee, and oozing blood like a lioness that has just devoured her prey. Linda broke the brief silence.

"You shouldn't have trusted her, Margaret."

"Why not? Robin is our friend. Right now, she's our guest. What's there that's not true?"

"I don't like it," Linda said, giving Robin the eye.

"Cool it," Margaret said. "What else would you like to know, Robin?" She took another sip from her mug. "Why did you hurt them?" Robin asked bluntly.

She was surprised by her own demeanor. The words just sprang out of her mouth naturally as if she was being guided by an internal radar.

"Hurt who, Robin? Who did I hurt?"

"Those people out there in the car lot. I saw them. I saw your face smudged with their blood. It was dripping from your lips as if you had slashed them with your own teeth. And then I saw them, or what remained of them, dangling from the car windows. You murdered them."

"Robin," she said, shaking her head, "you don't understand. You're rushing into judgment without knowing what you're talking about, honey."

"I gave you plenty of time to answer, didn't I?"

"I told you, you shouldn't have trusted her," Linda said again.

She got up quickly, her black eyes locked into Robin's, glaring with ire.

"Sit down," Margaret said.

"No, I'll take care of her for you. You should have never brought her in here."

"Sit down!"

Margaret made a jerky movement with her head to look at Linda. She suddenly became tense, demanding all the attention in the room. Linda sat back down quietly.

"Robin, you're upset, honey. You don't know what you're saying."

"I know damn well what I'm saying."

"I didn't hurt anybody, honey. Can't you understand?

Those people weren't hurt. The gazelles in the jungle, are they hurt when the leopard pierces their jugular with their canines? Of course not. They don't feel a thing. It's a natural act, like a tree that must fall to make timber. It's a natural process."

"Natural? You say natural? I say you're just bloody sick.

The whole bunch of you. What the heck do you mean natural? You feed off people, like beasts in the jungle. I say you're nothing but a murderer, Margaret, a cold-blooded murderer."

"Now what?" Linda yelled, looking at Margaret. "You're still gonna let her be after she's insulted all of us. Maybe you won't do anything but I will."

She made a move to pick up her feet but Margaret grabbed her arm quickly before she could get up.

"Stay put," Margaret said. "Haven't I taught you manners? We don't mistreat our guests. Robin is just confused. She's a confused young woman who hasn't experienced lust. She needs to be broken in, don't you see?"

"I'm not confused," Robin said and turned to put her cup away.

She looked around for a table. The rest of the room behind her was dark and she hesitatingly reached for the mantel on top of the brick hearth and placed the cup on it. Robin had not noticed it when she first came into the room. She had spent long minutes examining the room and yet she had missed it.

She felt disappointed with herself all of a sudden. Then she looked back at the group with Margaret sitting in the middle of them holding her mug to her lips. Robin had a fleeting thought about the contents in Margaret's cup. Was it coffee or chocolate? Silly, she thought. Of course it's coffee. Margaret made the first cup for herself and only made her chocolate when Robin asked for it. She began to walk away, heading for the door.

"I'm anything but confused," she said. "I'm not..."

She saw the room spin around her head. Suddenly she couldn't see anything, just darkness in front of her as if the last remnants of the night had abruptly crept into the room. She heard the thud of her head hitting the carpeted floor as she fell.

"I'm not confused," she wanted to say but the words wouldn't come out.

The first signs of dawn were filtering in through the Venetian blinds in the room but Robin would never see them. Her voluptuous body, long legged and wide hipped, was sprawled on the floor with legs spread eagle. Her long brown hair was flung around her face in disarray.

The autumn sun came up gently in the early morning, caressing the assortment of colorful leaves among the trees that grow abundantly in Englishtown this time of year. The soft cool breeze rushed in from the east, sporadically blowing dry leaves off the ground and creating a misty feeling in the air, as if surreal. It seemed as if the natural elements could converse with each other in a very subtle way, agreeing on what picture to paint and on what mood to convey. The large brown house, located at the foot of Maple Street in town, seemed perfectly suitable to this scenery as it stood serenely in the wide strip of land with a scant garden, mainly made of ferns and dark green ivy. A few feet to the rear was the bikes' parking spaces, set tight under a pine tree and with several bikes. Beyond this point, the foliage became dense and rows of pine trees and other evergreens grew so abundant that the area became an abundant huge meadow, a forest yard.

The area was known for its country homes and large acreage lots. You could still find home grown potatoes and plenty of cornfields in Englishtown. Hunters looking for rabbits and other small game could still be seen during the weekends prying the wooded areas. But the town had also achieved national notoriety through its local racetrack, attracting aficionados from all over the world who came to test their powerful engines and show off their car designs. The gigantic four-wheel drives could be heard roaring miles away as they plowed easily through mountains of metal rubber and jumped over flaming wreckage. There was a flavor of modern age to Englishtown mixed with a country background. The town had embraced progress and somehow managed to retain its original rural roots. Its small community enjoyed the best of two worlds, where crime was an oddity and the comforts of urban life were yet easily available. Maple Street was an untraveled road, to the west of the center of town. Most of the homes in the area were built on large acreage lots and accessible only from dirt driveways that sometimes spun a long distance into the woods before reaching a door. Privacy was well guarded. There was nothing unusual about a host of bikers, male or female, living in the old Victorian house at the end of the street. Some of the local residents knew it as the McCarter house because it had been built and occupied by that family since late in the nineteenth century. Stories had once floated around that the old patriarch McCarter, an able engineer, had custom built the house for his recluse wife and large entourage of children with the single purpose of keeping it in his family forever, as he understood the term. He built the house with all the amenities that nineteenth century engineering could offer so that its occupants would never need to leave it even for a trip into the local theater. The house had one. Whether by coincidence or a strange toss of fate, the McCarter wish had become true. The house was still a McCarter's, even after more than one hundred years after it was built. Restored and brought to modern standards by subsequent generations in the family, it still preserved its original imposing look, a wrap-around balcony on the second floor, long, rectangular windows following each other in close succession. William McCarter would have been proud if he could have seen his creation withstand time. It had survived, or better said, it had preserved time and its people, which had been his dream.

It was late afternoon when the young woman lying on the carpeted floor finally showed signs of life. Her beautiful body had lain sideways, resting on her right shoulder and hip. She moved her face slightly from side to side and stretched her legs. She opened her eyes and moved the strands of hair that covered her face. The room looked foreign to her and for a few seconds she could not remember how she got there. She sat up, holding her temples, as if believing that the pressure of her fingertips on her brain could bring her memory back. She had been in a deep sleep. She remembered the lonely ride in her bike from the Jersey shore, how she had met a group of friends in a central New Jersey town and then rode with them up north and back. She had met someone new—a new female rider who had shown up in the host's house. Robin was unsure how she was connected to them, but she had proved to be an able rider, cheerful and fearless. Robin had liked her and agreed to ride with her on her way south for a quick stop at her home. Everyone had told her not to miss an opportunity to see the McCarter house. They had said it was a landmark.

She remembered the others, several young men and women who had sat in a circle as if performing some bizarre ceremony. And she remembered something terrible too. She had seen the figures of people in the dark of night, bludgeoned to death by someone. She remembered seeing the woman's face, sadistic and bloody, as a panther after her kill. She remembered her name, Margaret.

Robin got up trembling. The gentle rays of the autumn afternoon sun filtered through the windows behind her, to the side of the hearth. She turned and looked around. A bookshelf filled the entire one side of the room, running from the front door all the way to the far wall. She caught a glimpse of the red oak front door and thought about running away. Her bike was outside. But she couldn't. She needed to know what had happened, who was here, and who these people were. She saw the stairway on the other side of the room but decided to check the entire bottom level first. She went into the kitchen. There was no sign of life. The sink was empty, and the kitchen counter was clean. It was as if no one had been here. Then she walked into the dining room where she saw a long rectangular cherry wood table and a matching china closet with prism glass. The walls were paneled in a light shade of cherry wood and right at the center of the ceiling hung a tear drop gold chandelier that dropped low at the center of the table. Despite her anxiety, Robin couldn't help but admire the room. It was that beautiful. She found another door that led directly into the living room. She went through it and climbed the stairway into the second floor. The brown wooden steps squeaked as she walked cautiously over them and she remembered the previous night when she heard the men and women descend noisily through them. She stopped at a landing on top of the stairs and looked at both sides. There were mahogany doors a few feet apart through the entire length of the hallway, symmetrically situated. Robin went left and turned the knob on the first door. The room was nicely furnished in Victorian style. The bed, sitting in almost at the center of the room, was canopied. The window at the end had soft white curtains tied with ribbons at the center, allowing plenty of daylight in the room. Robin walked inside and looked around. There was a single panel door, past the entrance of the room and Robin opened it. A few women's clothes hung inside. She went by the window and opened the door next to it. It led into a balcony. She looked down and saw several bikes parked under a big tree. Her bike was a few spots from the end and she felt relieved. She thought about just running down the stairs and getting away. But something held her back. Who were these people? Where were they?

She went back into the hallway and opened the next door. The room was exactly like the first one; it had the same type of furniture and the same setup. She looked everywhere—still nothing. Still could not see anything. She checked the next room, which was the last one on that side of the hallway and found nothing. Then she checked the doors past the stairway. There were three more rooms and the first two were exactly the same. The last bedroom wrapped itself around the entire east wing of the house. It had several windows, and the bed, sitting in the center of the floor, was exquisitely made with a red comforter and long red pillows under a high headboard. The wall-to-wall carpeting was also red. Robin stared at the furniture, looking for signs of life. She walked over the lopped portion of the room and found a door. She opened it and noticed a coiled wooden stairway that went up to a third floor. She hesitated for a moment but then began climbing the steps, trying subconsciously not to make any racket with her high-heeled boots. She came to a large area finished all in wood, from floor to ceiling, running the entire width of the house, with windows on both sides. It was busily furnished and had a Persian rug in the center. She walked until the end and found a door in the middle of the wall. She opened it and saw a room exactly like the one she was in that ran to the other end of the house. She stood there for a few moments surveying the area but saw no one. She turned back and went downstairs again, through the bedroom and into the hallway. She felt no fear at the moment, just an insatiable desire to know where the people had gone. As she reached downstairs, she looked up at the stairway and stood still. There was no sound. The entire house was, she decided, momentously lonely. She felt for the keys in the front pocket of her pants, took them out and opened the front door. She went under the tree, got on her bike, put on her helmet, and clicked the engine on. She looked back at all the windows behind her to see if the noise of the engine would get someone's attention but no faces appeared. She took a few steps back, dragging the bike, then she throttled up the engine and got on the road. Robin McManus was an only daughter. Her father had been an able biker and her mom a beautician. Robin had grown up alone with her mother after her father died in a motorcycle accident when she was five years old. Her mother closed the shop and moved from East Brunswick, a town in the central part of the state, to Cape May where her parents had retired. It was a lovely environment for a child to grow up in the early eighties. There was a personal touch in your everyday life, fewer children to one teacher, a more intimate relationship with your neighbors. You could feel the ocean breeze as you strolled outside your door and smell the salt in the air. It was a feeling Robin got so used to that she came to take it for granted. She grew up thinking that it was like that in the rest of the world. She was, of course, mistaken. But it was impossible for her to think that people just walked around without feeling the soft sea breeze caressing their faces. So when, as a teenager, she first visited the metropolitan areas in the north, she immediately felt there was something amiss. She couldn't identify what it was but felt the difference. It was an odd feeling of absence, like the one you get when someone is rubbing your back for a long time and then stops. When she returned home, she knew that she could never live anywhere far from the ocean. But she had her father's spirit and physical resilience. She had been a long-distance runner in High School and had been involved in just about any sport she could lay her hands on. Like most kids her age, she went for her learner's permit at sixteen and got her driver's license at seventeen. But the real driver's license, the one she truly longed for, she couldn't get until she became eighteen. It was her mother's nightmare. She had worked arduously to keep her daughter away from motorcycles to the point where she forbade her from ever riding one. And there she was, a few days after her eighteenth birthday, waving the plastic card at her friends when she thought her mother wasn't looking. Robin had gotten her motorcycle driver's license. The next step would be to see her riding and it didn't take her long. Robin saved not for a car but for a motorcycle. Her mother stood helplessly in their home's driveway one evening as she saw the Harley drive up and take a spot behind her own car. Robin was her father's child.

Heading south on the Garden State Highway, Robin leaned her head back slightly to hear the sound of the wind gliding through her cheeks. She looked at the long highway stretching ahead and thought about the night before. She had been impressed with Margaret McCarter. Margaret was witty and she appreciated witty people. She was great fun at the party, keeping the conversation animated and making herself very noticeable. She was a tall woman with long dark hair, probably in her forties, but who had firm, shapely limbs. Robin would have never guessed she was a biker. Her crew gave her away. They were all experienced riders, the ones you can pick out among a motley crowd. Robin kept thinking about last night. Before she passed out and the lights had gone dark, she thought she had seen them riding, or was it in the afternoon. She saw the group in her dreams, gathered outside and each one took their bikes, it came as no surprise. It happened that as they got on the highway, Margaret started to take the lead, not only on the road, but also in authority. That was a dangerous thing to do for a biker among a circle of friends who had been riding together for years. Nothing could rattle a group of bikers more than a shift in leadership. But somehow, Margaret got away with it and that impressed Robin. But there was something very persuasive about Margaret, something that delighted her listeners and made them trust her. Perhaps that was what Robin had seen the night before, a demonstration of Margaret's influence over the others who seemed to revere her.

On her way home, Robin rode her bike at a steady pace, about five miles under the speed limit. She moved back on her seat and relaxed, watching the road. She could hardly hear the radio with the sound of the engine roaring. Slowly, two other bikes came close to her in the middle lane. They were two men on red Kawasaki bikes, their engines shrieking as if on their last breath. As they came to be parallel to Robin, one of them waved and Robin waved back. Both wore full face open helmets with full graphics, one of the iron-cross, another of the rebel yell. Both wore dark glasses. The one on the lead yelled out to her. Robin could barely hear him.

"How far are you headed?"

"Cape May."

"Wanna ride together?"

"No, I'm okay," she declined politely.

He raced his engine so loud that it drowned out the sound of the other one. The bike stalled for a fraction of a second while the thrust of power disseminated through the engine. Then, its front wheel raised a few degrees, and the entire assemblage darted forward at incredible speed, with the rider bent forward over the handlebars. The other bike followed him shortly behind.

"Way to go," Robin said, knowing she couldn't hear even herself. "That engine has a short life ahead."

She stayed on the slow lane of the parkway, moving slightly under the speed limit and stopping only at the toll booths to pay the fare. It was dark when she finally reached the end of the parkway or exit 0 as people jokingly called it. She got on Lafayette and then turned east, making several turns. Her mother's street looked dark and deserted at this time of evening. The historic district of town, close to the harbor, was skirted mostly by colonial homes and every now and then an old two-floor Victorian that looked forlorn, as if nothing had happened in its confines for the past two hundred years. The robust sound of Robin's engine seemed an oddity in this tranquil setting. She throttled the engine as she neared the driveway, making noise that was sure to wake any napping head. She eased on the throttle and turned. The pole light by the front steps was already on with a bright white light that flooded the entire walkway among the twirling ivy covering the ground. Robin brought the bike a few feet behind the Ford SUV, parked at the entrance of the garage. She turned the engine off and leaned the bike on the kickstand. She came into the house through a back door after going through the fence gate that surrounded the house. It was a small porch that led into the country-looking kitchen, lit by a ceiling fan light.

"Robin, is that you?" asked the female voice from somewhere in the other side.

"It's me, Mom."

Robin took her helmet off and placed it on the table. She had picked it up last summer at a show and had never lost sight of it since then. It was a full-face open black helmet with a black chin strip. It wasn't fully protective, but Robin had chosen it for its looks.

"How are you doing, honey? How was the party?" her mother asked from an open door in the dining room. She had stepped into the kitchen quietly. Robin had pulled one of the spindle chairs from the table and sat down.

"Fine."

"Robin, what happened to you? You look all bruised." Her mother came near her. She was a tall woman, about 5.10 inches, with short light brown hair. Her face was very white, her skin smooth. She had peering black eyes, long eyelashes and a button-like nose. Nobody would have guessed that she was in her early fifties. She was a strikingly beautiful woman and her body did not seem to show any signs of aging under the blue Levi's and tight white blouse. She carried herself with much energy as she walked to the table. She held Robin's chin in her right hand and moved it sideways to get a better look.

"Nothing happened. I slept on a carpet. It's probably from the position I slept in."

"No way," her mother said. "That's not from laying down, honey. Come and see in the mirror."

"Mom, it's all right. It's nothing."

"How do you know, honey. You haven't even seen it.

That's okay, stay. I'll bring a mirror."

"Mom . . ."

But before she could formulate a protest, her mother was gone. She had walked hastily out of the kitchen into a small hallway on the side that led to the bathroom. She came back with a round makeup mirror.

"See?" she said, pointing to Robin's right jaw in the mirror and then slithering it towards her cheek. "Look at your neck, Robin. Here, you hold it."

She gave her the mirror and gently moved her tee-shirt collar to get a better look at her bruises. They were long black and blue streaks running from the neck up and small light purple blotches on her chin and left cheek.

"Mom, leave it. It's okay."

"You mean to tell me you knew about them, Robin?"

"Yes, Mom, I knew," Robin said, not really knowing why.

Helen McManus had been through a string of short relationships after her husband's death but nothing ever really fit. She weaned down as she got in her forties and now for the most part, she dated no one. She lived for her shop, a small beauty parlor in the historic Washington Mall section of town. She was well known, had a solid reputation, and people of all ages went to her for her golden touch. Men still sought her.

She was too beautiful of a woman to be ignored. But she had made up her mind. There was one most important person in her life and that was her daughter Robin. She had tried enough with relationships. Now she had set her course and lived only for her daughter.

Helen stood silently, trying to sort it all in. So, that's what it was. Robin would not even try to hide them. Shameful. "This is how girls are today," she thought. They don't feel shame. Everything has gone out in the open. And so, her innocent young daughter had broken loose. "Those bikers," she thought, "they're such a bad influence. This is how it always ended with them."

"Robin, the least you can do is be discreet about love marks. It's very unbecoming for a woman."

"Mom," Robin shrilled, shaking her head, "they are not love marks. I wasn't with anybody."

"Then what are they, Robin? They're scary."

"I don't know. I probably got them from the position I fell asleep in."

"You slept on a carpet you said?" "Yes."

"Why?"

"Because I was just tired and dropped."

"Were you drunk?"

"No."

"I know," Helen said. "It's those bikers. You hang around them and you end up in either of three ways, tattooed from head to toe, drunk, or a drug addict. Is that what you want for yourself, Robin? To end up like that? Bikers are nothing but trouble. I despise anything having to do with them."

There was silence for a few seconds as Robin kept trying to pull one of her boots off. She stopped tussling with it momentarily and looked up at her mother.

"You don't really believe that, Mom. You married one."

Helen looked towards the window. She could see the lighted driveway through the organdy cotton white curtains, and her black eyes suddenly seemed reflective.

"He was a different kind of biker," she finally said.

"Still a biker," Robin insisted.

"You don't know what you're saying, Robin."

"Mom, can you help me get my boots off?"

Robin stretched her right foot towards her. Helen reached down and grabbed her heel and the tip of the boot and slowly pulled it off.

"You've got to think about your future, Robin. And there isn't much of that in motorcycles."

Helen set her daughter's foot gently on the floor and picked up her other leg. She struggled for a moment until she pulled the other boot out.

"Have you ever watched American Chopper, Mom? Tell me those guys don't have a future."

"That's just show business, Robin. But back in the real world, motorcycles account for little. What do you have to look forward to as a biker? Tell me. You're going to ride and ride. And then what? What are you going to do after you finish riding? You're back in the same old doggie world that doesn't want you because you're a burden to society. That's the kind of world bikers live in. Time does not sit still, Robin. A couple of more years and you'll be in your mid-twenties. Your life is getting defined, Robin. You've got to come to terms with it. You've got to be prepared for life's inequities. That's what I'm talking about."

"Mom, I'm happy with my life. I don't rob or steal. I hold a steady job and I pay my bills like anybody else. True, I'm not a doctor or a lawyer but who says I need to be one to be happy? I'm happy just the way my life is. And most of all, I'm happy because I got you, Mom."

She looked straight into her eyes as she said it and smiled. It was a benevolent smile, like the smile of a child to her protective mother, the kind she knew could soften her mother's heart.

"Thank you, honey," Helen said, kissing her forehead. "You're everything to me, Robin. Don't you understand? That's why I worry about you so much. I can't help it. Those bikes are a bad influence. Sometimes I wish they didn't exist."

"Mom," Robin said thoughtfully. "When was the last time you rode? I can't remember ever seeing you ride."

"A long time ago," she said briskly.

"Do you know how it feels, Mom? Can you recall the feeling?"

"Yes, I can. But that's not what I'm saying."

"I know what you're saying," Robin said, slightly moving towards the table. Her hazel eyes shone under the light and her long auburn-brown hair hung handsomely in a narrow spread over the back of her neck. She had flat cheekbones, thick, sensual lips, and a chiseled chin.

"Robin, you're so beautiful, you know that?"

"Mom, think about it for a moment. Forget the everyday grind and feel the wind blowing in your face, the road, just stretching ahead as you roll down on it. Isn't it a beauty?"

Helen listened in silence as she held Robin's head by the temples. She looked past her, as if recollecting.

"I know, honey, I know."

"Mom, I'm so hungry," she said, pulling away. "I haven't eaten all day."

"You're joking, Robin."

"No, I fell asleep on the floor of this house and I slept all day. I slept till almost four and then drove here."

"Which house is it, Robin?"

Helen quickly walked to the stove behind Robin and opened the oven door. She retrieved a casserole and turned one of the electric burners on.

"It's this lady I met. She lives in this big house."

"Where did you meet her?"

"At the party. She was a guest there."

"Is she a biker?"

"Yeah, she is. She's pretty good too. She's daring."

"So where's the house? What does it look like?"

"I'm not sure, actually. It's somewhere in central Jersey. I followed her home last night. It's a very intriguing house. Quite big."

"So who does she live with?"

"She lives with some friends, young people. I mean, the house is so big that it could fit a battalion. I think she is the heiress to a big estate, I heard them say. The house is like a landmark in the area."

"It's nice to have money when you didn't work for it."

Helen took a wooden ladle from a set of utensils inside a flowered porcelain holder at the counter and stirred the sauce in the pot. She opened one of the cabinet doors, opened a box of Pipette pasta, and poured some to boil in another pot.

"It's nice to have money any darn way, Mom."

"Specially, if you did not work for it, Robin, when you're born into it. I say that facetiously, of course. It's actually the worst kind of money to have. It spoils you. People that are born into money never get to learn what it took to earn it."

"I wouldn't mind having some."

"I wish I could leave you millions, honey. Unfortunately, when I go, my estate will be small."

"I don't want you to go, Mom, ever. I'll go first."

"Don't say that even kidding, honey," Helen said vehemently, turning behind her. "I couldn't even imagine outliving my child."

There was a momentary silence between them. Helen's cell phone was vibrating on the table.

"Looks like you got a phone call, Mom."

"It's probably a customer. You can answer it, honey."

"Sure?"

"Sure, go ahead."

Robin picked up the small flip top phone and answered.

The female voice on the other end immediately took off, whining about her hair needs and how she had tried desperately to get to Helen's shop all day to no avail. She blamed her husband for all her quandaries. It was his fault for being away. She could never get anything done when he was away or then he was home.

"I think you want my mother," Robin finally said.

She handed the phone to her mother without turning around.

"Yes," Helen said as she stirred the pasta.

"I know Colleen, I know," she said. "But it's not the end of the world. I'm sure it can wait till tomorrow."

She waited, and the voice on the other end ranted so loudly that Robin could hear it from her chair.

"I'll be open for only four hours tomorrow. Ten to two.

That's it. If you're there by ten, I'm sure I'll get to you." She waited a few seconds until the voice faded.

"I'll see you tomorrow, Colleen. Don't worry, you'll survive."

She clicked the phone off and put it back on the table. "Mom, why are your friends so loud?"

"They're not friends, honey. They're acquaintances. They pay the bills."

"It's ridiculous, Mom. Does this lady really think that her hairdo is a cause for concern? Doesn't she have a life?"

"She has a life. She just doesn't know it. She is married and has grown children, but she also suffers from paranoia. Her hair is one of those things that trigger it. She's totally dependent on me. I have a bunch of ladies like that."

Helen took out some greens from the refrigerator and began cutting them up on a shopping board.

"Meatballs and pasta okay with you, Robin?"

"Whatever you have, Mom."

"I went Italian today. After I got home from the shop, I made the meatballs for lunch but never ate them. I had chicken salad instead. I was supposed to get back to the shop and close down, but I guess Irene will have to do it."

"Am I interfering with your day, Mom?"

"Of course, not, honey. Let my manager Irene close shop.

She doesn't mind."

Helen served Robin pasta with meatballs and salad. She placed some silverware on the table and some dressing bottles. Then, she sat on a chair across from her daughter and dialed a number from her cell phone.

"Irene," she said onto the phone, "I'm not going to be able to get back tonight. Just close up shop. We'll catch up tomorrow."

She waited a few moments, listening to her hysteria. "Let them be mad, Irene. I don't care. Anyway, honey, close up shop and go home. I'll be seeing you tomorrow, I guess."

She put the phone down on the table, which was covered with a pink tablecloth embroidered in white at the borders. She rested her right cheek on her open hand.

"So tell me about this house, Robin. What's it like?"

"It's huge, Mom. I've never seen such a big house. It's very Victorian with three floors. There's a lot of wood work in it.

The stairways and balconies are beautiful, all done in dark wood."

"I can picture it, Robin. I actually can picture that house in my mind."

"When did you last go to central Jersey, Mom?"

"Many years ago, honey."

"Would you like to ride with me down there one day?"

Helen looked down at the table, her intense black eyes focused on her daughter's plate. There were things in her past she would rather not talk about. It was too hurtful, too emotional. Cape May had been her savior at a time when she had been mentally torn down. And she had never traveled north of the city again, as if afraid to go into what she considered forbidden territory where the past would overcome her. On her travels, she would always cross the Delaware and fly out of Wilmington or go west towards Philadelphia, not unusual for a Cape May resident to do. But she could have just as easily gone north on the Garden State Parkway and fly from Atlantic City without ever leaving New Jersey. Only she knew the real reason. There was an impenetrable barrier north of her beloved city that she would never cross. Helen McManus knew her boundaries.

"You know, Robin, you be careful out there, honey. Perhaps you shouldn't ride to central Jersey, especially when there is so much to do around Delaware. If you want to ride, you can run across the coastlines and bump into clubs just about in every town you come across. And the whole time you'll have the Delaware Bay following you on your west flank, like a shadow. Try that scenario anywhere else in New Jersey."

"I know, Mom, but I like it up north. I have friends up there. Besides, I get a kick out of their fast-track lifestyle. They have so much energy."

"Robin, you're too much your father's daughter."

She said it without derision. She was him, adventuresome, inquisitive and thirsty for change. And it scared her. She wasn't prepared to deal with it again but knew she had to. She had been living most of her life trying to escape instability, and yet it always seemed that it had landed back at her doorstep.

This time she hadn't chosen it. She could be blamed for picking the wrong man. But this was her daughter, her flesh, and one thing she wouldn't do was deny her. If she had to face that world again, she would.

"Mom, you know you were crazy about him. Stop denying it."

She didn't answer. She watched her eat her pasta slowly, cut up the meatballs in small sections, and reach them one by one like her father used to do. How did she learn to do that? She wondered, where did it come from? Robin had hardly known her father, yet her mannerisms and eating habits were astonishingly similar to those of the man Helen had known and loved as a young girl. Life was remarkable in that way, she thought. He programmed your genes and fed them into your body. The rest was all small potatoes, she thought. No matter what they fed you or how they raised you, a gene was a gene and there was nothing you could do about it. Yet she had spent her life trying to change that.

"What are you doing tonight, Robin?"

"I don't have any plans."

"Not yet. How about sitting by the wharf with me for a while?"

Robin raised her head. Her hazel eyes seemed to glitter under the kitchen light that hung low over the two women's heads.

"Mom, are you feeling all right?"

Helen blinked momentarily, as if ridding herself of an ugly thought.

"Of course I'm all right. I just want to sit by the ocean and feel the water. I miss you."

"Mom, you work too hard."

"I know I do. I don't know what for. It only pays the bills."

"Well, I'll go. I'll sit with you. Aren't you going to have anything?"

"No, nothing after five. Let me go and change. I think I want to look a little more decent. I'm driving by the way."

"No!" Robin said, faking astonishment.

"You didn't really think I'd have it any other way, did you?"

"I was hoping you'd ride with me."

"No way."

She went inside and Robin heard her go upstairs. Robin finished her meal and made her way to the downstairs bathroom. She looked herself in the mirror. The black and blue streaks were really noticeable on the side of her face. She bent her head backwards and traced the thin black line down to her neck. She wondered how she got it. The whole episode at the McCarter house had been so bizarre that she had been trying to block it out of her mind. She tried not to think about what she had seen. But she did. She felt like confiding in someone and telling them the story. The thought of notifying the police had crossed her mind. Hadn't she been witness to a crime? If she could only tell her mother. But she knew she never would. She couldn't.

"Are you ready?" Helen asked, standing by the bathroom door. Robin became startled. "What's the matter, Robin? Are you nervous?"

"No, I'm okay, Mom. Ready for a run through the town with my best friend."

"Hey, I like that, honey. Come on, you're going to have to move your bike. I think I saw it is blocking my car."

"I know. I will."

Helen drove the black SUV into the bay area. She went on Delaware Avenue, turning left on Texas and picking up Route 109 towards the docks. She turned right into the Usher Marina right before the Cape May Canal bridge. She parked her car at the end of the lot bordering the ships' stores and facing the water a few yards away. Evening had set in that Saturday night. The area was now devoid of the summer tourists. Both women got out of the car and walked over the rocky shore to enjoy the outstanding view posed by the eastern waters. Helen loved it there. When her mind was often burdened, she came and sat alone over the rocks, just staring at the slow-moving string of boats careening on the bay and feeling the salty air on her face as though it was a therapy that took her hurting away. The two women stood near each other, each taking a spot over one of the slanting rocks, moist from the salty water in the waves.

"Isn't it beautiful, Mom?" Robin said.

"Gorgeous, honey."

The night had closed in on the ocean. The boats' flickering lights interrupted the subtle blend of water and sky far in the horizon. It was impossible to overlook the attraction posed by the tranquil scenery. Both women felt it and remained silent, engaged in their thoughts.

"Where are you going tonight, Robin?"

"I don't know yet, Mom. Maybe nowhere."

"You got lots of messages in our answering machine. Some are repeated. Did you call anybody while you were away?"

"My cell phone's been off since last night. I haven't checked any of my messages."

"Your cell phone's been off?"

Robin nodded.

"Let me check them now, Mom."

"Here, take my cell phone and call our number. You can retrieve them that way."

Robin flipped the cover open and dialed. Helen leaned her back on the rocky surface and watched the horizon, thinking that for now she needn't worry. Robin had no trip scheduled for that evening. The weather was getting colder, which meant soon, even now, her daughter could not ride anymore. She could feel safe for another season. Next spring, when the winter faded and sea breezes warmed up, making motorcycle riding possible, she would again have to endure the pain of seeing her daughter travel on the busy roads, and she would be worried for her safety.

Robin went through the phone messages one by one as her mother leaned her head back to feel the wind and relaxed. The cool night breeze kept tugging on her hair.

"There must be places in the world where people swim all year around," she said finally, not knowing whether Robin could hear her.

"There are, I'm sure."

"Where? Where would there be such a place?"

"I don't know exactly. Probably in the Pacific Ocean somewhere. Or in the Caribbean islands. It's always warm there."

"Even there," Helen said. "I think people take a break. It's got something to do with the water, not the temperature. I've heard that."

"What happens to their water? Their water is always beautiful and warm."

"Maybe it's a little bit of culture, too. You've got to have a break in the season. People need it. Their lifestyles would otherwise be too monotonous."

"Perhaps that's it."

Robin put the phone down and joined her mother in watching the bay. Neither of them said anything to each other as they stared at the faraway lights of the ships that kept going across the water. They stayed like this for a long time, sedulously watching the bay and not thinking about that evening or tomorrow but only that the bay was there for them and it would always be.

Chapter 2

Kenneth O'Gara was staying at a farm in Lancaster County, Pennsylvania. It had a large farmhouse and barn. It sat on elevated ground about three hundred feet from a twisting highway that ran rampant amongst the rolling hills, now dry corn fields, and trees of different colors and shades that grew in the region. He was lying still on his single bed, his head propped up on two pillows, as he held a large leather version of the King James Bible. He had spent the whole summer in Lancaster, living and working among the thriving Amish communities. What had been a curious encounter at the beginning of his stay was now an everyday occurrence. Daily he would pass one of the conspicuous black and brown horse carriages on the road. In town, he would occasionally have to pull to the left of the lane when passing a couple of Amish women, walking rapidly over the pavement. But it never bothered him. He actually came to admire them and sometimes felt tempted to visit their communities. He found the Amish girls he met attractive under their ever-present bonnets and their long dresses. At times he had thought that perhaps it could work. They were people of God and so was he.

Ken had been born in the cold suburbs of Detroit. When he was five, his family migrated to Chicago where his father's job as an electrician took him. There he finished the tenth grade, but in the mid-nineties, his father's job switched places again, this time to New York City. It was a hard adjustment, but the family bought a house in Yonkers and Ken suddenly found himself without school friends. School became a drag, not knowing anyone, but he found a new attraction. He loved the sound of the motorcycle engines as they sped down on one of the local highways. He could see them from his window.

Sometimes at night when he was lying in his room with the windows closed, he felt the rattle of the glass caused by the deep thrust of a Harley, speeding away on the high bridge. There was something almost mystic about the sound and Ken needed to explore it. But how? His father was an industrial electrician and his money went to support the family. There was not much left after the bills were paid. Ken befriended a kid who had a dirt bike and he let him ride it in the woods on weekends. At sixteen, he got his first job in a supermarket and every penny he made went to his savings account at a local bank. Someday, Ken O'Gara would own his own Harley.

However, among these cravings, Ken developed another interest. One that went almost unnoticed both by him and by his family until one day his mother realized there was no room to set foot in the yard. Ken had turned the grounds into a thick garden of corn, peppers, tomatoes, cabbage, garlic and a host of other vegetables. She thought that would be a whim that would pass soon, but by the end of that summer, there was no doubt in her mind that her son had more than a green thumb. The garden was so elaborate and fruitful that neighbors stopped by in the evenings to admire it. It was unimaginable for a boy of his time. Boys in the nineties did not grow gardens.

Ken's curiosity struck a third time. One day he was leaving school with his biking playmate when he saw a raggedy man preaching in the streets.

"Repent!" he yelled. "Repent to the Lord, and you will have everlasting life."

The sixteen-year-old and his companion were passing him by and they locked eyes with him. Ken instinctively stopped. His friend pulled him by the sleeve of his jacket until he almost dragged him.

"Son, you must read this book," the man said, waving a bible at him.

Ken stood there as his friend tried to get him to go. Somehow, the world was never the same. From then on, he had to know. He had to find out what it was all about.

Ken had been born a Catholic, but he was a non-practicing one. His family attended church during holidays and Christmas was always big at his house. But that was the extent of their religious practice.

Then unexpectedly, at seventeen, Ken became a born-again Christian. He studied the bible and went to church regularly. He became a settled teenager in love with motorcycles and farming and fearful of God. Such inconsistencies were rare in a kid his age, yet he thrived in them. He became skilled with motorcycle engines. His love for farming never waned and after High School, he went to work as a labor hand in the country in Illinois. Wherever he went, he remained a devout Christian who practiced his faith.

Ken had turned down an offer to ride to the West Coast the previous summer. There was nothing he could have wanted more, yet he had already committed himself to work as a farm hand in Lancaster County until autumn. He had to say no.

The invitation had come to him from a young, tattooed rider who lived in southern Pennsylvania and who had taken notice of Ken's impressive mechanical skills. Riders would always welcome a good bike mechanic to go along with them in a cross-country ride. Ken said no with a heavy heart. Perhaps the opportunity would not come again. It was summer and it was the ideal time to go if you lived in the northeast. But he couldn't break his commitment. The west would have to wait.

There was a knock at his door and Ken raised his head to listen.

"Yeah?"

"Ken, it's me, Johnny."

"Hi, Johnny, come on in."

The door to the room opened, and a young man wearing a long-sleeve shirt and brown work shoes came inside. He was tall, slim, and pale-faced. His curly black hair shone under the light bulb in the room. Ken put his Bible down and sat on the bed.

"I knew I'd find you here."

"Not hard to guess, right?" Ken said smiling.

Ken had a boyish look about him. His face was long and proportionate, with a well-defined chin, thin lips, brown eyes and straight black hair. He had wide muscular shoulders, and you could tell he was tall even when he was sitting down. He spoke as if he had known Johnny for a long time.

"They want to know if you could stay another two weeks," Johnny said.

"Really? I was beginning to pack."

"Yeah. They're running a few more cattle this way and they need more hay. You think you are up to it?"

Johnny had a bit of a drawl in his accent. He could have passed for a southerner. He drew his lips tight as he spoke to Ken.

"What happened to the other help?"

"They asked everyone else and nobody wants to stay."

"That's because it will get cold in the next few days. We're hitting October."

"I'll see that you get another room with heat if you stay," Johnny said.

"I can," Ken said, holding his bible tight and dropping his feet on the floor by the side of the bed.

"That's great, Ken. Martha will love it. She likes you a whole lot."

Looking relieved, Johnny stretched his arms and held his hands together above his head. The truth was that it had exasperated him to think Ken would turn him down and he dreaded to go back to his boss empty-handed. He had made a colossal error in leaving Ken for last and he had tried to mend it by playing the scene of an endearing boss. Actually, Martha Francis would not care one way or the other. She had recently become a widow and was going on her first year of running the farm without her husband. She had made Johnny Kelekes her manager, taking a big leap of faith, and did care who would be the one to stay as long as she had a body and the job got done. But her tolerance with Johnny was running low, perhaps the effects of her impromptu decision to fire the previous manager and replace him with Johnny. Johnny had thought much of himself when he got the position. It wasn't so much the money as the coveted status, the ability to tell people what to do.

"Does she really?" Ken asked, tongue in cheek.

Ken looked mischievous, like a second grader who had just played a trick on his teacher and knew he had gotten away with it.

"Yeah. I think we'd all miss you actually. We'd miss the sound of your bike coming up the highway making that rowdy noise."

"I'm glad to be missed. It's usually a good sign." "Well, at least you get to go. Me, I gotta stay here all

winter. How'd you like doing that, ah?"

"No, I guess I wouldn't be too happy about that. There can't be much to do around here in the winter."

"There's a bit of a slowdown, unless you are Amish, of course. Life goes on as usual for them."

"I prefer the big city in the winter," Ken said. "The heat works better."

He laughed and Johnny smiled slightly then made a quick gesture to go.

"Are you coming out for something hot to drink?" "I think I could use some chocolate."

Johnny opened the door and went out into an L-shaped hallway with five other doors for the rooms that housed the rest of the employees. In one side, there was a large rectangular room with several long tables that served as the dining room. Johnny walked hastily across the room, and Ken followed him. They entered the kitchen, and each got a Styrofoam cup. Ken made himself chocolate, and Johnny poured himself some coffee. They sat down at one of the tables in the center of the empty room.

"I kind of like the quiet season myself," Johnny said as if confessing a secret. "It kind of sets you on your tracks, you know. You sort of go on the gas that you saved during the past harvest season till next year. There's not that much to keep after, for me anyway, so I can't say it's all that bad."

"So, you stick it out because of the job, I guess," Ken said, taking a sip of his drink. "That's different. If this is what you want to do and you want to grow in it, I suppose you need to put in the time. You can't be a fair-weather foreman, right?"

Johnny did not respond. He took a drink from his coffee cup and looked down at the table.

"No, it's not that. I just don't mind the winter season that much."

"Very courageous of you. I admire your bravery."

Ken's, youthful face brightened with a playful look. He took another drink from his cup. Johnny notices it but went on as if he hadn't.

"So, what will you be doing this winter? Where are you going?"

"I'll probably be going south. I was hoping to land another farm job down in Georgia since their season is a lot longer than up here, but I think I waited too long. They don't need me now. I may have to go back to a motorcycle job, either there or in one of the Carolinas. Bikes are big down there."

"You're such a good mechanic that I don't know why you don't stick with it all the time."

"I like to break the monotony," Ken said chirpily, smiling again. "Unlike you, I have no stomach for inactivity. I gotta be on the move."

"Yeah. Well, the bike business must also have a season like farming. I don't see many riding in the middle of winter."

"Not here, of course. In the south, the weather does not get that cold, so it's almost an all-year-round business."

"What will you be doing exactly?"

"There's this shop in the Carolinas that builds custom made bikes. I worked there last winter putting the engines together and it was a good job. It's just a little demanding with the time guidelines. I left there to come here."

"You walked out of a shop, building engines to come here to roll hay in a farm. It sounds like you're all over the place, Ken."

"I enjoy mechanical work. I do it more for pleasure than out of need. Sure, I could have stayed. But I would have had to work under tremendous pressure, installing engines by the day, sometimes by the hour with a manager that does not know the first thing about bikes."

"But you're going back there."

"I may. I have two weeks to think about it," Ken said, laughing again.

Johnny acknowledged him this time, throwing his head back for a second and chuckling. He actually wished he could have kept Kenny through the entire winter. He needed someone here. Someone who he could boss around, have him feed the animals in the winter and maintain the barn. He would still try to make a go of it with Martha. He didn't know if he could but he felt it was only right. What good is a manager if he only has himself to manage? He needed other people around him so he could tell them what to do.

"If you can work on customized bikes, doesn't that mean you're pretty good? I mean, you must be, right? They're not just gonna hire any mechanic to build the bikes. It's gotta be somebody that knows the engines inside and out."

"Yeah. That is about right. But for me it's like a hobby, something I do out of pleasure. Something I enjoy. If I get into a situation where I'm working in a very unpleasant environment, then I may begin to hate the job and I don't want that. I don't want to lose that passion I feel for it."

"So, why are you going back then?"

"I'm not sure I will, actually. I'm only considering it because unfortunately, I may need the money after this season. But it's definitely not my first choice. I'd just rather go to a local motorcycle shop and work there through the winter, but this being the east, the shops don't have work all year round.

It's pretty seasonal, like farming."

"Ever consider being a farmer full time?"

"I'd have to own a farm to do that. Wouldn't you agree?" "Not really. You could have a job like mine or a sub-management job."

Ken took another drink from his cup.

"That wouldn't be farming, though. I like the open fields, harvesting and toiling the ground. That's farming for me. You see the ground open up and take the seed. Then it grows and it bears out fruit, like magic. I feel closer to God."

"Yeah. Well, for every laborer, there's always a support operation that's just as important. The planner never gets the seed if there isn't a supplier who brings it to him. The ground does not get to be furrowed if someone does not maintain the tractors. The managerial aspect of it is just as important, if not more, than the farming itself."

"I don't disagree, but it doesn't mean I have to like it."

He was again showing his teeth. His black eyes seemed to glimmer as he took another sip of chocolate.

"How would you like to stay for the whole winter?"

"Doing what?"

"You'd be working directly for me, just keeping up the farm until the spring. There would be a lot of trips to town, keeping up with the feeding of the animals, some inside renovations, maybe. You're good at that too."

Ken looked down in his cup for a moment, reflecting. He actually could see right through Johnny and thought about how miserable it would feel to have him tailing him all day long, ordering him everywhere he went. The harsh breeze of the up-coming winter would actually be the least of his problems. The job conditions would make his life more unbearable than any zero-degree weather, if it ever hit that low here.

"I appreciate it," Ken said, lifting his head. "I can't stay that long."

"Yeah. You're kind of turning into a drifter, Ken. You're almost there now."

"I'll have to look around for a girl to settle down. Maybe I'll get an Amish girl."

Ken was smiling at him again.

"You'll have to settle for a steady job before you do that. If you're interested in their kind, this may be the right place for that."

"Oh, it doesn't matter," Ken said, now seriously. "I just meant that as a joke. When the Lord blesses me with a bride, her race or ethnic background will be of no importance to me. As long as she's God fearing, I'll be happy."

"I've seen how you look at them," Johnny said with glee.

"Oh, I can't say that I'm not interested. I think they're great people. I admire them very much."

"Yeah. Well, this is your chance to find one. They're easier to talk to in the winter."

"I don't know that if I would stay for that reason, Johnny. I would hope that finding a mate would not be like a hunting expedition. I would want a partner and not a prey."

"Women seek men for dominance. We go after them to be subservient to us. It's in our nature. Look at the Amish who are living amongst us. What do the women do in that community, ah? They wear their long boring dresses and their bonnets and they clean their small simple houses, cook for their men and wash their clothes. The men do all the heavy work. When they get home after a day's work, what do you think they do? They yearn for attention from their women.

They want to be pleased and looked after. It's how their society functions. It's why it functions. So, when you look for a woman, what do you look for? You look for those traits that will make you happy. You look for obedience in a woman. A woman who's assertive and makes up her own mind will only get you into trouble."

He finished drinking his coffee in one gulp. Ken could see his tightly held lips as he guzzled down the last drops. Ken saw them stretch in what appeared to be an expression of infinite pleasure. The thought of knowing he had spoken true wisdom and that he knew it, and Ken didn't.

"Take my girl, for instance," Johnny went on. "You see her come to the farm to drive me to town. I don't ever drive her.

She has to serve me, take me around and help me do my chores. I trained her that way. She wants to marry. I told her she's gotta wait. When I feel like I've filled my cup, I may do it. But until then, she's gotta show me that she's gonna be a subservient wife. One that will speak when I speak and follow, not lead."

"I can't disagree with you more," Ken said. "I don't think the situation you describe brews happiness which is the main ingredient in a marriage."

"Yeah. Well, you're a bible boy, Ken. Doesn't it say in there that women need to do as they are told, follow their leader who is a man?"

"Not at all, no. Not in those terms."

"So, what does it say? What does the bible say?"

Ken vacillated. He felt uncomfortable about getting into a match of bible semantics with someone who was obviously contemptuous about its meaning. Johnny's mind was clearly made up, and Ken could not say anything that would make him change. Ken looked into his slightly slanted eyes under the curly black hair and decided in that instance that he would take him on.

"The bible tells women to be role models in their homes.

First of all, it tells them to love their husbands, then their children, then to be discreet, chaste, and then to be obedient.

God recognizes man's leading role in the home and because of that, it says that women should play their role well."

"See what I mean?"

"But by the same token, God tells men to be sober-minded, to be incorruptible, and impress even their opponents with their integrity. There is no room for a Christian to be abusive towards a woman or to take advantage of her. On the contrary, it compels men, above all, to love their women."

"I do that. I love my woman. I love her all the time."

"You can't love somebody you disrespect. A woman is not a pet. They're part of our bodies. They are our soulmates."

Johnny drew back a bit. Ken's comment came perilously close to calling him a chauvinist or even worse. But he felt trapped. If he complained and showed his anger, Ken could easily evade him by saying he was speaking figuratively, and not specifically about his relationship. And after all, he had put himself in the spotlight by talking about his own girl.

There was another reason, too. It was hard to imagine that the tall, muscular young man who picked up heavy bushels of corn during the day and rolled rolls of hay with ease could be a bible scholar. He seemed so curt and overpowering as he toiled the soil and in the evenings when Johnny heard him take off, his motorcycle thundering through the nearby highways, the gruff roar of the engine crept into his ears as if it came from the rider himself, rattling his body and intimidating his spirit.

Johnny knew he stood little chance of prevailing if it came to a showdown between the two. He had one thing going for himself: Ken's apparent devotion to religion. People of faith did not rely on their physical strength to get their point across. They used their beliefs. And they were supposed to turn the other cheek no matter what their size.

"I didn't say mine was a pet," Johnny said sharply. "She's practicing what you're teaching, Ken. She's learning to be obedient."

"Being obedient does not mean that a woman has to be a servant. She was meant to be your soulmate, not your servant. You are responsible for loving her and being her best friend. Are you really doing that? When you say she's being obedient, obedient to what? To your capricious desires? I'm afraid that is not what the bible means by the term obedience. I'll go a step further, if a woman is being physically abused, does that mean that she has to bear whatever punishment her husband will impose on her only because she needs to be obedient? Clearly, no. Obedient as meant in the bible is a two-way street word. It means to be obedient to the leading role of a good loving husband who is also obedient to her."

"Yeah. Well, my girl is not physically abused. I don't believe in hitting women. She's free to leave whenever she wants to."

"I didn't say you were."

Johnny nervously lifted his eyes from the table. He gave Ken a quick and edgy look, as if he was too burdened to actually look at the source of those bold comments. Then he switched his gaze back to the table and pretended he was drinking his last sip of coffee.

"I'll need you at the barn tomorrow. I want to pack as much hay as possible on the second level. That'll be our focus for the next few days until the upstairs is totally packed."

"Sure thing, Johnny," Ken said.

Johnny rose from the table, leaving his empty cup behind. He walked past the other tables stocked in a row in the room and disappeared into the dimly lit hallway. Ken remained seated, his elbows resting on the table and his hands recoiled under his chin. He could see his own shadow distortedly projected on the wall across from him. The only lights in the room came from the light fixture of marbleized glass at the center of each ceiling fan. Its rattan blades spun slowly above him, fanning a cool breeze, perhaps already too cool for this time of year. Ken thought about Johnny and the kind of relationship he was having with his girl. He had never seen them together, but it did not sound too good, at least not like anything he would want for himself. In the past few months, he had given the matter much thought and he had molded his wishes after the model relationships he had studied in the bible, like Abraham and his wife Sarah. Whenever he settled down, wherever he built his home, it would be with a soulmate who shared his thirst for the divine. Sometimes, he thought he was at the brink of finding one but only to be disappointed. He had not found the girl of his dreams even amongst his Christian brethren. He now believed that he did not need to confine his search to the church. A good mate could be found anywhere, in the city's suburbs just as well as in the solitary plains of the countryside, or even here, amongst a community of God-fearing people who secluded themselves from the rest of the world as the Amish did. Perhaps Johnny was right after all. Perhaps he had become infatuated with the idea of marrying an Amish girl. Perhaps he cared more about it than he could admit.

"Nah," he grumbled to himself. In two weeks, he would be packing his small bundle of clothes and riding on Highway 272 south to Maryland, then pick up Interstate 95 and head towards Virginia and the Carolinas.

He tossed his empty cup inside one of the garbage cans and headed slowly back to his room. There was not a soul around, and he wondered whether the others had already left. He lay in bed and tucked himself under the white sheets. He placed his bible on the nightstand and turned the light off. The room was dark, and he lay still under the sheets, knowing he would eventually doze off.

The next morning, Ken was up at 5:00 A.M. He moved the window shade aside. The first signs of dawn appeared as fragmented golden lines that crossed the sky and ran high above until they could no longer be seen. Ken watched clouds of dew rising from the fields. He remembered what Johnny had said the night before and regretted having to spend the whole day in the barn. It seemed that the weather would be very mild and he would miss a nice day.

He dressed quickly and grabbed a towel from the rack. He went into the bathroom at one end of the hallway, which was shared by five men. He washed his face with cold water and brushed his teeth. He dried himself with the towel and put it away in his room. Then he went into the kitchen and made himself some hot chocolate. He sat at one of the tables and drank alone. Then he heard one of the doors in the hallway opening. A short, swarthy man came out of the room and went towards the bathroom. He later passed by Ken and said good morning with a heavy Spanish accent. He took some coffee from the kitchen and sat across from him.

"Are you leaving this morning, Miguel?" Ken asked?

"Yeah. We're all leaving. Aren't you leaving?"

"No. I'm staying two more weeks," Ken said, raising his two fingers together.

"Oh, yeah? They asked you to stay?"

"They asked me, yes."

"It's gonna get cold in a month or so."

"It'll be all right," Ken said. "So, which way are you headed? Where are you going?"

"Back to Mexico."

"The others too?"

"Yes. Everyone. We're all going back to the same town.

We go back till the spring. Then we come back here. Will you be here next year?"

"Maybe. I don't know. I'm going south after I finish here. I think I may want to stay south a little longer this time. I sure wish I could go to Mexico with you guys."

"You can. You're welcome to come." "Is there farm work there?"

"Yeah. Some farm work but not much in the winter. It gets cold there too. Not as cold as here, but not very good for farming."

"What kind of things do you harvest down there?"

"Lots of corn. Some root vegetables, you know."

"Is the land good for farming?"

"It's very dry. Not as good as here."

Two other men had joined them. They were all very short of stature with very black, straight hair. One of them, named Raul, had a puffy face and he sat next to the other one, in front of Ken.

"Why do you wanna come to Mexico? Mexico is not like the United States," Raul said.

"I don't know. I'd like to go everywhere. I like to travel places."

"It's called a *rancho*."

"What does that mean?"

"Just many houses put together in the countryside. Everyone works the land."

"I think I would like to visit a place like that."

"Come with us."

Ken nodded in agreement. Yes, he would like to go very much. He would just as well go with them and live with one of their families in one of their flimsy country homes, walk the littered trails with them every morning and learn about farming their arid land. He'd probably be at their *fiestas* on weekends held in one of the open cattle houses where the men drank themselves into a stupor and the women cooked the spicy *tortillas* and *tamales*. He could easily become like one of them, carefree, indifferent and simple. Yet, he had a thirst for the word of God and a need to interchange his views. He had not yet preached. He had never preached. He thought he was not ripe for it. He was still discovering the word, learning to live by it. Traveling to a foreign land and living with the common folk would align with the Bible's teachings. Live simple and travel light. But his purpose had to be more than living like them. He needed to develop and grow in the word of God. Would they welcome him once his motives were known? That precisely was the challenge of adventure and the true nature of his calling. He smiled at the two men sitting across from him. One of the boarders who had been assigned to cook had gone into the kitchen to make breakfast and the smell of fried bacon and eggs filled the air.

"Of course I would go. I'd have no problem going."

"But you have to finish your two weeks now, man. That's a problem. We're leaving today. You'll have to find us on your own in Mexico."

"And that won't be an easy task, right?"

The quizzical look both men gave him told Ken they did not understand him.

"It would be hard for me to find you alone, right?"

"Right, right."

Ken laughed as the men repeated themselves, then all got up and headed towards the kitchen to pick up some breakfast. A thin man acting as chef was standing behind a table in the kitchen wearing an apron that seemed oversized for him. One of the other two men said something to him in Spanish, and suddenly, all three of them turned to Ken, smiling.

"What will you have," said the cook in very broken English.

"Scrambled eggs with toast. Thanks for cooking breakfast on your last day."

"It's okay," the cook said. "I have until eleven."

He turned to the other two and they quickly placed their orders in Spanish.

"What I wanna know," Raul said, "is what you do to get so big. You don't eat anything."

"I ealt just the right stuff," Ken said. "I stay away from the grease. It's not good for you."

The cook got busy filling their orders. The two Mexican men got a large amount of scrambled eggs with home fries.

They grabbed their plates and moved to the coffee pot to get some coffee. Ken went and sat by the table to wait for them. Out of the dimness of the hallway came Johnny Kelekes's, striding along and bending his head slightly with each step.

"Good morning," he said, pausing by Ken's table. "I see they're all going about their business as if it was just another day. They're all leaving today, you know. They shouldn't be making breakfast but getting packed."

"Ah, what's the harm?" Ken said, without looking up. "They gotta have breakfast anyway. Might as well have it here and leave with a full stomach."

"Yeah. That's 'cause you're not paying for it. Maybe we should deduct their bill from your pay."

"That would be okay with me. I wouldn't mind treating them."

Johnny said nothing. He strode towards the kitchen, ignoring the two short Mexican men who were walking towards Ken's table as he passed them. Johnny went around the table and began speaking to the cook in a high tone of voice. The two men sat on the table across from Ken and put their plates down.

"Why is Johnny so angry?" one of them asked.

"It's the early morning's blues."

"What does that mean, blues?"

"It means low spirits. Someone who's mad for no reason."

"Put everything away now!" they heard Johnny yell.

"But Mr. Johnny . . . " they heard the cook reply, as he struggled to look him in the face. Johnny towered over the slightly built man.

"I don't want to hear it. You knew you were leaving today.

What do you think we're running here? A Salvation Army center for Mexicans? No work, no breakfast."

Ken and the others watched from their table as Johnny grabbed the strings of the cook's apron. He lifted the small man off the ground like a toy and threw him against the wall. There was a loud crash as the impact of the body brought down pots and pans.

"Dirty Mexicans," Johnny was yelling. "Get back where you belong!"

Ken got up from his table and walked towards the kitchen. The other two men followed behind him.

"There's no breakfast for anybody this morning. What do you think this is? A restaurant? You all should have been on the road by now. Who the heck gave you permission to cook?"

"Wait a minute, Johnny," Ken said, standing behind the small table, the only object that separated them. "You can't treat people like that. I think you hurt him."

"Who the heck cares? Who's he to make himself at home?"

Ken walked quickly around the table and towards the wall. He and the other men reached down to touch the man on the floor. He was bleeding profusely from the nose. Ken moved his face from side to side, checking for scratches, but saw none. He knew immediately the injuries were internal.

"This man needs medical attention. We're going to have to call an ambulance."

"Just let him be. He'll be all right."

"No. You can't let him be. Either you call an ambulance or I'll call one myself."

"This has got nothing to do with you, Ken. Just go about your business and everything will be all right."

"It's got everything to do with me, I tell you. This man needs medical attention now."

"I ain't calling no ambulance. Let him lick his own wounds."

There was an icy silence as Ken got up from the floor where he had knelt to aid the bleeding man. All his 6 feet 2 inches stretched up slowly, his brown eyes were fixed on the pale-faced, arrogant, and very aggressive Johnny Kelekes, who had pitilessly maimed a submissive and cornered a man half his size.

"Then I'll call one," Ken said, walking towards him. He stood only a few inches away from Johnny.

"Ken, it's not your call. I know you are trying to help but this is not your call."

Ken retrieved his small flip Motorola phone from his pocket and handed it to one of the two men behind him.

"Dial 911," he said. "Hurry."

"Ken, I'm telling you again, stay away. This is not your affair."

Ken walked closer. Only an inch separated the two men now. Deep inside Johnny's preservation instinct made him wish the burly young man would not forsake the Christian principles that he so outwardly displayed. Although Johnny's desire to manage and control led him to be intolerant and to indiscriminately abuse others, at that moment he would have turned and walked away were it not for the hate fermenting inside of him.

"Why did you have to hurt him, Johnny? You know, you really hurt him."

"This people need to be shaken up, otherwise they take over the place. Look at them. They're supposed to be leaving this morning, but they're making breakfast and going about their business as if this was their house. It's pitiful. That's the same way they go about it in the entire country, as if it was theirs, roaming in and out as they please."

"Still, that was not a reason to hurt him, Johnny. You knew he couldn't fight you. You did it only because of that reason.

You wouldn't have tried it with me."

"You're not Mexican. I have nothing against you." "That's your reason for hurting him? Because he's Mexican?"

"You know what I mean."

Ken took a step forward and Johnny intuitively took one back. The two men would have bumped into each other if he hadn't. Johnny kept moving back.

"Listen, Kenny, I had no beef against you. You have nothing to do with this. Go about your business. Have breakfast if you want to. Then start at the barn like I told you."

"You know what I think, Johnny. I think you're a very little man. Smaller than that tiny Mexican man you have just beaten up. Perhaps you should learn about consequences, the consequences of your actions."

Ken turned to Raul who was using his phone.

"Did you get anyone," Ken asked.

"Someone is on the telephone now."

Ken grabbed the phone from him and put it on his ear.

"We need an ambulance here," he said. "Someone's been hurt pretty bad."

"Where are you exactly?" the operator asked from the other end.

"Halloway Farm. Off highway 272, south of the city. We also need a police escort here, too. It was an assault."

"We're sending them now. What is your name, sir?"

"Kenneth O'Gara."

Ken felt Johnny's hand, pulling on the sleeve of his jacket.

"Ken, don't! Don't!"

"Operator, I'm gonna have to hang up now."

"No, don't hang up," she said.

"I'm going to pass the phone to someone else who'll talk to you, okay?"

Ken gave the phone back to Raul and shook his arm free from Johnny's hold.

"Johnny, stay put and don't grab me again. You're making things worse."

"I won't let you! I won't let you!"

Johnny launched himself forward, sweepingly moving his right arm as if to shove Ken aside. It happened so fast that it caught Ken by surprise but he quickly recovered and grabbed his right arm first and then his left. Raul shuffled back into the wall to keep Johnny from reaching him. Ken held both of Johnny's arms behind his back and he wrapped his forearm around his neck in a choke hold to restrain him. Johnny was fighting back, trying to shake loose and kicking back with his feet but he was going nowhere. Ken had him.

"They're coming, Mr. Ken," Raul yelled with the phone still on his ear. "They're coming."

"Can you check on the cook?"

Raul knelt down by Miguel who was trying to place the cook's head into a comfortable position.

"How is he?" Ken asked.

Miguel just looked at him and shook his head.

"Do you know how to do CPR?" Ken said.

"What's CPR?" Raul asked.

"Resuscitation. To massage his chest to get a heartbeat going. Do you know how to do it?"

Both men shook their heads. The other two who had been sitting in a far table had now come close. They stood watching the cook on the floor bleeding.

"You guys are going to have to do something until the ambulance gets here. Get some clean cloth and wipe the blood. Clean him up."

"I'm telling you Ken. Let me go," Johnny was mumbling.

"Shut up," Ken said.

Johnny was still fighting him, kicking back and pulling forward, trying to get loose. Ken moved slightly aside, loosening the hold on his neck. Grabbing both arms tightly he shoved him away from the kitchen area and into one of the tables. Johnny kept resisting by kicking and jerking his body. Ken sat him on a chair and pulled his arms down in the back.

"You want to help yourself, Johnny? Stay still. If I don't get to Paco on the floor and he dies, there will be hell to pay for you, Johnny. Right now, it may be a question of assault only. That's pretty bad, considering you did not give that poor kid a chance and you had no reason to hurt him. But it's still a lot better for you than murder, Johnny. And that's what I think you'd be facing if Paco dies."

Johnny's face was cotton white. A glimpse of horror slowly grew on him.

"Ken, I . . . I never meant to get you involved. It had nothing to do with you."

"We're past that now, Johnny. Stay put."

Ken moved quickly away from him and went to check on Paco who was lying unconscious on the floor next to the wall. He saw how seriously he was injured. He had no abrasions on his face, but it was obvious that he had internal injuries. Ken got right to work. He moved Paco gently away from the wall and laid him flat on the wooden floor. He knelt at his side and began pumping his chest, his right hand in a fist and his left one open on top of it at the center of the chest. He counted five pumps and quickly put both of his open hands-on Paco's mouth, using them as a funnel. He bent down and blew air into Paco's lungs. Then he quickly went back to pumping his chest. He continued doing this for a long time, concentrating fully on his task. Finally, the faraway sound of sirens caught his attention and for a split second he thought to himself that he was almost done. Someone was coming. He looked at Paco's face as he prepared to blow into his lungs again. He saw no sign of life. He went on steadily until he felt the hand of the paramedic tugging on his tee shirt's sleeve.

"Let me take over," the heavyset man said and Ken moved aside.

Two other men had quickly set up a stretcher next to Paco and they carefully slid his body onto the stretcher. Then they lifted him while the other paramedic was still working on his chest. Ken caught a glimpse of Paco's face as the paramedics carried him away. He thought he saw his head move slightly and felt relieved. Then he looked around him. Johnny Kaleka's was still sitting on the chair where Ken had left him and the other men were crowding around two police officers who entered the room. Others were now coming in. Some of the Mexican men who were talking to them were crying.

"Sir, would you step over here, please?" one of the officers told Ken.

Ken joined the other men who had been answering questions from the officers.

"What do you know about what happened?"

He was tall and burly. His blue cap was tight over his forehead, and his blue eyes kept nervously hopping around the room. His voice sounded raspy, but the words came out fluently. He had now spotted Johnny, still sitting on the chair.

"There was an argument."

"Who had an argument? Did you have an argument?" "No. These two gentlemen and I were having breakfast when Johnny came in." "Who's Johnny?"

"Johnny is our manager. He's the man sitting back there."

"Okay. And what happened then?"

"Johnny came past us said good morning and then went to the kitchen. We heard him yelling at the cook. He didn't want the guys to have breakfast today because it was supposed to be their last day and he blew his top. Next thing we know is we see him shoving the cook against the wall. He's such a little man. He hit the wall and fell to the floor. We all came over to the other side of the table and I restrained Johnny. I made him sit down on the chair."

"Very good, friend. That's more or less what these guys have told me. By the way, that was some good work you did on that poor fellow, giving him CPR. You may have saved his life."

He broke from them and began walking towards Johnny.

"All right, sir, what is your name?"

The other officer followed. Suddenly, Johnny stood up from his chair and pointed his finger at Raul and the others.

"You lousy Mexicans! You bastards! You're all fired!"

"Sir, sit down," the first officer said.

Each of the two officers stood on either side of Johnny and waited a moment for his reaction to wind down. Johnny put his arms down slowly, looking shaken, then sat down again. The officers now stood in front of him. Ken and the others could not hear them so they retreated to one of the tables. Two more police officers walked into the room and headed towards the group. Then suddenly an older woman walked in hurriedly. She had held the entrance door to the hallway wide open before walking in and the pale light of the early morning engulfed the room momentarily. She hurriedly walked past their table and began speaking to the officers before reaching them. She was of medium height and wore her silver hair in a ponytail.

"What are you guys doing here? Why didn't I get a call?" she said loudly.

All four officers turned around to face her and one asked who she was.

"I'm Martha Francis. Why wasn't I told about this?" Ken and the others could not hear the officers' response.

They seemed a little taken aback by her quick entrance into the room.

"I don't care," she replied. "I should have been told about this."

She flipped her arms up as she spoke. She was a woman who was used to power. She had lived with it all her life. For her it was inconceivable that these men in blue would disturb her kingdom this early in the morning. She had been awakened by an aide who had rushed into her room to tell her about patrol cars, speeding through the driveway and then parking their vehicles around the gambrel-roofed brown hangar that housed the workers. She just caught a glimpse of them from the secluded window in her bedroom and that was enough to get her out of bed. She threw a light brown robe on and put on Chinese slippers. She had run the farm like a true Baroness, tolerating no mishap and demanding high standards of production. But she hardly knew her workers. She felt it was her manager's job.

"I want to know what happened."

"Please, sit down, and we will tell you what happened," one of the officers said loudly enough for Ken and the others to hear.

She had to retreat a few steps to reach one of the tables. She sat down at a table on the other side of the room and across from Ken.

"Everyone but the tall kid is out of here," she said. "I want them out of here right now."

"Wait a minute, madam," Ken heard one of the officers say, leaning forward to get close. "We have an investigation ongoing at this time. We still need to ask these gentlemen some questions."

"Ask them somewhere else, not in my property. I want them out of here."

One of the officers sat down in front of her with his back facing Ken's table. From that point on, Ken could not hear them. Ken saw Miguel bring a white handkerchief to his face to wipe the tears.

"Do you think Paco will be okay, Mr. Ken?"

Ken looked him in the eye.

"If you love your friend and you want him to be okay then pray to the Lord and he will be."

"Help us Ken."

Ken leaned forward on the table and uttered a prayer. He had his eyes closed and was startled by the officer's tug of his sleeve.

"Listen," the officer said, standing by their table. I don't believe we need you here for now. Ms. Francis does not really want these guys here, so perhaps it would be better if they outside. You can go about your daily chores on the farm."

"Am I free to leave?" Ken asked.

"Yes."

"Then I'm off with these guys. I'm done with the farm."

"Wait a minute. Ms. Francis wants you to stay."

"I won't. If you're done with me then I'm out of here." The officer hesitated a moment and looked over Martha Francis's table.

"Well, I guess that's up to you, Ken. I'll need an address from you."

Ken gave him his parents' address in New York. He truly did not know if he was going back to New York just yet. The officer did not seem to mind that he gave him an out-of-state address but he asked him for his cell phone number.

"Do you know where the ambulance took Paco?" Ken asked.

"Probably Lancaster General. I don't know for sure," the officer said. Then he spoke to the other men.

"All right, guys, you're gonna have to pick up your things. It's time to go."

They got up obediently and headed for their rooms.

"Aren't you getting their names?" Ken asked.

"What good is it to get any information from them? They'll probably give me false names anyway and then they'll all be in Mexico tomorrow. I've got your name. If I need any evidence it'll have to come from you."

"So what's going to happen?"

"I don't know yet. We're investigating."

Ken went into his room and began gathering his clothes. He did not have much, only some small garments and some items for his personal hygiene. He put everything into a duffle bag and zippered it tight. He threw the bag across his shoulder, grabbed his keys and bible, and went out the door. He noticed that the police were still questioning Johnny while Ms. Francis stood nearby, yelling objections as a lawyer in a courtroom.

Ken opened the front door and walked out into broad daylight. The sun was shining brightly and the misty autumn wind was already blowing. Parked next to the building was an older blue Ford pickup. Raul and the others were already hauling their bags into the rear of the truck. Ken walked to his bike parked nearby and placed his bag on the back of the seat. It was a customized metallic blue Harley VRSC with white fenders. The handlebars seemed shorter than usual and had a small red night beamer hanging under each side. The oval looking headlight was encased in shining white aluminum that matched the fenders. Ken mounted and slid the key into the ignition.

"Hey, guys," he said to the men in the truck, "I'm going to be going to the hospital to check on Paco. You can follow me."

He went south on Highway 222 then west on 30 until he intersected Lititz Pike. He passed Stauffer Park, moved west on 222 and got on North Duke Street, which lead towards the center of town where the hospital was located. He knew of the hospital's location from the time he had driven one of the farm hands to get stitches for a nasty slice on his forearm. Johnny had never been generous with medical treatment for the employees. Ken felt glad he had left. He did not know yet where he would go but that didn't bother him. His only concern at the moment was how Paco would fare with his wounds. The picture of the tiny man's face as he lay on the floor, oozing blood from his nostrils, haunted him.

He went into the parking garage on James Street and found a spot for his bike. The pick-up truck parked a few spaces away. Ken waited for the four guys to catch up to him. They entered through the hospital's main entrance, walked around the canopied semi-circle and then through the doors in the high glass bulwark in the center of the building. Ken went to the information desk and asked for the emergency room. The young woman dressed in blue gave him directions to go onto the other side of the building. As he entered the emergency room, a security guard stopped the group at the door. Ken told him they were looking for Paco. No one in the group knew his full name, not that the hospital would have known anyway. The guard called a nurse.

"Are you family?"

"We are friends," Ken said.

She looked at their faces one at a time, as if trying to detect any resemblance.

"He's in the trauma unit," she finally said. "He's suffered a skull fracture."

"Can we see him?" Ken asked.

"No, you can't. He's not conscious. He can't talk to you.

But we do need you to answer some questions. Can you come in for a few minutes?"

She took them past the security guard into one of the examining rooms. Inside, there were only two chairs and an examining bed covered with white paper. The room suddenly looked crowded with the five men standing around.

"I am going to get the patient's chart and will be right back," she said. "If you gentlemen could wait for a minute."

"Sure," Ken said.

She came back with a clipboard and she sat in one of the two chairs.

"Now, do you have any information about this patient? Anything at all?"

"All we know is that his name is Paco," Ken said. "He's worked at the Francis farm throughout the summer. He's a seasonal worker from Mexico. He came with these guys."

"Do they speak English?"

"Yes."

She gazed at the other men as if somehow the four of them formed part of another audience that she was addressing separate from Ken.

"Do you guys know his name?"

"His name is Paco," Miguel said with a heavy Spanish accent.

"What about his last name?"

"I don't know."

"Anybody?" she swept her eyes through the entire group.

"No," they all repeated.

"Does he have any family?"

"Not here," Miguel said. "His family is in Mexico."

"Where is he from in Mexico?"

"Rancho la Leona," Raúl said.

The nurse wrote down the name on the short form she was carrying. Most of the blocks were empty.

"Any contacts here in the U.S.?"

"What do you mean?" Raul asked, looking at Ken.

"She's asking you if there is anybody she could call on Paco. Any friends or relatives?" "No, nobody."

"So where did Paco work again?"

She was now addressing Ken and he answered her almost immediately.

"He worked at the Francis farm, off Highway 202, north of here. We all worked there. Today was supposed to have been his last day."

"Do you know how he was injured?"

The four Mexicans glanced at Ken. He looked straight at the nurse.

"Our foreman had a temper tantrum. He flung Paco against a wall and I guess he struck his head."

"Nice guy," the nurse said ironically. "Where's he now?"

"The police were questioning him when we left."

"Did you speak to the police? Did you tell them what you saw?"

"We did. Haven't they been here?"

"No, they have not. Not yet."

"So what can you tell us about Paco?" Ken said, "Is he going to be all right?"

"I don't know yet. He is seriously injured and he will need surgery. I just need to establish a contact."

"I can give you my cell number," Ken offered. Maybe I can help you reach his family."

"That would be nice."

Ken gave her his number and she wrote it on the form she was filling out. She was a woman well into her forties. Her face was attractive, long and slim, but the lower half of her cheeks was beginning to show some sagging. She seemed resigned with the little information that she had been able to obtain and she got up and looked at them indifferently.

"Maybe you guys could check with us later. Right now, there's nothing you can do."

She opened the door and held it open, waiting for them to leave the room. The security guard told them that they could leave through the emergency exit that was right in front of them. They all went outside and stood on the sidewalk talking. They were willing to wait until that evening but Raul, who was the spokesman for the group, seemed anxious to get going.

"We have no place to sleep tonight," he said. "We can't go back to the farm."

"We can wait till tonight," Miguel said.

"Tonight? You want to start driving tonight? You know how many hours we're going to be on the road? If we leave tonight, we'll have to stop a couple of hours later. Maybe we'll still be in Pennsylvania."

"Maybe we'll know more about Paco if we stay till tonight."

"I once went to a bar-restaurant near here," Ken said.

"Maybe we can have something to eat while we wait. You might as well. If you leave now without knowing how Paco is doing, you'll regret it later on. Stay a couple of hours."

They went around the rear of the hospital building and went out to North Duke Street. They went south on Duke, passing some old brick buildings. Two blocks down, they saw a large colonial bi-level entrance with a glass door that looked out of place on the facade. Ken grabbed one of the door handles and opened it. He walked in followed by the four men.

They entered a remodeled room with a large wooden counter that ended near the entrance. Despite the early hour there were already three people sitting at the counter. Ken pointed to a table near the wall.

"Here all right?"

"Yeah. Fine."

Each man pulled a chair out and sat down.

"Something to eat?" Ken asked them.

"No, nothing to eat," Miguel said. "We are gonna have a drink only."

A man wearing casual clothes came over to their table.

"Shall I bring you guys a menu?"

"They want something to drink," Ken said. "I want a turkey sandwich."

Just then, one of two men sitting at the bar counter turned to them. He was short and stocky and wore a short-sleeved blue donjon jacket. His exposed biceps were tattooed with several human faces, male and female.

"Hey, O'Gara, is that you?"

Ken turned. The man who had called his name had stood from his stool and came towards him. The other man sitting next to him had also turned. He was bigger and was dressed exactly as the first one. He had a silver skull and crisscross bones painted on the back of his jacket.

"How the heck are you, Ken? Still working at that lousy farm?"

"I'm fine, Dave. No, I'm not working there anymore. As a matter of fact, I'm on my way out of town."

"You're kidding me! You mean I would have missed you?

I've been looking for you. Couldn't find that lousy farm. I went up on 202 a couple of times but no, I couldn't find it. We need you."

"For what? What's going on?"

"We're gonna be going on a ride to Daytona with about ten clubs from the east. You haven't heard? It's being put together by Ron Mason. I'm sure you heard of him. He's got this crazy idea about putting together the biggest ride from the northeast ever to Daytona. They need some mechanics who can ride and fix."

Ken looked at Raul and the other three men, sitting at the table as if they hadn't heard him.

"This is Miguel," he said, pointing to him. "This is Raul and these two here are Daniel and Marco. They worked at the farm with me this season."

"Are you done now? Is the season over?"

"Yeah. They're actually on their way back to Mexico. One of our guys was hurt pretty bad this morning so we came to see him at the hospital."

"Really? What happened?"

"Our foreman got abusive and he hurt him. He hurt him pretty bad, actually."

"Are you serious? Who's this guy?"

"He's just somebody we worked under."

"Bastard. Can I buy you guys a beer?"

"No, not for me, thanks," Ken said. "Guys, this is Dave, a friend of mine."

"Come on, let's all have a beer. Join us at the counter."

Dave walked back to his seat. He pointed to the man sitting next to him.

"This here is Steve. He's the heck of a rider and knows more about bikes' braking systems than anybody I know. If your bike won't brake, this is the man to see," Dave laughed heartily and sat down, shuffling his body back and forth on the chair.

"Bartender," he called. "We've got some friends here. Need a beer for each one."

"I don't want a beer," Ken said. I'll have that sandwich."

"That's coming right up. Fellows," he said, turning to the Mexicans, "what will you have?"

"Bring us a bottle of rum," Raul said.

"We can't. We're gonna be driving," Miguel cautioned. "I'm not gonna be driving," Raul replied.

The bartender brought a bottle of José Cuervo and placed it on the counter with several shot glasses, holding them in each hand.

"Isn't that better than rum? You guys want the salt and the lemon, too?"

"Yes, if you have it," Raul said.

The bartender brought back a small plate of sliced limes and another with salt. Raul tried it first. He sprayed salt on the tip of his thumb and then squeezed a lemon slice on it. He lifted his hand and licked the mixture, then grabbed a shot glass of Tequila and quickly guzzled it down. Dave was the first non-Mexican to try it.

"I've never done it," he said, getting up from his chair and pouring himself a shot. "I've drunk Tequila but never had it like this."

He sprayed some salt on his thumb, squeezed a twist of lime on it and licked it. He took a shot down and groaned.

"Man! That is some nasty stuff! Steve, you want to try it?"

"No, man. I'll stick with my beer," Steve said, shaking his head.

"Come on, Ken. Try one."

"No, thanks. I'm only having a sandwich."

"Ken, you need a drink, man. You need to lighten up."

Ken was seated at Steve's other side. The bartender had slid a small plate with turkey slices on it, so Ken asked him for a Sprite.

"Ken," Dave said, "this is the ride of a lifetime. You can't miss it."

Ken did not respond.

"Steve, are you going?" Ken suddenly asked.

"Oh, yeah. I wouldn't miss that for the world."

"It's not going to be like the last time, Ken, I promise," Dave pleaded. "This is too big."

"It is," Steve repeated. "The whole northeast is coming out on this ride. This is major leagues."

"And they need mechanics badly, Ken. You could head a regiment with your skills. Think of the stature you're going to hold. You'll be right up there with the leaders."

It seemed like a long pause. He leaned his face forward and spoke to Dave over Steve.

"Who's going, Dave?"

"From Boston on down, Ken. This is big."

"Who's going?"

"The word is that troublemakers need not apply. This thing is going to be too much out in the open, Ken. There is no room for any trouble."

"Can you tell me some of the names?"

"They're picking them up as they come along all the way down to Baltimore. They have some riders from New York. Some of the Skyliners are going, not the whole club, though. The Mariners from Connecticut. I understand they're getting a lot of individual riders from Jersey. Some small clubs.

There's a club from Philadelphia, a couple more from Pennsylvania then Maryland. It looks real neat this time, Ken."

Ken took a drink. He had left his leather vest in his bike. His white tee-shirt exposed his muscled biceps and a wide chest that fit tight under the collar. Sitting straight on his chair, he looked impressive in comparison to the others. Steve drew back his head as he spoke.

"This is the ride of a lifetime, Ken. It's what you've been waiting for, kid."

Ken nodded politely. Yes, he had been longing for a run like that for years. He had missed many chances, including a ride to the west and one to Ontario. But he had made some short ones and that's where he had met Dave. He had never seen Steve before. He had regretted the run with Dave two years back. It had turned into a drug scene. Many critical situations developed on the road when drunken riders wrecked their machines and then depended on Ken and Dave, the only two mechanics on the road, to fix them. The trouble was that Dave too became a nuisance with the ugly stuff and Ken had to front all the maintenance alone. Over fifty bikes constantly needed repairs and there were only two mechanics, one of which became a total mess, hallucinating about alligators under the influence of LSD. Ken could have just driven away and called it quits, true. But even the State Rangers who tried to prevent the throng of riders from becoming a road disaster saw the sanity in him and begged him not to leave. He stayed. He got every engine back on the road while the Ranger police guided the bikers out of the local areas and into the deserted interstate Texan highways.

Then Ken thought his job was done and he turned around. He went east in the opposite direction and then north to Oklahoma, crossing over to the northern states through Kansas and Ohio. As much as he loved riding, he resolved that he would never again put himself in a situation where his integrity would be compromised. Ken was a man of God and he wanted to stay that way. He had made some rides since then, but mostly short ones, usually for a good cause that runs only intrastate, to the State capital. But he never stopped dreaming of the big one. He reached for his bottle again as he glanced at Dave who was having another Tequila shot.

"You plan on riding like that, Dave?" he said, making a gesture towards his glass.

"No, Ken. Come on, man. We're just relaxing here, man. I swear there won't be any booze. They'll kick me out if I drink. Besides, there are too many lady riders coming."

"Who says?"

"I know it. There are lots of them this time, not just riding but driving some pretty mean bikes. They're coming down from all over, New York, Jersey, Delaware. It's beginning to be a woman's sport too."

"It's always been," Ken said. "It just has never been recognized as one."

"Well, anyway, that got your attention, Ken, right?" "It's different, that's so."

"Listen, it would be me, you, and three other fellows as mechanics for the entire crew. Depending on the size, we could get more help. We'll have our own shop on wheels, together with three vans with all the tools you ever dreamed of."

"When is it happening?"

"It's already in motion in Boston. They'll be by here early next week. They're hitting New York Monday. They'll be on Jersey on Tuesday and then here by Wednesday. You can't leave now."

Ken finished his sandwich and guzzled down his Sprite.

"I can't leave, that is right," Ken said, chuckling. "I've got to see about Paco."

"You've gotta stay in this town till Wednesday, Ken. This is your chance. You don't want to miss this."

Ken got up from his stool with a smirk on his face. Yes, Dave could be right. This could be his chance. The chance he had been dreaming of. Dave had hit on his soft spot. But as a Christian he had learned to control his emotions. He would love to go on a long ride, but it would have to be with the right crowd and the right atmosphere. The joy of riding was a clean act for him, spiritual in a sense, and nothing could take from it. Or else he wouldn't have it.

Ken walked past Dave and stood between Raul and Miguel who were still sipping Tequilas.

"You guys ought to slow down. They won't let you see Paco if they smell any alcohol on you."

Raul and Miguel looked at each other, freezing for a moment. Then they broke into laughter. The alcohol had done its job fast. Their faces were red and their teary eyes shone like marbles.

"You're right, Ken" Raul said, slurring his words. "We gotta see about Paco. We gotta see about Paco."

Ken went to the two other men who had been quieter but had also drunk a great deal. Their swarthy skin seemed fiery and he could see the redness in the white of their eyes. He thought these guys would never make the road this evening.

"I'll see you all later," he said as he placed a five-dollar bill on the table by his plate.

"Ken, I'll get that, come on. If we're gonna be riding on the same team, we gotta share."

Ken was already at the door.

"I'll see you here later, right? You're not going anywhere.

You're staying with me!" Dave yelled after him.

Ken took a breath of the cool autumn air outside. He thought this was only the beginning of the coming season. In a few weeks from now, the cool breeze would turn into a gush of frosty air that would unmercifully bite into the skin. The sun would rarely show and the days would seem morbid and dark. If those bikers wanted to ride to Daytona, they better get going before it got too cold. He had never lived through a winter season in southern Pennsylvania but he could imagine how one could be.

Chapter 3

The most important intersections of the big highways in central New Jersey lie by the Raritan River. The New Jersey Turnpike, running in almost a straight line from New York City to the Delaware, traverses across Highway 18, a local State road, which then intersects Highway 1 a few yards to the west, just south of the big river. Commuters take exit 9 of the New Jersey Turnpike early in the morning to travel to their local destinations, most of them accessible through Highway 18 or Highway 1. The motorcycle caravan had started in Boston with a handful of bikes and rode through interstate highways until they reached Providence, Rhode Island. There it doubled in size to about 30 and from then on, the leaders decided to travel on local highways to avoid causing unwanted notoriety. When they reached New York City, they crossed over the Hudson through the Washington Bridge, causing a major traffic jam, then quickly got on Highway 1 and sprawled around the Fort Lee area to pick up another wave of riders.

The caravan went south on Highway 1 from there, stopping at the parking lot of a landmark movie theater overlooking the Raritan River, and only a few yards north of the intersection of Highway 1 and 18 in East Brunswick, New Jersey. The bikers had agreed that all New Jersey riders joining the caravan would wait at this location.

Ken O'Gara traveled from Long Island, New York, where he had spent two days with his parents after leaving Lancaster, and he decided to go alone to the prearranged location in the New Brunswick-East Brunswick area. He had been told that the caravan would re-organize itself at this point, where it was expected to grow to about one hundred riders. Since he left Lancaster, he had not spoken to Dave. He had debated over whether he would make the trip. He made contact with several riders in New York who told him that the caravan seemed destined to be one of the biggest motorcycle events ever. It was the baby of Ron Mason, a well-known and respected biker from Boston. The New York riders were scheduled to meet at Fort Lee, New Jersey, across the Hudson. It was planned that way to avoid the busy New York City traffic. But Ken preferred to make the downy ride on the Parkway alone. The ride was unusually leveled, only interrupted by a few toll booths, so he decided to ride by himself to Central Jersey and join the caravan there.

As he crossed the bridge over the Raritan River, Ken heard the roaring sound of the Harley engines in the distance. It was a distinctive sound that got inside you like the rush of a stormy wind. It flustered a person's emotions and rattled the body. Ken loved the sound. It was the reason he was here.

He looked ahead as he crossed over to the right lane, past fast-moving cars and saw the shine of the nickel mufflers and the metallic gas tanks, sparkling under the afternoon sun. Some bikes were just arriving and others had congregated in a circle in the theater's empty parking lot.

Ken raised his left arm to let the traffic behind him know that he was turning. He drove in through the uphill entrance to the parking lot and through the center lane until he was at the front of the movie theater building. He followed the arrows towards the left and reached the riders who had gathered on the southern portion of the lot. He slowed his engine down and looked for space to park. Several couples of men and women standing by their bikes and holding coffee cups came to greet him. Many of the men wore bandannas wrapped around their heads. The women wore their hair loose.

He brought his bike up close to the circle. He let his front tire roll parallel to the rear of another bike and then stopped. He released his kickstand and dismounted. He was wearing a black leather wide-collar jacket buttoned to the middle over a white t-shirt and blue donjon jeans over black boots.

"Mark Conners," a man said, introducing himself. He was tall and lean and he quickly extended his arm to shake Ken's hand. "You couldn't hook up with the caravan in New York?"

"Ken O'Gara" Ken said. "No, I got on the parkway alone."

"That's okay. The parkway gets pretty busy in the afternoon going south. So, you might have saved yourself some traffic."

Mark's companion was a woman in her thirties. Like him, she was lean and tall and welcomed Ken readily with repeated broad smiles.

"That's awesome, by the way," Mark said, pointing to Ken's bike.

Ken had put extra work into his silver fenders, which looked spotless under the sun. The metallic blue gas tank proved an affable contrast.

"Are you one of the mechanics?" Mark said.

"Yes."

"Sure glad to see someone handy come along."

"There will be more coming," Ken said.

"So, I hear. Well, we have someone actually. She's not officially a mechanic but she could easily do a darn good job of it," Mark said, turning. "Here she is."

Margaret strode along from the rear. Ken thought she was an older woman who looked as if the years had magically preserved her beauty. Her straight black hair went down over her shoulders, breaking at the back of the neck, each strand resting loosely on each breast. She had deep black eyes and very white skin. She was dressed in a black leather jacket, fitting snugly over her ample bust. Her black jeans were tucked inside very high leather boots that almost reached near the knees.

"I'm Margaret," she said, shaking his hand. "I see you brought your tools. We contributed a van. It's in the back. Maybe you can store your tool box in it. There's room."

"It's all right."

"That box pressing against your behind is going to make you feel very uncomfortable, believe me. By the time we reach Virginia, you'll need Preparation H."

She laughed and the others echoed her. Ken smiled back. Margaret inspected his bike.

"Come on," she said, turning to him. "I'll show you our trailer. You can put your box there. Bring your bike."

Ken grabbed his bike's handlebars, backed it up, and then carried it forward around the other bikes parked in a circle, with Margaret walking next to him.

"Do you ride much?" she asked.

"Whenever I can," he said. "I've gone as far as the Midwest. That's it."

"Never rode south?"

"No, never."

She shook her head in sympathy.

"You'll like this ride," she said. "It's a promising ride. Good for the lost souls."

She turned towards him, smiling impishly, then pointed to a grey van being towed by a pick-up. Ken parked his bike behind it.

"Hello," Ken said to the man reclined against the driver's door of the pickup tugging the small van. His big shoulders were visible under the black, tight jacket he was wearing. He seemed content in his reclining position and did not move.

"How're you doing?" he said. "I'm Zeke."

"Nice meeting you," Ken said, reaching for his hand.

"Zeke is dragging the trailer. You can put your toolbox inside. Go ahead."

Ken untied the straps holding his toolbox to the seat and retrieved it. Zeke reached quickly for the rear and opened the trailer's back cover. He carefully grabbed Ken's box and hopped inside to put it away.

"Don't worry, it'll be safe here," Margaret said. "Come, meet the others."

Two other men had already approached. Ken found himself staring at the scar on the left cheek of one of them.

"I'm Randall," the man said.

"And I'm John," the third one said. "We all ride together. Margaret keeps us safe."

"He's taking over," Margaret said. "He's a mechanic." "Oh, really?"

"You might want to wait for the caravan to get here. They might have other ideas about my role."

"Oh, you're it," Margaret said. "We heard from them already."

"You did?"

"You are Dave's friend, aren't you?" John asked.

"Yes. You may say I am. You know Dave?"

"Yes. Lancaster Dave," Margaret replied. "We know him very well. He told us about you. He said you are a super mechanic."

"I can fix my own bike. I don't know if I do as well with the others."

"You'll do just fine," she said throwing back her hand. "Here, come, meet the girls."

The three women stood beside each other, behind the men, reminiscent of a military formation. Ken said hello. The brunette in the middle spoke first.

"I'm Linda."

"I'm Flora."

"And I'm Donna."

"And don't forget our Robin," Margaret said, "sitting out there on her bike being bashful."

Ken saw her standing with a hand on the bike's handlebars, her wavy brown hair reaching down to her shoulders. She looked at him for a split of a second, enough for Ken to notice her large hazel eyes. She stood next to a chopper blue Harley Davidson Sportster with shiny white lace rims and chrome mirrors. She could have passed for a model advertising the awesome machine. She was tall, taller than any of the other three girls, and wore black jeans tucked under black leather boots that made her seem even taller. She wore a plain figure-hugging white blouse under a black leather vest. Her face was slightly slanted, with puffy cheeks and sensuous lips colored with a faint hint of heartbreak pink lipstick. Ken thought that had her bike been for sale, it would not have lasted long. He was so stunned by her beauty that he stood unconsciously frozen next to Margaret, not knowing what to say.

"Hello, would be nice," Margaret said with a chuckle.

"Hi," Ken said smiling.

"Hi," Robin replied, barely moving her lips.

* * *

Helen McManus did not sleep well that night after her daughter returned from her ride to Central Jersey. Her bedroom sat directly across from Robin's, with a small hallway between them. The only full bathroom in the house was next to Robin's bedroom, across from the bedroom that Helen's parents had occupied when they were alive. When Helen moved into the house, she had worked this arrangement with her parents. She wanted to be across from Robin's room. She could sleep with her door open, look directly across in the middle of the night, and have a full view of her treasured little girl who was only five at the time. This is how it all started and how it remained through the years. The only difference today was that her once innocent little girl had grown and with age came the desire for privacy and independence. The door to Robin's room was now closed, but her mother's, undaunted by time, remained open every night as if she could still see inside her daughter's room.

Helen heard her get up time and time again and walk out of her bedroom to use the bathroom. She was wearing her long white night gown. The first two times, Helen was hardly awake. She heard the rippling sound of the faucet and then water being flushed from the toilet as if she was in a dream. By the third time she was up. She put on her fluffy pink slippers and went to the single panel red mahogany door. She knocked on it gently, just three taps with the middle knuckle of the middle finger and waited.

"Robin, are you all right? Can I come in?"

There was silence for a moment and then her sentient voice.

"I'm all right, Mom. Go to sleep."

"Sure?"

"Sure."

She settled back on her double-size bed and slipped under her maroon flannel comforter. She thought about turning the TV set on and watching one of her favorite forensic file shows but decided against it. The noise could drown Robin's movements if she rose again and she meant to keep a vigil on her daughter tonight. She knew she would fall asleep fast but she knew also that she was a light sleeper and would be perceptive to the minutest sounds. A few minutes later, when Robin walked out of her bedroom again and went into the bathroom, she thought she heard belching repeatedly. She could hear the water from the faucet running but even that could not drown her daughter's groans. She got up quickly, put on her slippers, and ran towards the hallway.

"Robin, what's wrong? Do you need me?" There was no response.

"I'm coming in."

She opened the bathroom door and walked in. Robin was bending over the console bathroom sink, still spewing out the contents of her stomach. Helen wrapped a white hand towel around her neck, ready to wipe her face.

"Let it all out, Robin. Gee, it must be my food. I shouldn't have . . ."

She lifted Robin's head and rubbed her face with the towel.

As she swiveled herself around, she was shocked by what she saw. Robin's left side of the face was solid black. The streaks of black and blues she had seen earlier on her neck quickly traveled up on her face and covered the entire area of the left cheek, down to the jaw bone. Robin's eyes were swollen.

"Robin . . . I've got to get you to the hospital. You're having a bad reaction, I think. I don't know, actually."

"No, Mom. Leave me, please. Leave me."

She pulled away brusquely. She dragged herself towards the tub, pulling down on the shower curtain, and sat down on the tub sobbing.

"Robin, don't be upset. It's only a bad reaction to the food.

Come on. I've got to take you to the emergency room, and they will treat it right away. You'll get rid of it in no time."

"No!" she said, looking up. "I'm not going to any emergency! That's not what's wrong with me!"

"Robin, what's the matter? Why are you acting like this? It's only a reaction to the food. What do you think is wrong with you then?"

"Nothing!" she said, looking down. She sobbed, pressing her temples against her knees with her hands. Helen came closer and tried to lift her head, but she shrugged her away. Then she got up and quickly exited the bathroom. Before Helen could hold her, she ran into her bedroom and slammed the door.

"Robin, why are you acting like this? What's happened? Let me take care of you, please. It's nothing. Just a reaction. Please let me in."

Helen knocked on her door with the knuckles of her closed fist as she spoke.

"Robin, you're worrying me. Open the door, please. At least let me take care of you if you won't go to the hospital. Let me bring you some Mylanta, come on."

There was no response. Helen kept knocking.

"I'm not going away, Robin. Not until you speak to me.

Please let me know you're okay."

There was still no response. Helen was growing more anxious by the second.

"Robin, how about I bring you some tea from downstairs?

It'll help you get your stomach settled. You'll see. In the morning you'll be fine. Please let me do that for you."

Robin did not respond. Helen retreated, not sure if she was hearing her.

"I'll be right back with some tea, okay? Please don't move from where you are. I'll be right back."

She walked down the hall and took the stairway, skipping steps in her haste to get to the kitchen, and sliding her hand on to the reddish, shiny banister like a primary school child. She retrieved a mug from one of the kitchen cabinets and a box of green tea. She took one of the soft, silky bags from the box and dropped it in the mug. She filled the mug with tap water and placed it inside the microwave. She set the button at 90 seconds and waited impatiently as she listened to the rumbling sound of the microwave and until the beep came. Then she grabbed the cup and ran back upstairs. She felt agitated.

Nothing could be more upsetting to her than seeing her daughter in distress. Time seemed to have stood still since that fateful day when she and the five-year-old Robin had walked into this house. To Helen, Robin was still that same little girl.

"Robin? Open up. I brought you tea."

There was no response. Helen knocked on the door again and waited. Hearing nothing, she grabbed the knob and began turning it.

"Robin, I'm going to come in, okay? I'm bringing you tea."

She opened the door and entered the room but stopped near the bed, looking alarmed.

"Robin, where are you? Where did you go?"

The bed was empty. The covers had been tossed on the floor. The pillows were stocked high on top of each other. Helen felt her heart beating and pressure on the left side of her brain. She looked over to the end of the room and saw the curtains swaying from the night breeze. She quickly put the mug down on a dresser and walked towards the window. It was wide open. Horrified, she stuck her head out thinking the worst. She could see nothing on the ground in the darkness.

"Robin, are you there?"

She could hardly make out the bulk, by the side of the home's foundation, but she thought she saw it move and her heart sank thinking that Robin had fallen out of the window.

"Robin, I'm coming down."

She ran downstairs and went around the garden to reach the side of the house. What she saw stunned her. Sitting on the edge of the walkway, with both hands clutching against the cedar slates of the house, Robin was twisting her body and grimacing in pain. Helen took her by the shoulders and tried pulling her towards her.

"Robin, what happened? How did you get here? Are you hurt?"

Robin kept rubbing her upper body against the wall, throwing her head back and closing her eyes. Helen kept trying to pull her closer, but to no avail.

"Robin, you have to come inside. What's wrong?"

She began feeling it with her hands, in the neck and back, then down towards the hips and on her thighs.

"Are you sure you're not hurt? What happened? Did you fall?"

Robin kept twisting her head. She was in a world of her own, not responding to anything her mother said.

"Robin, let me call an ambulance, please. Something's wrong. You are hurt."

"No!" Robin suddenly snapped.

Helen stood up. She could not see her face in the dark and felt indecisive as to what to do. Her daughter could have a fracture and be reacting to the pain. By now she was sure Robin had suffered a terrible fall and could not stand up on her own. She would have to move her. No, better not. She could cause more damage if she disturbed her position. This required professional help. She felt like screaming but knew she could not lose her composure. She had to summon for help. She let go of Robin.

"Don't move, Robin. You may hurt yourself. Stay put for a minute while I go inside and get help. Hang on."

She started to walk away when she felt two hands hold her by the sides of her head. They jolted her vigorously and then she heard Robin yell.

"No! No!"

Helen was able to shake the grip, and as she turned, she saw Robin slide down onto the ground and fall on her knees, her hands open wide, crying.

"Robin, no, it's okay. It's okay."

Helen picked up Robin's face and brought it up to her shoulder.

"Robin, it's okay. You're just upset. Let's get inside the house. Come on."

"Oh, Mom," she managed to say. "I would never hurt you.

You know that."

"Robin, it's okay. It's okay. Come on."

Helen helped her get up and put her arm around her waist. They walked together on the cement walkway bordering the house. Helen helped her through the front steps and they both went inside. Helen helped her sit down in one of the living room chairs. The only light in the room came from a small shelf lamp in a brass-colored wall unit. Helen could see Robin's face faintly but she saw a terrible fear in her eyes. What was wrong with her daughter? She trembled at the thought that Robin could be losing her sanity.

"Calm down, Robin. Calm down. Are you in any pain?" "Mom, I'm sorry . . . out there."

"Robin, it's okay. It's nothing. What do you feel? What's wrong?"

"Mom, I don't know. Those women . . . that house."

"What house, Robin? What house?"

Her eyes lost focus momentarily, as if she had to think back.

She covered her face.

"Robin, it's okay. You don't have to think about it," she said, taking her hands. "You're home now. Don't think about it anymore."

"I don't know," Robin said, looking down. "I don't know what's happened to me."

Startled by this revelation, Helen took hold of her arms and helped her come up from the chair.

"Nothing's happened, Robin. Nothing. You're upset, that's so. Come on upstairs. Let's lie in bed together so you can get some sleep. Come on."

Robin was slowly getting up. Inside, Helen was dying to know who those women-riders were. It had to be riders again. Those rides that had made her life miserable were now hurting her little girl.

"Mom, I can't get them out of my head. I just can't."

"But you will, Robin. You will. Come on, let's go upstairs."

She took her left hand and passed her other arm around her waist. The two walked slowly up the stairs. Helen took her inside her own bedroom and had her lie in bed. She propped up two pillows by the headboard and got her the cup of tea she had brought earlier.

"Drink this, Robin. It'll calm you down."

She held the cup up to her lips and slowly made her drink. "Mom," she said. "Could you close the window?"

Helen looked back toward her daughter's room and remembered. She quickly put the mug on the night table beside the bed and rushed to Robin's bedroom. She grabbed both ends of the sash frame behind the curtains and brought the window down. The night breeze had made Robin's room chilly, and she closed the door behind her as she left, feeling as if she needed to protect her daughter from more than just the cold breeze. She sat at the edge of the bed and held the mug to Robin's lips again, making her drink.

"Mom, I'm so afraid," she said, looking deep into her mother's eyes.

"There's nothing to be afraid of, Robin. Nothing. I'm here with you. What is it, Robin? What are you afraid of?"

"Them," she said, her eyes fixed on the ceiling.

"Robin, this is only a bad dream. They, whoever they are, can't hurt you."

She said nothing for a moment, as if she needed to gather her thoughts. Then she let her eyes drop to the foot of the bed.

"Yes, they can," she said in a whisper.

Helen waited by the edge of the bed until she drank her tea.

She took the empty cup and set it on the night table. She brought her comforter up to Robin's chest, walked to the other side, and lay beside her. She took Robin's hand and held it with both of hers.

"Go to sleep," she said softly. "You had a bad dream, Robin. That's so."

She lay still on the bed for a few minutes, waiting until Robin fell asleep. When she saw her close her eyes, she relaxed, thinking that she could never fall asleep again. But as her eyelids drooped and she found herself dozing off, she thought that her internal alarm would sound off at the slightest disturbance and she felt good about that. She didn't recall hearing anything else. She woke up well past eight and she sat up in bed immediately. To her dismay, she noticed that the space next to her on the bed was empty. She ran barefooted and opened the door to Robin's bedroom. The bed was still unmade, as she had left it last night. There was no sign of Robin. She ran downstairs and went through the living room and kitchen calling Robin's name. Intuitively, she opened the kitchen door and looked outside. Her SUV was sitting in the driveway, in front of the garage doors. She opened the storm door and looked around. She remembered that the night before Robin had left her bike off the driveway, by the side of the house, it was gone after she had asked her to move it.

* * *

Margaret shoved Ken around, introducing him to the other riders who were standing near their bikes in small groups. She took control of him, handling him as if he was a pet. She grabbed his arm sensuously with one of her very feminine looking hands, coiling her fingers around his muscled forearm and pressing against the flesh with her violet-colored nails. Suddenly, Mark Conners placed himself in the front area of the lot, followed by Laura, to give them a talk.

"Listen, guys," he said, raising his voice. "I just heard from Ron. They're by Woodbridge. They'll be here in another ten minutes, so everyone get ready. If you have any coffee cups or disposables, please put them in the garbage dumps in front of the theatre. Do not leave any trash lying around. There are some patrols out there just waiting for us to screw up. We don't want to have anything that may hold us back. Be careful. Also, I know I said it before but I'll say it again. Check your gas tank. Make sure you have enough gas. Check your engines and your gear again. The word is we're not stopping until Philly and we're going to be traveling on Route One which is a busy highway, as you know. I'm sure Ron will give you a prep talk once he gets here."

More than half of the riders were female, and a good portion of those were riding their own bikes, like Margaret and her girlfriends. The rest rode saddled behind their men. On a long ride like this one, some riders furnished their bikes with parallel bars at the edge of their seats so that the passenger- rider could lean back on them for comfort.

"You must behave if you want to ride," Margaret said in a loud voice, mocking him.

There was murmuring laughter in the crowd. Mark broke in fast before it died.

"Listen up! This is no ordinary ride. We're going to Daytona. We're looking to be there for the races. We gotta keep our act together here. The cops will be waiting for us to make a mistake along the way. Remember, there will be over one hundred bikers riding in this thing. The State police will be looking to put us out at any time. We're a nuisance to them. I'm not saying you shouldn't enjoy the ride, but we got to keep it tight. We clean up after ourselves wherever we go. We don't get in trouble. We keep away from the booze while in route and we don't curse. This is how we're going to do it." He looked around the crowd to see the effect of his message.

Laura was next to him, her grayish hair blowing in the cool afternoon wind. "Oh, and one last thing," he said, as if reminding himself. "We take care of our women."

He looked down towards Margaret. She was apparently trying to deflate any wisdom in his lecture and goad the crowd. Mark put his arm around Laura and walked through the bikers. He was talking to them in the language they knew.

Women bikers were still not the norm and everyone knew it. Women riders, yes. But only as riders in the back of the seat with their arms wrapped around their male biker who was in charge of the machine and, more importantly, her safety.

"You boys better keep an eye on me," Margaret shot back. "I'm nutty."

Mark was already wading past the bikers, shaking hands with people as he marched along with Laura. He did not respond or couldn't. Ken had watched the exchange with interest and got bad vibes from it. He remembered his last phone conversation with Dave the day before. "At the first sign of trouble," he had warned him, "I'm gone. I'm in it only if it's a clean ride." But the farce he was watching was interesting and he wondered how it would play with the head of the caravan. He knew Ron Mason, the undisputed leader of the ride and his deputy, Phil Rocan. It was only because Ron Mason was in charge that Ken finally decided to go. Ron was a no-nonsense biker, extremely knowledgeable about bikes and with a sense of fairness. What he cared about was quality in the rider, comradeship on the road. Race or ethnic background played no part in Ron's decisions. His deputy in this ride, chosen by him, was Phil Rocan, a thirty-year-old African American man from Milwaukee, one of the ablest riders Ken had ever seen. How Ron felt about women bikers, Ken did not know, but he bet that he cared little whether they rode in back of someone or alone on their own bikes as long as they could do it with masterfully. Such was Ron Mason.

Ken gazed cautiously at the beauty he had met. Robin was standing by her bike, one hand on the handlebar and the other dropped at her side. A narrow strip of gauze was strapped around her free hand between her thumb and her forefingers.

"She's a hit, isn't she?" Margaret said next to him. "Come on, let's go talk to her some more."

They made their way back to Robin. Margaret seemed amused.

"I guess we're well protected now. We got Mark," she said sardonically, stretching her sensuous lips back.

"You weren't before?" Ken asked.

"No, it's all you males that are making us safe. Mark just nailed it when he said you have to take care of the women, right? That's why you're here too, isn't that right?"

"I wouldn't say so. I'm here to enjoy the ride. That's why I came. But of course, we gotta take care of each other, man or woman."

"You're not riding with anybody, I take it."

"No."

"Well, let's see what Mark has for you. But I say we'll need you riding behind our trailer. You'll have all the tools you need. The trailer is our contribution to the caravan."

"Are you gals in a club?"

"Yeah," Margaret said.

Ken had noticed Robin's reserve by now. Riders, male or female, usually weren't that shy. She seemed aloof, nodding in agreement to every question.

"It's called the club of the lost souls."

Margaret laughed. The other three girls giggled. The guys did eventually, too.

"Never heard of your club before. Sorry."

"That's okay, most people haven't, luckily for them. But we're here and growing. You'll get to know us."

"How did you get your experience with bikes, Ken?"

Linda had approached from behind Robin. Her black hair was shaggily combed.

"I've been in love with bikes since I was a kid. I learned to work on them."

"You might as well if you ride them, right?"

"Riding them is the easy part," Flora said. She was not as tall as the others. She wore her hair long and frizzed. "Margaret is good at it too."

The other girl, who had freckles on her face, wore an open black helmet with the straps hanging loose. Ken sensed their connection. They seemed like a tight pack.

"Caravan is coming," Flora cut in.

* * *

It was barely 9:00 when Robin drove her bike into the dirt driveway of the McCarter house. She had driven her blue Sportster on a tank of gas all the way from Cape May. She had sprung out of her bed right before dawn, boosted by some inner energy that she could never have explained. She rode on the parkway until exit 121, picked up Route 35 and went south, and then veered off onto Route 9. She went south towards the Englishtown area, following Margaret's path of two nights ago. She got off on a jug handle, went across the highway and into a local road. When she reached the dirt driveway, she did not hesitate. It was as if she was guided by an internal radar that told her exactly where to go. She drove her bike under the tree in the back and parked. She strapped her helmet on the seat. She walked slowly through the front walkway among large green ferns that bent sideways under the soft morning breeze and stopped at the red oak door. She pressed on the gold handle and popped the door open. She went inside. She walked across the living room and headed into the kitchen. The countertop was spotless and the sink empty, not a sign of untended kitchen ware. She looked down at the coffee table and saw the mug on its center, covered with a saucer. She uncovered the mug and took it by the handle, sure of its contents. She clicked the microwave door open and placed the mug inside. She set the timer on 50 seconds. She dragged one of the chairs away from the coffee table and sat down. She began sipping the hot chocolate, left ready for her on the table since the night before.

She felt warmer as she drank. The wind on the parkway had been rough on her face and her cheeks were red. She drank slowly, looking up at the oak cabinets that ran down from the ceiling, skirted on top by a wooden triangle valance. There was not one appliance out of place. The sink was empty, the strainer dry. A toaster and a shaker lay neatly on the counter against the wall. Whoever these people were, they picked up after themselves. Or maybe their aim was to keep the house empty, void of life and energy.

She finished her cup and slowly got up. She washed the mug and saucer in the sink and later dried them with a cloth. She placed them inside a cabinet and headed upstairs through the creaky stairway. She chose the last room at the end of the hallway. The bed set at the center of the room seemed heaven sent. It had a full canopy on top and its headboard was stacked with pillows. She closed the door behind her, sat on the bed, and began pulling her boots off. Then she slid off her pants and blouse, wearing only her panties and bras. She got under the burgundy comforter. She laid her head on the pillows, staring at the red top of the canopy. She felt totally at ease in this position and gradually fell into a deep sleep. The late morning's sun filtered in through the narrow creases forming in the drape at the window. Robin McManus had found her peace.

She woke up well after sundown, and she did not know exactly how. There was no noise, but she found herself staring at the deep black eyes of a face she had been dreaming about incessantly since she met her two nights before. She smiled the minute Robin opened her eyes.

"Did you sleep well?"

She rubbed her right cheek with her open hand. Robin blinked, assuring herself it was not a dream.

"Margaret?"

"I'm glad you're home, honey. Welcome. I've been waiting for you."

"Margaret . . . I . . ."

"It's all right, honey. Come on and shower. Flora has your bath ready. It's time to be up."

She took Robin's hand and helped her sit up. Then, holding her other hand, she waited for her to speak.

"I don't know what got into me, how I slept like this."

"You were tired honey. You needed to come home."

Robin lifted her chin. Her eyes gradually gained an air of awareness, as if they had been exposed to an act of revelation.

"Home?"

"Yes, honey. This is home. This is where you were meant to be."

"Sure?"

"Sure. Come on and shower. Then come downstairs. We'll be waiting for you.

"Margaret . . ."

"It's all right. Come on. I will help you."

She raised her by the tip of her hands and helped her take small steps, laying a hand on her back.

"You'll feel better after you shower. You will see."

She opened the bedroom door and let her out. They walked together to the end of the hallway, past the stairway. She stopped by a narrow mahogany door and opened it wide. It was a long, spacious room with walls tiled in pink ceramics and black borders. Flora was sitting on a vanity stool across from a multi-drawer chest and she smiled at them as they came in.

She was wearing a long black gown and her wavy brown hair spread casually over her face and shoulders. She stood up to receive them.

"Sleep well, Robin?"

"Yes but I'm still dizzy."

"I have a bath already for you. Come, come."

She took her by the hand, and Margaret let her go. An oval-shaped tub sat high against the end window. Flora took her up the two steps and let her stand on the landing near the tub, which was filled with warm water and small violet petunias floating on the surface. Margaret stayed back, watching them.

"It's all ready for you, honey. It's been waiting for you."

"I can't undress with people in the room," Robin said.

"I know, honey. I know."

Flora reached for the shower curtain, which was wrapped tightly against the edge of the window frame and slipped it across almost the entire length of the oval-shaped rim.

"Go ahead inside honey. You can have your privacy." Flora stepped back and sat on the stool again.

"Come downstairs when you're done. We have breakfast, ready," Margaret said as she left the room.

Robin stood quietly in the tub, as if re-thinking her position. She took a few minutes just staring at the floor then eventually moved the curtain aside and went inside to disrobe. Flora sat on her stool, hearing her splash small quantities of water on herself. A long time went by until she spoke.

"Do you want a bath towel, Robin?"

"Yes," she said from inside the curtain.

Flora arose and took a white towel from the dresser and a black bathrobe. Through a break in the curtain, she handed Robin the towel. She waited for Robin to dry up, then gave her the robe.

"You look disarming," she said, as she watched her step down from the tub.

"I feel so bare," Robin said. "I have no clothes to wear."

"Yes, you do," Flora said. "They are all ready for you."

She pointed to the high, narrow cherry wood lingerie chest near the dresser. She walked up to it and pulled one of its many drawers open.

"You have plenty to choose from," Flora said. "Pick what you like."

Robin went through the contents, taking a black tee-shirt and pants.

"I can't believe they're my size," Robin said, looking them over, surprised. "How can it be?"

"Everything is your size, honey. It's made for you. Interior clothes are underneath," she said and pulled out another drawer.

"Oh."

"Would you like me to step outside while you dress?"

"You don't mind?"

"Not one bit."

Flora went out of the room and closed the door behind her.

Robin stood in the center of the room facing the dresser's mirror and she stared at herself. She was wearing the black bathrobe, tight around the waist. It was a short skirt, reaching down to knee level, and exposing her legs. She turned slightly to gaze at her back, forgetting for a moment that she was not home. Then she got closer and examined her face, rubbing her hand over her jaw and chin. She saw no traces of the black botches running near her left cheek and neck. The spots were all gone. She got closer to the mirror and looked deep into her handsome hazel eyes. Where was she? What had happened? She got even closer, almost touching her nose with it and suddenly she remembered her clothes. She moved back, scared, and pulled her waistband loose. She shook her shoulders and the bathrobe fell to the floor. She saw the reflection of her nude body in the mirror. She could be a nine or a ten, but right now she could not see it. She took a pair of black bras from one of the lingerie drawers and put them on. Then she slipped on a pair of black panties and ran towards the tub. She retrieved her wallet from her pants pocket and reached into the vest for her phone. She felt the vibrations in her hand as she grabbed the silver gadget. She saw a familiar number on the bluish screen. It was her home. Her mother must have been calling her incessantly. She flipped the cover open and put it against her ear, but then she saw the room's front door open.

"Robin, are you ready?" Flora said from the doorway.

Robin dropped her hand down discreetly, still holding the phone.

"Yes. Almost, I mean. I'm coming."

She descended the two steps from the tub and went to the dresser. She took the tee-shirt from the vanity stool and slipped it on. She put on the pants and let the phone glide in her back pocket.

"I left my boots in the other room," she said.

"I got them for you," Flora said, flinging both hands from behind her back, each one holding a black boot.

Robin sat down on the vanity stool and Flora went behind her. She rose one foot at a time, pulling the boot in from behind Robin's shoulders.

"You look like a true rider of the night," she said.

"Am I?"

"We shall soon see."

Flora took her hand, and they both went out of the room, through the hallway and down the stairs. As they passed the living room, they could hear voices coming from the kitchen. The women were all sitting at the coffee table, drinking from mugs, while the three men stood behind them, leaning on the counter, also drinking.

"How's our sleeping beauty?" one of them said.

Robin could not remember his name. He had wide shoulders, dark skin and the most welcoming smile. Robin tried hard to remember him.

"Sit," one of the girls at the table said.

Robin gazed at her freckled face but could not remember her name either.

"I'm Donna," she said smiling. "That's Linda and that's Margaret," she said, pointing at them.

Linda nodded and Margaret smiled.

"Give her food," Margaret said to Flora. She has not eaten.

"Aren't we riding out?"

"After she's eaten."

Flora got busy at the counter and the guys moved away to give her more room. Flora toasted some bread and cut up some lettuce.

"Is turkey all right?" Flora asked.

Robin nodded, looking dazzled by all the treatment. "Doesn't anybody eat?" she asked.

All three women at the table traded looks.

"No, not tonight," Margaret said. "It's better we ride with an empty stomach."

"Where are you going?"

"There's talk about this major ride through the east coast. We're going to meet with a local club to formally enlist tonight."

"Where's the ride to?"

"Daytona."

"Wow, Daytona. I've always wanted to go to Daytona."

"Well, this is your chance."

"Would you come," Linda asked.

She was sitting next to her, and unlike Margaret, she seemed rather reserved, not sharing the enthusiasm of others towards Robin.

"Yes, I would."

"No questions asked?"

"No, no questions asked."

Flora set a plate on the table. "What will you drink?" Flora said.

"Oh, give her warm chocolate."

Robin grabbed the sandwich, a seeded roll with lettuce, tomato and turkey. She still felt weak from the previous night. Her whole body ached for some reason. But what was most prominent in her at the moment were those flashes of memory that kept coming in and out, haunting her. She kept seeing Helen McManus, her mother, wiping tears from her face as she stood in the driveway of their house. Then she would look up at the others and the vision would fade. She would see Margaret and notice her reassuring stare and she would feel confident again. It was as if it never happened. She felt suddenly nurtured and protected with an insatiable desire to learn more about them and follow them. She ate her sandwich as the others asked questions of Margaret, mainly about bikes. She drank the contents of her cup fast, then set it down at the table. Margaret looked instantly at her.

"Let's roll," she said.

The girls got up to leave. The men followed them out of the kitchen, all walking out in long strides, as if they needed to get somewhere in a hurry.

"Come on, Robin! Let's go! We're cruising," Margaret said without turning.

They went out through the house's main door and Robin followed them to the parking area. The first sound was that of Margaret's FLSTF Fat Boy roaring in a fury as she turned the engine on. There was no question she was in charge and she raised her left hand as a sign for the others to follow. Her midnight blue machine seemed invisible in the dark night, and were it not for its headlight, you would not know it was there. The other bikes came into life and they quickly got on the road, one after the other. Robin was still clicking her engine on when the last one of them pulled out. She could have taken off in the opposite direction at that moment. She had the freedom to do it. But she wouldn't. Something had trapped her inside and she reached into her back pocket to click off the vibrations of her phone so she could concentrate on what she was about to do. She needed to ride. She needed to follow Margaret and her gang even to the end of the earth. It was her destiny.

She tried to gain distance on the last two riders, riding side by side on the two-lane highway. The night was fresh. The autumn breeze splashed cool air on their cheeks, the most vulnerable part of a rider's face. But it felt good. Robin could not break in between the last two riders so she settled behind them, following them at a short distance. They went south on Highway 9 and then picked up Highway 18 north. No one was saying anything. Margaret was up in the lead, barely visible on her black clothes and black helmet. She rode alone in the front with Linda trailing a few feet behind. At an intersection, Margaret turned her right signal and they all followed her into a short street. At about the middle of the block, she took a turn left and went up on a steep driveway, next to a Cape Cod house. There was nothing parked on the road except what looked like a covered Harley Road King. Margaret went up the cinder block stairway on the side of the house and she knocked on the bottom of the storm door. A lean woman with a long face opened.

"Margaret," she said, her face becoming clearly visible as she flicked on an outside light to the side of the doorway.

"Hi, Laura. Mark in?"

"Yes. He's here. He's waiting for you. Did you bring your troops?"

"They're out here."

"Well, have them come in," she said, stretching her head out sideways of Margaret. "All you guys come in."

They went inside the small kitchen, which was paneled with narrow wooden planks that gave it an English Tudor flavor. There was a small round table in the center, and the woman waved for them to sit. There were not enough chairs for all of them, so all the girls sat down except Robin.

"I'll get Mark and some chairs. He's talking to someone now on the ride."

She disappeared into the small hallway.

"Should we get some chairs ourselves?" John said.

"No, we can stand for a little bit," Zeke said. "Maybe one for Robin."

"She could wait too," Linda said from the table.

Margaret gave her a look that didn't escape the others. Robin was not Linda's favorite but she had arrived as Margaret's pet. She was not to be touched.

"Guys," Laura called from the doorway. "Help me bring these in."

They carried some chairs into the kitchen and set them in a row against the wall. Mark walked in unannounced. He was tall, well over six feet and had very gray hair that grew copiously from the temples. He smiled as he came into the room and shook everyone's hand.

"What shall I get you guys? We have apple cider, Margaret. I know that's a favorite of yours."

"Give me whatever. Give them what they want."

"Well, we can make coffee," Laura cut in, standing at the door to the hallway. "But we have soda, juice. Whatever you want. Some wine?"

"I'll take wine," Zeke said.

"Us too," Randall and John said.

"We'll all have wine," Margaret said.

"What do we have here?" Mark paced the floor, looking towards Robin. "You joined this crowd, ah?"

"She wants to make the trip to Daytona."

"Oh, I see."

"She's a quite capable rider."

"I'm sure she is if she's riding with you. Is she officially in your club?"

"Yes," Margaret replied.

The others looked on, not knowing whether she was serious.

"Congratulations," Mark said to Robin. "That's quite an accomplishment, I want you to know. This group is quite demanding. They don't just take on anybody."

"Mark, tell us about the ride."

"It's the greatest thing ever put together. We got a pair of experienced bikers making it happen—Ron Mason from Boston and Phil Rocan from Milwaukee. You know Ron. What biker doesn't? He leads a pretty aggressive club but he's a clean guy, organized and devoted to his crew. If you're in Ron's ride, you'll be taken care of. That's the way he is. He runs a cohesive ride when he does one. But he's picky about his people. He doesn't just let everybody in. He chose Phil for his deputy. That in itself tells you something. Phil was in Jersey last summer when we did the bikers for leukemia. Phil is a tremendous organizer. The guy has a prodigious memory and can remember up to the minutest details. If you're a rider or have been a rider at some point, chances are Phil knows your name. And he's got Ron's ear on this one. So, if you're looking to be in this ride, Ron is gonna know everything about you even if he hasn't ever seen you."

Margaret had listened attentively but not with deference. She had obviously come here for a reason. She wanted her club to be in the ride and was looking for Mark to get her in, but she was not impressed by the organization's hierarchy. In fact, she resented it.

"All right, so these guys know our life history. Are we in the ride, yes or no?"

"You're in."

"Good."

Laura had served them wine in short glasses and she passed them out to them in twos. Margaret lifted hers and cheered.

"To the Conners," she said. "To us."

Then suddenly, they all hoorayed, loud and in unison. All, except Robin who sat back on her chair, lifting her glass in silence. Mark was a little startled by their reaction. Then the others began speaking.

"What do we do once we get to Daytona? Where are we going to stay?" Linda asked.

"That's the benefit of riding with Ron, like I was saying. He takes care of you. We have reservations by the beach. We do the run in town, a little bit of partying, and then we go to our rooms at night. We have a week down there."

"A week of parading and racing."

"We're not racing. We are watching the races," Mark said. "Some of us got different ideas," Donna said, speaking for the first time.

"Well, I'm gonna tell you right now," Mark said, getting serious. "Ron will not put up with it. If you're going on this ride thinking you're gonna race, don't go. This is a serious ride. It is a once-in-a-lifetime ride, and Ron is a disciplinarian. You've got to follow the rules. There is no racing."

"Mark, cool off, will you?" Margaret said." "It's not like we're gonna join the army."

"I'm telling you . . . "

"Can we have a cheer, please? We're not gonna race. We're gonna watch the races in Daytona."

She took on a serious air as she said it, solemn enough to convince Mark who waited a second and then took a sip from his glass. Margaret blinked both eyes while looking straight ahead. She raised her glass and the others followed. They waited for Mark to raise his glass to theirs.

"To Daytona," Margaret said. "To a good and peaceful ride."

They all had a drink, and then Mark spoke again.

"I would like to offer your mechanical skills if needed," he said. "Can I?"

"Sure."

"Okay. We're scheduled to leave next Tuesday. We'll be counting on you to bring a trailer. We're meeting the caravan by the cinemas at the intersection of one and eighteen."

Margaret stood up. There had been some small talk amongst the others which quickly faded as she got up. They said their goodbyes. Mark and Laura walked after them to the driveway and saw them leave. It was Margaret and Linda in the lead with two of the men after them followed by Donna and Flora and the last of the men behind them. Robin was last. They drove out of Mark's street and turned right towards Highway 18. The night was early, barely ten. No one said anything, even at the two intersections where they stopped in the highway. They veered right at the second light and took a local street onto the first intersection. They turned left, heading north again. The road was much darker, running parallel to highway 18, and bordered by a mixture of small industry and scattered houses. They went no further than a mile when the two bikers up front turned left and pulled into a large parking lot. They took a slot two spaces away from a car, parked right across from the entrance to an office building. Two of the others pulled in the space immediately to the car's left and the last two pulled up behind it. Not knowing what to do, Robin stopped a distance behind, waiting. Suddenly, everyone got off their bikes and moved toward the vehicle. There was the sound of glass shattering from both side windows and the rear one. All six of them went in at the same time, two from each side and two dragging themselves over the trunk. Their dark figures disappeared inside the vehicle and there was no human sound but the loud thud of jaws tearing and pulling flesh apart. Robin stayed on her bike with her engine running, watching it all from a distance. A few minutes later, all six of them came outside again, oddly stumping the ground as they tore and pulled on long threads of human intestines from each other. They made slobbering sounds with their mouths and savagely devoured everything in their hands. Gradually they stopped wavering and they stopped making those awful dribbling sounds. They stiffened their bodies and rubbed their hands as if to wipe off the blood and flesh residue. Robin was not sure if what she was seeing was a figment of her imagination. Hadn't she had one of Margaret's special drinks? Perhaps she had mixed angel dust with her chocolate. Yes, that was it. That had to be it. But then she was not even sure that the scene she had been a witness to was anything but ill-humored theatrics intended to confuse her and test her resolve. Was she in or was she out?

They mounted their bikes and throttled up their engines. They rode out of the parking lot in rows of two. Robin followed them. She had the urge to look inside the car to persuade herself that what she had seen was not a dream. She rolled her bike forward, past the rear of the car and then began arching out as she reached the front. She came almost to a full stop as she went by the driver's door. The driver's window was gone and on the seat there were only traces of what once had been a human body. A decapitated head with a large hole on top and some brain material. An arm hanging by the edge of the window. She gave gas to her engine and rode out of the parking lot, picking up speed to catch up with the others.

The lead riders kept a longer distance on the other four for some reason. Robin lagged behind. They turned left at the first intersection, heading south on Route 18. At a steady pace with no words being spoken, the pack seemed like any other average group of bikers out for a night ride, and without giving a hint of the horrible scene they had just left behind.

While stopped at a light for a few moments, Robin was able to catch up, coming close behind Donna and Randall. It was then that she heard their eccentric chorus.

"People are strange when you're a stranger faces look ugly when you're alone. Women seem wicked when you're unwanted, the streets are uneven when you're down. When you're strange faces come out of the rain, when you're strange, no one remembers your name, when you're strange. Da da da da, da da da da, da, da, da, da."

The light went green and Margaret's bike roared, followed by Linda's and then the others. Their voices seemed to fade behind the sound of the engines, but the murmur kept coming back, repeating the verses all the way through as they took Route 9 and went off into one of the local roads, turning on Maple Street and then into the driveway of the McCarter house. There was total darkness around it. The riders shoved their bikes into the parking slings under the tree and dismounted now quietly. Margaret walked through the entrance and turned the door open. A lamp by a window was the only light on. They all headed for the kitchen and Robin followed.

"What will it be?" Margaret said, standing by the cabinets after turning the kitchen light on.

"I'm doing the hosting tonight," Donna replied. "You're off Margaret."

"That's right. It is Monday. Wicked day of the week."

Donna took her by the shoulders and made her sit on one of the chairs while the others giggled.

"We take turns hosting," Donna said, looking up at Robin. "Your night will come too Robin."

There was a clicking sound at the kitchen entrance, coming from the living room, which they all heard but no one reacted to at first. Slowly, the long-barreled Flemington pump-action shotgun made its presence known as it verged into the room, held by a tall blonde woman who assertively pointed it at them. They all gazed at her with a look of awe, not fear. Margaret was the first to speak.

"What can we do for you?"

"I want my daughter back," she said. "Robin, come by me."

Helen McManus had made the dreaded trip to central Jersey, where she had not visited now for almost twenty years. The decision to travel north on the parkway into what she considered prohibited territory had been a real mind struggle for her. But once she decided, she did it without hesitation. Her daughter's safety was at stake, and even the unthinkable became a certainty when that was an issue. She did not waver in driving into the area she had spent almost a lifetime avoiding, just as now she would not vacillate to use lethal force if necessary to get her daughter back.

Margaret traded looks with Robin.

"Is that what this is? Is that what's causing you to threaten this fun-loving people with deadly force? Robin? Is that why you're here?"

"You know darn well why I'm here Margaret—you lousy devil. You made a big mistake when you touched my daughter. You have gotten away with enough, but not my daughter. I'm not gonna let you take her. Over my dead body."

"Helen, you didn't travel all the way out here from your foxhole to tell me that, did you?"

"I told you she was trouble," Linda said.

"Shhhhhhhh!" Margaret said. "This is not the time to talk. This is the time to listen."

"You're right, I didn't come here just to talk. I came prepared to use this if necessary." She pointed the barrel dead center at her chest then lifted her head towards her daughter who was standing near the entrance door. "Let's go Robin," Helen said. "Let's go."

"But Mom."

"Let's go, honey."

She grabbed Robin's arm with her left hand, still holding the shotgun with the other.

"You haven't changed, Helen," Margaret said almost casually. "You're just as beautiful as twenty years ago."

"And you're just as evil as then, Margaret. You should not be alive. You've hurt so many people."

"Hold your tongue, you ignorant creature," Linda said, standing up from her chair. "I will not have you denigrate Margaret that way!"

"Hold it," Margaret said, extending her arm. "Sit down.

There's no need. She's upset about her daughter being here. I guess we are not good enough company for her. But I say Robin ought to have something to say about that. She's an adult. Robin, what do you say, honey? You want to stay with us?"

"Shut up!" Helen said. "You're not playing your little mind games with my daughter, you devil. She's coming with me."

Helen pulled Robin closer and began retreating, still pointing the gun at them. Robin did not resist her, but her face grew painfully burdened as she looked at Margaret and then back at her mother.

"Don't look at her, Robin."

Helen had now worked her way into the living room from Margaret's and the others' view, but she still could not turn.

"You realize Helen," Margaret said from the kitchen, "you have already committed about three or four felonies. I could have you arrested at the snap of my fingers. You have broken into my home, threatened me and my friends with a gun, and are now kidnapping one of us."

"She's not one of you, Margaret," Helen yelled back, now standing by the front door, ready to leave. "She'll never be one of you. This time I won't let it happen. I'll kill you first."

"Watch that lashing tongue now, Helen. You're going to make me dial 911."

"Go ahead. Tell them to come to the McCarter house where they can find the evidence to all their unsolved crimes."

Helen tightened her grip on Robin's arm. She pressed down on the lock's bolt and opened the door. She darted into the dark night, dragging her daughter behind her, with a gun in hand, towards her SUV, which she had brought up all the way into the walkway. She opened the driver's door and pushed her daughter in, making her slide towards the passenger side. She got behind the wheel, turned the engine on and backed the vehicle up the driveway until she was in the street. Then she put the engine on drive and took off, tires screeching.

"Oh, Mom . . ."

Robin laid her head on her shoulder, looking agitated. "What am I going to do?"

"You're coming home with me, Robin. And don't ever, ever see this person again. They are evil, Robin. You hear me?

They are soulless."

"But Mom . . . I . . . ."

She rammed the gas pedal down, releasing all her ire into it as if somehow the truck was to blame. She was looking straight ahead, holding her shotgun in between her thighs, her face looking so tense that not one single muscle seemed to move. The SUV's tires slid on the dirt trail leaving a cloud of small pebbles and dust behind them. Then it took off like a rocket, making a raucous noise that sounded like the engine would blow up at any second. Helen negotiated the turn at the end of the driveway and the SUV's tires skidded on the pavement as they entered the road. Robin kept holding onto the passenger door and looking at her mother with amazement. She had never seen her drive like this. It did not seem she was trying to get away from them. She would have much rather stayed and faced the entire gang. Helen McManus was in a rage, releasing all her anger into the unlucky strap of metal that made up the SUV's accelerator, perhaps frustrated that she could not finish what she had come to do. But that was only because she had her daughter.

"Mom, my bike . . . my bike is in their yard."

"Forget your bike, Robin. Forget anything that these people have been a part of. Forget they ever existed."

"Mom, it's my bike. I need it."

"Forget it, I tell you. We'll get a new bike."

Helen kept looking straight ahead, not winking an eye, concentrating on the highway she had now turned into and speeding down the slightly curved slopes as if they were a racetrack. Robin was still amazed at the energy that flowed from her. The night was dark, moonless, and a cool breeze rubbed her face from the slightly cracked window. It was heaven sent. The right side of her face felt hot as when her mother had first discovered those awful black marks on it.

The breeze cooled her off. She laid her head back and closed her eyes, hearing the rove of the SUV's engine and felt happy that Helen McManus was her mother.

Chapter 4

The thundering sound crossing the Raritan River was unmistakable. It was a sound all bikers knew. Whenever more than twenty Harleys traveling together in short tow of each other, they make a rumble of a sound, like the thunder of a faraway storm, carrying itself slowly in the horizon. It now kept creeping closer. All of the riders in the parking lot had raised their heads, standing near each other in a group and looking for any sign of the caravan.

The first bike that became visible over the bridge was a yellow Harley Softail Chopper with street sweeper fenders. It was traveling a good distance ahead of the main pack, so it seemed it was going alone for a moment. The rider made the plodding curve after the bridge and raised his left arm parallel to the ground, indicating he was turning right. He slowed down and went up the sloped entrance to the theater's parking lot. He came to a full stop by arching his bike in front of the men and women standing by their bikes in the lot. He was wearing a black helmet and round sunglasses. He did not turn the engine off but lifted himself above ground and held onto the handlebars. He was tall and wore an un-zipped black leather jacket and white pullover shirt underneath. Both of his arms were busily tattooed.

"Hoity," he said, raising his right arm with his index and middle fingers extended in a sign of peace.

Everyone cheered and Mark Conners came to greet him. Just then they heard the buzzing sound of the other engines as they began entering the lot in two rows. The riders throttled up and rode around them, taking the space in the back and at the sides. The line seemed endless as more and more bikes, all traveling in pairs, came in. The sound of their engines drowned the human voices.

"I'm Mark Conners," Mark said, approaching the first rider. "Are you Ron?"

The man released his bike's kickstand and shook Mark's hand with his left foot.

"I'm Daniel O'Rourke," he said. "No, I'm not Ron. I was a scout in the lead. Ron and Phil were riding together with their women in the lead, so they should be in the parking lot already. I don't know where though."

He looked at both sides of the lot. A steady flow of bikes were rolling in, their engines roaring as they passed the entrance.

"Pretty hard to tell right now," he said and laughed.

They waited as more bikes drove in. Each man would take his bike as close to Conners' group as he could go, then turn it to face the highway. The next biker would parallel his bike to the last one. The lines kept getting longer until the last riders came in and both rows reached almost the entrance to the lot. The engines quieted down. Each man could now almost hear the rider next to him. Then two apple red Roadking Harleys with thunder header exhaust pipes and yellow flames painted on their gas tanks rolled in together through the center of the space between the two rows. Each bike carried a man driver and a woman passenger. They stopped by O'Rourke's bike.

The riders dismounted and secured their bikes to the ground with the kickstand. The women walked behind them, taking their helmets off.

"Are you Mark Conners?" one of the men yelled.

He stretched out his hand to Conners' before he could answer. He was tall and fit. He had his head wrapped in a red bandanna and wore stone-washed blue jeans and a black open vest with a motorcycle insignia in the back. He had a thin trimmed goatee. He laughed heartily as he locked hands with Conners.

"Glad to see you man. Glad to see you."

His companion was an African American man, taller than him, wearing the same outfit. His exposed arms looked massive even at a distance and he wasted no time to show off his strength when he squeezed Conner's hand so tightly that he had to pull back. There was a loud cheer from all the bikers.

Ron raised his left arm with an open hand and moved it from side to side to get their attention. The noise died down. Ron smiled. He was still wearing his open face black helmet with a strap on the chin. He walked casually in front of the crowd then turned around to face them.

"Daytona, here we come!" he yelled, lifting his close-fisted right hand, shaking it in the air.

The crowd cheered. It was a deep rumbling sound, fists shaking in the air. Ron walked around shaking their hands, asking for silence.

"We're gonna make the races, no doubt! We've picked up brothers and sisters from all over the East Coast. We've got riders from as far up as Maine. We've got them from Boston, Milwaukee, Chicago, Rhode Island, Connecticut, New York and now Jersey."

There was another yell from the crowd.

"Yes, sir, the Garden State. Whenever I've come here, my men and I have had the greatest reception. We've come on rides for charity. Last year we did one and we met some of your local clubs. People like Mark Conners, who's your local organizer in the area. Great guy to work with. So, when I called Mark and told him about our run and asked him if he could put some good riders together, he said to consider it done. He told me he didn't have to go out looking because he had just the right stuff already assembled. And that's what we were looking for in this ride. We want just the right stuff. We don't need heroes but we also don't need patsies. We want riders who care about each other. We want riders who will look after their fellow riders' bikes as if it was their own. If you are a selfish meathead who just wants to ride on your own and don't care about anybody else, you don't belong here.

Pack up and leave now while you still have time."

He looked around the crowd with a defiant look, then turned again.

"A thing about clicks: They're nice. We all have our clicks at home. I've got my own. But if you are here, it's because you are part of something much bigger, caravan 2005 to Daytona." There was a roar from the crowd. He went on. "You are here. That means you are part of this brotherhood and this brotherhood only. We're not going to let any local strife interfere with our purpose here. So, what I'm saying, if you came here as part of the Windbreakers, the Braves, or some other fraternity, I am going to ask you to put that aside for now. You're going into an adventure with many other guys and gals who deserve your loyalty and support. If you can't be faithful to them because of your own commitments, then you don't belong here. Clean up your slate. We don't force people to be here. Everyone here must be here voluntarily, and we don't want to interfere with your other commitments. If you have them, you're entitled to them. But they must remain at home if you are biking with us. Your pledge to the people in this run must come first. Phil, here is my deputy. He's gonna fill you in on all the details and he'll be assigning roles as we move along. Follow your leader and care about your fellow rider. I only make one rule in any run I lead and it's an obvious one. This is the way it goes, nobody, and I mean nobody, stays behind. If someone's bike breaks down, we have mechanics in the lineup who will fix it. In the meantime, you can ride with someone else, or we can get you another bike. If someone gets sick, we have medics who will fix you up. We wait until you're well enough to ride. Whatever your problem may be, all of the riders in this run are behind you. We are in this thing together."

He waved his left hand to Phil, who was standing a short distance away. The crowd hollered with delight. You could tell they connected well with Ron Mason, and already at this early stage, the caravan's newest members from East Brunswick, New Jersey, could not be told apart from their more seasoned counterparts.

* * *

Helen McManus rushed into the driveway of her Victorian home. It was past 1:00 A.M. and the house was dark. Helen did not try to hide the fact that she was armed. She exited the driver's door carrying her Flemington shotgun in one hand and quickly walked around the front of her SUV to help Robin out. Her daughter had slept most of the way but Helen was worried for her. She opened the passenger door and grabbed Robin by the hand, still brandishing the gun with her other one.

"Let's go, Robin. We're home."

"Oh, Mom... I..."

"It's all right, Robin. You don't have to say anything. Let's go inside."

Robin descended the SUV's step cautiously, holding her forehead. She removed her hand from her eyes.

"Mom, it's so dark."

"It's all right, Robin. Follow me."

Helen opened the gate, and both women went inside. They got in the house through the back door. Helen flicked a light switch, which turned the light on in the back porch. They went into the kitchen, and Robin sat down tiredly on one of the dinette chairs. Her mother patted her on the back.

"There's no time, Robin. There's no time. Come on upstairs."

"But Mom, I'm tired."

"You'll rest upstairs. Come on."

She gently pulled her hand, making her stand up. She tugged Robin through the living room, turning lights on as she went by, and then climbed the stairs to the second floor. It was a different Helen from the night before. Gentle and loving to her daughter but now determined, sure of what she must do.

She led Robin into her bedroom and made her lie on the bed. Robin did not resist. She seemed helpless as she sat at the edge, looking down. Only then did Helen notice the black streaks on the left side of Robin's face beginning to grow and she became alarmed. She must fight them. She must fight them to the end. She leaned her gun against the wall and helped Robin lie down. She tested the window, turning the lock in the middle, lifting the window up, then pushing it down and locking it again. She pulled on the window's sash and felt it secure. She opened Robin's closet door and squirmed with her clothes inside for a few seconds. She retrieved several of Robin's leather belts. She got to work quickly, binding her daughter's hands together and tying the other end on the board's pole.

"Mom, what are you doing to me?" Robin said, faintly opening her eyes.

Helen did not answer. She kept busy now tying her daughter's feet. She bound them separately, securing the other end of each belt with a knot around each bed pole.

"I'm saving you, Robin. I'm saving you from them."

She moved towards the head of the bed and spread her arms around her.

"Oh, Robin, how could this happen to me? How?"

"What Mom? What are you talking about?"

"It's she, Robin, she. It's Margaret McCarter again."

Robin kept her eyes open but unfocused, as if trying to visualize an image in her mind.

"Mom . . . Again? I don't . . . I don't . . ."

"You don't understand, Robin, I know. You can't understand in the state you're in. But I'm here to protect you. I will never let that woman near you. Over my dead body!"

She looked in the direction of the gun, as if to make sure it was still there, and tightly held Robin's hand. She knew it would be a long night. But she made up her mind that she would not let her daughter out of her sight. She watched her fall asleep and felt relieved. Perhaps it was not as lethal as she had made it out to be. There was no chair in the room. She took hold of the gun and moved the window blind aside. She had forgotten to turn on the twin outdoor security lights mounted on the east corner of the house when she came up, but she could see the ground downstairs. There was no movement, no sign of anyone. She put pressure on the window sash and felt it was secure. She watched Robin lying peacefully in bed for a few minutes longer before deciding to go downstairs to check on all the doors. It was the first time that she could recall ever doing this in her home. There had never been any reason to. Cape May was a peaceful town with hardly any crime. She went downstairs and locked the back door, then latched it. She did the same with the front door. Then she went back upstairs and glanced inside Robin's open bedroom from the hallway. Robin looked peacefully asleep. She gathered some underclothes from her bedroom and went into the bathroom for a shower. When she returned, she checked on Robin again. She decided she would lie down in her bed with the door open so she could see her daughter. She had put on some jeans and a t-shirt to be on the ready. She lay down on her bed, in her bedroom across from Robin's. She had her hand wrapped around the belly of her Flemington and kept her eyes on Robin. She had always been a light sleeper so she was not afraid when she began dozing off, her head tilting slightly to one side of the pillow. She kept coming back and looked straight ahead each time to see her daughter lying across the bed. In one of those occasions when she awoke, she thought she saw daylight penetrating the room from the window crevices. Could it be morning already? Then she jumped from her bed and her heart felt as though it skipped a beat when she noticed Robin's empty bed. She ran towards the room, pointing her shotgun. The strips of leather hung loosely from the bedposts. They seemed to have been ripped apart, as if beaten off by some animal. She quickly checked the window, and it was intact. There was no sign of forced entry. She looked around the room, growing anxious. She ran downstairs and went through every room. There was no sign of Robin. The door on the back porch was locked, but the latch had been released. She leaned her forehead against the frame of the door and cried, admitting defeat. Her Robin was gone. Deep inside, she knew the answer. Her daughter had left again to return to the Margaret McCarter's house. If she wanted her back, she would have to fight.

* * *

"All right, folks," Phil began, moving his immense body from side to side, "we don't have a lot of time for introductions because we have other riders waiting for us. I understand that there are bikers from throughout the State. I've known Conners, your local leader, for some time and he's an awesome rider. He tells me that one of you contributed a trailer to the run and I just wanna tell you that we appreciate that.

Conners? Who was that? Who brought the trailer?"

"It's Margaret," Mark said. "Margaret, come forward." Margaret stood next to Ken and the other women riders.

She waded through the web of bikes, making her way towards Phil. He looked with interest at the large, bosom-laden woman with high boots. She shook his hand and smiled slightly.

"Thank you," he said. "That was cool. We need to assign a mechanic to that trailer."

"We've got one," Margaret said. "We've got a good one, Ken O'Gara," she said.

The riders had begun dispersing, admiring each other's bikes and shaking hands with each other. Ken went towards Phil and shook his hand. They were of about the same height but Phil seemed much heavier.

"Is she your protégé, Ken?" Phil asked, amused.

"No. Actually, I'm from New York. I just met her."

"So, how'd you end up down here?"

"I drove late this morning."

"Oh, you must be Dave's friend?" "Yes."

"All right. You're up to it, Ken. You've worked with bikes long enough, I take it?"

"Yes."

"He's young but very experienced," Margaret commented, laughing maliciously.

Phil did not miss her evocative tone. He gave her an eyeful and quickly turned to Ken.

"Dave taught you a few things, ah?"

"I learned what I needed from him."

"We were thinking of assigning Ken to our trailer," Mark said, cutting in.

"Well, right now, we're a little short," Phil said. "That's why I'm surprised you didn't join us in Fort Lee, Ken. We could have used you during our run on the parkway. We were undermanned." Phil was looking him over. "But that's all right. We did manage. You're here. We're gonna have him run the line," Phil said, turning to Mark. "We're so short of mechanical help right now that we can't afford the luxury of having him guard a trailer. He's all I got for half the crew."

"I can help," Margaret said. "I do quite well with bikes."

Phil gave her a look from the ground up, his burly biceps flexing slightly as he held a clipboard.

"She's right, Phil," Mark said. "She's excellent with bikes."

"All right, Margaret. Why don't you ride by your own trailer until we get to Philly. We're picking up more mechanics there so we should be okay after that. Sorry, it's not that I don't want to use you, but these slots have already been assigned to experienced mechanics. Why don't you help Ken out until Philly then? We'll see what happens after that. All right, Ken," he said, turning to him, "you'll be covering the second half of the run until we get to Philly. Go with Dan.

He'll show you where your cut off point will be in the lineup. Dan, show him around."

Dan O'Rourke stumbled on his own feet. He shook Ken's hand. He had been standing, cross-armed near Phil, trying to listen to their conversation among the rattle going on around them. He put his hand flat on Ken's back and walked with him past one of the rows of bikes in the parking lot.

"The way it stands right now, Ken," he said, now putting his arm around his shoulder, "this purple Dyna Glider is riding right in the middle of the line. The rider is Gust Parker. Big stocky guy with oval sunglasses. He'll be riding across from that black Sportster over there," he pointed across from where they were standing. "And that'll be George Fletcher."

Ken felt elated at the preparations' precision and Dan's remarkable detailed plans. He suddenly felt happy about being in this run. It was neatly organized by people who took their jobs seriously. It had felt a little testy back there while Phil seemed to have admonished him for not having joined the caravan at its nearest cross point to his home area. Ken had understood immediately. Phil wasn't being petty. Phil was talking about unity in the run, precisely what Ron had hammered on. Ken had not thought of the caravan's needs but of his own. He had made a decision to ride alone and join them at a location other than his designated area. It had been, of course, an innocent decision, devoid of any ill intent. It was almost understandable for any young rider to venture on a ride alone and meet up with the group at whatever other location he wanted. But Phil was trying to tell him that it had been undisciplined, even selfish. In another young rider it might have caused rebellion, an impulse to cooperate even less and perhaps even to call it a day and walk away. Ken O'Gara was a Christian and humble by nature. He rationalized Phil's comments and moved on from there.

"You know every rider in this run?"

"Pretty much," he said proudly. "I have to pick up on all these new ones. I now know yours."

Ken saw him reach for his vest pocket. He pulled out a long sheet of paper, coiled in a roll. He rolled it around his index finger. There were names written in pairs with small letters on it. Dan rolled the paper until he came to a blank spot and then he wrote Ken's name on it.

"We're gonna put you right about here," Dan said, writing his name on the paper. "That's your spot."

"I thought I was to cruise the line back and forth."

"You are but that's your official spot. Where's your bike?"

"It's back there," Ken said, gesturing towards the East Brunswick club's bikes.

"Let's go have a look before the cops chase us out of here."

They waded through bikes now getting integrated information with the others. Ken pointed to the VSCR Harley with the white fenders, parked behind Margaret's trailer.

"This is you?"

"Yes."

"I like that metallic blue on the tank, man. Who did that?"

"I did it. I put it altogether."

"You built the bike yourself?"

"Yes"

"He's got talent, doesn't he?" Margaret said, suddenly coming up behind them.

Dan could have answered her by just turning his head but he turned himself around to face her. He had been wanting to do that all along while she was talking to Phil and he had to settle for watching her from a distance. Hearing her gruff voice right above his shoulder seemed exhilarating to him. He was already smiling when he laid eyes on her, as if wanting to portray an air of control over himself. But he was unprepared for her disarming beauty and felt a jolt when he looked into her deep black eyes, accentuated by the hair resting on her chest.

"He does," Dan admitted uneasily. "Yeah, he does."

"That's why we picked him. We needed someone like him for support. He came to us for that reason. That's why he wasn't in Fort Lee like you guys expected him to be. He came down here for us. You can tell Phil that."

"Oh, that? It's nothing. Don't worry about Phil. He always says things like that."

There was silence for a moment as Dan stared at her up and down. He suddenly became aware of the other three girls.

"And you gals are part of this club?"

"We are," she said nodding.

Dan looked them over and then noticed Robin, a distance behind the others, with wavy brown hair and hazel eyes that were nearing green.

"I hope you girls can handle these awesome machines," Dan said to Margaret.

"What a thing to say," Margaret quipped. "You think we can't because we're women?"

"No, that's not what I meant," Dan quickly corrected himself. "Those are pretty awesome bikes you gals are riding, that's so."

"Yeah, right," Linda blurted. "So is yours. What makes it any different for us?"

"Nothing. Nothing at all," Dan said. "I need your names so I can put them in the log."

He moved aside with a clipboard in hand and his long rolled up roster, ready to write. Linda crossed glances with Margaret.

"Tell him who you are," Margaret said.

"Linda," she said.

"Linda. Linda what?"

"Linda O'Malley."

"I'm Flora Rogers."

"And I'm Donna Sawyer."

"Who's the girl in the back?"

"She's Robin McManus," Margaret said.

"She can't speak?"

"I speak for her," Margaret said. "We're a team."

Dan ignored her and just kept moving around getting the names of the others and jotting them down quickly. Most of the riders were now at the ready on their bikes. A trooper came out of one of the State police cars parked at the front of the crowd. No one had paid them any attention. They looked around, still standing behind their open doors.

From the left side of the crowd emerged Ron Mason looking as tall as the two officers but slimmer. Beside him strode the long-haired woman who had ridden with him. She was as tall as Ron, Caucasian, wearing blue jeans and a loose shredded, purple faded tee shirt.

"Where are you guys headed?" asked the officer in the first car, walking away from the door.

"We're headed south," Ron said.

"South Jersey or south out of state?"

"Philly," Ron said, getting closer. He handed out a tattooed hand with a red silhouette of Janice Joplin above the wrist.

The officer did not look at it but shook his hand.

"How much time you think you'll be here?"

"Another fifteen minutes."

"All right. We want to get this parking lot vacant as soon as possible. This is a private lot."

"Well, we're on our way out. I'll see what I can do about getting us out of here sooner."

"That'll be nice," the officer said.

He went back inside his car and so did the trooper in the next car. The two cars went back on reverse at an accelerated rate of speed with their overhead lights turning. When they reached the entrance, each moved sideways slowly. They positioned themselves at an angle from the crowd.

"Get everybody in line, Phil," Ron said. "We're in a bad spot."

"Conners did not have his people counted, Ron. It might take us a few minutes. The heck with them," Phil said, motioning towards the trooper cars.

"I don't want to make a big splash, Phil. It'll get us in trouble even before we've even started. What's wrong with Conners anyway? He was supposed to have all his people organized and ready."

"We're still counting them. It's gonna be a little messy at the beginning."

"Well, let's get it going, Phil. We're out of time."

Phil walked towards the rear, where a few remaining bikers were still waiting to be assigned a spot in the line-up. He told them to move to the end of the line and get ready. Then he went looking for Dan, who was hustling back and forth, writing names on his log and telling people where to go.

"How's it looking, Dan?"

"It's getting there, Phil. It's getting there."

"We're gonna have to go, Dan. You'll have to log the rest while we're on the road. The boss wants us out of here."

Dan stopped cold.

"How am I gonna do that while riding, Phil? If I don't do it now, it's only gonna get me more backed up before the next stop."

"We'll get you help, Dan. We've gotta go, come on. Tell everybody to fall in line."

Dan didn't like half done jobs. He knew he was slow, but it was his nature to mull over things, and he fell behind on all runs that he ever made, no matter what his job was. And he had done many. They said he talked too much and perhaps did, but he did not like to leave things undone. It was not a good way to start a long ride. What was the hurry anyway?

They were not due in Philly until 4:00; besides, he was having fun talking to the women riders. He had never before been on a run with so many women. He needed to take his time. He kept rummaging for the slightest opportunity to speak to Margaret. Once they were on their way, he may lose sight of her. But Phil was right behind his tail, prodding him to get everybody moving.

"All right O'Gara," Dan said to Ken. "You found your spot already?"

"More or less."

"You're three spots behind Conners. Count three and you're it. Do me a favor and line up five people behind you, whoever you find. No matter. We gotta go."

Ken was already on his bike. He opened one of his leather saddlebags and fiddled with the contents. He pulled out his black bible and several personal items and kept fumbling inside until he found the earphone he was looking for. He placed everything back in and took a moment to carefully wipe the cover of his bible. As he belted his saddlebag, he looked up and noticed that Margaret was watching him. She and her girls were already on their bikes and had the engines roaring. Zeke, Randall and John were behind them. Margaret stared at him somberly. She moved her bike back cautiously, not taking her eyes off him. When she was a good ten feet away, she turned and led the others to the rear of the line that was slowly shaping into an arch around the southern portion of the theater's parking. Ken found Conners' bike and counted three spots back. He positioned himself behind the second rider after Mark. The caravan was formed in a double line, since the riders would ride in pairs in one lane. Ken's road mate rode in a blue Softail Harley, an awesome looking machine. He sat open-legged on his seat and reached out to hold Ken's rudder to keep it from sliding when he stretched back. Ken adjusted his phone headset. Dan had given him a Nextel which he clipped on his belt and wired it into his single ear headset."

In a few minutes, an endless line of bikers built up behind him. Ken tried to find Margaret's trailer at the end but did not see it. There was the high-pitched sound of a whistle coming from the front lines. Standing on top of his bike's seat, Phil was calling everyone's attention.

"All right, listen up! We can't hang around here any longer. The cops are chasing us out so fall in line if you haven't found a spot yet. We gotta go."

He pointed toward the front entrance. There were now four trooper cars ominously stationed there, leaving hardly any room for the bikers to squeeze by. Perhaps it was an implied provocation to scare the crowd into breaking up the run or simply it was the troopers' way of telling them to leave. They weren't welcome here. Ken wondered how two lines of Harley Davidson's bikes could get through the small opening at the gate. Most likely, Ron Mason would have to order his pack to break into single file to squeeze through. That seemed like the logical thing to do. Ron was trying to avoid a confrontation with law enforcement and prevent any mishaps that would threaten his caravan. It seemed like at this moment he was willing to "turn the other cheek." But Ron also had to prove a point to a crowd of impatient riders who did not appreciate being shunned by the police or by local interests. They would look up to their leader for guidance and their loyalty would depend highly on his performance at this early stage of the run. Run understood this. He was a seasoned rider despite his relatively young age and had built himself a reputation in the east coast for getting things done while taking no flak, like a tough old general leading his troops against the ties of bureaucratic conventionalism.

The caravan began moving, with most of the East Brunswick legion still unorganized, but riding at the tail end as an integral part of it. It wasn't the energetic beginning that most would expect of the grandest motorcycle caravan assembled on the east coast in recent memory, but it was a slow, thwarting leap of maybe ten to fifteen feet that promptly came to a halt. Those riding close enough to the front to be able to see watched how Ron and Phill came up to inches from the troopers' patrol cars and then stopped and roamed their Roadkings' engines ferociously. That was a signal to the rest. "We're coming through," they were saying. Like a stack of dominoes that falls artfully into place when the first piece is pushed slightly, the engines' loud roaming spread from row to row among the double formation, gradually and steadily, until it reached the very last bikes in the line. The sound was now a deafening roar that kept building up higher, gaining momentum with each incremental thrust. At that point, the troopers let them through. Ron and Phil's bikes, as a pair, darted forward past the entrance, and the ones behind them followed in perfect formation. There was excitement in the air. Ken followed his lead and went through the entrance, passing the troopers' cars standing only inches away. He and his paired rider both bent rhythmically as they turned slightly to the left, heading towards the main exit into the road. Two trooper cars had quickly gone onto Route 1 and positioned themselves in the middle of the road to stop the incoming traffic. As Ken made the exit and merged into the middle lane of Route 1, heading south, he could hardly see the first bike in the lineup. Ken unclipped his Nextel and pressed the talk button.

"Ken here," he said. "Dan, are you out there? Where are you?"

There was a pause and then his raucous voice came on.

"I'm out here in the back, keeping an eye on them."

"On whom?"

"The women. At the last minute, that foxy looking one made them come all the way to the rear. She seems to have a way with them, even with the men. I must say they fell into formation rather beautifully. The line is now straight all the way to the last bike. I'll keep in touch. I need to get some names now so I can fill out my log. Over."

Ken clipped his phone back in his belt. That Dan was a womanizer, Ken thought. Ken bet he would be hanging around the rear for the rest of the trip.

The afternoon breeze was cool. Ron had set the pace at about 45 miles per hour, it seemed. Traffic was beginning to catch up with them on the left lane, which meant that the troopers must have removed their blockade from the road by now and let the traffic move forward. Many commercial vehicles, such as eighteen-wheelers and regular trucks, traveled through that road. That was always a problem for bikers. Heavy traffic and bikes did not mix. Yet, on a run with so many bikers, the leaders preferred not to make too much of a fuss or else someone could summon the police for the sake of safety and that would jeopardize the run. Dan had given strict instructions about formation. They could not occupy more than one lane, no matter how many the riders, and nobody could interfere with the traffic on the roads.

"You think we will get there by Halloween?" the rider next to Ken said, jokingly.

"I think so."

"It's the first time I ever go on a run after August. It's rather unusual."

"But it's only early October," Ken said. "And we're going south where it's warm."

"Still. Just think how cold it will be when we get back."

"I haven't checked into the weather at all."

"No rain expected, I hear at least until Virginia. From there on, it's anybody's guess."

"Where's our first stop for the night? Do you know?"

"I think at the Virginia-North Carolina border. We're expected there tonight. They have the grounds reserved for us. By then we will have grown to about one hundred and twenty."

"Wow. I'm surprised we were placed this far."

"I don't think they could find any other place to accommodate us. It's too many of us."

Ken checked on his side mirror. He could see the flashing lights of a state trooper car all the way in the rear.

"Police is still behind us."

"Ron's not gonna like that. He doesn't want an escort."

"I'm afraid we're stuck with them all the way through. Every state police will be waiting for us at the state line. They all know we're coming."

"It's a shame. They should leave us alone."

"It's our size. It makes them nervous."

"It's the stereotype. They have us as trouble makers. They treat us as an event wherever we go, a dangerous happening. That's why they monitor us."

Ken nodded. Quietly, Ken thanked the Lord for allowing this ride to be a clean one. There were people from all over the east coast in the caravan. Many had never met the others before, yet it seemed that all of them had a genuine love for the clean sport of riding. So far, he had not seen any evidence of objectionable behavior. They were just bikers having clean fun and enjoying the ride. The early afternoon sun shone bright in the horizon, creating that misty feeling that only autumn can bring. The road had gradually whittled into two lanes in each direction and the traffic gradually started to build up on the outer lane. The trooper car had already reached the center of the caravan followed by a long line of trucks and cars eager to get through. The caravan's speed, controlled by the men in the front, seemed to slow down gradually.

"What's happening?" Ken yelled.

"It's probably a strategy by the front guys," his fellow rider said.

"How is that?"

"I think Ron may be trying to get rid of the cops. He doesn't like riding with them."

Their bikes kept getting closer to those in front of them, so they had to slow down. The trooper car had already reached the beginning of the line. Traffic was building up on the left lane. The bikers were suddenly bulwarked by an endless line of trucks that made it impossible for them to hear one another.

Ken heard the vague tinkle of his phone and picked up.

"Ken here."

"How're you guys holding up?" Dan said.

"We're slowing down, it seems."

"Gotta get rid of these cops. They're all over."

"Are they back there too?"

"At least four patrols have been behind us. Now they're switching on to the other lane."

"What's the harm? Let them be."

"Ron doesn't like it. He'll bring us down to five miles per hour if he has to."

"Is this how it's gonna be all the way down."

"Probably until we get to Virginia."

"Wow."

"Better for you. It's keeping the bikes healthy and running."

"I wanna get there, though."

"We will. By the way, that woman is some number, man. She's gotten control of this rear section pretty solidly. I don't know how. I think she's a control freak. She won't stop talking and keeps trying to move up on the line-up. I had to stop her. I think she could be trouble."

"She's a beautiful woman."

"That she is. I'm trying to keep her from making herself into a problem. Ron would never put up with that."

"Need any help?"

"No. But I may need to make my way up front. I may have to visit Ron. See you later."

Two more trooper cars had gone by the shoulder of the other side of the road as the caravan reached a gradual slowdown of about 35 miles per hour. The troopers had no choice but to pass them since trying to keep abreast of the bikers at this speed would make them back up the traffic on the other lane. They could not ask them to pull over in the middle of the highway either, because that would be chaotic. But still, Ken wasn't sure if Ron's strategy would drive the cops away. They probably would just sit at a spot farther down and wait.

The bikers kept the same pace for about twenty minutes until they reached the Princeton area then Ron and Phil picked up speed.

Apparently, the troopers had left. None were in the rear and none in the front. As the bikers moved ahead, the traffic behind them loosened up. Even the left lane did not seem congested anymore. They stopped at several traffic lights and still did not see any sign of the troopers. But as they entered the Trenton area and got near the boundary line with Pennsylvania, they came upon a cluster of state police vehicles parked in a row on the side of the road. Once the bikers passed them, the patrols followed them.

"I knew it," someone else said from the front. "Watch for the Pennsylvania troopers now. They'll be waiting for us as soon as we pass the state line."

"I don't know that I mind them that much," Ken yelled back

"It's harassing. We're just riding."

As they crossed the state line, the New Jersey troopers vanished, but when the bikers passed the area of Morrisville, they suddenly encountered a large detachment of the Pennsylvania State police, their vehicles waiting on the side. The bikers passed them at a normal speed, but as soon as the last biker had rolled by, the Pennsylvania troopers went on their tail. Some patrol cars switched over to the left lane, overtook the caravan, and switched back to the right lane in front of the lead bikers.

"They got us surrounded," Ken's fellow rider joked. "Where are we stopping in Philly, do you know?"

"Fairmount Park."

"Gee, that would be interesting. We'd definitely create havoc there."

"It's been planned ahead of time. I'm sure Ron will give us a prep talk about it but everyone knows what to do and what not to do. Don't litter. Don't drive in the grass, you know."

They kept traveling south. Shortly after the intersection of Route 611 with Route 1, the caravan turned right on a road that took them head on into the renowned park, known for its 18th century historic houses, scenic vistas and wildlife. They took a narrow road into the banks of the Schuylkill River that divided East and West Fairmount parks. Ron had asked his men to wait for him near the banks and that's where they were spotted. The Pennsylvania State police had lagged behind them, but their presence was noticeable as they collected on the road while the bikers rode right into a large parking lot, near spacious grassy fields. The two biker lanes broke up in two around the group of bikes near the center, each lane wrapping itself around them and coming to a halt at the end. Ron raised his arm as a signal to turn the engines off. Ken had barely got off his bike when a short and stocky fellow rushed to greet him.

"Ken, how the heck are you?"

"Hello, Dave."

"I didn't know if you'd come. You left so soon that day from Lancaster and I didn't hear from you. What happened to that Mexican guy that day?"

"He was hanging in."

"That's good. Those guys that you brought in stayed with us in the bar till late. They left drunk out of their minds."

"They came to the hospital later but couldn't get to see him. He was in ICU. They went back to Mexico."

"So what happened to that foreman?"

"I think he was charged. I am under subpoena to appear at the Grand Jury as a witness in October, after we come back."

"Grand juries can be wrecking. What do you plan on doing?"

"Telling the truth."

"Well, too bad someone's gonna have to go down. Anyway, where do they have you riding?"

"They put me in the middle for now. They were short of help."

"I'm not gonna have you in the middle. I want you to ride with me. Where are your tools?"

"These girls who've been riding in the rear have a trailer and they had me put my tools inside."

"I'll get that straightened out. Here's Steve, Ken."

"Nice seeing you, Ken."

"Nice seeing you too."

"Let's get Ken's tools," Dave said.

Ken noticed Dave's small Harley Davidson trailer set aside, tugged by a small pickup. Dave and Steve moved around the riders who had now dismounted and were once again getting acquainted. Because of the time, Ron had passed the word that it was okay to eat a quick lunch out here under the condition that everyone would pick up after themselves to keep the cops happy. Dave and Steve worked their way to the end of the line and Ken went with them. Dave recognized Margaret's trailer.

"Dave," Dan called from behind them. "Where're you going?"

"Dan O'Rourke," Dave said turning around. "How the heck are you?"

"I'm fine. Glad to see you. Desperate for help right now." The two men shook hands. Dan was holding his clipboard.

"I wanna talk to you about the line-up."

"So do I," Dave said. "What are you doing putting Ken in the middle. He rides with me. I'm the reason he's here."

"Wait a minute, Dave. We can't have mechanics riding together. We gotta spread them out. That's how Ron wants it."

"But we gotta ride near our tools, Dan. If a distress call comes, we go. That's how it's always done."

"Not this time, Dave. Ron wants it this way."

"What about our tools?"

"We spread the tool vans throughout the line up. Anyone who needs to use tools goes to the nearest van."

"I don't like that set up, Dan.

"All right, well Ken's tools are in the girls' van and they're all the way in the rear. I need them back."

"Oh, yeah, those girls. I think they're gonna stay in the rear too. They want to and that's all right. Ken is gonna be moved back a little bit so if he needs to use his tools, he'll be close anyway."

"That shouldn't be, Dan," Dave said, with reproach. "I wanna see that Margaret. And I want my van in the rear."

"All right, be careful. I think she bites."

Dave made his way past the crowd, shaking hands as he went along. Steve and Ken followed him. Margaret and her three girls were hanging around Zeke's pick-up, eating sandwiches. Robin was sitting on her own bike.

"Margaret," Dave called. "How are you kid? You look as great as ever."

He made a gesture to hug her, but she extended her hand to him instead.

"How are you, Dave?"

"You're riding with my friend Ken here?"

"If he's riding in the rear, I am, I guess," she said casually.

"You've got his tools in your van?"

"Who are you, his keeper?"

"Sort of. Can we have them? I'm gonna keep them in my van."

"Sure."

"Dave, don't do that," Dan said from behind them. "Leave everything as is. Ken is gonna be moved back in the line-up.

Come on, we got other things to worry about right now. Ken, would you mind?"

"No, I wouldn't. I wouldn't at all. Just tell me where I'm riding."

Ken glanced fleetingly at Robin. Her brown hair was blowing in the soft wind as she carelessly leaned back against the seat of her bike.

The caravan kept going south on Route 1 and picked up another load of riders near Gunpowder Falls, in the outskirts of Baltimore, then it veered east on Route 83, and went on Interstate Highway 95, heading south. They rode without incident past Richmond and picked up 301 by Emporia. Then they headed for campgrounds near Pleasant Hill, North Carolina, where Ron called it a night. Reservations had been made for them ahead of time. Two motels off the road had been booked completely for them. But Ron's bikers had grown to the astonishing number of one hundred and twenty- one, and Ron was forced to split the group into three sections to accommodate all its members. Ken, Dave and Steve were sent with the third group. They got rooms at a small motel north of town, a short distance from the other two. It was past 9:00 P.M. when they joined a bunch of other riders at the entrance of a fast-food restaurant where they sat down for a meal.

The word was that the riders would be allowed to gather at a near campground to discuss the travel plans for the next day. Ken knew that it was only a disguise for a party. Dave was already talking about bringing some supplies from his van, supplies that Ken knew were not related to his trade. He quietly slithered away from the men at the table and went outside. He went to his bike, parked among a long row of Harleys and opened his leather saddlebag. He retrieved some underwear, a toothbrush, paste and his bible. Then he headed for the room of his motel. He looked back across the restaurant and heard the happy chanting of some of the riders, telling themselves riding stories. Ken walked alone in the darkness and reached the walkway that edged the front of the motel building. It was pitch black inside the room. He turned on the light on a side table lamp and went in the bathroom. He took a shower and put on short pajamas. He had previously brought in a wrapping comforter in the room so he laid it on the floor and got himself inside, leaving the two beds in the room for Dave and Steve. He opened his bible to the book of Deuteronomy and began to read chapter 32. He had read the passage many times before but it seemed appropriate tonight. He did not know why. He longed to read a summary of God's work for his people, his greatness and his righteousness. Ken felt that as he had done for others, he would do for himself. With these thoughts and one occasional far away laughter, he fell asleep.

* * *

The dawn of the morning before the ride, Margaret sat on the carpeted floor of the living room of her Englishtown home. She was surrounded by the three men, John, Randall and Zeke at one side, and the three women, Linda, Flora and Donna on the other. They had made the circle large enough so that it could fit another person in Margaret's spot. Robin McManus was sitting cross-legged across from Margaret, holding her hands open, as if waiting to receive a blessing. Margaret looked solemn as she held a black sheaf in her hand, tied. It was still dark outside and there was very little light in the room.

"There is no power like that of the body and mind together," Margaret said dryly. "In order to believe that, you have to dispose of everything you ever had. How you were raised, what you learned in your past years, all has to be trashed away. You have to start from a clean slate. You are a new person. All those stories you heard about humans carrying their souls with them to their death have to be done away with. Whether they are true or not, it won't matter anymore. The secret is to renounce the soul while you are still living. Then you will realize your true potential. You will do things you could never imagine you could do. You'll be entering a brand-new world of opportunity and pleasure, where the everyday hideous concerns that worry you now won't mean a thing. You'll experience freedom as you never have before. You'll be the owner of your own self. You'll really own yourself. You owe no loyalty to life or tradition.

Gone are the narcissistic faces that made you their slave, under the pretext of love. Love. What humans call love is nothing but an apology for their demand for an absolute connection to other people. It is their zeal for dependency and involvement. They call it love. You can call it slavery. But from now on you can be free. You don't have to depend on your spirit. You can make it go. Release it. You are lucky, Robin. You are about to enter a world that very few people have known. You've heard me say it before, 'those who live by the sword will die by the sword.' But it is a different kind of life, Robin.

And it is also a different kind of death. You live free, to your full potential, independent. You die graciously, happy, as in the end of a happy story. The sword is your keeper, and not your curse as humans would have you believe. This is the sword that lets you live free and experience your full potential."

Margaret retrieved a narrow blade from the black sheaf. The silver blade shone against the faint light of the night lamp near them as she swept the air with it in fast nymph-like strokes. Robin did not move. The marks on her neck had returned. She had noticed them on the rear-view mirror of the car Flora had driven her in. She had walked out of her mother's house in a daze and bolted the house's rear door open. As she opened the door to leave, she found Flora standing there, smiling broadly as if she knew all along this moment would come. The moment of surrender to your destiny. "It is your destiny," she had said to her in the car.

Robin did not really understand it. All she knew was that she felt relieved when she saw Flora, as if she had been saved from a great catastrophe that was going to befall her. And the anxiety she had felt as she lay tied in her bed and desperately trying to free herself was all gone suddenly. She had thought about the tapestry in Margaret's living room, its wolf howling in the night and imagined that she was him. She visualized the sharp scissors showing majestically from his open mouth and knew she could be him. She was him. And she bit into the leather and cloth straps holding her, cutting them up viciously as if she was dying of hunger. She felt a thirst, a need to be relieved from the enigma that haunted her. And there was only one place where she could get relief, where her senses drove her to, almost automatically. She did not even consider that she had no means of travel. She was only thinking of getting away, running out into the road and driving to the McCarter house, anyway she could. When she saw Flora standing outside the door, she felt relief. Flora was there to take her back. She had been waiting.

Robin had sat in the pickup quietly feeling respite from her anxiety. She was on her way home. Then as they got close to the McCarter house, she felt the vibrations of her cell phone in her pants pocket and that made her remember Helen, her mother. She had walked out on her mother again. She was thinking rationally now. She was no longer in a dream. She waited until the pickup stopped at the back of the mystical house. Flora opened the driver's door and Robin tilted her head forward to look at herself in the rearview mirror. "You look lovely," Flora had said. But she wasn't looking at her face. She was looking at those ugly black marks growing up on her neck and reaching her left cheek. Where did they come from? She must find out. Perhaps Margaret knew.

She saw Margaret in the kitchen as soon as they came in the house, smiling at her. She was happy to see her, her eyes said. She wanted a drink, she knew, her eyes told her. Robin saw her turn back and reach for a mug from a cabinet. She poured a bag of chocolate powder in the mug and then warm milk. Then, as if an afterthought, she sprayed the cup with crystalline particles that glittered in the dark as they dropped from her fingers. They could have been sugar grains or confetti sprinkles, Robin thought. Margaret was treating her like a starved child. She was nurturing her every need, fulfilling her fantasies. And then for a moment she had the most terrible fear that the white grains could be angel dust.

She had never tried angel dust. But Margaret wouldn't do that, no. It couldn't be. She had rubbed the left side of her jaw and imagined that those particles were an actual form of poison meant to enter her bloodstream and coagulate her blood slowly until her entire body was black and she would die a horrible painful death from gangrene. What a terrible imagination she had.

"This is your master," Margaret was saying as she flung the blade back and forth. "Now you must build your relationship on it. You will live by it. It is your best friend. It is the key to your existence. Your friendship to it must be sealed with your own blood. It's the only language that the blade understands. Blood is its life."

Margaret laid the blade on top of Robin's open hands. Robin felt the cold iron rub against her skin but did not react to it. Then Margaret slithered the sharp blade vertically through the base of one hand. Robin pulled back. Blood quickly flowed onto her palm and she looked down at it horrified.

"I'm bleeding . . ."

"You need to bleed. It is your spirit that's leaving you. Let it go. Let it leave you."

Margaret kept the blood-stained blade on Robin's hands. Robin kept looking down, not knowing what to do. It was a bizarre scene. She had known of the ceremony but had not expected its gruesomeness. She went along with it as if it was insignificant, not realizing its intended meaning, not even knowing its details. She was under the influence of a strange force that dominated her will like no other emotion had before. She did not understand it. It kept her in need, in need of being in the McCarter house as if it was her heaven. There was no place in the world where she would rather be. But the weak signals of the real world outside kept coming in, as when her mother would try to contact her through her cell phone, or she would look out the window and have a fleeting thought that there was a life out there. Now she was a million miles away from the real world. She was seeing herself bleed and did not know what it meant.

"Are you willing, Robin? Are you willing to abandon your soul?"

"Margaret, I'm bleeding. Please make it stop!"

"Tell me, Robin. Are you willing to join us? Are you willing to be like us? Tell me."

"Margaret, I'm bleeding. I'm bleeding!"

She kept looking down at her bloody hands, now both covered in blood.

"Blood is good, Robin. It is good. It means you're getting rid of your soul, like unwanted waste. Let it go. Let it leave you."

"Margaret, I can't . . . I can't . . ."

Robin dropped her head, opened her mouth, and felt faint. She slumped down, her face landing on Margaret's thigh. Margaret pulled herself back and sheathed the blade, then hung its string around her neck. There was an absolute silence in the room as the others looked on.

"She's still fighting us, Margaret," Linda said. "She is still not ours. She's holding back."

"Let her be. She will come to us."

"Should we help her?" one of the others said. "She's bleeding pretty badly."

"Wrap the wound up so the bleeding stops," Margaret said. "Come on, let's go."

Flora ran quickly upstairs and came back with gauze, iodine and towels. She wiped Robin's hands, then she tied gauze around her wrist and hand to cover the wound. It was not a deep cut and she was able to stop the bleeding quickly. Robin had passed out more as a result of shock. She was slowly coming to as Margaret began to lecture them.

"We're in the ride for pleasure. We join them but we don't follow them. We're our own. We play with them. They think they're in charge but only you know the truth. They're funnies believing that their ride will make them immortal. That's all they have, the ride. Once they finish it and go back home, they will be in the same old world as before. They have to answer to an authority, work their bodies for food and struggle to survive. They think they're free. Imagine that.

"We toy with them. We don't hurt them unless they're hostile towards us. If we have to feed off them, we do it with finesse. We leave nothing behind."

"Has anybody ever tried to leave you after joining," Robin's voice came from the floor, unexpectedly.

"Margaret, you're not going to let her ask, are you?" Linda yelled. "She's got no right."

"Hush," Margaret replied.

Margaret smiled at Robin. She bent down to touch her face in a sort of maternal gesture that the others found unbecoming of her. She grabbed Robin's shoulders and helped her sit up.

"Actually, yes, someone did. A long time ago."

"And what happened to her?"

"Him," she corrected her. "He lived like we live but in a different way. He was a rebel at heart. He was totally fearless and beautiful. But when the soul leaves the body, you can't get it back. Strange things can happen if you don't follow your needs."

"What happened to him?"

"He became a casualty."

Margaret was rubbing her temples gently, as if Robin was a child. Linda and the others watched in amazement, not knowing what to make of it.

Chapter 5

Ken woke up with the light of day. The sun was barely out. He walked through the grass field and headed for the restaurant at the other end. He was not sure whether there was any service at the restaurant this early, but he went anyway. There was hardly anyone inside, only two men sitting at a small table drinking coffee. Ken sat at another table. He was next to a window and he could see through the open blinds. A young woman came to his table to take his order.

"Eggs, sunny side up," he said, "some oatmeal and a cup of hot chocolate."

"You don't want to see the menu?" she asked methodically.

"No, thank you. I'm fine with that."

It was a cool morning. The breeze had picked up during the night, and ghost winds had sporadically swept through the maple trees at the rear of both buildings, pouring a stream of auburn-colored leaves on the ground.

"Actually, I don't know if they have chocolate, sir. But I'll try to find you some. I guess it's still not cold enough," she said smiling as she went to get his order. Ken looked around for a newspaper. There was a stack of them at the cash register. He grabbed one and took it to his table. The headlines announced the latest bombings in Iraq. Other articles commented about the effect of oil prices on travel. As a dependent of the not too far away 95, Pleasant Hill was highly dependent on tourism. Ken read in the article that some gas stations were beginning to feel the pinch. Travelers had begun to cut back on the driving. There was a small article at the bottom of the page that announced the upcoming arrival to the town of Ron's riders. Ken read it.

Local residents voiced their concern about having their town invaded by a throng of bikers, much larger than any other that they had ever seen. And they were not just passing by. Two entire motels had been booked in advance by the bikers, and then when they ran out of room, another one had welcomed the rest. A town councilman called irresponsible the decisions to accommodate the bikers as irresponsible. But the report concluded that the owners were business men who need not answer to anyone. As long as the bikers paid for their lodgings, they had as much right to be there as anybody else.

"Good morning," Dave said, from the door. "Did you sleep well?"

"I slept fine."

"You're up early. We don't get going till 10:00."

Dave, accompanied by Steve, went to his table. The waitress had just returned with Ken's order. She placed it on the table in front of him.

"Would you guys want to see the menu?" she said.

"No, we'd like to go ahead and order."

"All right."

She pulled a small pad from her apron pocket and waited for their orders.

"Oh, the cops are here again," Dave said.

Three police cars had pulled into the parking slots at their motel building. One of them seemed to belong to the local police and the others were state highway patrols.

"Ron is not gonna like that," Steve said.

"If that ain't harassment," Dave observed. "Three police cars at our doorstep to make sure that we get going. Isn't that a crime?"

"What will it be?" the waitress asked.

Some officers stepped out of their cars and they crowded themselves around their vehicles. Other police cars had also arrived at the parking lot.

"It looks like trouble to me," Steve said.

"Did anything happen last night while I was sleeping?" Ken asked, looking sideways into the motel's building.

"Nothing," Dave retorted. "We were as quiet as the elderly."

"Do you gentlemen want your order now?" the waitress asked impatiently.

"I think you guys should place your order if you want to eat," Ken said, smiling to the waitress.

"We were just waiting to see what was going to happen outside," Steve said.

"Well, you're gonna eat breakfast anyway," Ken said. "You might as well not keep the young lady waiting."

"Gimme scrambled," Dave finally said, "with bacon, toast and home fries. I don't know what Steve wants."

"Some coffee, sir?"

"Oh, yeah, some coffee."

She turned to Steve who continued to stare down towards the lot, oblivious to their conversation.

"Sir?"

"All right," he said, looking up at her. "I'll have scrambled with bacon. Some home fries too."

"Coffee, sir?"

"Yes."

She glanced quickly at the motel's parking lot and tore the order forms from her pad, then went towards the kitchen. As she was about to push the swing door open, one man dressed in a suit and tie accompanied by two officers wearing the uniform of the North Carolina Highway Patrol came through the door.

"Hoity," the suited man said to the waitress who stopped short of pushing the kitchen door open.

"You gentlemen want a table?" she asked them.

"No," the suited man said, coming towards her with the patrolmen following. "Let's go inside for a minute."

"I wonder what these guys want now," Dave commented. "Our run is peaceful and they're after us like wolves. It's just not right."

"It's aggravating," Steve said. "There's no need for them to be here, following us at every step we take."

Ken shrugged his shoulders and drank a sip of hot chocolate.

"I suppose it has to do with the image we portray," Ken said. "But it's not all that bad. Anytime there is a large amount of people together as we have, there is a need for law enforcement."

"Why? If you're not doing anything wrong."

"The potential is there with big crowds. For instance, what did you guys do last night?" Ken asked.

"We stayed outside in the campgrounds with the others. We had a great time."

"All one hundred and twenty of you?"

"Pretty much, yeah. Even those girl riders were there. Why didn't you come?"

"Were you guys drinking?"

"A little bit."

The kitchen door in the back swung open and the three men came into the dining room. One of the patrolmen waved to the two men at another table.

"Gentlemen," he said to them, "would you come here for a second please?"

The two men did not look like bikers, but the officers had apparently linked them with Ken and his friends.

"Just take a seat at this table over here, next to these fellows," the suited man said with a very pronounced southern drawl, pointing to the table next to Ken's.

He had a gangly-looking body that stretched well over six feet. The officers standing behind him looked as tall as he. The suited man spoke first.

"You fellows are with the bike run, I take it."

"Yes," Ken said, taking the initiative.

"Do any of you know Dan O'Rourke?"

"Sure, we do," Ken said, speaking first. "He's one of the coordinators on the ride."

"When did you see him last?"

"I spoke to him by phone right before I turned in last night through the phone," Ken said, pointing to his Nextel. "We were in touch all day throughout the trip."

"At what time did you speak to him?" "Oh, sometime after ten, I guess."

"What did he say when you talked to him?"

"Nothing much. I made the call. He was out with the rest of the guys, and I just checked with him to see if he needed anything. I told him I was going to sleep."

"Which one of you guys was with him?"

"I think we all were," Dave said looking around at the others.

"Until what time were you there?"

"I guess until midnight or maybe a little bit later."

"Is there anything wrong officer?" Steve finally asked, looking up.

"Yes. They found Mr. O'Rourke's remains in the woods this morning."

"What?" Dave said in amazement.

All five of them looked at each other in disbelief. Dan had proved that he could be trusted with handling the most important aspect of the run. He had been responsible for the positions of the riders in the line, and for the supplies and the repairs that would be needed. Every rider knew that when something was wrong the person to call was Dan O'Rourke. Who would have hurt a man like that?

"What happened?" Ken asked.

"That's what we're trying to find out. We're hoping you guys can clear up a few things." The detective reached into his shirt pocket and retrieved a small notebook.

"Now, from what you're telling me, all you guys, except you," he said, pointing to Ken, "were outside at the campsite when Dan was there. Let's get a sense of timing here. What time did you leave the campsite, sir?"

He was pointing at Dave.

"It was me and Steve here. We shared the room with Ken who was already sleeping so Steve and I left together, probably after midnight. It was late."

"Was Dan still there when you left?"

"Yes, he was."

"Who was with him?"

"He was with no one in particular. Dan didn't just hang out. That's his thing. He doesn't get too attached. Except that he was spending time with some of the girl bikers. I guess he took a liking to them."

"How about you guys?" the officer asked the two men at the other table.

"We left together too. I'd say about 12:30 A.M."

"Was Dan still at the campsite when you left?"

"Yes."

The detective pulled a chair from Ken's table and sat down across from them. The other officers stayed behind him.

"What is your name son?" the detective said.

"Ken O'Gara."

"And why were you not with the others last night?"

"I went to my room."

"I know you did. But why?"

"I don't drink, and I was tired. I checked with Dan before I settled in. I knew my teammates here, Steve and Dave, would be with the others, so I stayed in the room alone and went to sleep."

"How many of you guys are staying at this motel?"

"Oh, I don't know," Dave said. "Probably around twenty."

"What happened? You couldn't get a room over at the first two motels?"

"No, there were too many of us."

At this time, a man and a woman entered the room. They were carrying their helmets in their hands and looked as if they had just woken up. They had walked through the open grass field outside and past several highway patrol officers who had now gathered near the entrance.

"Sir and madam," one of the officers said. "If you would please, come this way."

The man was wearing only a tee-shirt over his overgrown stomach. He had long gray hair and clear glasses. With his sea-blue eyes, he looked right at the officers.

"Did you guys decide to join us in the run, is that it?"

"No that's not it, sir. That's not it at all. I don't even know how to ride. Madam, if you'll step this way, please," he said, moving slightly backwards and pointing to the table where the others were sitting.

"We want to ask you a few questions," the detective said, getting up. "See if you can help us retrace last night's events a little bit."

"Why? What's happened?" the gray-haired man asked.

He and the woman had sat down next to the men at the table. "It seems that for some reason someone did not want to see

Dan O'Rourke make the ride to Daytona."

"Something's happened to Dan?"

"He's dead," Dave said.

The detective watched the exchange intently. A few more riders came in followed by more officers. Dave's phone made a scruffy sound, signaling that someone was on the line. Dave picked up.

"Dave here."

He put the receiver to his ear.

"John Murray here," the voice said. "Looks like we're gonna need some mechanical help. One of the girl's bikes seems to have busted a chain drive. She's at the Day's Inn second motel. We need you. Can you get here?"

"I'll try," Ken said, looking at one of the officers.

The detective waved for him to release the phone and he grabbed it.

"This is Detective Leany here. Who's this?" "John Murray. What do you want with my men?"

"You'll have to hold up on whatever it is that you want. I'm questioning these guys right now," the officer said.

"We still got a ride to do, officer."

"Not for now you don't," he said, putting down the phone. "Are we under arrest?" Dave asked.

"We haven't decided yet."

"Well, why don't you go on and decide, man? If it's true our friend is dead, we'd like to find out about it and pay our respects. Stop playing games with us."

The detective glanced at the officers, as if deciding what to do next. His eyes showed his intention to act, but the officers were sending him a warning. The situation had to be handled with kid gloves, or they could end up with a riot. One hundred and twenty-one bikers was a lot to handle.

"Right now," Detective Leany said cautiously, "we are calling the shots. There has been a death, apparently a homicide and it's being investigated. If some people need to be brought in for questioning, it will be done. But we haven't decided. For the time being, you are just going to have to remain here. We will let you know when you can leave."

"Did anyone here see Dan O'Rourke leaving camp last night?"

No one answered.

"That means that you all left the campsite last night, I presume, it was to go to your rooms, while Mr. O'Rourke still remained there, is that right?"

Other bikers had gradually entered the restaurant. A group of about fifteen of them had gathered at the tables near Ken and the others. Most were men but some were women who had been riding with their husbands or boyfriends. A few were middle aged couples who were in for enjoyment of the long cruise. Everyone kept silent.

"I guess that's affirmative," Dave said.

The detective eyed him with obvious displeasure, still feeling sour over the previous exchange. He resented the way Dave had defied him. With the other two officers, he moved away from the crowd.

"I think we should separate them from the others," Detective Leany said.

"Detective, that may not be practical for a number of reasons," one patrolman said. "First, I don't think we could manage it without making some arrests right on the spot.

Some of them are going to rebel against us. I can already sense that. If that happens, we'll need help. It's just too many of them. Secondly, I'm not sure that splitting this group from the rest will make the investigation any easier. In fact, if they all get together, we may learn more from their reactions than if we keep them apart. They will be talking among themselves and that's what we need to watch. Anyway, it's your call."

Detective Leany turned and walked back towards the table.

"Is any of you gentlemen a member of a gang?"

"You think that because we're bikers we must be in a gang?" Dave asked, mocking him.

"I didn't say that. Are you?"

"Of course not," the grey-haired man said from his spot at the table. "We're pleasure riders. Some of us are even family men. We're out here to enjoy the ride. If one of us has been hurt, then we'd like to know about it. So, we'd like to get the facts straight. You are not telling us much but you are asking us questions which we can't answer. We've been sleeping all night."

"That's right!" Dave said.

"Let's get on to the other motels," another man said.

The riders sitting at the tables got up and they and the others in the room got ready to leave. A few more just arriving remained at the entrance.

"Wait," Detective Leany said. "You can't leave just yet.

We have to get everyone's name."

The other patrolmen who had come into the room had subconsciously formed a chain in the forefront.

"What are you gonna do?" yelled Steve, "Arrest everybody?"

"Let's go!" someone else said.

They all made for the door. Detective Leany sensed it was better not to interfere. He left the center of the room and joined the other officers. More than twenty riding men and women had gathered outside the restaurant.

"They told us Dan O'Rourke is dead," Roy McGreevy said. He was the man with the gray hair.

"For those of you who didn't get to hear what the detective said inside, he didn't tell us how it happened. He told us that they found Dan in the woods nearby. I think the cops are sort of baffling us by not telling us everything. I guess it's their job to try to hunt for the facts. I can't think of any reason why anyone in this run would want to hurt a man like Dan O'Rourke, or anybody else for that matter. I don't think we are a rowdy crowd. Otherwise, I would not be part of this run. And right now, I'm not even concerned about the crime that was committed. I'm just concerned because a friend of mine has been hurt and I want to find out what happened. I am sure you all do too. So, as a leader of this segment of our run, I say that we get on our bikes and report to Ron and Phil right now and find out what the hell happened. I'm not asking you to be rebellious with the officers. They're here because they have a job to do and that's fine. But we're going to join our other teammates and stick together. Don't make any trouble with the patrolmen. If they tell you to do something, just do it.

Avoid a confrontation with them and let's try to get on to the other motels and join the others."

He made a gesture with his free hand to wade through them. Everyone went back to their rooms in the motel and gathered their belongings. Then quietly they went to their bikes, parked right across from their doors and cranked their engines into life. Several patrol cars had flanked them at each end of the parking lot. Roy, with his wife in the back, took the lead on his black Softtail Classic. He put on his blue aviator goggles and drove slowly out of the lot into highway 301.

They were only a few minutes away from the motels where Ron and Phil were staying with the rest of the caravan. The two buildings were side by side, right off the highway. Roy lifted his left hand as a signal that he was turning left. Several Roadkings followed him. Dave, Steve and Ken had spread themselves out through the formation, ready to take care of any mechanical problem that could arise. Roy turned into the short driveway leading into the parking spaces across from the two buildings. Highway patrols were stopped right at the edge of the road, facing each other and leaving a small opening between them, barely wide enough for a car to go through it. Roy and his group got in the lot without disruption.

* * *

It was almost 5:00 A.M. that morning when Robin felt someone's pull tugging her covers on the bed. It was Flora. She was sharing a room with Flora and Donna. Margaret and Linda had slept in another room and the men too. Robin opened her eyes and waited, wishing no one was there, and that she was only having a dream.

"Robin, wake up," Flora whispered. "Margaret wants to take you out. Come on."

She raised her head slowly.

"What time is it?"

"It's still dark out. She's waiting for you in her room. Come on. Dress up."

She pushed off the covers and got up. Suddenly, she felt very energetic, eager to know what Margaret wanted. She had slept only about three hours but did not feel tired. She put clothes on while Flora watched her. For some reason, the boss wanted to see her. She opened the front door and went to the next room.

"You called?" she said.

Margaret was dressed all in black. She took Robin's hand as soon as she came in.

"It's time, Robin."

She was holding a black concave sheath in her hand tied to a string. She slipped the string around Robin's neck.

"This will be your best friend from now on. Remember, this is how you stay alive. You never use it wastefully. That, you must never do. You use it to feed your body. Now you must come with us. You need to prove yourself tonight."

She led her to the door of the room, followed by Linda.

Flora went ahead of them but then went back into her room. The three women went to the back of the building. There was hardly any flat space. The ground began a steady slope a few feet from the rear wall of the building. Dense foliage began to emerge as the three women began climbing. They ran into a thick assortment of pine trees. Linda led the way, followed by Margaret who kept holding Robin's hand, guiding her as if she was a child. They climbed up to the top of the hill and then stopped. The woods made it very hard to see. No one said anything and Robin could not imagine why they had stopped walking. A short distance ahead she noticed the small glow of a cigarette. Someone was there. Margaret let go off her hand and moved in front of Linda. She walked a few steps ahead of them towards the light and then she removed her top with both hands in one swift motion.

"Dan, I'm here," she said.

There was no response for a few seconds but then Robin heard the voice of a man.

"I . . . can't believe you actually came," the voice said. It sounded unsteady, showing signs of inebriation. "Sit down. . . let's share a joint. Wow, what have we got there, honey?"

Robin smelled the burnt marijuana aroma as soon as he spoke. Then she felt Linda's hand grabbing her arm. It was not a gentle hold like Margaret's but rough, as if she did not really want to touch her and was doing it only because she had been told to.

"I'll share everything with you tonight, Dan," she heard Margaret say.

She saw her sit down. "Oh, honey . . ."

Linda got closer. Robin could see Margaret reach out towards the man with both hands. She and Linda kept walking, getting closer to them. They were only a step away. Margaret was kissing him, holding his head then suddenly she reached towards her bosom with one hand and Robin heard the snap of the blade as Margaret retrieved it from the sheath and then the dashing sound of it cutting through the man's throat. Linda let go off Robin's hand and rushed forward, moving in front of Margaret. Both women bent down over the man's body, ripping his entrails open. Robin could not see it but could hear them, slashing and tearing away. For a moment, it seemed as if they had forgotten about her but then suddenly Margaret turned towards her, still kneeling on the ground.

"Come on, Robin," she said. "It's time to feed."

Robin could not see her face in the darkness but felt her gaze upon her as if she was a guard.

"Come on, I said. It's time."

Robin took a step forward, and she felt the vibrations of her cell phone in her pants pocket, rubbing against her thigh. She stopped. It must be her mother trying to reach her. Her mind traveled quickly to the Victorian house near the ocean, miles away from here. Yes, she had a home and a good life. What was she doing here?

"Robin, I'm waiting for you. Come on. You must feed," Margaret said.

Robin could not take another step. The vibrations of her cell phone seemed to be getting more intense, like an alarm clock that was waking her from a deep sleep. She saw Linda look up.

"Damn her, Margaret! Make her do it!"

"Hush! Let her come on her own. Come on, Robin. You need to feed."

Robin did not move a muscle. She heard the sound of footsteps threshing the grass behind her, but she was so shaken she could not even turn. Donna came past her first, then Flora, and then the three men. They all knelt on the ground next to Margaret and Linda. They got busy pulling and tearing the body like wild dogs.

"Come on, Robin," Margaret said. "We're waiting for you."

"I told you, Margaret," Linda said. "You should have never let her in. Never!"

"Shut up."

Margaret got up. Robin saw the blood in her face.

Margaret grabbed her hand gently. Robin felt the vibrations of her phone, still going.

"Come on, honey. It's all right."

Robin noticed Margaret's long black hair, its tips soggy from the blood rubbing against the exposed nipples of her breasts.

"No . . ." she managed to say.

It was the last thing she remembered. Everything turned black, blacker than the night around them and then she felt her head hit the ground like that first night in the McCarter house when she had passed out to sleep.

* * *

Another detective was interviewing Ron inside his room. The first-person Roy saw was the tall and lankly John Murray with his long hair in a ponytail. He was standing on the devil strip to the building, pacing and talking agitatedly to the riders around him.

"I thought it'd be best to bring my pack to you," Roy said.

Murray looked up at him, as if momentarily dazed.

"Right, right. Good move, man. I'm glad you're here."

"I think the cops were trying to split us."

"That's it!" John Murray said, pointing his index finger at him. "That's exactly it, man. They want to keep us apart, break our cohesion. They figure that someone will break down and point fingers if they do that. That way they get a suspect.

It's tunnel vision, man. Police tunnel vision as usual."

"So, what happened?"

"We don't know everything yet. When he didn't turn up this morning, his roommates went looking for him and they found body parts in the woods."

He pointed to a wooded area, high on a bank behind the motel buildings. You could see it was not a leisure area. One had to have a purpose to climb the high banks and go into the woods. Roy felt immediately that Dan did not just wander up there aimlessly. He must have been with someone.

"Was anybody with him last night?"

"We all were with him at the camp site," John Murray said, pointing to the picnic area aside of the two motel buildings.

"Is that it?" Roy said.

"Yeah, that's it. You mean you weren't there?"

"My wife and I went straight to the restaurant at our motel. There was no room here."

"Yeah, the place was packed. We all jammed outside till pretty late. I can't recall who Dan was with but the girls who saw him last said he left a little bit after midnight."

"What about his roommates? Didn't they see him in the room last night?"

"The police have been questioning them. But they didn't see him going in. Most of us were pretty exhausted last night, you know, riding all day. So, you can't blame people for not paying too much attention. They just went to sleep."

Murray shook his head. There were several cops walking in the woods, looking for clues.

"I do need O'Gara for some mechanical work. We've got bike trouble with someone at the other building."

He pointed toward the second motel.

"I'll take care of it," Ken said. "I need to get my tools, though."

"Where are they?" Murray asked.

"They're inside the girls' trailer."

"You mean Margaret's trailer?"

"Yes."

"All right. Well, go and see them. They're in the last rooms, second building. You'll run into them out there. One of their bikes needs work."

Ken got on his bike and drove through the parking lot. He rode slowly near the parking slots, in front of the rooms' doors until he reached the end. No one was outside, but he spotted a Blue Harley Sportster with its chain off. He pulled his bike next to it. He noticed the trailer parked a few feet away.

Ken knocked at the last door of the building. A familiar face opened it. Ken recognized her as one of the girls he had seen the day before with Margaret.

"Hi, I'm Ken. I was sent to work on a bike."

"Yes, I know who you are. I'm Flora," she said.

Her long face with bony features could have been attractive if her restless eyes just sat still for a second. She seemed full of energy.

"Is the blue Sportster the one that needs work?"

"Yes. Let me get you the owner. She's inside."

"Robin, come out here, please. They sent a mechanic to fix your bike."

She turned and smiled at him. "Right? You are a mechanic?"

"Yes. I need to go into your trailer. My tools are in there."

"Zeke has the keys. I'll have Robin bring them out to you."

Ken recognized her at once. She strolled out of the room, tall and graceful, and handed Ken a set of keys without saying a word. She did not have any makeup and her skin looked very pale. There were black rings under her eyes. She was dressed all in black. She stood by her bike while Ken opened the back door of the trailer with the key and retrieved his toolbox.

"It looks like you got a busted chain," Ken said, kneeling down by the rear tire. "How did it happen?"

"I don't know."

"If you were riding when it happened, you definitely would know," Ken said, staring down at the flap of the black chain hanging loose around the center of the wheel. "Maybe it was already weak and it tore right at the moment when you stopped the engine. When did you notice it?"

"This morning," she said, without looking up.

"You drove it straight here from the highway last night?"

"Yes."

"I'll have to get it replaced. Let me just retrieve it and then I'll go get a new one from Dave's trailer. Is your bike working okay otherwise?"

"Yes."

Ken smiled at her. He could not meet her eyes. She was staring down. Ken opened his toolbox and grabbed his ratchet socket wrench. He locked it into the center bolt in the middle of the wheel and began turning it. He stopped momentarily and slid his toolbox some distance away from him. He sat down on the pavement, made himself comfortable and went on with his work. He kept talking to her as though she was in front of him.

"Well, thank God it's nothing serious," he said. "You've heard what happened with Dan, I guess?"

"Yes."

"It is so tragic. I'm still kind of numb from the news. Dan seemed to be a good man. I only met him yesterday and yet I feel like I've known him for a long time. May the Lord keep his soul."

She did not answer. Ken kept silent, subconsciously waiting for her answer.

"His soul?" she muttered.

"I'm sorry?" he asked, as if he hadn't heard her.

She said nothing, and he turned to face her. Her beautiful hazel eyes showed the lethargy of the early morning rise. Ken felt the same disconcert she had portrayed the day before when he had first laid eyes on her. It was a disarming feeling triggered by her raw beauty, her flocks of brown hair hanging loosely on the side of her face, her thin waist and firm bosom, her wide hips and long legs, standing there like a goddess.

"It's a real shame," he said, turning back to the wheel. "I hope that the cops do their job fast and find out what really happened."

Ken went on with his work. He pulled the shock away from the wheel's axle after turning the bolt loose. Once more he had the urge to turn around. But then his thoughts were interrupted by another female voice.

"Robin, get inside," Margaret ordered, walking toward her.

She was wearing her black hair loose and untidy, looking as if she had just awakened.

"Good morning, Margaret," Ken said cheerfully.

Ken saw her grab Robin by her wrist and tug her as if that of a child. Ken hauled the bolt out, letting the bike's shock absorber hang loose then stood up, holding onto the wrench. He watched as Margaret steered Robin into the open door of the room. The door shut and then it opened again quickly. Margaret came out.

"Where's Dave?" she asked.

"With the others by the restaurant." "Is he coming?"

"I don't expect him to. I'll be going to see him in a minute to get a new chain from his trailer for this bike."

"I want him here," she said resolutely. "Call him." Ken hesitated.

"Is anything the matter?"

"No, nothing's the matter. I just want him here."

"All right. Let me call him and see if I can get him."

Ken grabbed his phone. He was not sure if she had been utterly rude or merely upset because of the recent events. He dialed Dave's extension and waited. She turned brusquely from him, and he heard her grumble angrily.

"I don't want anybody else to touch her bike."

"What's this all about Margaret? What's troubling you?"

"Nothing. Stay away from my riders. You keep preaching to them and there will be hell to pay."

She spoke with her back turned. She turned and Ken saw the look of abhorrence in her fiery black eyes, staring him down with contempt. Ken heard Dave's wobbly voice on the phone's speaker.

"What's up?"

"How is it going out there? Anything on Dan, yet?"

"No, they're still investigating. What's up with that bike?" "It has a busted chain. I'm gonna need you to send someone with a new one." "How did that happen?"

"Don't know yet. It's a real mystery so far. Can you come down with a spare?"

"What model?"

"A Sportster. Looks like an x18831."

"All right. We'll do. You have it ready?"

"Yes. It's ready to be mounted. I just need the new chain."

"All right."

Margaret hadn't taken her eyes off him.

"What's the harm in preaching, Margaret? I admit that I am really hooked on preaching. Perhaps I overdo my welcome that way. But it does you no harm, Margaret. I thank the Lord for giving me the courage to preach. I am only trying to save your soul."

"I don't want to hear it. Keep it away from my riders. Keep it away from me or else I will deal with you personally."

"Why, you are not a believer?" "Shut up."

"Big mistake, Margaret. You start living when you meet the Lord."

"I said shut up. I already told you, I want Dave to do the job. I don't want you touching her bike. Get out of here."

Ken smiled faintly. At his young age, he had already met many obstinate non-believers. He rationalized Margaret's behavior as part of her thirst for control. Motorcycle clubs leaders were like that. Ken thought that Margaret was a club leader obsessed by control of her turf. She guarded her riders as a tigress protecting her cubs. Still, he found something disturbing in her sudden shift. What had caused her to change?

"Murray sent me over. He's expecting me to do the job."

"Never mind that," she said, getting closer to him. "I'll handle Murray and I'll handle Dave. Get out of here now."

Ken put his wrench away inside his toolbox and slapped it shut. He picked up the box by the handle and looked back at her as he walked away. She was standing there like an owl, watching his every move. He went up to his bike and placed the box on his lap. He looked back at her again. She hadn't moved an inch.

"Good bye, Margaret. I'm sure we'll meet again during the run."

"You hope not."

He smiled slightly at her, as if hoping that his benevolence would win her over. Then he clicked his bike's engine on.

"I'll pray for you."

She didn't answer him. She just watched him leave. Ken thought Margaret had had a bad morning. The scriptures had trained him to be humble, so he quickly put things into perspective. First and foremost, he was to bear no animosity toward anyone. Whatever was going through Margaret's mind, it would be of no consequence in the larger scheme of things. The important thing was to focus on one's purpose as a Christian and leave it at that. Perhaps it was nothing more than a stint of frustration directed towards the men of the caravan. He had heard Margaret when she addressed the crowd the day before. Her comments were feminist and antagonizing. She seemed oversensitive and craving control. Dave was coming out as Ken parked behind his trailer to put his toolbox away.

"What are you doing here?"

"Margaret only wants you to do the job," Ken said.

"Is her bike the one with the busted chain?"

"No, it's one of her girls. She doesn't want anyone else working on it but you. She seemed upset at me."

"Ah, it's nothing. Margaret's like that. She's too protective with her team, that's so. Don't let it bother you. I'll go over there and set her straight. Where is she anyway?"

"Knock on the last door of the ground floor at the second motel. She might still be out there waiting for you."

"All right. I'll be back. I'll go out there and see what's bothering the old fox. You hang here with the other guys while I'm gone."

They saw Detective Leany getting out of a patrol car. The rumor was that some riders were still being questioned inside Ron's room. But no one knew what was going to happen. Murray saw the detective coming.

"What could they want now?"

"Oh, we're here to harass you a little bit," Detective Leany said, teasingly, before Roy could answer.

Dave got on his bike and left.

"Where is he going in such a hurry?" Detective Leany said. "He's going to work on a bike," Ken said.

"I heard you on the phone this morning," Leany said. "Come to think of it. We'd like to get a look at that bike too. Whose is it?"

"Belongs to one of the girl riders." "Which one?"

"It's down by the end of the second motel. You wanna go down and look at it, be my guest. Maybe you can help out with the repairs, too."

"No, we don't do repairs. We observe. All right, who wants to volunteer to take us there?"

He waited a few seconds and then randomly pointed at Ken. "You," he said. "You were in the other motel this morning.

You were the one who got the call from this guy, right? Let's go. Come with us."

Ken followed them into their patrol car and they had him sit in the rear.

"It's too bad what happened to your friend," the detective said, just as they were pulling in.

"What exactly happened?" Ken asked.

"No, I'm doing the questioning. I want you to tell me what happened."

"I wish I knew."

"Really? You mean to tell us that you didn't know anything about it until we told you?"

"That's right."

Ken could see he was fishing around.

"All right. Let's get out there," the detective said.

Dave was sitting on the floor, behind the bike's rear tire.

Three girls and a guy from Margaret's crew were standing by him. Neither Margaret nor Robin were there.

"What happened?" Detective Leany asked.

"A busted chain, if you must know," Dave said without looking up. "What are you doing with Ken?"

"He's our guide. He brought us here. Whose bike is it?"

"Belongs to one of the girls'."

"And how did this happen?"

"Don't have a clue. Who can tell with chains? They bust when you least expect it, sometimes for no reason at all."

"Some rough riding maybe?"

"We haven't done any rough riding, but we rode all day yesterday. Chains are like people. They get tired and break down. That's probably what happened."

A short distance west of them, some members of the forensic team, dressed in blue overalls, were descending from the embankment, slowly making their way into the parking lot.

"Which one of you owns this bike?"

"Robin," Linda said.

"Where is she?"

"She is inside."

"I want to talk to her."

Ken crouched next to Dave and began to help him mount the new chain on the sprocket.

"We need to take the pipes off to get to the other end."

"Why didn't you do that first?"

"I was talking to Margaret."

Linda and the others went inside the room. The two officers wandered a few steps away, watching the forensic people enter their vehicle.

"What did you ever do to that woman?" Dave whispered. "Not a thing, Dave."

"She's awfully bitter at you."

"Where is she now? How come she is not here?"

"I heard she was the first one questioned this morning. They had her in Ron's room for a good hour all because she was with Dan last night. She's awfully irritated about that."

"What's this about not letting me work on the bike? What do I have to do with her being questioned?"

"Apparently, she's an atheist. She found out that you are religious and that upset her."

"I only mean well."

"Ken," Dave said, lifting his head. "You haven't been preaching to her, have you?"

"No."

"Well, don't. Not to anyone around here."

"That wasn't part of our deal, Dave. I can't help but manifest how I feel about the Lord."

"Oh, stop with that. Here comes that other one now. The one who owns the bike. She's a fox if you asked me."

Robin was walking in front of Linda and the other two women. Ken was able to make eye contact with her as he looked his way. He nodded to greet her. Surprisingly, she nodded back. The two officers were walking back to the bike.

"And who might you be, young lady?" Detective Leany asked.

"That's Robin," Linda snapped.

"Well, she can talk by herself, can't she?"

"I'm Robin," she said quickly.

"What's the matter? Why are you upset?"

"I'm not."

"Looks could be deceiving, I guess."

"So, what do you want from Robin?" Linda asked.

"You're definitely too young to be Robin's mother," the other officer said. "Perhaps you should let her speak." "Robin," Detective Leany began, "what happened to your bike?"

"It's got a busted chain," she glanced at Ken as he unplugged the exhaust pipe.

"And how did that happen?" "I don't know."

"You don't know? And how did you discover it?" "It was like that this morning," Linda said.

"Excuse me," Detective Leany said. "Let her answer, please. If we need to ask you something, we will."

"I tried to ride this morning and it wouldn't go. That's when I found out."

The officers had gotten closer to the bike, almost brushing up against Dave.

"When did you ride your bike last before this morning?"

"Last night when we drove in."

"And your bike was fine then, right."

"Yes."

"Did someone ride it after you last night?"

"No."

Detective Leany waved for Robin to follow him and his officer. The three walked slowly away with Robin in the middle. They were talking to her softly and the others could not hear them.

"Where are they going?" Linda asked.

Dave and Ken looked at the others. The man with square shoulders, standing next to the three girls, seemed pleasant enough and the other two girls seemed easygoing. But Linda looked indisposed.

"They're fishing for answers," Dave said.

She glanced discouragingly at them then turned to Ken. "And what are you doing here? Margaret told you not to work on Robin's bike."

"Robin would want me to work on her bike."

"No, she wouldn't. If she wanted your help she would have asked you."

"Are you speaking for her?"

"Yes."

"Well, maybe you shouldn't. Like the detective said, she can speak her own mind."

"I won't let you touch her bike," she said, moving towards him.

"Hold it," Dave said. "He is with me. If he does not work, I don't work either."

In a moment of frustration, Dave bent down and picked up his toolbox.

"Ken, let's go. We're not wanted here."

Dave's bike was parked a short distance away. He was riding an elegant customized black FLHXI Street Glide. He clicked the engine before hopping on the seat. The engine's roar made the officers turn towards them. Dave got on the bike and Ken sat behind him. Dave drove the bike in a semi- circle and then raced back towards the restaurant area.

"What did those cops want with you?" Murray asked Ken.

"They asked the usual questions," Ken said. "They were just fishing for clues."

"I wanna see Phil," Dave said. "Where is he?"

"He's up in Ron's room sitting through some police questioning. We can't interrupt him. What's the matter?"

Dave hesitated. Ron had replaced Dan quickly, he thought. But that was his nature. Ron was a born leader and as soon as he heard that Dan was dead, he named someone to take his place and maintain the caravan's ranking order. That was how he looked after his people. Dave wondered if Murray was yet twenty-five. Standing about six feet tall with his light brown hair tied into a long ponytail, Murray reminded him of a rocker from the seventies. It didn't seem that long ago since he himself had looked like that. Dave pondered how to answer him without making too much of it.

"The girl who leads the women's biker club doesn't want Ken to fix their bikes. I don't know why. So, I'm not touching that bike. Ken is with me and if she doesn't want him, she can't have me either or any of my men. Let them fix their own bikes."

"Wait a minute," Murray said. "What's this all about?"

"I don't know. Why don't you ask her? All I'm saying is that if any of my men is not good enough for her, then no one in the entire group is and we won't work on their bikes."

"You can't do that, Dave. This is the kind of thing that Ron was talking about. We're all part of a team. There cannot be any friction among us."

"Right, and it works both ways."

"So, you're telling me that the bike is not fixed?"

"Right."

"Dave, you gotta get back there. We gotta get that bike running regardless to whom it may belong."

"I'm not doing it."

"Ken, we don't have time for this nonsense."

"Murray, I'm sorry," Ken said.

"We can't have dissention in the ranks, Ken. Ron will not tolerate it."

"Ken!" Dave said brusquely. "You've done nothing wrong! Don't go on blaming yourself. It's not Ken, Murray," he said, facing him. "He's done nothing wrong. For some reason that witch with the big chest that runs the show down there does not like Ken because he's religious. I don't know what she's got against men of religion. She flatly told Ken to leave. She doesn't want him working on her girl's bike. She sent for me. I went and I had Ken help me anyway. One of the other women didn't want Ken to touch anything so I left and I ain't going back. We are a team."

Dave threw his hand down for emphasis then walked away from Murray and went to sit on his van. A group of around thirty bikers, standing by, had watched the exchange.

"Oh, man," Murray lamented. "I cannot take this to Phil or Ron. Not now anyway. We've got enough problems as it is and we must be ready to roll at a moment's call. I'm gonna have to take care of this myself. Hey, Roy, can you take over while I go down there and speak to the girls. I'm gonna find out what the problem is. Maybe I can take one of you guys to help me with that bike. Anybody?"

No one made a move. Dave carried a lot of weight around the riders. All of them knew him and if it came to choosing sides between Murray and him, they would side with Dave. Murray looked around until he realized that no one was going to follow him. He hopped on his Dyna Low Rider and sped off towards the other building. Ron had just placed him on the job, and he hated having to return to him with a complaint.

Specially with something as silly as this. He noticed the detective talking to Robin. This was not good. Then he noticed the blue

Sportster with the muffler pipes out and the chain hanging loose. He thought that must be it. He parked his bike and walked toward the girls near the bike.

"Okay, girls whose bike is it?"

"It's Robin's," Linda said, looking indifferently at him. "Who are you?"

"I'm John Murray. I'm taking Dan O'Rourke's place in the line-up and I'm in charge of detail."

"Well, your mechanic was here earlier and he started work on the bike then decided to take off."

"Well, before we get to that, where's Robin?" "Robin is right there," she said, pointing towards the detective and the police officer with the girl in the middle. "They're still questioning her."

"Are you the leader of this club?"

"No, it's Margaret."

"Can I speak to her?"

"She's resting in her room. She does not want to be disturbed."

He glanced at the young man with them.

"I didn't get your name?"

"I'm Zeke. This is Donna, and that's Flora. The one you already met is Linda."

"You got any tools around?"

"Sure. We brought our own van."

"Can you and I give it a try? Maybe we can put this thing together ourselves."

Murray paced around the bike, thoughtfully examining the open shaft. Zeke looked toward Linda, as if asking for her approval.

"Actually," Linda said, "Margaret could have taken care of the bike herself. She's quite capable. We waited for your man to do it and he walked out on us."

"Yeah, well. I'd just rather get the bike going right now.

Zeke, you think you can get some of those tools, man?"

"Sure."

Linda nodded, and Zeke went to the van. He returned with a silver toolbox. Murray had squatted by the rear tire, examining the broken chain.

"It's really a simple job," Murray said to him. "We just gotta unbolt the cover from the drive to get to the other end of the chain."

"That sounds simple enough," Zeke said.

"Do we have a new chain?"

"Yes, it's right on the other side."

The detective and his officer strode back toward them with Robin.

"It looks like you fellows are doing a good job. Finally putting this thing back together. That other fellow that you sent he didn't work out, ah?"

Murray stood from his crouching position.

"So, you officers appreciate bikes after all. Are you finished with your questioning?"

Murray glanced at Robin. She had remained in the back of the others. For the first time Murray really noticed her.

"As a matter of fact, no," Detective Leany said, "we find Robin's story quite unconvincing, you might say, which leads me into my next question. I am going to need to talk to the rest of these young girls here, but first I need to see that other one. Where is she?"

"Who?" Linda asked from behind him.

"Your leader," the detective said, turning.

"Margaret can't come out right now. She's resting."

"Well then I'll go to her. You girls are not saying she wouldn't cooperate, are you?"

"Margaret was questioned this morning," Linda said. "I know that. Where is she?"

Linda pointed to her room.

"What we'd like you to do," Detective Leany said, "is to remain here until I finish with Margaret. I want to ask you girls a few questions too."

Detective Leany and the officer crossed over the parking lot and reached the walkway that ran along the rooms, heading for the last door in the building. Murray and Zeke went on working with the bike.

"Jerks," Linda said, as soon as they were out of reach. "Margaret is not going to be happy. That'll be the second time they wake her up this morning."

"What the heck is wrong with your Margaret, anyway?" Murray suddenly asked. "She's sleeping in this late morning while everybody else is out here walking on eggs. I tell you something, she sure rubbed my boy Dave the wrong way."

"Your Dave is incompetent," Linda said. "He and that other one."

"We can't have this kind of dissention going on. Ron doesn't like it. You can't find better mechanics than those guys. What could Margaret possibly have against them? By gosh, they hardly even talked to her. Now she's got Dave all bent out of shape over this. He wouldn't even come back here to finish the bike."

"What a pity," Flora said, looking at her friends.

"Yes," Donna agreed.

Murray thought them to be all good-looking women and they seemed to blend together in a perspicacious sort of way. Murray liked that. It was team work. The entire caravan should be like that. That's what riding wall all about. If you rode with people like that, nothing could hurt you, nothing could touch you. Small problems like the police asking questions about an alleged murder could never shake a true cohesive team like Ron had envisioned. He admired the women riders. They were a team. He felt disappointment for Dave and Ken for their not knowing how to handle them. A little compromising and gentle touch was all that was needed.

"You think I can get a word with Margaret after these guys are done? Maybe I can get things warmed up between everybody. It would be a shame to have any discord."

"Yeah, maybe," Linda said. "What do they want from Margaret now? She's already told them everything they want to know."

"Maybe they got something else to ask her now that they interviewed your other friend there," Murray said, looking at Robin.

"What did you tell them, Robin?" Linda said.

"Nothing."

"You were with them for an awful long time," Linda said coarsely. "What were they asking you about?"

"About my bike mostly."

"And what did you tell them?"

"That I found it broken this morning."

"What did you tell them about Margaret, Robin?"

"Nothing."

Murray felt the tension in the air and he walked in between the two women.

"Cool it, now," Murray said. "We are all under stress around here. First, we lose one of our own on the first day of the ride, and then we have these cops going around asking questions, making everybody feel guilty. It's really nobody's fault. These guys are just looking for anything they can to hang their hats on. They got nothing so they're going into our personal lives. But we can't let them get to us. We gotta stay together. Come on girls."

Linda retreated only at the sound of a new red Street Bob.

The rider pulled up right alongside them.

"Ron wants everyone to gather in front of the restaurant, Murray," the rider said. "He's gonna make an announcement."

"All right girls," Murray said, looking around. "This means you too. Round up everyone and let's go."

"Zeke, ready?"

He had left Zeke to assemble the cover and the muffler after mounting the new chain.

"Just about."

"Let Robin try it. It's her bike." "Robin, hold it. We need Margaret."

She heard her but she wasn't listening. She mounted her bike even while Zeke was still hooking the pipes.

"Robin!"

"Let her be," Murray said. "Let her try it. Ready Zeke?"

"Yeah, go ahead. Robin, crank up the engine, slowly."

She clicked the engine on and it roared. Murray and Zeke stood back a bit admiring the bike.

"The Sportster is a beautiful bike," Murray said out loud. "It sure is. This one's got it all. Beautiful rims, twin exhausts."

Robin put the bike in gear. She took off, first straight then in a circle until she reached the roadway. She picked up speed and her front wheel lifted slightly off the pavement. She went towards the first motel area.

"Where is she going?" Linda said, agitated.

"Wherever she wants to," Murray said. "She's free. That's why she has a Sportster. It's an awesome machine, made for those who love freedom."

Robin drove straight through the drive, next to the room's doors, picking up more speed. She was doing well over fifty. She only slowed down when she reached Dave's trailer where Dave, Steve and Ken were sitting, listening to Roy and a group of other riders. She came to a full stop, a few feet past them, then turned and rode her bike right behind the trailer.

"Nice to see it's running again," Ken said, getting up. "Sorry we couldn't finish the job."

She smiled faintly but said nothing to him. Ken came closer and bent down to look at the chain.

"He did a great job," Ken said.

"Yeah, that's fine," Dave said. "How does it feel?"

"Good."

She was sitting on the bike with the engine running. Ken stood up and saw her profile, thinking she was more beautiful than ever.

"Listen up, guys!" Roy said from his spot near the others. "Ron is coming out with Phil. Gather everybody around. I think we're gonna have an announcement."

Phil came ahead of him, walking like the morbid giant that he was, wearing an open vest with nothing under despite the chilly wind. Ron was behind him, a bit shorter and showing the strains of a difficult morning. They came by David's van, and someone wheeled in a red touring model and held it straight for him. Ron climbed on top of the seat. His tall figure towered way above the crowd's heads. He could see down to the last rider at the end of the parking lot from this vantage point.

"All right, folks, listen up!" he began. "Come on down closer so you can hear me. I'm not so good at shouting this morning after what we've been through."

Slowly, the men and women gathered closer. They packed in every inch of available space in the immediate area, crowding around David's van. Ken put his hand on Robin's handlebar, pointing to her ignition.

She clicked the engine off. Ken leaned on her front tire to listen to Ron.

"By now you all know that we've lost Dan," Ron went on. "It's been a terrible tragedy and a terrible loss to this ride. As you probably know, Dan's body was found in those woods right in front of you by that embankment."

He pointed to the sloping trees across from them, in the back of the motels.

"It seems that somebody wanted to do Dan some real harm from the way they have described his injuries to me. I can't even imagine why anyone would want to harm a guy like that. He was my friend and your friend and, as you know, a darn good rider and a superb organizer. In the few hours that we were on the road, Dan had already mastered all the details of our formation, knew the riders by name and organized the run so that it was running flawlessly last night when we got here. Somewhere in one of our stops back there, I said something to you that I meant from the bottom of my heart. I said that we wouldn't leave any rider behind. I said that and I meant it.

And at the same time, I will say this to you: there is nothing, absolutely nothing that will prevent this run from being carried to its completion. This run is going to Daytona and it will get to Daytona."

He was interrupted by a round of applause that turned into cheers. People in the crowd shook their closed fists in the air. Ron took his time to survey the crowd. Some last stragglers were coming in. Slowly making their way through the lot by the first motel, Ron noticed two highway patrol cars, a sinister reminder that the investigation was still ongoing and that the caravan was not free to leave. Ron went on.

"And part of the reason for that is that Danny O'Rourke wanted it that way. He joined us all the way back in Boston and he dreamed of making history by being part of this run, the longest motorcycle run ever undertaken in America. And he has. Dan O'Rourke has made history because he has now become the spirit of this run. We are not going to leave Dan behind. We are gonna take his spirit with us and he will be our guide all the way through, till we get to Daytona."

There was a loud cheer and then gradually the unmistakable sound of Harley engines, including Robin's, exploding in the air, roaring away, as if somehow trying to reach Dan O'Rourke, wherever he was, to let him know that they would do him the honor of reaching Daytona in his name.

Chapter 6

The wind picked up in the afternoon and by the time Ron got word from the highway patrol that they were free to ride on, it had turned into a ghostly bash that made road conditions hazardous, especially for motorcycles. Yet Ron did not hesitate to make his decision to go. The state had taken possession of Dan's scanty remains and they would not be released until forensics completed a thorough investigation. Ron had made arrangements for Dan's family back in Boston to receive his remains once the state was done. Detective Foley had compromised with the bikers to avoid what seemed like a real riot. All one hundred and twenty of the riders would be free to go, but they would be under subpoena power from the State of North Carolina. It had really all been a power play. There was no evidence that anyone in the caravan had been involved, and Dan's death, as grotesque as it may have seemed, could not be pinned on anyone. The riders who found him had said his entrails had been consumed, as if by some hungry beast that had simply devoured them. He was recognizable only through his clothes.

The caravan got going late in the afternoon. It took highway 301 north, then turned west on 48 until it reached Interstate Highway 95. It headed south. As the bikers rode on, no one knew how far they would get this day. After all, the delay had fouled up the leaders' former plans. The original plan called for them to spend the night in Georgia, where reservations had been made previously, but that no longer seemed possible. They had gotten started too late and evening would set in soon. Traveling at night would be too hazardous for such a large group of bikers, and it would most likely be impeded by the highway patrols that now roamed ominously all around them. There was a certain feeling of uncertainty among the riders as they rode quietly on the highway. Ken had been moved further up the line as Dave spread his mechanics throughout the line-up. Ken was now about ten riders from the head of the caravan. He rode next to a heavy-set man driving a sky-blue Touring model. It was a good half hour of riding before Ken's phone rang again.

"Ken here," he said, picking up.

"Dave here," the scruffy voice from the phone speaker said. "Everything okay?"

"So far."

"Everything's running fine in the middle. I just checked with Steve and he's got nothing to report."

"You have any idea where we're stopping for the night?"

"We have gas for three hours. My guess is we're stopping right after the border."

"That would be South of the Border, no?"

"Ron wouldn't stop there. That's a tourist's spot."

"So where do you think?"

"Phil just called. He said they're taking care of it. They want to make sure it's okay with the highway patrol since they got us under their sights. My guess is we'll camp out for the night somewhere."

"That'll be neat, no?"

"Yeah, but some riders might not be ready for it."

"That's true. Do we have enough tents?"

"I think so. You'll fit in ours. Don't worry."

"I'm not. I just pray it doesn't rain."

"I'm sure Ron and Phil will check into the weather before they venture us up into the wilderness. They're neat about things like that. Anyway, I'll keep in touch. Call me if anything."

"All right."

The caravan drove on the right lane of the highway, engines running at a slow, steady speed. The vastness of the flat land seemed consuming, permeating a feeling of endlessness, as if the ride would go on forever. Ken noticed the first signs for Rocky Mount as he found himself wondering whether this same quietness prevailed among the riders in David's sector, at the end of the line. At this very moment, David was wondering with some degree of astonishment about the women's club in front of him. Margaret and her club had taken over the tail end of the caravan, riding in pairs in the lane with Dave riding solo behind them. Margaret started the racket and the others quickly joined in.

"People are strange when you're a stranger, faces look ugly when you're alone," she sang out loud.

"Women seem wicked when you're unwanted. Streets are uneven when you're down. When you're strange. Faces come out of the rain when you're strange," the others echoed out loud. "When you're strange. When you're strange. Da, da, da, da, da, da, da, da, da, da, da, da, da, da."

There was a sad feeling among the riders after Dan's tragic death. There had been no hollers of joy from anyone since they got on the highway and even the engines were keeping the thrust down. But Margaret and her crew seemed to be having a ball. Dave straightened himself on the bike's seat, regretting to have assigned himself to the rear of the caravan. He picked his phone and dialed Ken's number again.

"I'm feeling real uneasy back here," he said. "You wanna switch spots? That beauty you like is back here."

"I wouldn't have a problem going back there if you want me to."

"All right. I'll come up to you in a few minutes. Just remember though, no preaching around Margaret."

There was no answer from the other end, but Dave knew immediately something bad had happened from the change in engine pitch. Ken heard a pop that sounded like a firecracker. He intuitively looked at the rider next to him and saw his blue Touring shaking out of control. Its rear tire had blown out.

"Steer to the shoulder!" Ken yelled. "Stay on it! Stay on it!"

The rider could not re-gain control. The bikers behind them were trying to slow down to keep from colliding. But even a gradual slowdown could be awfully dangerous in such a long line-up because of the potential domino effect. Ken knew it and he reacted quickly. Moving close to the Touring, he grabbed its left handle bar to help the rider gain control, steering it toward the shoulder. Ken's own bike began to shake from the impact but he held on. He steered the Touring hard toward the shoulder, with his bike almost pinned next to it. They both went into the shoulder and then into the low ditch as the rest of the caravan passed them by. The Touring became too difficult to handle as it went down towards the ditch. Ken held on to it for as long as he could but then it lost stability and it went down, dragging the rider with it. Ken released it to keep himself from crashing but it was too late.

His bike was at a thirty-degree angle from the ground and as it hit the bottom of the ditch its rear tire slid sideways. Ken let himself go to keep his right leg from being dragged under and he was ejected. A second later, he was face down on the ground. He shook his head and immediately got up. The Touring had ended up a few feet behind him. It had actually started to climb the other slope of the ditch after hitting bottom. Its rider had not been as lucky as Ken. The bike was lying on one side and the rider was trapped underneath the big engine. Ken ran up towards him and grabbed him from the shoulders, then thought better of it.

"Are you hurt? I'm sorry, I never got your name?"

"I don't know. My right leg is under the engine. It feels like it's on fire. I'm Mike."

"I'm Ken. Mike, don't try to move, okay? I'm going to try to lift the bike. Hang on."

Ken turned the engine off. With one hand, he grabbed the right handlebar and the gas tank.

"I'm going to push it up, Mike. As soon as I do, you try to drag yourself back if you can. Ready? On the count of three."

Ken pulled up. He was a strong man, used to handling heavy equipment as a hired farm hand. Yet, he could only lift the bike up a few degrees with Mike on it.

"Can you slide back Mike? Can you move?"

He was a large bulky man. He slid his body on the seat of the bike back but his lower body did not drag. Just then Ken became aware of the buzzing sound of the bikes engines passing them by on the road. They were still trying to slow down.

"How does your right leg feel?" "Not good, man. I can't feel it."

Ken looked at his leg. The seams of his pants were torn and the lower portion of the leg was turned backwards. Ken marveled at its position. Then he noticed the blood around the knee area and the object protruding out of the calf. That had to be a bone, Ken thought. The leg was fractured.

"Stop, Mike. Don't put any weight on that leg. Let's do something else. Let me lower the bike a little bit. You slide yourself back on the ground to get away from the bike but don't use your right leg, just let itself dangle out from under the bike."

"Is it that bad Ken?"

"No, buddy. It's not. Just do what I'm telling you. You'll be all right."

"I wish we had some help. It's starting to hurt me now."

"Help will be here, I'm sure. The whole bike line up has to come to a stop. I'm sure the riders in the rear will be the first ones here once they stop."

Just then Ken's phone started buzzing.

"Hold on Mike, hold on."

He turned around, slowly shifted his hands, and grabbed the bike's gas tank from behind him. The phone kept ringing.

"Go ahead, Mike, slide down."

Slowly, Mike worked his way backwards and out of the bike with both hands in front of him, grabbing onto the seat.

"Careful now Mike, you're going to be off the bike in a second. You need to hold on steady or you'll fall. I can't reach you until you're off the bike."

Mike had thrown his head back and closed his eyes in pain. "A little more Mike. Just a little more and you're off the bike."

As he reached the end of the seat, his large body slid down slowly on the rear fender, but the weight of his right leg kept him from coming off completely. He shrieked from the pain.

"Drag yourself back, Mike. I'm gonna try to move the bike up now that you're off."

Ken lifted the bike. He grabbed one handlebar and rolled the bike until it was out of reach of Mike's leg. Then he released the kickstand out to lean it over and ran back to Mike.

"Mike, don't move anymore. Stay still until I get some help."

"Ken!" he heard a female voice call from the top of the ditch. The bank wasn't deep, but she seemed to be standing so much higher to Ken at the moment. She was sitting on her bike at the crest with the engine running. Her long brown hair was clasped by her helmet on top.

"Are you all right?" she asked.

"Robin. We're going to need some help moving him. His leg is fractured. Can you get us some help?"

She looked towards Mike's lower body and noticed his bloody leg with the pants torn.

"They're coming," she said and dismounted. She released the kickstand and walked down toward them at the bottom of the ditch.

"We should not move him. His leg could get worse," Ken said. "We need a stretcher."

Mike had thrown his head back and was moaning in pain.

They heard the bike's engines racing above them. "Ken," Dave yelled, getting off his bike. "Are you all right?"

"Mike's hurt. We need to get him to a hospital."

Dave ran down the embankment and knelt near Mike. He wiped the sweat off his forehead with a bandanna. He pulled his phone and dialed an extension. Other riders had now reached the ditch and were surrounding them.

"Murray," Dave said into the phone. "Someone's hurt. We need to get him to a hospital. He's gotta busted leg."

There was silence at the other end as Murray sorted the information in his head. A female's voice called from the top of the ditch.

"Robin!"

Margaret was on her bike looking down at them. Ken made an attempt to go to Robin, but she was already walking away from them and up the embankment. He followed her with his eyes until she reached the top and disappeared. Margaret was staring down at him. The hatred in her gaze left him no doubt that it would be a fight to the death. The green, flat valleys of the Carolinas would roll forever into the horizon, their supple stillness reigning among travelers on the road, and like them, Margaret McCarter would never leave him alone. She would stand in between him and Robin like a fortress, impeding his pass and he could never dream of having her. Robin was a prohibited prize.

"Leave it alone, Ken," Dave said, grabbing him. "We're gonna have to move Mike. Come on."

Margaret vanished from the top. Murray's voice came on Dave's phone.

"All right. Can you guys move him?"

"Why can't you get an ambulance down here? He needs to be taken to a hospital."

"The Rocky Mount first aid squad has been notified. But in the meantime, can you get him on the road?"

"I think we can," Steve said.

"All right boys. Let's all lend a hand. We're gonna have to be careful not to move his leg."

Ken and two other bikers took hold of Mike's leg from underneath to keep it from slanting or jerking away. Others lifted his body. They carried him towards the top.

"Someone lay a blanket on the ground so we can put him down until First Aid gets here," Dave said.

One rider laid a comforter on the shoulder of the road and the others laid Mike on it. A rider brought in a light blanket and unfolded it. He laid it down gently on top of Mike, covering him up to the chest. Ken knelt down near him again.

"How are you holding up, Mike?" Ken said.

He opened his eyes. He painfully moved his hand from under the blanket and he grabbed onto Ken's wrist. His hand was massive and fat and it wrapped itself easily around Ken's wrist. Mike lifted his head and spoke to him in between breaths.

"That was some driving you did back there, Ken. Thanks."

"You'll be all right, Mike. It's only a scratch, as they say."

"I'm afraid it's a little more than that," he said, gnashing his teeth. "I'm done for, Ken. I'll never make the run."

"Ah, there'll be other runs. That's not important. What's important right now is to get that leg in a cast, Mike, so it doesn't buckle on you and you can ride again."

"Yeah, it would be a bomber if I can't ride again."

"Where are you from, Mike?"

"I'm from Boston."

"We'll bring your bike back. Don't worry about that."

They heard the faint sound of sirens coming from the north side of the highway. They were a slow revolving sound, working their way to a crescendo and then slowing down to a low volume as first aid sirens normally do. Two highway patrols pulled over on the shoulder of the highway behind them. An officer jumped out quickly out of one. The caravan had filled the road's shoulder ahead for as far as the eye could see.

"What is it fellows? What happened to him?" the officer asked.

"He had a blow out and lost control of his bike," Ken said. "I tried to help him and we both ended up on the ditch. I was able to free myself from under my bike but Mike got dragged under his Touring. It's a heavy bike and it tore his right leg pretty badly."

"Well, First Aid is coming. But we're gonna need you guys to get moving. We can't have the shoulder congested like this. We need to keep it empty."

"It's better than stopping the whole line-up on the regular lane. That would really have been a scene," Steve said roguishly.

The officer gave him an eyeful.

"That would have definitely got you one hundred and twenty summons perhaps even some complaints for inciting a riot. You're close as it is right now."

"All right, gentlemen," another officer said, "whoever is in charge here is gonna have to get things moving. We want that shoulder cleared right away."

"We can't get moving until we see about our friend here, officer," Dave said. "We are not gonna leave him by the side of the road like an animal. We got a motto here that we do not leave any riders behind."

"I think you're gonna have to leave this one," the officer said, looking at Mike on the ground.

"All right, folks," the other officer said, spreading his hands. "Let's move back and away from the injured. First Aid is here."

The ambulance pulled onto the shoulder, right behind them. It was a square van with overhead lights on the roof. Two men in overalls jumped out and immediately went to work on Mike. They pulled up his blanket and looked underneath.

"We need the stretcher," one of them said, pulling his walkie-talkie from his belt.

Another First Aid man went back to the ambulance. From the other end of the shoulder came the sound of a Touring Harley, traveling on the ditch of the road and heading towards them. Ron Mason wore no helmet. A woman, also without helmet, wrapped her arms around his waist. He drove his bike right up to the ambulance. He climbed off and let his woman companion handle the bike. He stood watching the medics take the stretcher holding Mike inside the ambulance.

"How badly is he hurt?"

"Looks like a fractured leg, Ron."

He looked around their faces and spoke to Ken.

"I heard about the driving you did back there, Ken. That was awesome. I wanna thank you for your comradery."

He stretched out his hand to him then turned to Roy.

"We need to send a rider with that ambulance. Mike is all by himself."

"I'll go, Ron," Dave said, raising his hand.

"No, we need you around here. We're gonna get going and we need all the mechanical help we can get with us. We'll leave a rider behind to look after Mike, make sure he's okay and then he can catch up to us later. It's a sacrifice but it's part of what we do. We can't abandon our riders. Do I have any volunteers?"

He looked around the crowd, which kept growing as more riders came in from the shoulder. The two officers retreated a few steps back, giving the group some privacy. A couple of young men in the back raised their hands.

"All right, Sullivan," he said, pointing to a young man with long black frizzled hair. "You got it. Get your Harley going and follow the ambulance. Murray, give him a phone. Make sure he stays in touch."

Murray broke from the crowd and went with the young man, walking hastily through the labyrinth of bikes, gathered in the shoulder. Margaret and her girls were hanging by their bikes, at the end of the line.

"All right," Ron went on. "We've taken care of our mate. Sullivan will stay with him at the hospital and contact his family. Dave, you take care of Mike's bike now. Where can we carry it?"

"We can get it in the back of a pickup."

Ron pointed to Margaret's pickup. Zeke was leaning against it.

"Whose pickup is that?" Ron asked.

"It's our club's," Margaret said quickly.

"Do you have any room in there?"

"Hardly," Margaret said.

"There's room in there," Dave said. "There's plenty of room."

"All right. You wanna get Mike's bike in there, guys? I'm hoping he can ride it on our way back north."

She looked Dave over as one would look over a prize. Then she turned to Zeke and asked him to help the others. Ron moved over to the two officers who were standing by the sidelines, anxiously waiting to talk to him.

"We have to get your line-up going," one of them said. "We can't have you create a parking lot on the shoulder. Traffic is building up. You're going to have to get going."

"We will," Ron said. "Just minor adjustments. We'll get going in a few moments."

He talked bluntly to them, as if they weren't real cops. Ron watched the ambulance speed away on the highway, and shortly thereafter, the healthy roar of a Harley engine took off from the middle of the pack. The blue Soft Tail caught up to the ambulance in no time as the two vehicles disappeared down the highway.

"We can get that bike in the back of the truck, Ron," Dave said, rushing up to him after having checked Zeke's pickup. "It'll fit just fine."

"Good. Load it up then and let's get going. We gotta hit the border tonight."

Ken, Dave and several guys went down to the bottom of the ditch and picked up Mike's bike. The bike's right side had been pretty banged up, and at least one pipe was out of place. They rolled it up to the shoulder and pushed it next to the truck. Dave climbed inside with two other guys. It took four men on the ground and three in the truck to bring the huge machine over the side of the truck and lay it inside.

"All right, folks," Ron said. "Everyone make sure you check your tires and give one of our mechanics a yell if you need anything. We don't want any more blow outs. We've taken care of Mike for now. But we gotta get rolling again. At this rate, we're never gonna make Daytona anytime soon."

Ron walked up to Ken and tapped him on the shoulder.

"That was good work, Ken."

Ron's girl was right beside him, smiling at Ken. She was a tall brunette dressed in a white tank top under an open leather jacket. Ron's Touring roared into life, moving abruptly through the shoulder, working its way through the maze of bikes and men clogging up the road.

"Ken, you move up to the same spot. Steve will follow you in the middle and I'll take the rear. Is your bike all right?"

"I think so."

Ken looked past him. The women's club was gathered at the rear. Ken worked his way down to the ditch and picked up his bike. It had made a soft landing when Ken ejected from it but sustained no damage except for a broken mirror. Two riders had come down with him and they helped him bring it up. By then the caravan's engines were going full throttle and Ken took his spot close to the front of the line-up. The riders in the front began swiveling onto the highway's right lane from the shoulder, like the head of a snake, followed gradually by the rest of the line.

Ken fell into place on the line-up and noticed the empty spot next to him where Mike had been riding. The falling back into line had happened so fast that Murray did not have time to re-arrange the line-up. Ken felt awkward about the void and he called on Dave.

"Ken, here," he said into his phone. "Are they going to fill Mike's spot?"

"Nope," Dave said. "I've got an empty spot next to me too and it's gonna stay. I think Ron wants it like that in memory of the riders who occupied it. Ron is thoughtful about things like that."

"That means there must be another empty spot in the line-up for that other rider that went with Mike, no?"

"Yeah. We got three. And I hope there will be no more."

"Right," Ken said. "How is it going back there?"

"Oh, the same. The women are singing their way through this thing, as if nothing happened. It's spooky."

"It's a long way to South Carolina. Do we have any planned stops that you know of?"

"We're getting gas by Smithfield. That's about an hour south of here."

"All right then. Keep in touch."

* * *

The sun was setting down by the time the caravan passed Smithfield. Murray called all the mechanics and they passed the word. They would fall in double file at the exit for Smithfield. Ron had a station in mind because it had a large, paved area facing the meadows, and he could swing his riders inside without backing up traffic. They went into the exit ramp and stopped at the crossroads. Then they went right.

Already a patrol man had stopped his vehicle at the intersection and was guiding traffic. One by one the bikes passed through the pumps and filled up their tanks. Ken waited for Dave, who was the very last rider in the line-up.

"Don't fall out of line too long. Ron wants to keep going."

"Have any idea where we are stopping for the night?"

"I think it's gonna be west of Dillon, South Carolina. We lost our reservation in Georgia, so Ron made arrangements for a hard camp out in the wilderness, near one of the creeks. He found someone whose family owns land there."

"Oh, that'll be neat."

"It may be darn cold," Dave said. "No running water and nothing to eat except what we may get going on a fire. If you're not fond of country, you won't like it."

"I'm okay."

"Some of the others around here may have a hard time with the accommodations."

Margaret's club passed by them, and one of the girls looked over. Ken wasn't sure whether she was Flora or Donna. These two always confused him. But he looked past them, searching for Robin. She hadn't noticed him as she sat on her bike, but one of her domineering companions did, and she moved quickly in, manipulating her bike to place herself between Ken's and Robin's.

"What do you want down here?" she asked.

The voluptuous Margaret now blocking his path seemed pretty resolute leaving no doubt that she deemed Robin her possession. Why, Ken did not know. But it did not matter. The die had been cast. Ken knew he would have to go through her, as one goes through a hurdle. How intractable and uncompromising that hurdle would be remained to be seen!

"Robin," Ken said.

"Take off."

Dave pulled his bike alongside Ken's.

"Ken," Dave said. "It's okay. Leave it alone for now."

"No," Margaret said, pointing her finger at Dave. "Not now, not ever. I don't think I noticed you back there earning up stripes with Ron Mason. Keep away from our business.

Keep away from our club. You're not welcome."

"If it was up to me," Dave replied, "I would have you kicked out. I wouldn't give a damn about you. I think you're a bunch of freaks. It's only because you're part of this run but let me tell you, I've just about had it with you."

"Really? Is that why you meddle in our business constantly? Because of you, we have to carry someone else's bike now." Dave had an impulse to call Murray and ask him to re-assign him but he thought better of it. He had promised Ron his support back in Boston and he would make good on his promise. He would just have to handle Margaret.

"Margaret, we're all in this caravan. We all have to do our part."

"That's right. We all have to do our parts. Right girls?"

Linda, Flora and Donna chuckled. Even the three guys who Ken noticed together for the first time laughed heartily.

"I hope that is your true sentiment, Margaret. Strange things can happen on the road when you're riding and you never know when you might need a hand from a fellow rider."

She smiled pointedly at him.

"You never know, that is right," she said, still smiling.

Dave did not allow himself to think what she meant.

"I'll be in touch," Ken said, interrupting his thoughts, and rode his bike out towards the front of the line.

He took his spot in the line-up, which was moving sporadically as each bike went through the pumps. Slowly, as the riders finished filling up, the caravan made its way back to 95 and headed south. Dave buzzed Ken a few moments later to confirm they would be going non-stop until they passed the state line to South Carolina. He hoped it would be a smooth, uneventful ride. The riders were still feeling unsettled about what happened. The unnatural silence prevailed among most ranks and hardly a word had been spoken as the caravan began seeing the signs for Fayetteville, accessible through route 87 and a web of local routes. Humorous billboards announcing the glitzy conglomerate of motels, stores and games that make up

South of the Border began crowding the highway. Experienced riders from the west compared it to a watering hole. An oasis in the middle of the unrelenting vastness of the Carolinas. A welcome break in the monotony of the trip, but one that most riders did not actually use as a stop. It was thought to be too touristy, flocked by families and children, looking for the games and the fast foods. Motorcycle riders did not seem quite fitting in this scenario, especially a caravan of Ron Mason's size.

"Who's this Pedro that we see on the signs?" Ken heard the couple behind him say.

"He's the little guy with the big hat and the poncho. I guess he had too much tequila."

"I'd be curious to stop just to see him," the man said.

"That's probably the trick," Ken said. "The billboards work this character up the kazoo. He's appealing to the children and he keeps popping up as you go along to the point where he grows up on you. By the time you hit South of the Border, you want to stop to see this guy, whether he even exists. It works."

"I bet. I'm anxious to see him myself."

The caravan reached the state line as a gaudy, gigantic hat with glimmering lights on top became visible. To their left were the bright lights of the complex, mostly stores with large neon signs, restaurants and motels. It was flashy but they passed them in a few seconds. Then they bore on the sign welcoming them to South Carolina.

"The boss says to pass the word," Dave said.

"We're getting off by Dillon, west on Highway 9."

"And then what?"

"We're getting off near the creeks that flank the highway. One biker's family owns 50 acres here so we're gonna camp out."

"All right. I'll spread the word."

Ken maneuvered his bike to the center of the lane and worked his way up the line-up, telling each rider the plan. He went up two spots from the lead then slowed the pace to retreat to his original spot, letting the first couple of riders behind him know the plan too. Then he phoned Dave back to let him know.

The riders up front put on their signals to turn right as they came up to Highway 9. The caravan made its way slowly into the road, going west. It was already dark and the lack of lights on the highway made it hard to see. But Ron and Phil were apparently familiar with the area. The lead riders pulled suddenly onto the shoulder and the others followed. Two highway patrols swerved quickly past them and stopped a few feet away. Ron waited for the officers to come to him.

"What's the plan here?" one officer said in a very heavy southern accent. His uniform was not visible in the dark and his partner, walking close behind him, was shining a flashlight at the men.

"We are resting if that's okay with you," Ron said. "You guys rest, don't you?"

"We rest, sir, at the appropriate time and with the appropriate accommodations."

"Well, we have the appropriate accommodations, officer, and they're right here."

Ron pointed towards the right side of the road.

"There is nothing there but woods, sir."

"We're camping out here, officer."

"It's private property, sir. You can't camp out on somebody else's land."

Ron dismounted from his bike and his girl rider moved up on the seat to grab the handlebars.

"Hey, McClure," Ron called waving his hand in the dark. "Can you come here for a second?"

He was a burly young man whose face features could not be seen in the dark.

"The officer here wants to know who owns this property," Ron said, pointing again to the side of the road.

"My family does—the entire strip from here on west for about 3 miles, and about 3 miles deep. There's a shack near one of the creeks and a well. The grounds around the shack were flattened last year to get them ready for camping. We can reach them from the trail that comes off the road right about here. I've stayed here before."

There was silence for a moment as the officer looked him over, then looked back at Ron.

"You got tents?"

"We sure do," Ron said.

"Well, it may sound like we're overbearing but believe it or not the South Carolina Patrol is actually looking after your own well-being. We don't want to have another Pleasant Hill tragedy over here."

"We stayed inside a motel at Pleasant Hill, officer," Ron said. "We were supposed to be safe there and look what happened."

"I understand what you're saying, sir. I understand. But we still gotta make sure the public is safe. How're you going to be able to get down to the campsite?"

"The trail starts off right here," Ron said, pointing. "We're gonna drive our bikes through it till we reach the cabin and then we'll camp out."

"Is there any electricity down there?" the officer asked McClure.

"No, there isn't, sir."

"And how are you people going to see in the dark? What are you going to be using for light? No fires are allowed in the woods. You know that, right?"

"Officer, you could join us in camp. You could watch us. It would probably be a lot safer for us."

"No, I'm afraid not. We're not in the business of camping out with people. We're only going to do our jobs and that's it."

"The North Carolina Patrol was in the business of camping this morning. They camped in our parking lot for most of the day."

"Not the South Carolina Patrol, sir. Anyway, you want to get going. We don't want you to create a traffic jam here.

Lots of folks are driving home from work at this time."

Ron got on his bike and pointed to McClure.

"All right, McClure, you lead the way."

They went single file on a dirt trail that sprang out among the trees on the side of the highway. It got pitch dark inside and all they could see was the thin stretch of path illuminated by their bikes' headlights. They got to an open space in the forest, and McClure stopped. He steered his handlebars to the side and shone into the small wooden cabin with his bike's headlight. He released the kickstand and got off the bike.

"I'll get lights going in the cabin," he said to Ron.

Ron turned to the riders behind them and asked everyone to put their bikes in a circle around the cabin. Those who had tents would have to share them with others. No one was to be left out without a roof in the field. Everyone got busy parking their bikes as McClure lit an oil lamp inside the cabin. Dave backed his trailer close to the cabin. He brought out his tan Expedition tent and folded it into a big heap. Ron stood on the roof of one of the pickups and spoke to the riders.

"Everyone find a spot in the open area. Don't straddle too far from the cabin. We'll try to set up a station here, so if anyone needs any drinking water or supplies, just come over. I'm sorry about tonight's accommodations but it's the best I could do under the circumstances. I couldn't have you keep going all night. Luckily, the weather will be pleasant and we should all have an adventurous but pleasant time. Again, I encourage you to be good neighbors and help anyone who might need a hand. So, everyone choose a spot and have a good night. We'll get going tomorrow morning around 8:00. If everything goes right, we should hit Daytona around 4:00 in the afternoon."

Ron waited momentarily to hear the crowd's reaction but got none. Then he jumped off the roof of the pickup and mingled with the crowd.

"These riders are getting fatigued," Dave said, as he spread the heavy cloth of his tent on the ground.

"What makes you say that?" Ken asked.

"You can see they're not reacting anymore. I see the first signs of discontent building up."

"Not a good thing," Steve commented.

Ken got the orange groundhog stakes clamped into the ground while Dave began clipping the bottom ends of the tent to them. Steve got under the fabric and raised the rear section, cinching the guy chords around it and past the ridge on top to the other side. Ken and Dave placed a support pole underneath and quickly moved to the forward sections. The tent was spacious but really meant only for two. Ken would offer to sleep out in the open but knew Dave would never let him. They worked quickly, extending the tent's flat end at the entrance. Dave and Steve brought their sleeping bags and supplies from their van. Ken went to his bike and unwrapped his comforter from the seat. He retrieved his bible and pajamas from one of his leather saddle bags. Dave and Steve set their sleeping bags parallel to each other and Ken set his comforter at their feet. Their tent was a good hundred feet from the cabin where McClure and the others had gotten a gas lamp going. It shone inside, spreading some light to the surrounding area where a crowd had gathered, chatting in low voices. McClure and some of the others had set up refreshments and snacks inside. Some of the bikers had brought wine bottles which they started to serve to the crowd in mugs. Ken went inside the cabin with Dave and Steve. The cabin was small, made of pine tree planks. There was one single bed and a brick stove. The McClure family had built it as a retreat for short stays and fishing trips. McClure lit a fire in the stove and set a coffee pot to boil on top. There was no place to sit and the men were gathering in a circle near the doors, mugs in hand.

"Got a mug, Ken?" Dave said.

"I can get one," Ken said. "What are they serving?"

"Looks like coffee."

"Nah. I could go for some hot chocolate though." "They have it," Steve said. "Tea too. Bring your mug."

Ken stepped out of the cabin and went down the two steps at the entrance. As he did, he ran into Linda and Margaret, who were coming inside. They did not look at him, and neither did the two other girls who followed them, but Robin, who walked alone behind them, smiled at him. He retrieved a yellow mug from his saddle bags and returned to the cabin.

"They have heard from Mike," Dave said.

"Really? How's he doing?"

"He's doing much better. Sullivan called and reported to Ron. He said they did surgery on his leg. His leg bone tore out of the skin completely right below the knee. They had to open his leg up to put the bone back together. He's now all stitched up but doing well. He's out of surgery."

"Great news," Ken said.

"He remembered you, Ken. He sent a message with Sullivan to tell you thanks."

"I did nothing that you would not have done."

"That's why I want you on my team. Here," Dave said, looking down at his mug. "Give me that. I'll get you your chocolate."

Ken made a gesture to resist but Dave pulled it from him and he quickly moved to the front of the crowd.

"Give me a hot chocolate," Dave called to the two men by the stove.

"Hey," one of them said. "That's only the second request I got for one of them. The first one was from that young lady over there."

He pointed towards Robin, standing near the only window in the room where Margaret and her crew had gathered.

"This is not for me," Dave said, handing him Ken's mug. "It's Ken O'Gara's."

He gave Ken a nod.

"That was great defensive driving out there today, Ken. I'm glad you're with us in the run."

Ken nodded back, but his attention was on Robin.

Margaret noticed it. The man filled Ken's mug and handed it back to him.

"Maybe you ought to sit by the window with her," he said. "If there are only two of you with the same choice of drinks in a whole regiment of 120 riders it's pretty miraculous if you ask me."

He showed a set of outgrown teeth when he smiled.

"Leave it alone, Reilly," Dave said, drinking his coffee. "Don't go there."

But Reilly had already taken a step back, trying to get a better look at Robin. It was obvious he had been drinking.

"Do you mind?" he said to Margaret. "You're obstructing the view."

"I know."

"Hey, honey," he called past her. Can I introduce you to my friend, Ken O'Gara? He's a great mechanic—the greatest there is—and he drinks chocolate like you."

He laughed haughtily and turned back towards Ken and Dave.

"Sorry, Dave. Didn't mean to deflect you. You're a great mechanic too. But after what Ken did out there today, he's gotta a leg up on you, at least on the riding."

He was laughing again. Ken and Dave went outside. The room was getting very crowded, and people were forming a line to come in. Ken looked back over his shoulder, aside of Margaret, and saw Robin's brown hair, reaching past her upper back. He was smitten by her beauty again. As if by magic, she felt it and turned slightly towards him, but Margaret was standing between them, like a wolf guarding her prey and obstructing Ken's view.

"I wonder what's with that woman," Dave said outside. "What woman?"

"Margaret."

"She's pretty unfriendly," Steve said.

"Worse than that," Dave said. "Something's not right. The way she carries herself with those others like she owns them."

"A fine-looking woman," Steve went on.

"Yes. That's what Dan thought too."

"Did he?" Ken asked. "Dan O'Rourke thought that?"

"I think Dan may have had the hots for her. You saw how he stuck to the rear of the line like glue, following her."

"Poor Dan," Steve lamented. "He was like that, very much into women. A regular guy who loved motorcycles and women. Nothing wrong with that."

"No, nothing's wrong with that," Dave repeated. "I wish we knew what happened, though. It doesn't seem fair that we just took off without really finding out."

"You mean you don't know?"

He was a tall rider with saddle-knee-high boots, blue jeans, black undershirt and a black vest. Both of his arms were tattooed from shoulder to wrist with busy arrangements of human faces and flower designs. He had strolled carelessly toward them, holding his coffee mug.

"We sure don't," Dave said. "And I don't know of anyone who does. There's been no official version released about it that I know of."

"He was attacked by a wild animal," the man said. "He went for a walk in the woods and he was jumped by some beast. A wolf maybe."

"There are no wolves in North Carolina, man. Dan's death had nothing to do with a wolf. We're probably never gonna know what happened if you ask me. Dan's case is going to be forgotten like any other unsolved murder."

"My name is Larry Donovan, by the way," he said, shaking their hands. "I'm telling you it was the work of some wild animal. I'm surprised you guys did not hear it."

"Stop," Dave said.

Margaret and her girls crossed by them, heading for their tent. The three men marched in last and Dave looked at them with interest.

"I wonder what kind of guys these are. They seem to follow that woman like sheep."

"So do the other women," Steve said.

"Wine fellows?"

Two riders holding bottles and empty paper cups stopped by them on their way to the cabin. The night was not cold but breezy, lending itself to a tepid drink. Dave accepted a cup, and Steve and the other man did, too.

"How about you?" they said to Ken.

"Thanks. I'll pass."

"I know it ain't much, man, but it's better than spending the night dry."

"Thanks. I'll pass anyway."

Dave was staring at him, almost as a taunt. He smiled slightly as he drank.

"Ken is a clean guy," Steve said. "He doesn't drink alcohol."

"Hmmm. Interesting. A biker who doesn't drink. What do you do when we stop?"

All of them laughed together and Ken took a sip from his mug.

"I don't drink," Ken said. "That's what I do."

"Well, tonight is kind of an exception and it should be for all of us. We've been through a lot. We lost one of our mates.

Almost lost another one out on the road today and would probably have had it not been for you, and then here we are in the middle of nowhere with no real food to speak of, all one hundred and twenty of us. I say it deserves an exception. You sure you don't want some, man?"

"Sure. Thank you."

A man and a woman approached them and asked for a sip.

"What time do you fellows think we'll get going tomorrow?"

"I'd say Ron will have us out of here by 8:00," Dave said. "He wants to get on the road early to make Daytona while it is still light outside. We were supposed to have been there tonight."

"Tonight? No way," said Donovan. "We would have never made it there tonight."

"We could have if we had left Pleasant Hill early but we lost too much time."

"Hey guys," Ken said. "I'm going to get going. I'll turn the light on in the tent and do some reading. I'll see you there."

They said goodnight, and Ken made his way through the maze of tents already up on the grounds, with riders crowded around them, drinking and telling stories of past runs. So many tents had gone up in the short time that passed since he helped Dave and Steve put up theirs that he suddenly lost his bearings. There was no rhyme or reason for where they had been erected, mostly at random and as close to the occupants' bikes as possible. Ken made a few wrong turns and had to backtrack until he ran into Dave's orange tent and slipped the entrance's cover aside to get in. He got inside his blue comforter and lay flat on the ground. He reached for his bible that he had left inside and opened it to his bookmark in chapter 5 of the book of John. Pinned against a bundle of pages was a small compact reading lamp, enclosed in a plastic case. Ken retrieved the flexible arm with a small fluorescent bulb at its end and the light flicked on. He began reading.

". . . and Jesus went up to Jerusalem." Ken's attention focused only on the story. The voices of the men and women congregated outside did not disturb him. He could only hear Jesus talking to the infirm man, lying on the ground. "Jesus said to him, 'Rise, take up your bed and walk.' And immediately the man was made well, took up his bed and walked."

Ken read the entire chapter. The voices outside seemed to quiet down gradually. A long time must have passed as he fell asleep. He suddenly raised his head and opened his eyes. The open bible was resting on his chest with the battery light still shining. He heard snoring and looked up to see Dave and Steve sleeping inside their Expedition bags. He sat up on the floor and pushed the light rod into the case. It was pitch-black in the room. He looked at the glowing numbers on his wristwatch, which showed almost 4:00 A.M. He was usually a sound sleeper, hardly ever waking up during the night, so he found himself wondering why he was awake. He laid his head back and tried to go to sleep but the thought kept coming back to him. He felt for his bible underneath and pulled the light rod on. He was still on the book of John.

"Therefore, they sought to take Him, but no one laid a hand on Him, because his hour had not yet come."

He thought he heard a ruffling sound outside, as that of an object moving on the grass. He wondered if that was what had waken him up. He waited a few seconds and he heard it again. He pulled himself up and subconsciously he held on to his bible. The tent was short in height and he had to crawl to get to the entrance. He un-zippered the curtain-entrance and tossed it aside. As soon as he stuck his face out, he noticed her hazel eyes looking at him. She was blocking his path out of the tent and he had to bring himself up from the ground. He felt an intrigue as he brought himself up to face her. She said nothing to him at first, just stared at him as he spoke.

"You are Robin, right? You're with the other girls."

"I've come to warn you," she said. "You must leave the tent now. They're coming for you."

"Who?"

"They are. Margaret and the others."

What was she talking about? She seemed upset. He had gauged her as being discontent with the others. Perhaps she had finally left the club and was looking for help. He was glad of that. He never thought she belonged with them and was eager to help her. But why had she chosen him?

"You don't understand," she said, showing signs of agitation. "Margaret and her riders are going to kill you. They don't like you. Margaret especially hates you. And if they find you they will finish you off. You won't be able to escape. Leave now. Run away and hide until the morning and then pack your things and leave before they get you."

"Why are you telling me this?"

"I don't know. I don't want to see you hurt."

He intuitively moved his closed hand, holding his bible. He had not realized he had crawled out of the tent carrying it.

"Why would Margaret want to hurt me? I've done nothing to her."

"Because of that," she said, pointing to his bible.

Robin just stood there, so close to him, he could smell her breath. He reached out to touch her and she moved away. She suddenly began running through the tents without looking back and Ken went after her. She was not running aimlessly but weaving through the narrow spaces towards the clearing. Then she ran towards the woods and he began catching up to her. She cut through the clearings between the trees but when they reached the high grass, she stumbled and fell. He was right behind her. He threw himself after her and both fell side by side on a thick layer of grass. He grabbed her by the shoulders and lifted her up. He wanted to look her in the face and ask her why she was running and how she had gotten involved with the "Lost Souls."

"Robin! Robin!"

"Leave me alone," she said.

"Robin, what's wrong? What's happening?"

She did not answer him. But she came closer to him slowly until her head rubbed his shoulder and she rested it on it. He put his bible down and again grabbed her by the shoulders with both hands. Her face was pale and there were black rings under her eyes. He shook her shoulders.

"What does it all mean, Robin? Who are these people?"

"They're after you, Ken. You must leave the caravan."

"I won't leave the caravan, Robin. Why should I? What do these people want?"

"Feed. That's what they call it. They feed off people. It's what they do to release their hate and to survive."

"Look, Robin," he said. "Look at me. You're not dreaming this up, are you?"

"It is real, very real."

Then she bowed her head down to her chest and wept. She wept alone without getting close to him, but then gradually she leaned against him. She cried, burying herself amidst his arms as he embraced her, pulling her closer. He threaded his fingers through her hair and remained quiet, thinking about what she had just said. Her sobs were intense and they drowned her words. He caressed her head with his open hand, giving her time to answer.

"It's too . . . late," she finally said. "It's too late for me. I have to feed."

Ken grabbed her by the arms, placing her face across from his.

"What is it Robin? What do you feed yourself with?"

"Human flesh."

He was jolted a bit by her answer but quickly recovered.

He wasn't letting her go. "You eat human flesh?"

"I haven't yet. But I will. I have to. I've given up my soul. I can't survive without it."

Her face looked frazzled from crying.

"Nobody has the power to give up his own soul. It's something only the Lord can take, Robin. You're living a lie. As for feeding off human flesh, it would be an evil thing to do. Whoever's done it will need to answer for it. It is a crime. We will have to report them, whoever they are."

She struggled to say something but merely stared at him in silence. He was still holding her by the shoulders. Gradually, she leaned forward and rested her face on his left shoulder.

She sobbed for a few seconds while Ken caressed her hair. Then she pulled back and spoke again in despair.

"Ken, they're going to feed off your friends tonight! They're going to! Your friends are in danger! You must do something to stop them! Hurry!"

"Robin, what are you talking about?"

"Margaret and the others. They're going to feed off your friends. Come quickly! We have to stop them!"

She got up abruptly, pulling his hand.

"Hurry! Hurry!"

She ran back towards camp, pulling him by the hand. He followed her asking himself why he didn't stop her and make her see that it was all in her head. That it was all a dream. Some kind of lunacy that this club had managed to infuse in her brain. But as he felt his chest pounding from the run, it occurred to him that the beautiful Robin could actually be a disturbed young woman. What a disappointment it would be. He had banked so much on her. Her beauty was so raw, so rich that you could never have imagined there was any fault in her. She wiggled her way through the tents, as if she knew exactly where to go. They met no one in their path. The darkness of the night made everything hardly visible. She stopped running and Ken noticed the reflection of the lantern's light inside the orange-colored tent. He knew immediately that there was something wrong. He moved in front of her and held her back. She was sobbing and held onto his hand, looking agitated.

"It's too late," she said. "It's too late. They were here already."

Ken pulled the tent cover's entrance aside. It had been left unzipped but that could have been his own doing when he ran out after Robin. He crouched to get inside through the opening and Robin came behind him. What he saw made his stomach turn. The lantern was thrown on the floor with its flame still burning. Miraculously the tent had not caught on fire. The sleeping bags had all been shredded into pieces and left hanging like an omen from the top of the tent. Ken took a step forward holding back his distress. He had to see what had become of Dave and Steve. Spread on the ground like litter, the body parts that remained had been torn or chopped into small pieces. Blood was spattered everywhere. Despite his shock, Dave tried to look for clues. But the scene looked more like that of an explosion that had blown his companions to bits, tearing everything else apart around them like paper. Only it wasn't the work of ammunition. Ken knew right away this was a deliberate and malicious act of destruction by someone who had calculated it with outstanding accuracy. Still searching for a trace of his friends, he bent forward, looking over every spot in the tent.

"Ken, don't," she said behind him. "There is nothing left.

You're not going to find anything. They're gone. Let's get help. Come."

He turned around. Their faces were about an inch from each other, and he held her hand tightly, as if they had known each other for years. He followed her out of the tent and turned towards the tent once more.

"May God have mercy on their souls," he murmured.

Then she pulled on his arm and ran in front of him. They headed towards the cabin. She stopped in front of a grey elliptically shaped tent.

"This is Ron's tent," she said.

He looked at her quickly, surprised that she knew so much.

"Ron," he called, moving the entrance aside. "We got trouble. Come on out."

There was no movement inside and he crouched to get a glimpse.

"Ron! Ron! Wake up! We got trouble."

Ron was lying on top of his bag with a light blanket on top. Next to him was another sleeping bag, which Ken imagined to be his woman-rider's. Ken saw movement from another figure lying by Ron's feet.

"What's the matter? What's wrong?" the voice said.

Phil had unzipped his sleeping bag and sat up. There was a woman inside of it. Ken noticed his arms rise up in the dark and his open hands rub on his eyes. Phil had gone to sleep early in the night, anticipating a long day of driving the next day, and had settled near Ron and his girlfriend. Phil didn't get particularly excited about emergencies. His nature was unemotional to everything. Besides, what could possibly be emergent about some riders in the middle of the woods?

"We got trouble in camp, Phil," Ken said. "Steve and Dave are dead. We have to call the highway patrol."

Then Phil remembered the events of the night before and the scenes of Dan's murder flashed through his mind. He looked over Ron's side. He was also beginning to rise and slowly slipped himself out of his bag. Phil crawled out of the tent and came outside.

"What are you saying, now? Who's dead?"

"It's Dave. Dave and Steve. They came to get us, Phil.

Robin came to warn me and we went away for a few minutes. When we came back we found Steve and Dave slaughtered."

Ron had also come outside and had caught part of the conversation.

"Call 911 now!" Robin said. "It's them. It's them."

"No, wait a minute," Ron said. "Let's not call anyone yet. Let's find out what happened first. Who's them?" he asked Robin. "Who are you talking about?"

"It's them! I know it's them," she repeated. Ken exchanged glances with Phil and Ron. "I think we need to notify the patrol, Ron."

Ron and Phil were still both barefooted, standing by the tent's entrance. They both seemed to hesitate a moment.

"Take us to your tent," Ron said after a few seconds.

Ken took the lead, and Robin walked right alongside him. "Don't you think we ought to wake the people in camp? They may be in danger."

"No, not yet," Ron said. "Keep it quiet until we find out what's happening."

"It's them," Robin said, "I know it's them."

Ken pressed her hand tightly and picked up the pace, walking ahead of her. He moved fast through the grass and among the tents scattered a few feet from each other until he spotted the light shining low from the ground. He saw movement in a tent nearby and was immediately on guard. But the man who had crawled out from inside was yawning. He had been awakened by their voices before. Ken stood at the entrance of Dave's tent and pointed.

"That's it. It's here. Come inside."

Phil went in first, hunkering down to get his big body inside. Then Ron went in, crouching and going through the entrance. Ken went in after them. He held onto Robin's hand. She was shaking from the thought of having to see the crime scene once again, but the thought of remaining outside by herself, if only for a few minutes, infused pure terror in her. She had found warmth in Ken, a security she had not known for days. She bent down while holding Ken's hand and walked inside. Ron and Phil were standing in the middle of the tent, looking around the shreds of clothing, hanging from the top of the tent, and trying to make sense of it all. Neither one of them spoke but when Ron saw the torn pieces of the two men's bodies, it proved too much for him. He backed up, holding his open hand over his eyes. Then Phil tried. As soon as he got a glimpse of the bloodied grass and the chunks of fleshy material stuck on the walls of the tent, he stooped down, his face almost hitting the ground and he began to vomit. The sight of the big man crouching over and vomiting in the center of the tent was almost comical. The others crawled outside.

"We have to wake everyone up, Ron," Ken said. "Someone else could be in danger."

"Wait," Ron said, gesturing with his hand as he looked down. "You know," he said cautiously, "who could do a thing like that? Who would be capable of killing people this way? What the heck is going on here?"

"I know who did it," Robin said resolutely.

He watched her, noticing her weary face with swollen eyes, partially visible in the darkness of the early morning. A chilly wind rubbed their faces and Ron laid his hand on her shoulder.

"All right. Don't go anywhere. Stay with Ken until the police get here."

Phil had worked his way out of the tent. He looked disheveled and took a second to gain his composure.

"You have your phone with you, Phil?" Ron said.

"No."

"Ron, I got a phone," another voice said. It was the man Ken had seen leaving his tent earlier. He came towards them and handed Ron a cell phone.

Ron grabbed the phone and dialed 911. He put the ear piece up to his ear and waited.

"Hello. This is Ron Mason. I'm with the motorcycle caravan west of Dillon, off Route 9. Can you call the State Patrol, please?"

There were a few seconds of silence as the operator asked Ron about the nature of the emergency.

"It looks like two of our riders have been killed."

Chapter 7

The patrol cars had entered the camp through the trail off Route 9. The cars had to bear down on the bushes that flanked the narrow path, unsuitable for any vehicle except hardly a motorcycle. They had stopped in single file right at the entrance of the cabin. Several uniformed officers got out, led by a detective who wore a tight Stetson hat. He was tall and low on weight. An early forties man who kept fit and who had made a name for himself in the department with his radar senses. He could spot trouble a mile away. He walked up to Ron although he wore nothing identifying him as the ride's leader.

"All right, sir, what have we here? You now confirmed what the patrolmen told you last night. These woods are not a very hospitable place for strangers. That's why we got motels on the road to welcome our travelers. Venturing off onto the wilderness has never been a good idea for the tourists."

"Two of our men are dead, Detective. They were killed."

"Now, whatever makes you say that? Dead, maybe. But killed is a pretty wild assumption. I wouldn't just go there yet."

"They were killed," Robin said from above Ken's shoulder. "And we know who did it."

"Ohhh!" the detective let out. "That's even more reckless to say. And who might you be, young lady?"

He was peering towards her, tilting his head slightly to the side as he spoke.

"I'm Robin. And I know who killed them. I can take you to them."

"I sure hope so. Now," he said turning to Ron, "do you know anything about this?"

Ron looked indifferently towards Robin, standing meekly beside Ken O'Gara, as if she were a child he was protecting. He had heard her ramble on several times about how much she knew but didn't pay her much mind. She had sounded detached and incoherent and Ron had thought she was probably in a state of shock, not to be taken seriously. Now, as she went on to face the captain and repeat to him what she had been saying all along, it dawned on him that maybe after all she may hold the key to the whole affair. Ron was beginning to suspect that his caravan was in real trouble and that they had a murderer in their ranks. He had fought hard to keep the caravan going, even in Pleasant Hill, when they dealt with Dan's murder, he resisted the troopers' idea that the ride could not go on, that it was just too dangerous, and he prevailed. He knew then that he had won, or thought he did, and he guided his riders out of the troublesome state. But never in a thousand years could he dream that he would be facing the same situation again as soon as he crossed the state line. He had actually thought he was home free, that as long as he was out of the north, his riders would not be bothered again. Ron had this hang up about state lines, something he had developed in his many years of travel. Maybe it was superstition, maybe just plain old luck. But it had always seemed to work for him. He had to cross the state line. As long as he did, it would be a new beginning, a new adventure that would wipe out the old one and make the slate clean. That was why he was delighted to learn that one of his riders had access to land just a few miles past the boundary line of the two states and he plunged into the chance. But something had gone awry. Something had not worked. Here, he was facing the same situation again. He combed the strands of his bushy hair with his fingers and looked up at the captain.

"I've heard her say it before."

"And what do you think? Does she have something there or is she totally off the wall?"

"I guess you should check it out," Ron said, looking defeated.

The detective looked serious for the first time since his arrival, contracting his forehead as if to concentrate.

"You should have listened back there, Ron. You could have dispersed."

"Disperse? Disperse?"

"Yes, disperse without reaping the entire project at the seams. Now it's too late. You know that, don't you?"

Ron looked him in the eye, still not ready to give up. "Why don't you go and check the scene out, Detective? Take her if you need to. She might be of help."

"All right, men," the detective said, looking about him. "Those of you who are here will stay here and not move an inch, is that understood? Those of you who have woken up will stay up. Those who are sleeping still will stay sleeping. But no one among you leaves this spot until I come back with this young woman, all right?"

He waved to Robin to come to him. She hesitated, still standing behind Ken.

"I think I'm gonna need to go with her," Ken said. "She's still in shock. I was with her through the whole thing."

The detective looked him up and then nodded approvingly.

"Good," he said. "Let's go."

Ken went ahead of the detective and Robin hung to his arm, walking behind him. The detective waved for some of the patrolmen to come along and they followed the group after Ron and Phil who had quietly fallen into line. It was still dark out and to make your way through the clutter of tents required tact. Robin moved ahead of Ken, still holding his arm but now leading the way. It was as if she had a sense of recognition over the others. This did not escape the detective's attention; he followed them with interest. No one said a word as they worked their way through the narrow spaces, but a shuffle here and there told everyone that some in camp were beginning to awake from the noises of the nervous footsteps passing by their tents. Robin stopped in front of the orange tent, still showing the light from the ground and giving one the distinct feeling that something was amiss. Robin pointed to the tent and retreated behind Ken, clutching her hand on his shoulder. The detective went first. He slipped on a pair of gloves and brushed the flap of the entrance aside. He bent his lean body down and went in followed by two of his troopers.

"Nobody touches anything," they heard him say.

Ron and Phillip pulled back from the group and began discussing the situation in low voices. Robin clung to Ken as if he was her only connection to reality. Ken did not encourage her, but he did not discourage her. He had been so attracted to Robin since the first moment he saw her, yet, things had unfolded so fast, so unexpectedly for them both that Ken was in a state of disbelief. He waited eagerly for the officers inside, knowing full well what they would find but still hoping that perhaps some miraculous discovery would end this nightmare and bring his friends back. Just a couple of hours ago, he had laid peacefully next to his two friends, sharing their tent. Were it not for Robin, he would be sharing his friends' fate right now. He asked himself why the Lord had spared him. What had he done to deserve life? But then again, it was how the Lord worked. There was no point in asking. Trusting the ways of the creator, as he, the Christian that he was, had learned to do was the only answer. He remembered Dave seeking him out for this trip, cajoling him to come. Ken had had his doubts and thought that the ride would turn into a drinking binge but never in his wildest dreams had he imagined that murder would be involved. But here he was, standing in front of Dave's tent, waiting for the South Carolina authorities to make an inspection and render an opinion of what had happened. At the sight of the first officer crawling out of the tent, Ken cringed inside, feeling the pain of his friends' loss with more intensity than ever before.

The detective came first, then his troopers. The two troopers turned around immediately and each backed to the sides of the tent, got on their knees and made deep, gurgling sounds with their mouths and vomited. The detective stood quiet, with no expression, waiting for his men to gain their composure.

"You fellows are going to have to excuse my men. It's pretty nasty inside. Now," he said, turning his attention to Robin, "young lady, you were saying that you know who did this. Is that what you said?"

She looked at him from above Ken's shoulder. "I know they killed them. I know it."

The detective stared at her somberly.

"All right, then, why don't you show them to me? Show me where they are. You too," he said to Ken, "come along. Let's go."

Robin took Ken's hand and led the way. The detective waved for Ron and Phil to follow them, then yelled out to his men to come.

"Come on guys," he said. "I may need your expert marksmanship. We're going to meet the bandits. Let's go."

Robin was already walking. She did not go further into the camp but sideways, heading for the outer perimeters. She worked her way through the tents and stopped by an outfitter wall tent, standing a few feet away from the others bordering the camp. It was a large tent, rectangular in shape, fitting six to eight people. Robin pointed to it.

"That's them. They're inside."

The detective took his time observing the tent. His two officers had now gained their composure and stood restlessly behind him. He was looking for any sign of light inside or any movement that would reveal a human presence. But there was nothing. The first breaks of dawn were beginning to show in the far horizon, red streaks of crimson scattered in small and gaseous shapes across the eastern sky, slowly making their way to the west. The detective suddenly turned to Robin.

"What's your name?" he asked in a low voice.

"Robin."

"And where are you from, honey?"

"New Jersey."

"Where in New Jersey?"

"Cape May."

The detective's face lit up.

"Oh, you mean that beautiful colonial town by the bay at the tip end of the state. What's an attractive young woman from Cape May doing in a motorcycle caravan? Are you a biker?"

She nodded, unwilling to commit herself to a verbal answer. "Are you part of a club? Is there a club of riders from Cape May in this caravan?"

"No," she said. "I'm the only one from Cape May."

"What's the name of your club, honey?"

"The Lost Souls."

"The Lost Souls? Interesting."

"So, now tell me, why do you think the people inside that tent had anything to do with what happened back there?"

"Because they were planning to go there. I was with them when they planned it. That's my tent too. They were planning this for tonight. They were going to take me with them. They were going to kill them, all three of them. They hate Ken especially."

"For what reason? What's their reason for wanting to kill three fellow riders? Is there some sort of rivalry between the clubs or what?"

She looked straight at him when answering.

"They found out that Ken is a Christian. They hate that. It's a threat to their survival."

"It's a threat to their survival," the detective repeated pensively, looking down.

Ken was listening attentively to their conversation, standing right between them, as Robin still stood partially behind him and spoke to the detective from above his shoulder.

"Why is it a threat to their survival," the detective now asked, lifting his head. "What are we talking about here, loony stuff? Are these people in some kind of evil cult that does not agree with Christianity?"

"Yes."

"So much so that they have to go out and kill?"

"They have to feed anyway but with Christians they have to kill."

"Look, young lady, I don't know if everything you're telling me is true or if it's a product of your own ordeal here tonight. We will get to that. The story that you're telling me is pretty far-fetched and I find it unbelievable, quite frankly. I would imagine that if there was any meat to it, Ron Mason would know something about it."

He turned towards Ron who was standing to his right, aside one of his officers.

"Ron, do you know anything about this?"

"No, detective. The riders in this tent joined us in central Jersey. They are pretty sharp riders actually. They were different in that half of them are women riders. I mean, we have other women riders in the caravan but these acted rather exclusively in that they kept to themselves and insisted on riding at the tail end of the line-up. I let them because I did not see anything particularly wrong with it. I thought they may have been rather timid, so I let it pass, thinking they would eventually grow into the crowd and blend in. And I think it started happening last night. I noticed that they were hanging out with the rest of the riders at the cabin. So I didn't see anything unfitting in them and I certainly had no clue that they could be involved in any hate crime otherwise they would have never been allowed to join us."

"I hear you, Ron. But it looks like we may have some situation now that involves these folks and we are going to have to investigate it. Obviously, there has been a crime committed and this is the first lead we get. As a first order of business, I am going to ask this young lady to stay with one of my officers for now. You are not to leave his company, Robin," he said to her directly and waved for one of his men to move next to her. "The other trooper and I are going to enter that tent and we're going to search it. After we are through, and depending on what happens inside, you will have to take a ride with us to the station. We are going to have a long talk."

He unclipped his walkie-talkie from his belt and got someone on.

"I'm at the eastern end of the camp," he said in a low voice. "Trooper Duffy and I are going inside a tent. Possible suspects inside. It's a grey outfitter wall tent. Looks like it came out of the Civil War. It's sitting by itself, a few feet from the others.

I want four men here right away with firepower. They must come quietly. Understood?"

"I read you, detective," said the voice from the other end. "We'll do."

He turned his gaze to the other trooper next to Ken and waved for him to move forward.

"You folks move back," he said to the others.

The detective took one side of the tent's entrance and the trooper stood by the other. He reached for the canvas but noticed that the entrance was zippered from inside. He looked over the middle crack to find an opening, but the flap entrance was tucked securely. If they were going to get in, they would have to cut an opening. Detective Foley was not in the business of reaping tents. He had been a detective for almost twenty years now and had done countless searches. But breaking into a tent, he could not remember ever doing. He wondered for a moment about the legal issues involved. But there was no question in his mind that the situation, as depicted at the moment, called for an emergency entrance. Two people were dead and there was direct knowledge from someone that the occupants inside had been involved. He signaled to Trooper Duffy to hand him his switchblade. Trooper Duffy tossed it from his position at the other side of the entrance. Detective Foley opened it and took a step back, deciding on the best possible spot to cut an opening. He slashed the knife into the canvas by the middle of the entrance, as high as the height of his shoulders. The blade went into the canvas, making a dry thump, then he turned it and cut horizontally a couple of feet, then vertically until he reached the bottom. The blade made a thrashing sound as it cut through. Detective Foley handed the blade back to Trooper Duffy as he reached for his service issued 38 pistol and quickly slithered inside through the opening followed by the trooper. The two took opposite sides inside the tent, aiming their guns. There was no movement among the several bulky sleeping bags scattered inside the tent. Only one was empty and Detective Foley quickly rationalized it must be Robin's. There was already one thing she said that was true. Then he nodded to Trooper Duffy and yelled in a high voice.

"All right! Everyone up! This is the South Carolina State Police! Everyone on your feet!"

There was no movement from the sleeping bags at the forefront, so Detective Foley walked towards them, bending his head forward to fit in.

"Detective," Trooper Duffy said, "be careful."

Detective Foley bent close to the first sleeping bag he came across. The woman lying in it was not tucked inside the bag but on top of it. She was covered with a blue blanket up to her shoulders and slept quite peacefully. Detective Foley almost felt bad about waking her up and stood watching her for a second. She looked attractive with her brownish curly hair spread out on the sides of her head. Then he gently poked her midsection with the barrel of his gun.

"Wake up, honey. We need you up."

She reacted by opening her eyes. He smiled, still pointing his gun at her. She sat up quickly, finally realizing that the man in front of her had a gun and he was aiming it at her.

"Yes. What is it?" she said groggily.

"I'm Detective Foley. Get up. Put on some clothes and let's go outside. We need your friends here too."

She tossed the covers aside and rose. Detective Foley had his eyes on her, watching her every move. Her face seemed frazzled. He looked for other signs of sleep.

"Do you have a gun?"

She shook her head and waited for him to tell her what to do.

"Go outside, honey. Just walk outside with the other officers. Go ahead."

She walked through the opening at the entrance and Foley moved towards the others. Some were already rising and Detective Foley wasted no time in warning them.

"Go easy, you guys. Don't make any sudden movements if you don't want to get shot. Let's make this real easy. We don't want you to get hurt. We just want you to go outside so you can answer some questions."

"Why? What's this all about?"

The detective saw her stand up from the rear of the tent and pointed his gun at her. She got up carelessly, unconcerned about the danger she faced. Her long black hair spread loosely over her chest like a blanket, and her face, unlike that of the others, was energetic and vigilant.

"No funny moves honey," Detective Foley said. "Get up slowly. Let me see your entire body and then walk outside with the troopers. We'll let you know what we'll be doing next."

"Why? Why do we have to walk outside?" she asked, still in a sitting position.

Detective Foley looked at her with a smirk on his face. He knew instantly that the young woman at the rear of the tent was not a follower. Her beauty and radiance struck him. Just awakened in the early hours of dawn, she seemed like a picture of authority, questioning the trespassers to her kingdom.

"Right now, it's because I say so, honey. Let's go. On your feet."

She gave him a look of disdain that the detective blamed on the inconvenience he had sprung on her and her companions. But she was not ready to comply without at least questioning his motives.

"This better be good, Detective. You're interrupting my crew's night sleep. We have a long day of riding ahead."

"Oh, I know what I'm interrupting all right. Your crew is just going to have to do with little sleep this morning. As for the riding, I'm not sure if there'll be any of it going on today. Let's go outside. Get up so I can see you."

"Not until I'm dressed, Detective. I don't make it a habit of walking nude in the dark."

Detective Foley walked up to her sleeping bag and without warning he wrenched away the sheet covering her. She made no effort to stop him. She wore transparent black lingerie with some type of embroidery that the detective could not distinguish well in the darkness but he could see the contours of her breasts. He looked around for any garments he could throw her but saw none.

"Let's go," he said. "Find yourself some clothes to wear. I want you outside with the others."

"Are you going to be asking me about my sleeping habits?"

"We'll be asking you anything we want to know."

"I'm usually discreet about my dreams," she said.

She fidgeted with the contents of her sleeping bag and Detective Foley motioned for her to move. She stood up, revealing the rest of her body. Her lingerie only reached the top of her thighs and her long legs were bare. She smiled sardonically at the detective. The fact that she did not show the slightest tinge of fear did not escape the detective's attention.

"Come on, get some clothes on. This is not a burlesque show we're running here."

"I thought you would want me exactly as I was, Detective. Don't you want to preserve the evidence?"

"Evidence? Evidence of what?"

"I don't know. Whatever it is you have in mind."

"Let's go. Enough said. Put on some clothes."

She bent over provocatively, taking her time to find more suitable attire. The detective waited a few feet behind her.

The others had already cleared the tent. Trooper Duffy waited at the other side of the tent, still pointing his gun at her. She put on a pair of black jeans that she slithered slowly over her bare buttocks. Then she turned to face Detective Foley again.

"Am I decent enough now?"

"Put on a shirt," he said.

"Okay," she said, smiling again.

She stooped over her sleeping bag, this time facing the detective, and as she did, she gave him a glimpse of her low cleavage. She grabbed an oversized black tee shirt from the floor and threw it on.

"Let's go," the detective said.

There were four troopers outside guarding the men and women who had gotten out of the tent. Trooper Duffy went out first, followed by Margaret and then Detective Foley. They brought her by the others with the troopers around them.

"What is your name, Madam?" Detective Foley asked her. "If you must know, it's Margaret."

"And this is your club?"

"I lead them, if that's what you mean."

"Is everyone here?"

She looked obliquely from him towards the group around them and laid eyes on Robin who was standing next to Ken, leaning on his shoulder.

"We're missing someone," she said. "Robin belongs here," she pointed towards her.

"Her? No, I'm not worried about her right now. She stays where she is for now."

"She's part of our club."

"Maybe. We'll see about that soon." He raised his head high to speak to his men. "All right, troops. Take these people over to the cabin inside the camp and get them seats. I'll be over in a few minutes. None of them is to leave the area until questioned. Go."

They all began walking ahead with the troopers at the sides.

Margaret managed to take the center spot among them.

"Does that mean we're under arrest?" she asked as she was led away.

"Not yet," Detective Foley replied.

Detective Foley pulled out his walkie-talkie.

"We need some lab people here," he said. "It's a pretty bad crime scene and I'm sealing it right now. Send me six more men to guard the scene and meet me by the cabin they got in this camp. It's over at the center."

Detective Foley stayed near Ron and the others. Some other riders had now come out of their tents and joined them. Over ten people were outside, wondering what all the fuzz was about.

"Ron, we're going to need you and Phil at the cabin. I don't know how long this is gonna take but it does not look like a quickie."

"All right," Ron said and turned around to the other riders who had come to join them. "It looks like something's happened guys and girls. We're gonna be delayed again."

"Delayed again?" one voice said. "I thought it was smooth sailing all day."

"No, I'm afraid not. We've run into a few bumps."

"I thought we had already done that," someone else said. "We all came for the ride to Daytona and it seems we're spending our time talking to police officers instead of riding."

"What else has happened now?" someone else asked.

"It's best that you guys wait until everyone is here. Phil is going to make an announcement. I'm gonna be at the cabin meeting with the troopers."

"Let's go," Detective Foley said. "Phil, you'll join us later. Come on, Robin, you're coming too."

She grabbed Ken's arm, not wanting to let go. Ken took her hand and walked with her, following the detective and Ron. Phil stayed behind, responding to the moaning of riders who complained they were not being told enough. Dawn had fully broken, and there were men and women riders standing in groups along the path to the cabin. Some had conglomerated around the steps to the cabin, holding coffee cups. Everyone went silent as Ron and the detective stepped into the small porch.

"What's going on, Ron?" one voice asked from the crowd.

Ron turned around before going inside.

"Go to the end of this trail," Ron said. "Phil will tell you what's going on."

There was a murmur in the crowd as Ron held the storm door open at the cabin's entrance for Detective Foley. Ken and Robin went in and then there were yelps of discontent in the crowd. Ron positioned himself at the center of the room where Margaret and her crew sat looking rather disconnected. Four troopers kept pacing the floor around them, checking their seats and looking at their laps. Detective Foley stopped to look behind him to make sure Ken and Robin were in the room.

"All right, folks," Detective Foley said. "The reason we have you here is to ask you some questions. First thing we wanna know is where you folks have been all night. Now, be careful how you answer because I'm gonna hold you to it. Whatever you tell me I'm going to assume is true. So if you tell me you were in your tent that means you were in your tent. If it turns out later that you were somewhere else or somebody saw you somewhere else, you've got a problem. So, let me start with you, young lady."

He casually dropped his left hand and pointed his index finger at Linda.

"Wait a minute, Detective," Margaret said, sitting in the middle of them. "What's all this about? Why are you questioning us?"

"We're questioning you like we are going to question everyone else."

"Why are we the first ones to be questioned?"

"Maybe we like you better than the others. You have a bigger tent."

"Detective," Margaret said shrewdly. "Last time I checked, we have a right not to answer questions from the police if we do not want to. There is such a thing as the Fifth Amendment."

Detective Foley smiled and turned his back to her. He spoke with a hint of sarcasm.

"You're absolutely right, ah . . ."

He did a quick about face and looked at her.

"I'm sorry. I never got to learn your name although we did meet."

"Margaret," she said dryly.

"Margaret, you're absolutely right. There is such a thing as the Fifth Amendment and you don't have to incriminate yourself by answering any questions from the police. So, if you believe that you would be incriminating yourself, then by all means do not answer. I wouldn't want you to make my job any easier. I like a challenge in what I do, which of course brings me to the question of what exactly you think would cause you to be incriminated. Do you know something I don't?"

She had been watching him attentively. She knew where he was leading and she sought to stop him dead on his tracks.

"Precisely. We don't. We don't know what game you're playing here and what you're looking for. Usually, when the police ask you questions, it's because they're looking for an answer to an unsolved mystery, perhaps a crime. And if that's the case, we don't want to be blamed for something we did not do."

"That fast, ah? You're in denial mode that fast. I haven't even told you that anything has happened and you're already denying. What are you denying exactly? I have not mentioned that anything's happened, have I?"

"We have been sleeping all night," Linda said suddenly. "If anything's happened, none of us would know about it. We have not read the paper yet."

She drew a downcast stare from Margaret.

"Are you speaking for yourself or the whole group?" Detective Foley asked.

"The whole group."

"I see. Well, how do you know what everyone else was doing if you were sleeping?"

"We all went to sleep at the same time until you woke us up."

"Did you say all?"

"Yes, I said all."

"Including that young lady back there," he said, pointing to Robin.

She slowly squeezed herself behind Ken's shoulder like a shy child. Linda looked startled and was going to respond but Margaret cut in.

"She wasn't with us," she said.

"And how did that come to be? She is part of your group, isn't she?"

There was a quick exchange of glances between Margaret and Linda.

"I guess she was out with him," Margaret said somberly. "How long was she out?" Detective Foley asked.

"I don't know. We were all sleeping."

"When did you notice her missing?"

"She. . ." Linda started to say but Margaret interrupted her.

"When you guys woke us up," Margaret said.

"Really? What is your name?" Detective Foley asked, pointing to Linda.

"Linda."

"When did you first notice her missing?"

"Like Margaret said, when you guys came in."

"Interesting. So none of you guys know how long she was missing. Not you, not you, not you."

He pointed randomly to some of the others.

"Isn't it odd that she goes missing in the middle of the night, and none of you have noticed it?"

"No, it's not odd at all," Margaret said. "She's free to do what she wants when she wants to."

"And where was she? Do you know?"

"No, we don't know. I guess she was out with her man."

Margaret gazed towards Ken, looking for Robin. Her face was partially hidden behind Ken's shoulder. Margaret's disdain was visible all over her face. Her eyes spit out fire.

"What time did you guys all turn in?"

"Probably twelve, eleven thirty."

"Kind of early on a night like last night."

"We were anticipating a long ride today so we tried to get some sleep."

"Was Robin with you?"

"She was," Margaret said.

"That must mean she left you later, no?"

"I guess," Margaret said, looking bored. "What do you want with us, Detective Foley? This conversation is getting monotonous. We'd much rather get on with the riding. Ron is anxious to get us to Daytona."

"I'm afraid riding is not an option now. Not until we get some answers at least."

"Okay. Answers to what, our sleeping habits?"

"Guys," Detective Foley said to the other troopers. No one is to leave this room while I'm gone."

He pointed directly to Robin. "Young lady, let's go outside."

He grabbed her elbow and she jerked away from him, holding onto Ken's shoulder.

"Let's go," Detective Foley said. "I'll go in with her," Ken said.

Detective Foley gazed at him thinking of Robin's dependence on a man he did not know. Perhaps it was no harm that he came along. After all, he seemed to have played a role in the events.

"Let's go."

The three of them went out of the cabin and through the crowd that was building up outside. Detective Foley led the way. The troopers' cars were lined up in a row, not far from the cabin, on the trail that led out to the road. Detective Foley went to the second one and opened the passenger door for them.

"You guys sit in the back."

He closed the door after them. Then he went around the front of the vehicle and sat on the passenger side of the front seat. Another trooper sat behind the wheel. He shuffled his body back and forth for a few seconds to get into a comfortable sitting position. He reclined his back against the door, slapped his hand across the edge of the seat and leaned his head against the window glass.

"All right, Robin," he said. "You want to tell me what the heck is going on in here? You tell me that these people went out in the middle of the night to commit murder. It turns out they weren't, but you, in fact, were missing from their tent in the middle of the night. How do you explain it?"

"It's not true!" she said excitedly. "That's not how it happened. We were all going out there. We were together inside. I ran off from them because I wanted to warn Ken that they were coming."

"What were you doing with them?"

She looked down at her lap. Her attractive hazel eyes were wet with tears.

"I don't know. I don't know. I . . . I can't explain it. I've been with them for the ride but I don't want to be."

Ken exchanged glances with the detective. Ken was getting ready to speak but the detective held him up.

"They have some sort of hold on you? Is that what you're going to tell me? A young woman rider trapped by the Lost Souls' club. Is that it? Is that the name?"

"Detective," Ken said. "I think there's something to it. I've seen it."

"What have you seen?"

"I went to sleep early. I fell asleep while reading and woke up in the middle of the night, or rather, early this morning.

Something woke me up but I didn't know it. Perhaps it was intuition, self-preservation, now that I look back on it. I don't know. But some noise made me go outside the tent. When I did, I found Robin there."

"She was there?" Detective Foley asked, pointing to Robin.

"She was just standing there in front of the tent."

"I came to warn him," Robin said quickly. "They want to get him because he's a Christian."

"Robin told me they were coming and then she ran away from me. I caught up with her in the woods. Robin was a mess. I tried to comfort her. Then suddenly she said that she knew they were going to kill Dave and Steve and she ran back toward the camp to try to stop them. I went after her but it was too late when we got to the tent."

"Did you see them? Did you see them at the tent?"

"No."

"When was the last time you saw Steve and Dave?"

"When I got up to go outside. They were sleeping."

"Are you sure about that?"

"Yes."

Detective Foley looked over Robin's way. She was sitting next to Ken, leaning against him like a battered child.

Detective Foley thought fast. He knew enough about motorcycle gangs to know that rivalry and descent can stir violence, but the minute he heard Robin's reasoning for her club to go after Ken, he became disillusioned. Then he felt the suspicion that always spurred him to dig further and do his job. He had not come to these dark woods to hear stories about religious rivalries.

"Listen, whatever your creed may be, whatever your reasons for being here, I don't care. But two people were killed out there, practically disintegrated by some brutal murderer. Things like that just don't happen out of the blue. Someone planned this and did it very meticulously. I am going to just assume that. In the absence of some natural disaster that is not present here, people do not fade away as these people have done. It doesn't happen that way. So, let's start like this," he said, pausing to turn his attention to Robin. "Why were you with these people? If you knew that they were out to get Steve and Dave, why didn't you report it to some authority?"

She hunched down momentarily, but she then lifted her head up.

"I did. I went to Ken. And I had no choice but to be with them."

"What do you mean you had no choice? You always have a choice? You were in their club. If it hadn't been for the fact that Ken was involved, you would have joined them, isn't that right?"

"No," she said rigidly. "He was the main reason they were going? They wanted him mostly."

"And not the others? If they wanted him, why did they get the others when he wasn't there? And what's all this business about him being Christian? What does that have to do with anything?"

"They could have only gotten him in his sleep. Once he was awake they couldn't touch him."

"What?"

"He believes. They're terrified of someone like that. But even that I think only goes so far. Margaret can change it."

Detective Foley shook his head from side to side. He was beginning to lose patience.

"How long have you been a man of God, Ken?"

"Oh, for a quite a long time. Since I was in high school." "And you really think the fact that you are religious has an effect on these people?"

"I don't know. That's what Robin's telling you. I have noticed the animosity towards me, from Margaret especially. It started out well between me and her when I met her. But then later as we rode along she became extremely abrasive."

"It's because you're religious, Ken," Robin told him. "She found out. Everyone in the club was barred from talking to you."

"All right," Detective Foley said, lifting his hand. "What's this business about being asleep or awake? I don't understand."

The trooper behind the wheel traded looks with the detective then shook his head from side to side in amazement.

"I don't know," Ken said. "I don't know about that."

"What's going on between you two? Are you boyfriend and girlfriend? What's your relationship?"

Ken and Robin looked at each other.

"I don't really know," Ken said.

Detective Foley did not say anything else. He had the good fortune to sense that these two were onto something that they couldn't even put into words at the moment. Better leave it alone. But a crime had been committed here. He could not afford to leave anything alone. The static sound of a radio came on and the trooper sitting at the driver's seat, picked up the receiver from his belt.

"Yap, car number ten here," he said. "What's up?"

"The lab people are here," the voice said.

"Take them to the tent," Detective Foley said.

"We'll be there in a minute."

"Take them to the tent," the trooper said.

"How long have you been with the club?" Detective Foley asked Robin.

"A few weeks."

"Since the summer?"

"Yes. Since the end of the summer."

"What made you join the club?"

"I don't know."

"You don't know. Okay. Well, tell me this, how do you know so much about what was going to happen last night? You said you knew, right?"

"They were going to kill Ken and his friends."

"With a minor correction, you were supposed to go along too. But what I want to know is what was said and why."

"Nothing was said. We just knew."

"What?"

Detective Foley jerked his head back, faking surprise. Robin was not hiding anymore. She seemed stern, her beautiful hazel eyes showing the strain of fatigue with black rings around them. Her long brown hair seemed untidy, hanging in tangled threads on both sides of her face. Detective Foley stared at her sensual lips and her chiseled chin, thinking she could have been a model and how wasteful it was that she was here. She looked straight at him, probably for the first time since they had met and said nothing.

"You don't expect me to believe that, do you?"

Detective Foley ran his eyes by Ken who merely looked on, waiting for Robin to respond.

"They feed and when they are going to, you just know."

"How do you mean?"

"They can't survive if they don't feed."

Detective Foley looked towards the trooper, still sitting behind the wheel, and shook his head.

"Now, I've just had about enough of these hallucinations. This is serious stuff we're discussing here. You'll do yourself a favor by answering coherently. I want a logical answer to my questions. If you are on angel dust or some other crazy crap, I don't particularly care. This stuff we are discussing is for sober people. What I want to know is very simple. You said you knew your club was going to kill Ken and I guess also Steve and Dave. How do you know that? What did you see that leads you to believe that?"

"They were after Ken."

"Fine. So he was lucky to have gone out with you; otherwise, he wouldn't be here, right? But how do you know that they were going after him and the others? Just how do you know that?"

"I just knew."

Detective Foley moved his head from side to side in frustration. He turned to the trooper.

"Call them. See if they got any medical personnel out there. If they don't, just have them send us some paramedics. We need to have her tested."

He set himself straight on the seat, looking straight ahead as if he was a passenger in the patrol car as it was being driven down the road.

"I'm going back to the cabin," the detective said.

"Where do you want us?" Ken asked from the rear as Detective Foley opened the door to leave.

"Hang in here with the trooper until further notice," he said without looking back.

Detective Foley headed back towards the cabin. He met Ron and Phil near the steps among a crowd of bikers that was now getting very loud. Ron and Phil were speaking to the group from the top step into the small porch of the cabin. Detective Foley stopped and raised his hand. Ron signaled for the crowd to move back. Then he and Phil stepped sideways and went by the detective.

"I need to talk to you guys," Detective Foley said. "What now, Ron?" one of the riders said.

"I'll know more in a minute, guys. Let us talk to the detective."

Detective Foley walked along with them, moving away from the crowd. They headed back to the patrol cars. Detective Foley opened the rear door of the first car on the line and waved them in. He took the passenger side on the front seat, next to a trooper who sat behind the wheel. The morning was fresh and the sun was now shining in full force.

"Looks like you got a dreadful mess out there, Ron. I'm afraid you can't walk away from this one."

"Detective, if we don't figure out this thing within the next two hours or so, we're both going to have a real mess. We got one hundred and sixteen riders in these woods, itching to go to Daytona. What do you think is going to happen if we don't take off?"

"If your boys and gals get out of line, Ron, we got the room for them," Detective Foley said, smiling back at him.

"Come on, detective. You know what I'm talking about. Do you really want to have this thing escalate into a crisis? This has to be solved locally and fast before it gets out of hand."

Ron leaned forward in his seat as he spoke. He slithered his fingers through his copious black hair as if it could really change his hairstyle.

"Unfortunately, Ron, it seems to me we've got ourselves a double murder investigation out there. The crime lab people are here already. They have to be. I have no choice. This is ugly, Ron."

"It has to be handled, detective. That's so. It has to be handled with care. You don't think I feel bad about what's happened. I've got two of my best mechanics dead out there."

"And you don't think we're handling it, Ron? You don't think my men are doing their job?"

"Do you have any suspects?"

"I wouldn't call them that just yet. At least not until the crime lab people are done."

They heard static on the trooper's radio. He unclipped the radio from his belt and raised it.

"Car number 3 here," he said.

"Is Detective Foley in there?" the voice at the other end said.

"He's sitting right here."

"Detective, are we secure?"

"Yes," the detective said, getting his face closer to the radio. "What's up?"

"I have the technicians out here working on the scene. They have been able to piece together several body parts. We need an identification on the bodies. Looks like two."

"All right, hang on a minute," he said, turning to the trooper.

"Go see the couple sitting in the next car. Bring the guy sitting in the back out. His name is Ken. Bring him over here and I'll talk to him."

Detective Foley turned to Ron and Phil, smiling pleasantly. "This is always the unpleasant part. The gory scenes where you have to put the severed heads back on the body and see if they fit. Too bad, Ron. It could have been a nice run for you. Actually, Ron, I'm seeing similarities between this and what happened to you guys in North Carolina. I think you got some killers in your ranks."

"Detective," the trooper said at the window.

"Looks like we're having a problem with the girl in the back of the car. She won't let the fellow go alone. She's holding onto him for dear life."

Inside the car, Detective Foley turned to Ron and Phillip.

"Do you know this girl?"

"Hardly," Ron said. "She came with the women's club from Jersey."

"She's not very loyal. She keeps accusing her club of murder."

"She's obviously upset, detective."

"Upset? No, I think it goes beyond upset. I think your girl is deranged, Ron, totally deranged."

Detective Foley looked out the window and addressed the trooper.

"Make sure those two stay together the whole time, then bring them back here for questioning. Tell some of the medical personnel to examine the girl after they get back. I think she needs treatment."

The trooper walked back to the other car and opened the rear door.

"All right," he said. "You both are going."

Ken had not expected to be called for the job. He was not quite ready for it. But he had now been asked; as always, it was a matter of doing the right thing for him. If this is what the police needed, he would do it. It would be a step up in the investigation of the murders, and those who committed them, whoever they were, needed to be found and punished. Yes, he would go.

"I'll walk you two out there," the trooper said. "Now, the crime scene might be a little too tough for you madam. You may wanna let him go inside the tent by himself."

"I can handle it."

The trooper walked in behind them, and they disappeared among the winding trails, twisting their way around the tents.

"Who are these people, Ron? Where do they come from?"

"It's a club from central Jersey. They were brought into the run by Mark Conners, a rider from that area who heads a middle-aged club."

"What do you know about the girls?" "I'm told they're good riders."

"Ever met them before this run?"

"No."

"Is that how you're running this ride, Ron? Aren't you getting careless at a time when you're supposed to be at your peak?"

"Detective, it's utterly impossible to know every single rider. I do know most of them but that's really not so important. We usually deal with the head of the club. In this case it was Mark Conners."

"The club comes from a town in central New Jersey called East Brunswick," Philip said. He had been listening quietly to the exchange, deferring to Ron in his role as leader of the caravan. Detective Foley had ignored him completely but now that the burly man had spoken, he turned his attention to him.

"Do you know them?"

"I know of them."

"How did they get in your ride?"

Phil had a look of ennui about himself. His eyes focused tranquilly on the detective as he spoke without emotion but unhesitatingly.

"They came in through Mark Conners, as Ron said. They are a tight club. They ride together a lot."

"Who's this girl, Robin?"

"She's one of their women riders. She joined the club recently. I think she's from the shore. When we got the original roster from Mark, he said there were seven members, then it went up to eight and she was the extra one. She's pretty new in the club."

"She's not from their area."

"I don't think she's from the central part of the state like the others."

"Don't you find that odd?"

"Not really. It happens all the time."

"What's different about it," Detective Foley said, "is that she is a long distance from where the club operates. If my geography of New Jersey serves me right, she would be about three- or four-hours' drive from their headquarters. That's a far distance in such a small state. How did she team up with them being so far away?"

"I don't know. I don't find that to be a big deal. The club is largely known to be a woman-rider's club, which may be why she joined them. Maybe they don't have women riders where she is. I don't know. Anyway, how does that relate to what's happening here?"

"It's actually the detachment, Phil. That's what's curious about it. Something doesn't match. The others seem to be pretty tight, like you said, but this one is at odds with them. You've heard her. She's accusing them of murder. I see the inconsistencies."

"Maybe. I don't know. I think this girl is bordering on the deranged right now, probably affected by what's happened. I don't think you can give a lot of weight to her accusations."

"That's a very sharp observation, Phil. I noticed that myself and that's why I'm having the medical people evaluate her. But the story itself of what transpired is bizarre. We have Ken verifying that she went out to warn him. Then she runs off and he goes after her. It does not make sense. Of course, the story doesn't end there. A few minutes later, Dave and Steve turn up dead. Is it coincidental? I can't just discard Robin's accusations. These guys and women in the club are persons of interest to this case right now. They're definitely within the zone. Tell me this Phil, since you seem to be the personnel man around here, how did Ken and Robin team up?"

"They didn't before. The girls have pretty much been keeping to themselves since we've been riding. Ken is a good guy. I think he probably was attracted to Robin, but the two haven't connected until now."

"Hmmm. Ron, what do you say?"

"It's like Phil says, Detective. We don't know anything else. It's just a girls' club."

"Just a girls' club," the detective repeated. "Just a girls' club."

A trooper came up to the driver's window of the car and tapped on it. The detective waved for him to open the door. "Detective, there's a team of about five people in the tent right now and they have been going through everything feverishly. So far, they're drawing a blank on fingerprints. They find none whatsoever."

Detective Foley made an empty gesture, staying still for a few seconds then slowly shifting his body on the passenger seat. He spoke without giving a hint of discomfort.

"Ah, it's too soon to tell. Let them go through the whole tent then talk to me."

"Detective, they've gone through a lot of it already. Nothing's turned up. Of course, they're going to find prints on the sleeping bags because that's where the guys were sleeping. But that's not where they're looking."

"Wait for me," the detective said. "I'm gonna be going out there in a minute with you."

"All right."

"Well, Ron," the detective said, turning. "I guess Daytona is off."

"Detective, are you going to detain us all?"

"No, but I can't let you go on. There have been three murders in this ride in less than two days. If I let you go, who knows what will happen next?"

"We can be in Daytona tonight."

"And then what, you think you'll be any safer there?"

"We would have reached our goal. Nothing can hurt us then."

Detective Foley laughed quietly.

"Are you superstitious, Ron?"

"Somewhat."

"Ron," Phil suddenly said, "I just realized we got no mechanics left except Ken."

Ron looked down, meditating.

"Actually, we have someone else if need be."

"Who?"

"Margaret McCarter."

At the mention of her name, Detective Foley picked up his head and stared at him energetically, as if Ron, with his resourceful answer, had reminded him of her.

"You know more about her than you care to say, right?"

Chapter 8

The caravan, now short five riders, headed down south on Route 95, about ten miles south of Dillon. It had left the camp well past five and traveled east on highway 9 until it merged into 95. After a grueling morning and an anxious afternoon of pleading, Detective Foley had unexpectedly decided to let them move on. Ron could not figure him out and neither could Phil. They had talked privately between themselves and decided that the ride was dead. There was no way it could go on. Two people had been gruesomely murdered the night before and they had previously lost Daniel O'Rourke under circumstances they all knew could not have been accidental. There was a killer on the loose, Ron and Phil had thought, and they didn't know how to point him out. But after a rigorous search, evidence gathering, and testing, Detective Foley had abruptly said he wanted them out of the area. The girl who had so adamantly accused Margaret's club of slaying Dave and Steve was obviously deranged, Detective Foley had concluded. How it came to be that she knew so much detail about them, he did not know, or apparently did not think it was important. It could simply be a feud building up inside the entrails of the gang, and when it came to motorcycles, Detective Foley thought feuds were the rule of the day. He had seen many pass by in his day as they traveled down through his state. Nevertheless, even Phil and Ron, who were the most concerned about keeping the ride going, thought the State Patrol should stay involved. In two different instances now, riders had been killed. They were even disappointed when Detective Foley sent them on their way. It was anomalous for the lawman to be so passive in the prosecution of a crime. But Ron was not going to argue with them. Yet, safety measures were to be taken. Ron was not going to give anybody a chance for another road killing. So before the bikers got underway, the word came down, no matter what the time or the circumstances, there would be no more camping or stopping for the night. They would drive straight to Daytona.

At Ken's request, Robin had taken the spot next to him on the line-up. Robin's relationship with Margaret's club had deteriorated, and she refused to ride with them. Since the incident, she had clung to Ken like a lost child, almost begging for his protection, and Ken had countered with delicate affection. Something had happened back there in those woods that had driven the beautiful girl into his arms. Perhaps it had been the sudden fear of finding herself alone amidst friends who were now strangers. Ken did not know. But he wasn't going to turn her away even if he thought he was being used. From the moment he saw her, it had been like a lightning bolt for him. Whether it had been the same for her, he did not know, but she had come to him. She had picked him out of all the men in the run and he would not let her down. Ken saw it as he saw everything else in his life. It had been God's will. He had set the path for him by placing Robin under his protection, and the rest had no consequence for him.

The two rode next to each other on the road, Ken closer to the open lane and Robin riding close to the curve. Ken had now snugged his phone in a cradle mobile mount set on his handlebar. He was the only official mechanic left on the run, and Ron asked him to be extra vigilant. He needed him to keep the engines running. If there was a breakdown and it could not be fixed on the spot, Ron had given him instructions to place the bike in Dave's van and keep moving. Two spots up the line-up, Dave's van was being towed by another rider who had given up his bike to drive the pickup towing the van. All of Dave's tools were now Ken's responsibility.

Ken's phone made a rumpling noise that sounded like paper being torn as a voice came on its speaker.

"Ken, you there?"

It was Ron calling him.

"Yeah, I'm here," Ken said, putting the phone on his ear.

"Any trouble?"

"We'll be by Florence in a few minutes, then it will be all dead space until we reach Savannah. I'm gonna try to push them through without stopping for gas until then. I don't know if I'll make it but

I'm gonna try. I'm gonna depend on you to check on the riders and see who needs to gas up. Maybe we can fill whoever's tank is low from the supply tanks in the van without stopping the other riders. If it happens that a rider is low, pull him to the rear, fill his tank up and then catch up to us. You think you can manage that?"

"Sure can, Ron. I'll call the pick-up driver now and check on that gas tank. We'll have to siphon the gas into smaller containers for any fill up that we might need."

"By the way, for all the checkups they did, those cracker heads missed the gas tanks we're carrying in the van. Imagine that, two one-hundred-gallon tanks inside a van full of gasoline and they miss them. That goes to show you how thorough they were in their investigation."

"I hear you."

"All right, so go up and down the line now to check up on people. Make sure no one is running low."

"We'll do, Ron."

"Okay."

Ken put the phone down and stared at Robin. The twilight was beginning to set in and her face features were fading in the sunless scenery. Her long brown hair, trapped under the edges of her helmet, flapped up and down on the back of her neck. She was holding on to her handlebars, looking straight ahead, and her profile seemed to Ken like one of those Roman chiseled heads staring solemnly ahead, past the tides of time, as if it could see forever. She was beautiful.

"I have to run up and down the line," Ken said to her, raising his voice over the roar of the engines. She looked baffled for a second but then reacted.

"Can I follow you Ken?"

"No, it's best that you stay on this spot. I'll be back in a few minutes. Ron wants me to check up on the gas situation."

"Can I please go?"

Ken shook his head. Moving up and down a line-up of more than one hundred riders was dangerous enough for one. It would be impossible for two riders to do. But Ken felt her despair and felt sorry for her. She was so frightened. He stretched out his hand and wrapped it around her wrist.

"I will be back in no time."

In order to ride the line-up, the biker needs to get on the next lane of the highway and then increase or decrease speed, depending on whether he wants to move forward or back. If traffic builds up behind him, the rider has to squeeze in the line-up or move up to the front to allow vehicles to pass him. Ken checked for traffic behind him and then merged into the left lane. He decided to work his way up to the front of the line at first.

"How are you folks doing with gas?" he said to the first pair of riders he met after his spot. They were a young man and a woman, both riding Soft Tails. They had gotten on this spot during the last reshuffling of the line-up at Dillon.

"We are showing three fourths of a full tank," the rider on the left said.

"That's good," Ken replied. "Just let me know when it gets to a quarter. We'll have to pull you out of the line-up and give you some fuel."

"How far are we going until we stop?" the young man asked.

"Ron wants to try to go as far as Savannah."

"Whew! Let's hope."

"I hear you," Ken said. "Well, see you guys later."

Ken throttled up his engine and moved up to the next riders. He was taking mental notes as he went along, telling those who had phones to stay in touch and let him know at the first sign of concern. Anyone who was less than a half tank full would need to drop on the shoulder and get to the rear of the line where Ken had sent Dave's truck and trailer carrying the supplies. Ken worked his way up to Ron and Phil, out in the very front. Both men were riding their touring bikes with their women behind them, braced to their mid-section.

"How are you guys with gas?" Ken asked Ron.

"You don't need to worry about us," Ron said, leaning over the side of his Roadking. "You know the type of tanks we got in these babies. How is it back there?"

"So far, pretty good. I came up on the line from my spot. I have to work my way back to the rear now. I'll keep you posted."

"Let's keep them moving Ken. No matter what, let's keep them moving."

"Ken," Phil yelled from the other side, "call us when you get to the girls' club. If they give you any problems, I'll go down there."

"All right, guys. Let me jump in front of you."

There were car headlights moving towards him in the rear and Ken cruised a few feet in front of Ron and Phil, then went onto the shoulder where he slowed down to almost a halt, letting the entire caravan pass him by. He got back on the right lane, behind Dave's van. He checked for traffic on the left lane and moved up to the pick-up driver's window.

"How goes it man?" the driver yelled out to him.

He was wearing a dark bandanna wrapped around his head. Ken could not see his face features in the darkness that had now blanketed them. But he detected a slight odor of alcohol in his breath.

"Be careful with that," Ken said.

"What's that?"

"Alcohol."

"Oh, that. It gets pretty lonesome out here, man. I had to give up my bike to drive this and on top of it I'm driving right behind those lunatics."

He tipped his chin, pointing towards Margaret's club riding in front of him. Ken could not see them. Their van was behind them, being tugged by their small pickup. He could hear the hum made by their voices as they sang. Ken got ready to move up.

"Put it away," Ken said to the driver. "All we need is for a trooper to stop you and find you drinking. The whole caravan would pay for it."

Ken moved up slowly, reaching Zeke at the wheel of the pickup. He was riding with his window down.

"Are you okay with gas?" Ken asked him.

"Take off, man. We don't need you."

Ken did not answer him. He kept moving slowly up the line.

"Do yourself a favor, bible boy, skip our club."

Ken was already by his front fender and could hardly hear him. The others' singing was now clearly audible.

" . . . Faces come out of the rain when you're strange . . ."

The first couple he came across was Randall and Donna. Ken had to yell to be heard. "How're you doing with gas?"

". . . When you're strange no one remembers your name . . ."

He moved up to Flora and John, next in the line and got the same reception. He worked his way up to the first couple, Linda and Margaret.

"Are you okay with gas?"

Linda was riding on the outer side of the lane and Margaret to her right. Linda turned to him and spat at him. The small saliva bubbles broke up in the air, hastily dissipating into the wind.

" . . . When you're strange. People are strange when you're a stranger . . ."

Linda rode on her Dyna Wyde Glide and Margaret her FXDBI Street Bob with the high handlebars. Ken noticed that they moved at exactly the same speed and both front wheels were perfectly symmetrical to each other. It was impressive showmanship and skillful riding. Ken moved up gradually, showing no reaction to their discourtesy. The sound of their voices became muffled as he moved on the line.

"How're you doing tonight?" Ken asked the heavy-set man, riding a Touring. He was Ron McGreevy, and his wife Silvia was next to him, riding a Dyna Low Rider. Ken remembered them from the caravan's stop at Pleasant Hill and their discussions with the police the morning of Dan O'Rourke's murder.

"We're fine. A little tired of the singing back there. I wish they switched to another song."

"I guess it's not that simple once you get locked into Jim Morrison and the Doors."

"They could try 'Light my Fire.'"

Ken laughed. They were good-natured people going on an adventurous ride where they had lived through the unfortunate experience of seeing three of their teammates murdered. Disappointment was written all over their faces. Yet, they were still riding, perhaps hoping that the arrival at Daytona would expunge all traces of ill feelings from their memories and they would remember only the races and the pride of having made the trip. Ken asked them about their gas tanks and told them to watch their gauges. Then he moved to the next couple. It happened when he had worked his way well into the middle of the line-up. He heard an intense roar behind him and knew instantly it was not a car engine. He had no rear-view mirror so he had to turn to see. The bike was hardly a hundred feet away from him but was coming at breakneck speed. He knew instantly that if he stayed in his position, the bike would collide with him. He did not have enough speed on his engine to make a run for it so he slid onto the outer side of the lane, hoping the bike would miss him. By the time it passed him, the bike's front wheel was doing a wheelie, up in the air, and it had picked up speed. Ken knew then the driver had no intentions of avoiding him. The bike was on a crash course. As it passed him, he thought he recognized her slim figure, dressed all in black and leaning back on the bike. It was Linda. She passed him while riding on her rear tire. Ken thought he saw another bike driving on the shoulder also doing a wheelie. That had to be Margaret. He saw Linda's bike ride on the line-up. Its rear red light got dimmer as the bike got farther away, but then its beam intensified, a sign that it was stopping. That would be just about where Ken's spot was on the line. Robin. The name came to him like a flare in the dark night sky. They were after Robin. He rolled his throttle up to maximum and his bike roared. His back wheel screeched on the pavement. He went from 40 miles an hour to over 100 in seconds; he was right alongside Linda's bike in less than a minute. She had moved onto Ken's spot and kept trying to edge her way towards Robin while Margaret rode on the shoulder, a few feet away, yelling.

"You have to come back, Robin. I've come for you. Come on!"

"Robin, move up!" Ken said, "Squeeze in between the next two riders."

She turned nervously, unsure that the maneuver would work or that she could even attempt it. The riders in front of her turned back, surprised by the commotion.

"You can do it, Robin! You can! There's room! Go!"

As Linda kept trying to close in, Robin rolled her throttle up suddenly and her bike jumped forward, narrowly squeezing in between the next two riders. Linda's bike went into Robin's previous position on the line-up. Then it was Ken going on the offensive and he moved into the empty spot next to Linda. He got close to her bike to the point where their legs touched. Linda was holding on but Ken kept pushing her sideways. The front wheels of their bikes rubbed against each other for a moment. Both shook out of control. Ken held on to his handlebars and gained equilibrium again. Linda's bike lost its path and went right towards the shoulder where it passed near Margaret's. Ken yelled for Robin to fall back into line. She slowed her engine down and squeezed back.

"Stay on that side," Ken said. "I'll take the side closer to the shoulder in case they come back."

The female rider in front of them moved her bike in between them.

"What was that all about? What's happening?"

"The girls' club in the rear is after Robin," Ken said. "It's not horseplay. They're serious."

"Wow. That was crazy. They could have got us all killed. Why? What's going on?"

"They want Robin back."

She turned sideways to get a glimpse of Robin.

"How long were you in their club?" the woman asked.

"I was never an official member."

"You weren't?"

"No."

"What kind of a club is this?"

She did not respond. She was sobbing slightly but loud enough that the woman could hear her.

"Look, I think you may want to tell Ron about this. We really can't have this going on. If these girls are as crazy as they seem, they should not be riding with us. They could do major mayhem here. Imagine if they crash in the middle of the line-up. Everyone in the back could come stumbling down like a set of dominoes. It's scary."

She moved up and took her place in the line, next to her male rider. Ken got on his phone and dialed Ron's line.

"It's Ken," he said into the speaker, bringing it close.

"What's all the commotion back there? Rumors traveled down the pipe already. What's happened?"

"It's Margaret's club. They came while I was gone and tried to take Robin."

"How many were there?"

"Two of the girls. Margaret was one of them. I was able to run them off to the shoulder. They were all right. They didn't get hurt."

"All right," Ron said on the speaker. "I'll send Phil down there to straighten them out. This can't go on."

"I agree. I'm afraid to leave my spot now, Ron. I think they'll come back again if they know I'm gone."

"Stay put."

Ken put the phone down. He couldn't see Robin's face well but he could see the fear in her eyes.

"I won't let them take you, Robin," he said, extending his hand out to her.

"Ken, you realize what you're doing? You've practically signed your death sentence tonight."

"Trust God, Robin. Only he can decide who's to live and who's to die."

She paused, looking ahead. The rider in front of Ken looked fidgety on his seat, shifting his body from side to side.

"But this is real danger, Ken," she yelled. "These people are vicious. They can hurt you."

The rider up front turned. "What do they want?" he asked.

"They want Robin back," Ken said. "They won't let go of her."

"What did Ron say?"

"He is sending Phil back there to talk to them," Ken said. "He's trying to quiet them down."

"I think Ron has to get tough," the woman-rider next to him said. "We can't have these people endangering the rest of us for no reason."

"Ken," Robin called out. "I think I should drop from the ride."

Ken thought he heard a slight dwindle in her engine throttle and he stiffened his body on his seat. Slowing a bike down in the middle of the line-up could be suicidal. A rider must always preserve his speed on a caravan to maintain a distance between him and the rider behind him. Any sudden stop could be catastrophic.

"Robin, you don't want to do that. I won't let you."

"But, Ken, it's no use. I can't beat them. . ."

"You can Robin. Yes, you can."

Ken heard other engines roaring in the back, and he instantly looked. He saw the two headlights moving at a fast speed on the shoulder. Then suddenly their headlights beamed down as the bikes' rear tires came up doing a stoppie. Then they touched down as they passed him and Robin on the shoulder. Ken and Robin merged into the left lane.

"Stay on course," Ken said, putting out his hand. "Don't speed up. They'll lose us."

"Ken, they're out to hurt you because you're with me. Maybe I should go back," she said.

They saw the two bikes gradually slowing down on the shoulder until they returned to the vacant spot left in Ken and Robin's line-up.

"Don't let them in," Ken murmured to himself, hoping the caravan would magically shrink and close the open space. But confusion and fear were beginning to spread among the riders. The man and woman who had been traveling in front of them were now sliding their bikes into the left lane, trying to get away. Some of the others in the rear were merging onto the left lane. The caravan was fragmenting. Ken kept an eye on Margaret's riders, still on the shoulder.

"We're going to switch spots," Ken said to Robin. "You get on this side, fast!"

He maneuvered his bike in front of hers and she moved onto his spot. Margaret's riders were taking a swing at him. They came in fast, leaning over their right sides, trying to brush up against Ken's bike as they zoomed by. Ken swung his bike far into the left as the first rider skirted near him. It missed him by a few feet. The second one came right behind the first, arching wider towards Ken but still missing him. He had arched well into the middle of the lane and as he tried to bring the bike back he came dangerously close to the woman's bike which had now moved onto the left lane, in front of Ken. The biker stumbled as it tried to avoid hitting her. His bike shook from side to side, then suddenly flipped out of control. It's rear went up and swung forward doing a complete summersault. Then it rolled on its side at first in a straight line, then curving to the right with the rider trapped under it. It dragged towards the right lane through the empty spots left by Ken and the others who had moved to the left lane. It went into the shoulder, drawing sparks from the pavement as the bike's frame scraped the asphalt. It disappeared into the shallow ditch at the side of the road. A few seconds later, they heard the explosion behind them. Ken looked back and saw the narrow flames shoot up with waves of twinkling sparks underneath them resembling holiday fireworks. The entire bike line-up behind Ken was a mass of confusion. Some bikes had quickly gone onto the left lane and others had gone to the shoulder. Riders were no longer riding in couples. Groups of bikers heaped together in disarray, speeding towards the front. Others had pulled back on the left lane, trying to get away from the crowd, while others were on the median dividing the north and south sides of the highway. Ken thought he recognized the headlight of Margaret's other rider's bike as they passed him. It was just beginning to gain speed again from the shoulder. Ken waved at Robin.

"I'm going to get on the right lane again, Robin. He's coming back."

"Ken, no! Stay!"

"No, it's okay Robin. You stay where you are."

Ken merged into the right lane, looking at the bike's Sturgis' round headlight coming behind him. It was racing fast towards him and as it got close, the rider leaned on his right side, trying to draw his bike closer to Ken's. Ken waited until it glided close. He turned his engine's throttle up and yanked his clutch. His bike's rear shot up like an arrow and for a few seconds, Ken was riding on his bike's front wheel. The other bike slithered underneath him, missing its target and then losing stability. It kept sliding on its side through the left lane, missing another bike by inches and then kept going out of control onto the shrubbery separating north and south. There was a loud crash followed by an explosion and then orange-colored flames that rose furiously over the trees as the gas tank exploded. Immediately after that they heard an even louder explosion coming from the rear, so loud that it sent vibrations over the entire line-up.

Ken turned back to look. The flames were thicker and higher than any of the other two explosions.

"That had to be a Touring or a truck," he said almost subconsciously to the biker who had ended up at his side on the right lane. Ken couldn't see his face in the dark but his voice came through clear.

"Whose bike could it have been?"

"I don't know."

"Think we should go down there and see?"

"I think we should. Only I can't leave Robin behind."

He looked over to his side. She was riding on the left lane next to a lady rider.

"I'll watch her!" she said.

"Thank you. We're going to pull into the rear. That's where all the trouble is coming from."

"Go ahead," she said.

Ken and the other rider pulled onto the shoulder. They slowed down almost to a walking pace, waiting for the other bikes to pass them. Ken quickly got on his phone.

"Ron! Ron! We've got trouble."

"I know Ken. I'm right here," the answer came fast. "I can see your bike. I'm right in front of you."

Ken looked up and saw the rear round read light of Ron's Touring, moving on the shoulder. Ken turned to the rider next to him.

"What is your name?"

"I'm James Callaghan," he said, his face barely visible in the dark. "Yours?"

"Ken O'Gara. A pleasure to meet you."

They got right behind Ron's bike. There was no room on the shoulder for the three of them to ride side by side.

"We gotta get on to the rear," Ron said. "I haven't heard back from Phil. What the heck happened in there?"

"Two of them went down," Ken said. "Both bikes exploded."

"I know. But why?"

"It's Margaret's club. They've gone berserk. They've been trying to get Robin back. She must have sent those two riders to get to me. I think they were on a suicide mission."

"Where's Robin now?"

"She's up by the middle. I left someone with her."

The tail end of the line was now passing them. They saw Steve's pickup tugging his tool van but no sign of Margaret and her riders.

"Where did they go?" Ron said.

"My guess is that after that attack, they would have dropped out. They're probably way back."

"Phil, Phil, come in!" Ron yelled into his phone.

"Ron, why don't we ride towards the explosion back there?

We gotta see what that was about."

Ron had now stopped his bike and Ken and James did also. "All right, boys. We're gonna be riding against traffic.

What gets me the most is there is not one single patrolman around. Where are they when you need them?"

Ron pressed one button on his phone.

"Conners, are you out there? Conners come in."

"Yeah, Ron. I'm here."

"Where are you in the line-up, Mark?"

"There is no line-up, Ron. It's a mass hurled together like cattle, riding in all directions."

"I know, Mark. I'm in the rear with Ken and another rider. I'm gonna try to find Phil and then I'm gonna get those women if it's the last thing I do. You're gonna have to take over. Get in front of the line. Stop the caravan on the shoulder and get people to line up again. It's your show. We're gonna be busy back here. We'll meet up with you later."

"Ron, these people will not want to fall back in line anymore. Everybody's scared."

"Scared? When did you hear of riders being scared?"

Maybe your club is scared, Mark. That's another thing I want to talk to you about, how did you get these freaks into your club, Mark? Where the heck did they come from?"

"They're not in my club, Ron. I told you that."

"I need to know that you're gonna straighten my line-up, Mark. It's either that or I get somebody else."

"All right."

Ron put the phone down and turned his bike around. The woman riding in the back of him rolled her index finger in the air as a sign for the others to move. Ken wondered how she could still be riding with him after all that had happened.

"Let's go, boys," she said. Ron should have let me straighten out those women from the beginning. I told him they were trouble."

James and Ken followed him. They drove on the shoulder, Ron in front of them and James and Ken riding parallel to each other. Their headlights must have presented a frightful sight to oncoming cars suddenly facing them in the opposite direction and probably thinking for a second or so that they had gone the wrong way. Those are normal reactions for a driver on a dark interstate highway at night. It gets lonely on the road and the mind grinds with the repetitive motions of holding the wheel and watching the road. Any sudden shift in the monotonous scenery can twirl the brain out of control. The riders saw that reaction now from drivers in cars coming up the road. They were riding steadily until they noticed the bikes' headlights facing them. One car clicked its high beams as it passed them on the outer lane. Another swiveled momentarily inside his lane, while the driver figured out what to do. Yet another blew its horn and quickly turned into the next lane perhaps thinking he was traveling against traffic, spun, and went into the grass of the mid area, mowing the high weeds with its mudguards.

"Let's hurry up," Ron said. "The longer we are riding this road this way, the more likely we could cause an accident. We have enough of those already."

"Are they?" Ken asked.

"What do you mean?"

"Are they really accidents?"

"No, of course not. We've got three murders and a freaky woman motorcycle club that's gone haywire. No, I'd say that's not an accident."

"What did Phil say?" Ken asked.

"Nothing. He was at the rear with his woman, trying to talk sense to this Margaret and her people. I don't know that he got very far."

They were coming on to the spot of the explosion. The fire was still burning quietly on the shoulder of the road. The flames were weak and burning out, but there was a trace of thick smoke, visible even in the dark of night, trailing all the way up into the sky. They stopped their bikes a few feet away and dismounted. As they walked towards the wreck they recognized Phil's Touring bike. It was lying sideways on the shoulder. Pinned against its midsection were two charred bulges in a crouched position. Ron got very close despite the flames. They were clearly human bodies unrecognizable in their present state, just burned slumps sitting immobile. Ron finally turned around towards the others.

"It's Phil and his rider," Ron said, solemnly.

"How can you even tell, Ron," his girlfriend said.

"I can't Cherry, but who else would it be? It's his bike."

She looked up and down the highway. There was no sign of other wreckage. No sign of Margaret and her crew.

"So where did they go?"

"I don't know," Ron said looking at each of them individually. "Everyone be careful. Keep your eyes open."

He walked back to his bike and retrieved something from one of the saddlebags. He placed the object discreetly inside his vest pocket before turning around.

"I wish they showed themselves, Ron," Cherry said.

One half of her face was visible under the reflection of the flames. Tears were rolling down her face. She wore a yellow tank top under a black vest. She was tall, almost reaching six feet. Her face was large but not chubby. She had beautiful blue eyes and dirty blond strands of hair protruding from under her head bandanna.

"Ron, Tammy was my friend. How am I going to explain this to her folks?"

Ron walked up to her and threw his left arm around her.

"I wanna get those creeps if it's the last thing I do," she said in between sobs.

"Be cool, Cherry. We all wanna get them. Look at him," he said getting closer to Phil's bike. "The man was like my brother. We have been riding together for years. He hasn't missed one run with me for fifteen years. How am I going to call his folks in Milwaukee and tell them what happened?"

"The bike looks pretty much intact," James said, bending down near the wreckage. "No sign of impact that I can see."

Phil and his passenger's left legs were still pinned on the foot rest as if they had been going on a pleasure ride right before they were consumed by the fire.

"Look at the tank," Ron said.

The inside was totally exposed and its top was gone. Small flames still burned inside.

"That gas tank looks like it's been hit by a missile. This was pure execution. Phil must have been caught by surprise. They could have never got to him otherwise."

"Ron," Ken said. "Have you seen these people in action? They are pretty vicious. I don't think it is a question of strength. It's something beyond that. And I pretty much figured out that they are after two people. First, they want Robin back, and second, they want to get me. I think the best thing for the caravan at this point is for Robin and I to break off. We're endangering the others."

"I won't have that in my run, Ken. Anybody has something against one of my riders, he has to go through me too."

"No, Ron. Too many people have died already."

"I won't have it, Ken. I just won't. By the way, that was a heck of a ride you did out there tonight, kid. You licked the heck out of them."

"I never intended to hurt them. I just got out of their way."

"Well you did. You got two of them out of the way."

Ken put his head down. For the first time it dawned upon him that he may have been responsible for two people's deaths. It wasn't calculated, true. He was only guilty of very defensive, mastery driving that two very reckless bikers could not measure up to. But still in his mind, he had been the cause of their deaths. He felt a rush of adrenaline travel down from his head to his feet. He needed to say a prayer.

* * *

The caravan was stalled for a good two hours. It took Ron a while to get the patrol on the scene. Before he had resented their presence but now he craved them. His best friend had been killed and now the notion had been driven home that there was a group of sinister women and men out there hunting for them, looking to do them harm. Ron wanted the patrol to take definitive action. This time he wanted them involved. But the patrols were sluggish at this point. When they first arrived, they seemed reluctant to declare the matter urgent. Motorcycle mishaps were hardly a matter of urgency.

Highway 95 was full of constant crashes and gory accidents. The highway patrol thought it was more important to get the riders back on the road and not have them linger around, creating chaos and holding up traffic. The line had to get moving right away. Surprisingly, Ron was in no hurry to get his people out. There had been four murders already and he wanted a resolution. Like Robin before, he pointed towards Margaret's club for being involved. But where were they? The patrolmen examined the crash scene and determined that it was a one-man accident. Unfortunate but by far not murder. Yes, there had been others, they knew, but previous patrols had determined that the riders should move on, apparently not seeing serious grounds for detaining anyone. And so, it must be this time. Ron felt frustrated and thought he was arguing against himself. But he could not go on exposing his riders to danger. He wanted protection for them. Seeing no action from the patrolmen, he took the offensive. He left two of his riders well equipped with phones and money to make arrangements for Phil's remains and those of his companion to be shipped back north to their families. Then he named section heads, severing allegiances and ignoring rivalries among competing clubs. This was now a matter of survival and he did not care who got offended or what lines he crossed. He procured a gun for every leader of a section and gave them instructions on what to do. He was seeing to it that from now on his riders would not be victimized. When the caravan finally got going, someone thought to ask where they were in the state. Ron did not know. In the Carolinas, the distances could stretch for so long that you could get lost in the monotony of the landscape. Someone said they were near Fayetteville. Others thought they had passed it already. Ron got on the lead, saving the vacant spot next to him in Phil's memory. He let his engine run with an excessive roar and the entire line-up followed, filling the highway with a thundering boom that seemed to symbolize the caravan's resolve and presage their future. They had lost some of their best, but they were still going. They were not stopping. Daytona was their destination. Try as anybody might, their destiny would be fulfilled. Ron took his feet off the ground and rolled his bike forward, feeling the bulk of his gun on his breast pocket as he leaned forward. He turned back and made an announcement.

"Next stop is Savannah! Who cares where we are now!"

The riders behind him hurrahed. It seemed the caravan was anything but done.

Ken rode next to Robin for the first ten minutes but then moved up towards the front of the line, talking to the riders at each spot on the line-up as he went along.

"We're about one hour from Savannah," he said to the man and the woman riders. "We'll be there in no time. Do you think you have enough gas?"

"We're both running on a little below half a tank," she said.

"All right. You should be fine. I'll be around."

"He kept checking on everyone as he went along, then he went on the shoulder and slowed to a walking pace until the entire caravan passed him. Dave's pick up was the last one on the line-up. Ken came up to the driver's window and talked to the driver. He was driving with the window down and he saw Ken before Ken saw him.

"You ought to be careful when making your rounds, man," he said, nervously switching between the road and him. "You could be taken for one of those freaks. Everybody is nervous after what happened."

"You're all alone back here," Ken said. "You're probably a little more nervous than the rest of them. If that club were to re-appear, I think you would be the first to see them coming from the rear."

"Don't remind me. I'm ready for them though. It's not gonna be easy to take me."

Ken knew that Ron had gone to extreme measures, but he had not been present during any of Ron's individual sessions with some of the crew.

"What instructions do you have?" "To shoot on sight."

Ken thought it was not a very good way for riders to be thinking. He kept his bike on course for a few seconds just thinking it through. If others in the caravan thought this way, the probability of seeing a shoot-out war at any moment was pretty high. He had not seen anybody holding a gun but was sure Ron had one. And he probably had instructed everyone to shoot at Margaret and her people if they spotted them. Ken decided to move up fast on the line-up and finish his run. He would tell Robin to stay where she was. He would ride the rest of the way in back of Dave's pickup just so he could be the first to meet Margaret and her crew if they showed.

It was well after midnight when they began seeing the signs for Savannah, Georgia. Ron's voice came on Ken's phone and his directive to get off at the next exit spread fast through the line. All riders welcomed it. They had been riding hard under much stress and needed a break. More importantly, they all wanted to feel that they had made progress despite all the setbacks and that they were only a stone's throw from their goal.

The bikes went in double file formation into the gas pumps. The line of over one hundred riders twisted around the entrance of the six-pump station, just off the highway, then went straight back onto the road, causing some small traffic to back up, even at this late hour. Ron had pulled his touring to the side inside the lot and surrounded himself by his newly named captain-riders and his only mechanic, Ken O'Gara.

"What's gonna be our planned course of travel after we gas up?" Mark Conners asked. "Everyone is screaming for a break."

"Listen up," Ron said. It is midnight, I know. But we are about one hour from the Florida State line, then maybe twenty minutes from Jacksonville, which at this time of night will be a breeze to cross. There is no traffic. We can be in Daytona in another hour after that. So we're talking two and a half hours. That's not bad at all."

"Ron, everyone is fatigued. It's not so much the riding as the stress we've been under," Don Connelly said.

He was a muscled, short man, standing near his bike and wearing no helmet. Ron had picked him to ride the last segment of the caravan, right now the most vulnerable spot in the line-up.

"I hear you," Ron said. "But if we stop now, I'd be exposing everyone to more danger than we've ever seen before. Those things are out there, man. And they'll come after us with a vengeance wherever we happen to stop. Besides that, where am I going to put my riders at this time? We didn't plan on being here at this hour, so no reservations were made anywhere between here and Daytona. According to our plans, we were supposed to be in Daytona tonight."

"Ron," one of the others said, "the fear with this girl club is that they might attack us if we stop, right? Supposedly, we now think they were behind Steve's and David's deaths. And now Phil's too. But they have already attacked us while we were moving, so what's stopping them from attacking us while we are pulling through the last stretch of the ride?"

"Nothing," Ron replied. "I just think we have more of a defense if we are moving. Chances are that if we get lucky enough and find somewhere to sleep for the rest of the night, many of us will be obliterated in our sleep."

"We could have sentries, Ron," another man said. He was an African American, tall with an exposed shaved head. "So far, these things have hit us because we had no clue what they were up to. We weren't expecting it."

"From what I understand, Manny, these things get more bizarre at night and when they're off the bikes. Would you not agree with that Mark?"

Ron pointed to him. Mark was easy to spot in the crowd of seven men. He was taller than any other, lean, with gray, bushy hair that dropped rashly over his forehead. The others turned to him.

"Ron, I don't really know. It's as much of a surprise to you as it is to me. What can I say? I don't know who these people are anymore."

"But you brought them in here, Mark. You've gotta know something about them."

"I know them only as very able riders, especially Margaret who's been with me on other rides. There's never been any indication that they are anything else but that. And by the way, that's what I feel they are even now. I think we're making too much out of this whole thing. There's nothing supernatural about these people. They're humans just like all of us."

"We're making too much of this you said?" one other rider asked. "We've got four of our people dead out there, not to mention that two of their own got killed today. That's six people who have died on this ride and all because of all those women."

"Hold it now," Don Connolly cut in. "There are three guys riding with them."

"Two now," Manny corrected him. "One was one of the ones who died in the highway."

"All right, two."

"There are three girls and two guys left." Mark turned to Ken.

"It's more like four girls, Ken, isn't it?"

"Robin was never in with them, Mark. She was the one who pointed them to the cops. They're after Robin."

"That's another thing I don't get, Ron," another rider said, getting off his bike. He had a look of anger about him. "Why are we riding with this girl among us when she started out with the women's club? I think we're placing the enemy right in the middle of us. In fact, that may be why the others are after us with such ferocity. Why is she with us?"

"She's Ken O'Gara's girl. That's all I know. Ken tells me she's not part of it and that's good enough for me. You all know Ken, don't you?"

All heads turned to Ken and he quickly spoke.

"Robin is of no danger to anyone here. Robin was a captive of the women's club until she was able to break off from them last night. Now, I will say this. I made it very clear to Ron that I do not want to endanger anyone here and I'd rather go on alone with Robin. Ron has insisted that I stay with the ride, but I don't have a problem breaking off if you guys don't want her here."

"It's not you we have a problem with," Manny said. "You showed us what stuff you're made of tonight. You put two of them away. It's she that we are concerned about."

"If I ride, she rides with me," Ken said.

"Ken, is she really that important to you, man?" Don Connolly asked.

"She is."

They all looked at each other and Cherry, standing next to Ron, smiled at him.

"People, let's get on the road," Ron said. "Everyone keep their eyes open, especially in the rear. Don't give them a chance to run up the line. At the first sign of them, fire away. I'm sending two of you guys to the rear, to ride behind the truck as an escort. That will be Manny and Scott. I know you guys are crazy and got eyes in the back of your heads. No one can get past you. Let's go!"

The group went into different directions, taking their positions in the line-up. Bikers had been passing through the gas pumps six at a time and now were lining up on the local road leading back to 95. Ron drove his bike to the front of the line and got on the phone as he waited. He had wired an earpiece and microphone set to his phone. He had also seen to it that all his captains were wired. Communications were vital at this point. When the last group of riders filled their tanks up and got on the tail end of the line, someone called Ron and he gave the signal with his right arm up to move on.

The caravan rode fast on 95, heading south. Florida travelers who made the long trip from the northeast usually felt relieved as they rode past the wetlands and bridges of the eastern coast of Georgia. The highway felt smoother, more akin to their vehicles. The shrubbery seemed more welcoming. Time seemed to move faster. Perhaps it was all psychological knowing that the sunshine state's line was less than an hour away. It was a little past one and Scott and Manny, riding in back of Dave's trailer, had been checking their watches methodically every few minutes. They each kept a constant vigil on their side mirrors, trying to spot any motorcycle headlights in the distance coming from behind them. But they had seen nothing. They heard a vague drone and looked back but saw nothing.

"What's that?" Scott asked, trying to see Manny's face in the darkness.

Manny leaned his head back to listen.

"It's a murmur."

The hum's pitch seemed to increase slightly over the sounds of the engines. Like a faraway echo, it became more audible, and Scott suddenly yelled.

"Those are human voices," he said. "Slow down! Let's pull back from the trailer."

He pulled out an automatic pistol from his vest pocket. Manny did the same. They slowed their engines, and the van quickly gained distance on them. Gradually, the words became decipherable to them.

"People are strange when you're stranger . . . when you're alone . . . women seem wicked . . . when you're strange . . . no one remembers your name . . . ."

"It's those freaks again!" Scott said.

"See them?"

"I don't see anything," he said gazing at his mirror first then looking back. "You?"

"They're definitely behind us somewhere but I can't see them."

"Jump on the left lane. There's a car far behind us. I bet you they're behind it."

They both merged into the left lane and slowed their engines even more. Then Manny made a startling observation.

"That's not a car. It's a pick up." "I'll be darned if it's not theirs."

"It is. Keep pulling back. Let's put it out of commission."

They flicked their lights off and pulled their bikes to the edge of the left lane to avoid being noticed.

"It's probably no use, Scott. They must have seen us already."

"But they don't see us now."

The truck was getting close, now about two hundred feet away, and coming closer as Scott and Manny maintained their slow speed to let him catch up. The two men seemed totally fearless, out on a mission to destroy. Suddenly, they heard the loud roar of motorcycle engines behind the pickup, exploding into life, and an array of headlights, moving fretfully in different directions.

"They've seen us!" Scott yelled. "They're coming! Let's get the truck!"

They both turned at the same time. The shots from their handguns sounded like pops from champagne bottles. They fired in unison, two or three times. At first, there was no reaction, no sign that they had hit a target, but then the two headlights veered abruptly to one side of the road, then the other, as the vehicle went apparently out of control. The mushy sound of tire threads dragging on the pavement let them know that the vehicle's tires had been hit and it was now riding on its bare chrome wheels. The truck tumbled from side to side, grazing dangerously close to the bikes that had shot out in front of it. It seemed to head straight into the shoulder when suddenly it turned sharply towards the middle of the road again, did two full spins and then flipped, plummeting towards the other side on its roof and sweeping one of the bikes on the left lane. The trailer must have gotten disengaged at that point, for it went in the other direction towards the shoulder of the road with a deep rumble. There was a loud bang as the pick-up smashed several trees on the median, disappearing in the bushes and miraculously not catching on fire.

"Let's go!" Scott said.

The two rolled up their throttles, making their engines roar with fury. They quickly gained speed, moving fast on the left lane. They slowed down only when the long trail of red lights made by the caravan's bikes became visible.

"Don't get too close," Manny said. "Our job is to keep these things away from them."

Scott said nothing. He looked back and saw no trace of their headlights. They had left the crash far behind.

"You think we put a dent in them?" he asked.

"That was awesome, man," Manny replied. "The truck swiped one of them clean. They're killing each other."

"Yeah, it was sharp. It seemed to go too easy, don't you think?"

"No, it didn't. We just hit them right, man."

They had dropped down to a slow pace of under 50 miles per hour, dragging their engines a little. In an apparent sudden need to relieve themselves, they veered off towards the median and gradually left the highway, slowing down to a walking pace. That is how it would have seemed to any passerby. They came to a halt among the high trees in the median and dismounted their bikes. Neither man knew what hit him. They were jumped from behind by two dark figures which instantly slit their throats with Bub Worrell field knives that they retrieved from slings hanging from their necks. They ripped through the men's skin at the base of their necks, slashing deep wedges of exposed flesh that oozed profusely with blood. The men fell to the ground but the two figures were right behind them, one on top of each. They had slit their blades into their black leather pouches and they now tore up their victims' flesh ferociously with their bare hands. The men's heads were first to come off, then the two worked their way down through the men's upper bodies, ripping and tearing, pulling their tracheas and working down to the mid sections. They pulled the men's guts, devouring the intestines like hungry beasts. They opened and closed their jaws, each time swallowing bloody body parts, making the gory sound of teeth clamping down on bare flesh. Nothing was spared. They threw their hands up in the air in frenzy as they fed. They kept moving down to the men's lower bodies. There was no sound on the lonely highway other than the incessant, gluttonous chomping of their teeth on the bloody spoils.

The driver in Dave's truck had seen Manny and Scott pull back on his side mirror. He thought it a deliberate maneuver on their part but did not know why. He watched as their bikes' headlights disappeared in the distance. He waited a few more minutes before he decided to call Ron. He picked up his phone and dialed.

"It's Gerry Brudy here, Ron."

"What's up?"

"Manny and Scott dropped out of sight. It's been a while."

"See anything else? Hear anything?"

"No, nothing."

"All right. Keep your eyes open. I'll send someone back there."

Ron thought of Ken immediately. He was not sure why. Ken was, after all, his mechanic, so he had to save him for the mechanical emergencies that were sure to come. But the young man had shown such prominent skill in his handling of the previous crisis that he had earned his respect. Truly, he did not think anyone else surpassed his riding skills in the entire caravan.

"Ken," Ron said on his Nextel. "I need a favor from you, man."

"Sure."

"I need you to go to the rear and check up on Manny and Scott. They have dropped out of sight for quite a while. I wanna make sure they're all right. I'll ring the riders in front and back of you so they can keep an eye on Robin while you're gone. Deal?"

"Sure. No problem." Ken put down his phone.

"Robin, I'm going to check the rear. Ron wants me to."

"Ken, no!" she said alarmed. "It's a trap. They're back there. I know they are!"

"It'll be all right, Robin. I'm just checking up on Manny and Scott. You stay put. I'll be back in no time."

He looked at her with those mischievous brown eyes that she had long longed for. She knew then and there she could not afford to lose him. He was the reason she was alive. She would die for him. She saw him smile and then merge into the left lane. She heard the sound of his engine reduce speed and drop back in distance. She waited a few seconds. The couple riding in front of her turned towards her.

"Stay put, Robin. Ken will be back."

She waited until they turned, then drove her bike towards the shoulder and dropped speed. The caravan was going past her faster and faster as she slowed down to almost a halt. She was right alongside Dave's truck now, and she could hear Ken's voice questioning the driver.

"How long ago was it?" he asked.

"I don't know, ten or fifteen minutes."

"You haven't heard anything?"

"No."

"All right. I'm going to go back there to try to find them. I'll give you a call if I do."

"Are you armed?"

"No."

"Are you nuts? You can't go back there without a gun. Here, take mine."

He pulled a pistol from underneath the seat but Ken stopped him.

"I don't want a gun. You take care of yourself. Keep your eyes open."

"But what if . . ."

Ken slowed down and dropped back out of sight. But he was not alone. As soon as he cleared the van, he was startled by the bike riding parallel to him on the shoulder. His heart skipped a bit until he recognized Robin as the rider.

"You should have stayed, Robin. You're in danger out here."

"I won't let you go alone, Ken. I'm the cause of why they're after you to begin with."

They stared at each other, now riding closer on the right lane. There was a feeling of tenderness between them, as if they had suddenly discovered what had connected them and how fate had intertwined their lives. It was them, Margaret's club that had brought them together, and it was them that they were now preparing to do battle with. They both knew it.

Ken turned up his throttle and drove ahead.

"Let's get on the shoulder. We're going back there."

He arched his bike towards the left lane so he could have a wider angle to turn around. He swung in a half circle and got on the shoulder. Robin followed him. The two rode alongside each other on the road's shoulder in the opposite direction of traffic. The road was empty but their headlights made a bizarre sight for any lone traveler heading north on the highway at that moment. Suddenly Ken turned to Robin.

"Turn off your headlight," he said and flicked his off. "That way they won't see us."

"But they can, Ken. They can."

"How's that?"

"They are creatures of the night. They come alive at night. Darkness nurtures them."

They were doing well over 40. Ken was on the side closer to the lane and kept busy looking at the road and around him, searching for any signs of trouble. Something caught his eye ahead in the wooded area dividing the roads. A wide area of weeds and small shrubbery seemed to have been mowed down, wiped by some powerful impact. Ken was immediately on guard and put out his hand down at waist length as a signal to Robin to slow down. He cautiously moved into the first lane and then the second. He pulled into the grass, right in front of the disrupted vegetation and spotted the bulk of the pickup under the gleam of the moonlight, lying belly up, its front fender twisted around the trunk of a pine tree where it had seemed to end its deadly trajectory. Not far from it was another grisly figure, this one a bike pinned in between two trees.

"This looks like there was a war out here," he said, turning back to Robin. "It must have just happened. There is still smoke coming out of that truck."

"They're close by, Ken."

"Who was in that truck?"

"One of Margaret's men."

"What about the bike?"

"It's one of theirs too."

Ken reflected on the scene quietly for a moment. He was trying to decide whether they should back up further on the road, but then he concluded that if Manny and Scott had caused the wreck, they must be somewhere south of here since Margaret's club had to be moving in a southerly direction. But he hadn't seen them on his way up.

"Robin," he said. "Let's go south a little bit."

She stepped back, rolling her bike backwards. She did not say anything. She felt their presence but she wasn't afraid. He was with her and that was enough. She did not try to understand why he wanted to go south to find Manny and Scott. She was only thinking that she had him and that she would be safe as long as she was with him. He turned his bike around and waited for her to catch up to him. They went slowly on the highway's left lane with Ken watching the woods carefully. They went no more than a mile when he noticed one bike lying on its side a few feet into the woods and then another one, lying farther down. He pulled into the grassy area and she followed him. They both were silent as they stopped. He dismounted and released the bike's kickstand.

"I'm going to see what happened. You stay here."

"No," she said. "I'm going with you."

She left her bike near his with the engine still running and leaned it on the kickstand. They walked through the weeds towards the first bike. There were no tracks on the grass that they could see. It all seemed as if it had been a normal stop on the side of the road. Except for the downed bikes, that is. Ken went near the first one. It appeared to have slid through the ground on its side but it was intact. There was not even a scratch in it. He looked farther down towards the other bike and midway through he noticed the first sign of disturbance. He had no idea what it was. It was a dark, long object hanging loose over the top of the thin weeds. He got closer. *No, it couldn't be*, he thought. Then the headlights of a passing vehicle flooded the area with its beams and it left him no doubt.

"Is this what I think it is?"

Robin was right behind him and she had seen it too. She grabbed his hand as a gesture of intimacy. He turned and tried to make her walk back.

"Maybe you shouldn't see this."

"I can handle it, Ken. I know what it is. It's somebody's arm. There will be other small body parts around but that's all you're going to find," she said, surprising him.

"What do you mean?"

"They leave nothing but bones behind, Ken. They're cannibals, predators who feed on other humans. They eat their victims, pilfer the organs and feast over them, scrap the bones and devour everything until there's nothing left but traces of blood and some bones if you're lucky. It's not deliberately planned. For them it's just feeding, Ken. They feed. It's how they live."

Ken looked back. There was blood on the edges of the coarsely severed base of the forearm and the badly mutilated fingers, extending out over the weeds' sultry tops like a piece of wet cloth left out to dry. Ken went by the other bike. He saw traces of blood on the grass around it and felt the slippery coat of fleshy material rubbed off on the grass. He walked back in horror, realizing he was walking on the men's mutilated body parts. He was in a state of shock when he turned to Robin.

"Do you see anything else?"

She shook her head in silence. Ken went towards the other bike and paced around it.

"You're not going to find anything else, Ken. Those men are gone."

Ken took a few steps back to get a good view of both bikes and bent his head down.

"Lord, have mercy on their souls," he prayed. "They were men who loved to ride, were not perfect, and probably did not know you, Lord. Only you with your infinite wisdom and power can judge them. Please have mercy on them."

He turned decisively away from the scene, grabbing Robin by her hand and headed back to the edge of the road.

"Robin," he said, in deep thought. "Have you ever fed?"

She turned to him quietly, her hazel eyes now clearly visible in the opaque moonlight.

"Never, Ken. I saw them do it and wanted to leave but couldn't. Their influence is so overbearing. It's something they do to you. I don't know how. They're still trying, Ken. I feel their presence, all of them ganging up around me but I'm with you. You hold them back, Ken. There's something about you that they fear."

"You need to trust the Lord. Then maybe they'll fear you too. No one can have any power over you when you have God on your side."

"I wish I had your faith," Robin said, holding his hand tight. They were standing by their bikes, hearing nothing but the soft rattling of their engines. Ken looked back towards the woods. He could see the glare made by other cars traveling on the north side of the highway on the other side. He needed to report to Ron. He hadn't even thought about the danger of having Margaret and her riders still roaming around. He took his phone out and dialed.

"Ron, it's Ken here."

"What's up, Ken?" the voice from the other end said.

"I found the club's truck smashed against some trees and one of their bikes—no sign of survivors. A little bit south of there I found Manny's and Scott's bikes. They must have stopped for some reason because their bikes are intact. No sign of any crash. There's nothing left of them, Ron."

"What do you mean?"

"It's like Dave and Steve, Ron. It's as if some animal devoured them. There are a couple of body parts around but that's it. What do I do?"

"Get back to us immediately, Ken. Get away from there."

"But what about the patrols? Shouldn't we notify them?"

"I will take care of that. Listen, blast your way back here. I don't want you hanging around there alone. Get back."

Ken raised his eyes towards Robin. Ron was right. Out here, he and Robin were an easy prey for Margaret and her predators.

"Ron wants us back right away. He's afraid for us."

Ken got on his bike and moved it into the highway, heading north. He made a full turn around going into the right lane, extending his left foot sideways, dragging his boot on the road, and going south. Robin followed shortly behind him.

"Stay close to me. Keep your eyes open."

"I don't think they're after us right now. They could have got to us here if they had wanted to."

"I thought they were always after us."

"They are. But they'll choose their timing. They're in no hurry. They've fed."

Ken looked ahead and throttled up his engine. It was not a sudden boost of power but a gradual increase that made the engine reach 50 in a few seconds. Robin was keeping up with him, traveling right alongside of him. Ken turned to her abruptly.

"Why is it called feeding?" he yelled over the wind.

"They use the term casually. It's something they need to do to survive."

"Why humans?"

"I'm not entirely sure. It's something having to do with the soul. That's why they call themselves 'the Lost Souls.'"

Ken went up to 70. Robin was right beside him, keeping up. The caravan had gotten a good jump on them and he wanted to catch up. He was not afraid, but his imagination bordered surreal. He had seen the bikes and the blood, but had it really happened? But more than that and even more important was Robin's role. How did she know so much? If the club was as deadly as it seemed to be how could she get away? Ken didn't doubt her, no. But questions were beginning to take shape in his mind. Had he rushed into believing Robin? Could she still be part of them? He concentrated on the road, thinking it through and imagining her face in his mind with its raw beauty, just as he had seen her that first day at the theater's parking lot and wished he could have gone back in time. He wished he could have talked to her that day and convinced her to go with him to Lancaster, where it could all be peaceful and he could work again as a hired hand. They didn't have to go on this run. They didn't have to be any part of this.

"There they are," she shouted. "I see them."

A long row of double red dots stretched down on the horizon for what seemed miles. The caravan was moving steadily but at a moderate pace. Ken decided to let Ron know.

"I'm coming up to the tail end," he said into his phone. "You want to let the pick-up driver know. I don't want him to shoot me."

"He knows you're coming. He's been told. But all right," Ron said. "Come on down and take your spot in the line-up."

"Ron," Ken said. "Can you let us guard the rear, Robin and me?"

"Ken, you're my only mechanic right now."

"You're afraid you might lose me back here, Ron? Is that what you mean?"

"Well, now that you mention it, yes. It's too vulnerable of a spot, Ken. I can't afford to lose you."

"Ron, you know we are the target of these attacks. It doesn't matter where we are. They'll come for us and find us. I think it's safer for everyone if we stay back."

"No, Ken."

"Yes, Ron. I think we can fight them off pretty well. We've proven that."

There was silence at the other end and Ken felt confident he had him. He waited.

"You stay in touch," he said. We're reaching the Florida State line now."

"That means we got about another hour, no?"

"An hour and some minutes. Stay in touch."

Ken and Robin came close behind Dave's trailer. Ken motioned to Robin to stay in her position and he moved up on the left lane to reach the truck's driver. The driver stared right at him before Ken came to his window. He looked edgy.

"What happened to Manny and Scott?"

"They're gone."

Ken saw the fear in his eyes. He kept moving his right arm holding his pistol.

"I'm going to stay back here with Robin. It's okay with Ron."

Gerry gave a sigh of relief. Ken saw him grab the wheel with both hands all of a sudden.

"I never got your name," Ken said.

"I'm Gerry, man. Gerry Brudy. Glad to meet you. If we make it to Daytona, I'll buy you a drink."

"Oh, we'll make it all right. The main thing is to stay cool. Don't lose your composure."

"That's pretty hard, man. We're fighting for our lives here.

How can you stay so relaxed?"

"Faith. You must have faith. Leave it all in God's hands."

Gerry suddenly looked uncertain, and Ken felt his gaze on him, as if he had a hard time believing what he had just heard. It was a look Ken had seen many times. The look of a disbeliever. But this was a time of fear when the least pious finds it consoling to think of the Almighty, and it is a good time for a leap of faith. Ken saw him shake his head.

"I can't believe Manny and Scott are gone, man. They were just right here a few minutes ago. Are you sure, man?"

Ken nodded.

"Unfortunately. Ron notified the state patrol."

"Why don't we stop? It seems the farther we go, the worse it gets."

"Ron doesn't want to. And I guess I can't blame him. If we stop, we'll be more vulnerable. It's best to keep going."

A cluster of tall buildings sneaked up on them. There was hardly any traffic on the road and the rows of the buildings' lit windows looked lifeless with no one inside. Ken had not realized that they had passed the Florida state line. The caravan had reached Jacksonville. Ken looked at his wrist watch. It was not even five minutes past two. Despite everything that had happened, Ron's timing had been incredibly accurate. Ken felt a deep admiration for Ron at the moment. Ron had the grit-tight capacity to keep the riders together. He thought that if Margaret and her club had wanted to disperse the caravan, all they had to do was go after Ron. He was the rock that kept the ride going. Yet that hadn't happened. The vicious group had carried sporadic attacks only on him. They tried to take Robin, but apparently, they did not intend to harm her. Ken wondered about the group's obsession with her. Why was Robin so important to them? He decided that if they made it to Daytona, he needed to have a real talk with Robin. He let his bike lose speed just a bit and slowly drifted back to the rear of the truck. Robin was riding her bike a short distance behind the trailer. Ken lost more speed and merged into the lane. He took the spot next to Robin. They were going through inclined sections of the highway that cut right through the heart of the city.

"Ever been in Jacksonville before Robin?" he asked.

"No."

"It's usually very crowded. We're lucky to have hit it at this hour. There's nobody in the streets."

"It's so much not like Florida."

"It's their New York. They're proud of it. They say their state doesn't just have the exotic beaches. It's got big cities too."

"How much longer do you figure?"

"By Ron's estimate, another hour. We go on 95 till we hit 40, then we go east, and we pour right into the Daytona beaches. You'll be impressed. It's a great vacation spot."

"Where is Ron putting us?"

"I don't know that just yet. I imagine it's been set up for a while. We'll find out soon. How do you feel anyway?"

"More sure of myself but nervous about Daytona. I don't know what to expect there."

"There will be lots of other riders there. They have races going. Tomorrow, I'm sure we'll parade through the town."

She did not answer. She was thinking this was her first night away from Margaret's club. She couldn't help but wonder over the state of affairs at their camp or wherever they might be. She felt compassion for their losses. After all, she was sure Margaret wasn't one of them. Three of their riders had been killed or whatever happened to people like them when they met the end. Margaret had said that you didn't die. You never died for as long as you fed. But you must feed to survive. She tried to guess who might have been the couple whose bikes exploded in the highway when Ken evaded them. She thought Randall and Donna had been riding in pairs. But it could have been Flora and John too. Maybe even Linda and Margaret. But no, that couldn't be. Generals do not go to battle. They send their sergeants. She had liked Flora and wished deep inside it wasn't her. Flora still had a human side to her. She could be kind and caring unlike the others. Then she thought about the truck that collided back there and figured it was Zeke inside. Margaret had trusted him with the truck and van, he and nobody else. But whose was the other bike that crashed? Could it be by some miracle have been Linda? She wished. No, she knew it wasn't. It was either John, Donna, Randall, or Flora. She was sure Linda and Margaret would not go so foolishly. They had a higher calling. Besides, the gory discovery she and Ken made in the woods left no doubt it was Margaret's work.

The caravan made its way out of the 295 loop, circling the city, and kept going south on 95. At that point, Ken's phone rang again. It was Ron.

"We have some minor problems with a couple of the bikes," he said. "I do not want to stop. Let's try to ride it, but I'd like you to go and take a look. We've got a Softail Chopper, similar to O'Rourke's bike, that's grinding a little bit. He's in row 9. There's also a Street Glider, brand new, that's having a transmission drag. Hard to understand with a brand-new machine like that. They're on row 29. Can you take care of that? See what you can do and give me a report on it?"

"I sure can, Ron. Now, what about Gerry? How do I handle him?"

"The truck driver you mean?"

"Yes. He's extremely edgy. I think he's liable to start shooting at the slightest disturbance. That man should not have a gun, Ron."

"We're too close to Daytona now for me to replace him. At this point, he just has to hang on. Tell him you'll be right back and to stay cool. I'll ring him."

"Ron, wait . . ."

Ken had been startled by Robin who was waving for him to put the phone down.

"Ron, I hear them. They're back there."

Ken saw the arctic expression in Robin's face, showing fear and determination at the same time. She kept looking back. Ken turned and saw nothing but the dark highway behind them.

"I don't see anything, Robin."

"I hear them. Listen."

He sat still on his seat listening to the steady humming of his engine and then gradually, just a pitch above he heard the barely audible buzz of their voices singing merrily and in unison."

"Faces come out of the rain when you're strange. No one remembers your name. When you're strange. When you're strange. Da da da da da . . ."

"They're still at it. I can't believe it."

Ken picked up his Nextel again.

"Ron, these girls are still in back of us. We can hear them singing but I can't see them."

"All right, hang in tight, Ken. I'm sending two riders back there to cover you. Don't lose it now. Remember, they've gotten some of our guys but we've been getting them back too. They're not immortal. By my count there should only be three left, am I right?"

"I think so."

"All right. Wait for Don Connolly and Russell Hayes. These guys are riding right by you. They'll be there in a second."

Ken clipped his phone onto his belt. He reached out towards Robin and grabbed her wrist. She stared at him, her eyes glowing with a deep, disquieting fear.

"You know, Robin, for a moment back there when you were with me, I thought you were the strong one. It seemed like you were able to read these things pretty well. Why are you letting yourself go now, kid? They won't hurt you, Robin. Don't worry. I won't let them."

"You can't stop them, Ken," she said. "Nobody can."

"Yes, we can. There's always somebody who can, Robin. These people are not invincible. You've seen that. If they get close, we'll chase them back."

"Ken, whatever you do don't let them touch you. If they do, they'll get you. They're very strong."

"Anyway, just stay here. I'm going to see about Gerry.

Slide a little to the left if you want. I won't go far."

He waded slowly into the left lane then moved up to the pickup's driver's window. Gerry glanced at him nervously.

"What's up?"

"They're back there, Gerry."

"Oh, no. Not again. How do you know?"

He grabbed the gun sitting by his lap. He lifted it up to chest level and pointed it towards the windshield as if expecting someone to jump on his hood.

"We can hear them singing back there. I think they're a good distance away. We cannot see their headlights."

"Maybe they're riding with their lights off."

Just then Don Connolly and Russell Hayes came into view. They were riding their bikes on the left lane, slowing down to get to the rear. The odd effect of seeing the rear of their bikes coming closer gave them the impression that they were riding backwards. Ken saw Gerry pull out his gun through the window and fire. Ken grabbed his wrist quickly and diverted his aim in time before the second shot was fired. It busted the truck's windshield.

"Stop! Those are our riders. Keep the gun down!"

The first shot had done some damage. It cracked the rear red light of Russell's brand new black FLHXI Street Glider and then went right through its rear mudguard. The bike stalled and weaned and Russell had to fight the handlebars to keep it standing. Then he turned around, pointing a gun towards the truck.

"No, don't shoot," Ken yelled. "Gerry made a mistake. He didn't mean it."

"You pervert!" Russell yelled, pointing his gun at Gerry. "You busted my bike. What's wrong with you boy?"

Russell pulled out his .38 from his vest's pocket. Russell's bike was weaving from side to side and he was losing control of it. Don

Connolly let his bike roll back out of the way. Ken moved quickly into the left lane and grabbed Russell's handlebar.

"Hold on tight!" Ken told him.

The two were riding dangerously close, with Ken holding onto one of his handlebars and trying to gain control of the bike. In the confusion, Russell had dropped his gun. The bike began to stabilize as it lost speed. They were drifting back from the caravan. Robin slowed down to keep pace with them.

"Ken, you can't stop. They're back there."

"Robin, tell Gerry to turn back and bring the truck here."

Ken and Russell moved out of the left lane into the grass, coming to a full stop. Don Connolly was right behind them with his phone cocked to his ear.

"I think you just got a busted tire," Ken said.

Russell jumped off and released the kickstand.

"My brand-new bike! I'll kill him! I'll kill him!"

"Listen, guys. Ron is on the other end," Don yelled behind them. He wants us out of here now."

"What are you talking about?" Russell said frenetically. "I'm not leaving my bike out here."

"Wait," Ken said, "I sent Robin for Gerry. He'll bring the truck with the van. We'll put your bike in the van. I'll have a spare installed in no time."

"Listen, Ken," Connolly said. "We don't have time. Ron wants us out of here."

They saw the bike's headlight heading towards them. It was driving in the left lane, opposite traffic, with the engine thundering. She screeched her tires as she came to a stop.

"Ken, he won't stop!" Robin said. "He won't turn around!"

"Miserable wretch," Russell said. "I'll get him."

"Listen, Russell," Ken said. "We got no choice at this point. Come back with me. I'll get the truck and get your bike later. Come on."

"Let's go, guys," Connolly yelled nervously. "Those things are out there."

Ken released the kickstand on Russell's bike and laid it on its side on the grass.

"What are you doing?"

"Let's make it look like it was an accident. In case they do come, maybe they'll ride off."

"Good idea," Connolly said. "Let's go!"

Ken got on his bike and Russell sat behind him. Robin and Connolly were behind them with Connolly watching his rear repetitively. Ken throttled up his engine. His rear tire sank from the weight of the two men, but it gained top speed in seconds, and the red lights of the caravan became visible again ahead of them. Robin caught up with Ken.

"Ken, you're not really serious about going back there. Are you?"

"Yes."

"Ken, they're out there. Margaret is out there. I could hear them."

"It'll be all right Robin."

"Ken, I'm going with you."

They locked eyes, just before they reached the rear of Dave's Harley's van. Ken disappeared from her view as he went on the shoulder of the road and approached the pickup from the passenger's side. As soon as he reached the window, Gerry was pointing the gun at him.

"Gerry, stop the truck! Put the gun down!"

"I can't hear you guys. I ain't stopping for nobody."

Connelly came up slowly on his driver's window and reached inside the cabin with his right hand, bracing Gerry's neck with the muzzle of his handgun. Ken could see the terror in Gerry's eyes as he made a faint head movement to turn and was stopped by the gun.

"Stop the truck right now or I'll spill your brains all over the dashboard," Connolly said, loud enough to be heard over the sound of the engines.

The truck maintained its speed for a few seconds, but as Connolly pressed the gun harder against him, Gerry began slowing down. The caravan's red lights began to scurry away from them. The truck came to a full stop on the right lane without pulling onto the shoulder. As soon as it did, Russell jumped off the back of Ken's bike and ran around the front of the pickup.

"Drop your gun and step out," Connolly was saying to Gerry.

Gerry opened his door and stepped outside. Russell was waiting for him in the middle of the road.

"You bastard!"

He did not give him time to speak. He struck him on the left cheek and Gerry fell back against the pickup's window, then slid down and his arm got caught on the side mirror. His body wobbled against the door in shock. Ken stepped in front of Russell and held him back.

"Let him be, Russell. Let him be."

"The guy is a traitor. He doesn't belong in this run."

"Let Ron decide that. Right now, we need to get back there.

Get behind the wheel. Come on."

"Listen, guys," Connolly said. "Ron doesn't want us to go back there. It's not a good idea."

Ken helped Gerry to his feet. His cheek had ballooned to the size of a regular potato. Ken held him to keep him from falling.

"Is your bike in the van, Gerry?"

"Yeah."

"You're gonna have to get it out, buddy, and ride it," Connolly said. "Let's go. Get it out. Let Ron figure out what he's gonna do with you. You're through driving the truck."

Russell got inside the truck's cabin ready to drive it on the shoulder. Ken opened the rear door for Gerry and helped him take his bike outside. Gerry got it started it and rode off to catch up to the caravan.

"All right," Ken yelled from his bike on the other side. "You're clear with traffic in the back, Russell. You're going to have to pull more onto the shoulder and then U-turn, slowly."

The pick-up went past the shoulder into the grass then arched widely, coming up on the highway in a U-turn. It was a dangerous maneuver on an interstate highway, especially when you are dragging a van behind you and you are going to go opposite the flow of traffic. The pick-up got back on the shoulder, now heading north with Ken, Robin and Connolly trailing behind it. Two cars traveling south passed them on the left lane, the sound of their horns echoing in the distance for long seconds.

"Last call, guys," Connolly said from the rear, "Ron does not want us back there. He wants us back in the line-up."

Ken and Robin ignored him. Ken could hear his phone ringing but was not picking up. He respected Ron but understood Russell's point. Nothing can be as dear to a biker than his own machine. And Russell was acting on impulse. Leaving your bike behind on the side of the road was unimaginable, like leaving your best friend, and despite the danger, it was something you just did not think about doing. At this point, the adrenalin was flowing and it was best to ride on it. Ken let the phone ring.

Russell slowed down as they came near the spot where they had left his bike. He went off the shoulder towards the shallow ditch to gain enough room to turn.

"Careful on the ditch!" Ken said. "It's soggy ground around here."

He wasn't sure if he could be heard. The pick-up drove back on the highway and turned swiftly around with the van quavering behind it. Russell swerved over the left lane and went into the grass, stopping right in front of his downed bike. He jumped out of the pick-up and went for his bike. Ken was already opening the van's rear door.

"Slide back a little bit," Ken said to Robin and Connolly. "Shine your headlights towards me so we can see what we're doing here."

Russell had gotten the bike on its wheels. Between him and Ken, they dragged it towards the rear of the van. They moved fast, positioning the bike by the van's open door. Ken jumped inside and got an access ramp. The two of them rolled the bike inside through the ramp and secured it on one of the rails that had been set up on the sides of the truck.

"It's more than a busted tire, unfortunately," Ken said while strapping her up to the clasps on the wall of the van.

"Darn," Russell said. "I think I rode on the flat for too long. That idiot busted my light too."

"I'll have that replaced in no time, Russell, once we get to Daytona."

"Ken! Ken!" Robin kept yelling. "They're behind us! I hear them!"

Russell and Ken perked their heads, trying to hear the slight murmur, barely audible.

"No one remembers your name when you're strange, when you're strange . . ."

"Let's get out of here, Russell!"

Ken jumped and got on his bike next to Robin. Connolly was behind them, making his bike's engine roar.

"Let's go! Let's go!" he kept egging them.

The truck took off into the left lane, spitting small pebbles and dust from the ground as it got going. Ken and Robin raced their engines, tagging right behind the van. Suddenly, they heard two pops and then two more. Connolly had lost his nerve and began shooting at the empty highway behind him. There was no sign of a headlight, only the importunate sound of the voices singing the same haunting melody.

"Faces come out of the rain, when you're strange. No one remembers your name, when you're strange, when you're strange. When you're strange. Da da da da . . ."

"Stop that!" Ken said, turning around. "You could hurt someone else back there. They're not visible."

"I don't care!" he said. "They are out there!"

Connelly turned again and snapped another shot towards the rear. They could still hear their voices, keeping the same pitch despite the distance Ken and the others had now gained.

"Where are they?" Connelly said. "Where?"

Ken slid his bike towards the left lane to get a view of the road ahead. There was still no sign of the caravan but they were making good speed and there was no sense in pushing Russell to go any faster. The pick-up was much harder to maneuver with the trailer behind it. The faster it traveled, the less stable it became.

"You're doing just fine!" Ken yelled towards his window. "Don't push it too hard Russell. We don't need another accident."

Ken saw him nod and he merged back onto the right lane, next to Robin. She was finding out what he was all about. She wasn't scared by the humming anymore. She was with Ken. He had liberated her. No longer did she feel that she was the property of the Lost Souls. The night was old already and she had not felt any of the effects of those horrible signs, calling her into the arms of the bizarre woman and her followers. Maybe she had crossed the barrier back to sanity. Maybe Ken had rescued her from her insecurity. She was free again, free again! She leaned her head back and felt the night breeze brush against her face and sweep her strands of hair, jutting out from under her helmet. She fell in love with riding again and for the first time since she had started on this run, she rode with joy and elation, as she had always done before and learned to do as a little girl when her father carried her behind him.

"They're out there!" Connolly yelled. "They're still out there!"

He turned once more and fired his gun three times until he ran out of ammunition. Ken turned and saw nothing behind them. The highway was dark, stretching for miles. Perhaps it was only an illusion, a trick of the imagination. Margaret and her girls were not there. They had retreated if only momentarily and were only playing a game of cat and mouse at the moment.

"You've emptied it, right? Now put it away. They are not out there. They're not coming for us."

"What makes you so sure?"

"I sense it. They're not out to get us right now. They want us to reach Daytona first."

"Why?"

"I don't know. It seems that's where they're headed. That's why they joined us, no?"

"Well, I don't want to be in Daytona knowing those things are looking for us. There must be a better place to stay."

"You can break away from the caravan if you want."

"No. That, I won't do. Anyone of us alone will be an easy target for those things. The caravan is our protection. They'll crucify you alone."

"Perhaps not."

"If you know so much about these things, why don't you make them disappear?"

"I think in time we will."

Ken said it and looked over Robin's way. She smiled. She had understood. The time would come when the two of them would have to face them alone. That's how it had to be. And she would be there next to him.

They had now reached the rear of the caravan, and Russell slowed down. Ken drove his bike by the pickup's window.

"Everything okay?"

"Yeah. We made it. I'm glad I got my bike. Where do you think that yellow Gerry went?"

"Don't know, probably up on the line, as far to the front as he can get, I guess."

Ken picked up his Nextel and listened to Ron's tense voice about to lecture him.

"Where have you all been?"

"We went and got Russell's bike. It's a brand-new Street Glider, custom made."

"It could be a Touring with gold plated wheels for all I care. You don't just jeopardize life for a bike. What's wrong with you guys?"

"We couldn't leave it behind. That would have been cowardly."

"Did you meet any of those things back there?"

"No."

"So, where the heck are they now?"

"They are coming with us to Daytona. They're somewhere behind us."

"I swear the patrols better get involved down there. Whatever happened to all the cops we had following us when we started the trip? Right? Now we need them and they're not here."

"Are we coming onto Daytona soon?"

"We'll be getting off highway 95 in a few minutes."

"And how about lodging? Where do we go?"

"It's all set up. Phil did a lot of it himself. We have the entire hotel for ourselves, facing the beach. We were supposed to have been there early in the evening. It's all right though. I just confirmed it. They're waiting for us."

"That'll be a big relief to many people around here."

"Anyway, hang tight down there and no more escapades, you hear me?"

"We'll do Ron."

The caravan traveled uneventfully on the highway. If the riders were distressed, they did not show it. The whole line-up was moving steadily, keeping a close distance between each other and looking remarkably uniform, like a military formation. At a long stretch of the road, Ken could see past the entire rows of red lights down to the first bike that Ron was riding. For a few moments, there was no memory of the horrible moments they had lived through and the unnerving voices still audible in the rear. There was a gradual slowdown in the line-up as the bikes in the front got off on an exit. The caravan took Route 40 east, heading for the coast.

"I thought we'd be getting off on the International Speedway Boulevard," Connolly said. "Now we're going to go on this narrow road, dark as a cave, while being hunted by those things. What's Ron thinking?"

"I don't know the area," Ken said.

"He is probably looking to hook up with Route 1 again. It runs right alongside the beach," Robin said.

"We could have gotten it through 92 and it would have led us straight into Daytona without any turns," Connolly complained.

Connolly was right about the local highway. There was not much room to maneuver and as soon as the caravan got off the ramp, they backed up traffic behind them. The road had two lanes, one in each direction, leaving very little room for overtaking. But even more notable was its poor lighting. If Margaret and her gang wanted to surprise them, this would be the place for it. Ken looked behind him and saw a row of cars straddling slowly to keep the pace. They could not pass them if they wanted to. The bike's line-up was just too long.

"I wouldn't worry about that club right now. Local traffic is behind us. Besides, I think we'll hit the beach in a few minutes and then have plenty of lights."

Robin was right when she told him. The caravan came onto Route 1 near Ormond Beach and turned right, heading south. Immediately they began seeing the high-rises east of them, lit with a large variety of color lights. There was a rush of activity still on the road. A throng of motorcycles kept coming in the other direction. They soon began stopping at the sight of the caravan. Ron had put together the longest trail of bikes ever to ride and they were being acknowledged. Some riders waved, others yelled encouragement. The men and women in the run began getting their spirits up. They kept going at snail's pace until they came onto Main Street where they turned and passed the Halifax River, then went right on South Atlantic Avenue, right along the beach line. They finally stopped by a white rectangular building with large windows in the front, facing the beach. Ken looked at his watch. It was 2:00 A.M.

They were told to park on the north side of the building. The men who Ron had chosen last as section leaders came around to direct the traffic. The riders were sure to fill the suites of the hotel. Because the rooms had been reserved long before, there were no other guests. One by one, couples checked themselves at the lobby and were assigned to their rooms. It was as if, by some strange secret decree, the riders stayed in the same order as on the road, and Russell, Kevin, Robin, and Connolly were the last four to check in. Russell and Connolly went first, then Robin and Ken checked in.

"Are you taking a double?" the attendant asked.

Ken and Robin looked at each other. They had not considered this moment. Ken finally spoke.

"We'll take what you have."

"Sorry, it's two singles in this room. I guess originally that's what it was going to be. Now," the man said, looking beyond them. "I know that some riders are missing but are you the last ones? Seems I'm missing a whole club. They had special reservations. Two girls to a room and then three guys on one. Odd, isn't it?"

He chuckled behind the glass window. He was young with bushy hair, yet as soon as he smiled, he seemed to look older, as if his tease had uncovered his age. Robin and Ken looked at each other again.

"My guess is they'll be here," Ken said. "Maybe the arrangement will not be quite the same."

They went upstairs into their room. There were two single beds near the door across from a dresser with a television on top. The sliding door at the end of the room gave them a view of the ocean. The moon, still visible on the eastern sky, reflected on the quiet ocean with a silvery trail that seemed to sparkle as the waves swayed.

"You can't ask for a better view," Ken said, walking towards the window.

"No, you can't," she said, agreeing. "Can I go first please?"

She looked his way, pointing to the bathroom. Ken smiled at her. It had been a long, traumatic sixteen hours that had tried everyone's patience. Like everyone else, Ken had held his liquids just to end the trip. His bladder was ready to burst but he waved to Robin who seemed in dire need of relieve too. Perhaps there was a bit of chivalry involved. He watched her go inside then opened the door to the balcony and sat on one of the wicker chairs to feel the breeze. The night was beautiful, he thought. Ron had really picked one of the best spots on the beach for his riders. Tomorrow, large crowds would gather around just to get a word with Ron's people. The word would spread like wildfire that they had made it and they would all suddenly become trophies in everyone else's eyes. Ken reflected on what had happened, the lives that had been lost. For a moment he tried to imagine that it had not happened. It was always during those moments that he sought the comfort of prayer and the guidance of the word of God. He did just that. He bowed his head in the darkness and closed his eyes, thinking only of his Creator and giving Him praise for having survived the trip, asking Him for guidance. He must have been in this position for a long time, or so it seemed, when he was startled by Robin's tapping on the door's glass. Robin must have just gotten out of the shower. As soon as he opened the door and faced her, he knew something was terribly wrong. She was trembling. She was wearing a white bathrobe over her underclothes, untied at the waist. Her hair was dripping wet and her eyes were tearful. What shocked Ken the most was the black coloring of her skin running from the left side of her face to her neck.

"What happened? Did you fall?"

Her entire body was shaking. Her mouth twisted and she squeezed her shoulders, as if trying to bring them together. Her body appeared to be slumping. Ken thought she would fall, and he grabbed her by the shoulders.

"Be careful, Robin. Come on, lay down. Let me put you in bed. I'll get help."

He tried making her walk but she did not move. She was shaking so violently that she was making him shudder. Ken held her under her armpits and dragged her to the first bed in the room, near the door. Robin was trying to speak. She kept shaking her head and mumbled the words.

"Nooo..." she said, "no."

"Robin, you might be running a temperature," he said, feeling her forehead. "You feel warm."

He helped her sit down on the bed. She was still shaking. He slowly laid her head on the pillow and brought her feet up on the bed. Her body was trembling, making the bed vibrate.

"Ken," she said unexpectedly. "You'll have to help me."

"Of course, I will, Robin. Let me go get some water and a thermometer."

"No," she wailed, making an effort to lift her head. "No, Ken, don't leave me."

She was looking at him wide-eyed and grabbed his wrist in despair.

"Ken, you must promise me something. It's my only hope. I'm going to be getting much worse through the night. You have to do something for me. I want you to tie me. Tie my arms and feet to the bed. You got to make sure I don't get out of bed and don't ever leave me alone in the room."

Ken was silent. He noticed that the blackness in her skin seemed to be spreading. He watched her as she teetered on the bed.

"Robin, does this have anything to do with Margaret?"

"Yes," she answered, crying. "I need help."

"I'm right here, Robin. They can't hurt you."

"No, Ken. You must tie me. I'll run away. Please, do it now."

He waited, standing by the bed, looking down on her. She was shaking more violently now, lifting her head and biting her lips as she fought to stay still. She pulled the waistband from the bathrobe and handed it to him with a shivering hand. He still hesitated.

"You have to do it, Ken. You have to."

He tied her feet with the waistband to the end poles of the bed. He did not have much to work with so he took his own belt off and tied one of her arms to one side of the headboard. Then he found her jeans, took her thin black belt, and used it to tie her other hand. She was looking at him and moaning slightly. He reached into his bike's saddlebag that he had brought up with him and took out his black leather-bound bible. He pulled the chair from the dresser and set it at the foot of the bed. He sat down and began reading out loud from the book of Matthew. He had no idea what the rest of the morning would bring but let himself be guided by his faith.

Chapter 9

The two women and one man moved stealthily through the inn's stairway. There was light at each floor section of the stairs coming from a spotlight installed above each window facing the ocean. But it was too dim to make their faces. Two of them dropped back as they reached the next set of stairs and looked down through the window. There were three floors from the ground and the hotel lights at the entrance beamed against wide sections of the beach, reaching as far as the incoming waves. Two bulges lying on the wet sand were visible as the tide pulled back. They were half buried in the sand. The foaming sea water completely covered them as the tide moved back in. They were two motorcycles, one a Harley blue Sportster, and the other one a VRSC model with white fenders. The man and woman at the window gave each other a smirk, then went on climbing the stairs. The woman ahead of them had reached the next floor and without turning, she stretched her right hand out as a sign for them to stop. She opened the door to the hallway and walked towards the first door. She knocked.

Ken O'Gara was sitting back on the dresser's chair with both feet resting on the footboard of Robin's bed. His bible was spread open on his thighs. He had dozed off a few times as Robin seemed to go into a deep sleep but he kept waking up every so often. Robin's condition seemed to have stabilized to the point where Ken had second thoughts about keeping her tied. He had not wanted to do it. But Robin had been so adamant that he truly had been concerned not to follow her demands for fear of what would happen. This was all foreign to him. Was someone to walk through the door and ask him why Robin was tied to the bed, he would not have an answer. He did not know what ailed Robin specifically. Was it some kind of curse? But in this day and age that did not seem like a credible explanation. And he worried about what to do. Every time he opened his eyes he watched Robin's position on the bed. Was she too uncomfortable? Were the belts in her hands and feet wrapped too tight? He guessed that he must wait for morning. Something told him that the answer to the whole riddle would come in the morning. He had started to read from his bible when he dozed off again. The knock on the door had him up in a second, and his mind raced through a dozen scenarios that could explain Robin's very peculiar position to whoever was there. As he got up, he felt pain running through his back from his crouched position on the chair. His neck was stiff. He looked at this watch and noticed it was past 5:00. He pushed down on the nickel lever latch of the elegant single panel door. Standing before him was one of the most beautiful women he had ever seen.

Margaret wore black jeans tied with a wide black leather belt and silver buckle. Her silky black hair came over her shoulders and parted in two strands that dispersed at each side of her chest. She wore a black tank top that outlined two bulky, erect nipples in her bosom area. Her stomach was flat and her hips were ample and firm. Her beautiful thighs connected to a pair of long legs booted up to the knee. Her mouth partially open, as if in amazement, and her dazzling black eyes, rendered a picture of lust hardly capable of being duplicated. She had very white skin that seemed to gleam in the darkness of the night. She was staring right at him as the door opened.

"What have you done with my girl?"

Ken stood speechless at the center of the doorway, holding the door. On his left hand was his bible. He had not for a flashing second thought about Margaret and her gang despite the obvious fact that they were still around. But now it had all come down to greet him. Of course, they would not give up.

Margaret and her friends would not be scared off merely because they had lost four of their mates. They weren't leaving without Robin. Ken instinctively stared at her body. He would have never guessed that the specimen before him was that of a woman fifty-three years old. But he thought quickly. Margaret was here and she had come for Robin. He shook inside.

"What do you want with us, Margaret?"

"You know what I want, Ken."

Her eyes glimmered as she stepped into the room, causing him to retreat. A shriek came from Robin's bed, which made Margaret turn. Robin had lifted her head momentarily, then flung her head back into the belts, binding her hands. She bit them like a wild animal and tried to get loose. Margaret turned to Ken.

"What do we have here? What are you doing to my girl, Ken? Are you holding her captive? I know. The convulsions can get pretty violent. It's not a pretty sight. That's what happens to those who have a taste of me. They cannot break away once they've had me. They're powerless. That's why it's no use in fighting me, Ken. You're mine too."

"Margaret, get out," Ken said, lifting his bible. She laughed.

"Is that what you think this is, Ken? Is that it? Do you really think it would work? A flash of a cross and I'd be gone running like a scary cat? You are fantasizing, Ken. That's Hollywood you're thinking of. In the real world, those things don't happen. You've got to do better than that."

She moved towards him and he backed off.

"Ken, don't touch her!" Robin yelled.

The other two entered the room at that point. They were Randall and Linda, and Robin recognized them immediately.

"Ken, look out!"

Ken kept retreating until his back touched the dresser.

"Ken, don't you see you don't have any choice? You've stolen my girl. You've led me on a tragic chase. But it's useless, Ken. You know, I must give you this, Ken, you're a pretty good rider. I like good riders. I like to lead them. Think of it this way, Ken. Fifty years from now, no one will remember you, no matter how good of a rider you were, unless of course you rode with me. At least then, people will say, this man must have been good. He rode during the time of Margaret McCarter."

Ken knew he was out of time. Linda and Randall were by Margaret's side now, closing in on him. He had no idea how the three of them would confront him or what their means of violence would be. They did not appear to be armed. They seemed after all like just regular human beings. He thought about that as he reached back into the dresser with his left hand to set his bible down. As he did, he inadvertently pushed the dresser lamp sideways. It tilted over the dresser's top and came crashing onto the floor. Everything went dark all of a sudden. There was no other light in the room. Ken jumped back over the chair in the darkness, escaping Margaret's flailing hand. She had thrown it towards him like a bear's claw, missing him by the skin of his teeth. As he moved back, his feet got tangled on the lamp's electrical cord, knocking it out of the outlet. The chord made a sapping sound as it sprung back and small blue and red sparks glistened from the outlet. It went pitch dark inside the room. Ken saw the three dark figures hesitate, then they lunged towards him like vats in a cave. He picked up the chair now in front of him and swung it at them. It seemed to have no effect. They kept charging towards him. Then suddenly, out of nowhere, he saw a flame flare up. Margaret and her gang moaned and scurried back. Robin had gotten her hands loose and was holding a lighter in her hand with the burning flame. Living with the creatures, Robin had learned their weaknesses. Ken realized the flame's effect right away. He quickly untied Robin's feet. She jumped off the bed, holding the lighter up. She was starting to shake.

"Keep the flame burning, Robin," he said.

He quickly grabbed one of the sheets from the bed and brought it close to the lighter's flame. He could hear Margaret and the other two groan hysterically at the sight of the fire slowly smoldering the sheet. The three were scrambled at the corner of the room near the window. Ken flaunted the blazing sheet in the air for a second, and they yelped frantically, moving back and forth like rats trapped in a room. One of them made for the sliding door leading into the balcony, pushed it open and leaped outside. The others followed. Ken went behind them. Their yelling got louder and could now be heard throughout the beach. Ken held the sheet by its end and tossed it at them. Yelling wildly, the three of them jumped from the balcony.

Ken watched them fall on the ground and roll away in the sand. They got up without looking back and ran along the shoreline, disappearing in the darkness.

He went inside the room. Robin was still holding the lighter in the dark, sobbing. He took it from her and held her close to him.

"Now we can fight them back, Robin. We know how."

She covered her eyes with her hands. They heard voices in the hallway and the sound of footsteps coming up the stairway.

"What happened?"

It was Connolly. Ron had left sentries on each floor, expecting more trouble.

"They were here," Ken said.

Connolly flicked the light on in the room. He was holding his 38 with his right hand, and he stared Ken and Robin down, as if he needed to convince himself that they were not threatening.

"They were here? Where are they now?"

"They jumped out from the balcony, Connolly. We chased them out with fire. They're afraid of fire."

Connolly took his time, pondering over what Ken had just said.

"Is that so? You realize you are the first known to have survived an attack by those women?"

"You mean by not fleeing from them, Connolly."

Ken remembered when Connolly had looked for ways to dodge an encounter with Margaret and her gang only a few hours before. He had grudgingly run along with Russell, Kevin and Robin to retrieve Russell's bike but played no active role. In fact, his fear made him a liability when he suddenly started shooting the wind as they made their way back to the line-up. Here he was now pretentiously considering Ken's story doubtful. Connolly raised his chin up, apparently annoyed by Ken's comment.

"This does not make you a hero, Ken, you know."

"It also does not make me a coward, Connolly. I think you should call Ron now."

People had started to pour into the room. Everyone was tired but on edge, and at least on this floor, most riders had been woken up by the disturbance.

"Everyone should go back to your rooms," Connolly said. "No one's been hurt."

"Are those women here?" someone from the crowd asked. "Are they here?"

"No, they're not here," Connolly said. "Nothing's happened. It's between Ken and his girl. Come on, everyone go back to your rooms."

Some of the riders began dispersing, most walking barefooted out of the room, holding up towels and wearing light clothes. Russell had worked his way through the crowd to see Ken.

"Ken, is everything all right?"

"Yes, we're all right. We're going to go out for a breath of fresh air," Ken said.

"I'll join you, man. Can't get much sleep with everything that's happened."

Ken retrieved his bible from the dresser. Connolly met him at the door.

"Where are you going on the beach?"

"Just out, Connolly. It's not safe here."

He took Robin by the hand and then remembered something.

"Robin," he said, "let's take a blanket."

Robin had read his thoughts. She looked weak, but inside, she felt determined to follow him. She took the cover and sheet from Ken's bed, still untouched, and followed him out the door. They walked down the stairway into the beach area, followed by Russell.

"What happened?" Russell said outside.

"They came back. They almost had us. We fought them with fire and they ran off for now."

"What do they want? I don't understand."

"They want me, Russell" Robin said. "They won't give up until they have me. And they want to get me."

"But why? What have you done?"

"I guess they see me as a threat because I'm keeping Robin from them. But I'm gonna make sure no one else gets hurt."

He and Robin were spreading the sheet on the sand, only a few feet away from the water.

"What's that?" Russell said above their heads.

The three of them turned towards the ocean. As a wave came in, it splashed on the two heavy objects partially buried in the sand. They slowly paced towards them, ignoring the water that reached their feet, then their shins, and up to their knees as the next tide came in. Ken's heart sank as he recognized the shine of his silver fenders, glimmering from beneath the sea water under the moonlight. Next to it, he saw Robin's blue Sportster with its front wheel buried half-way through. Margaret had made sure they could not get away by wrecking their bikes.

"What happened here?" Russell said.

"Those are our bikes," Ken said confidently. "They destroyed our bikes."

"What?"

"Very malicious. Once the engines are exposed to the sea water, they're ruined. It's more ruthless than burning them."

Robin held onto his arm and laid her head on his shoulder.

"Who could do such a thing to beautiful machines like those?" Russell wondered out loud.

"It's them. They are after us."

Ken turned around, looking towards the hotel.

"Listen, Russell, you better get back. Robin and I are gonna stay out here. I think we know how to keep them away until the morning."

"Ken, you're nuts. You can't do this alone. Let's go back into the hotel."

"If we go back, we'll only put the rest of you in jeopardy. No, we'll stick it out here. Come on, Robin, let's pick up some wood to make a bone fire."

They strode through the sand on their bare feet. Ken found the first log, half buried in the wet sand. Russell came behind them, still unsure of what was happening.

"I'm not leaving you out here," he said. "You helped me get my bike last night. I'm not forgetting it."

"The wood is going to be wet, Robin," Ken said, looking at her. "We'll need some dry leaves or paper to get the fire going."

Russell stopped behind them.

"I have the answer," he said. "I'll siphon some gasoline from my tank."

"Good thinking," Ken told him, turning. "You go get us the fuel and we'll get the wood set up."

"Will you be all right out here?"

"We got our weapons," Ken said, flicking the lighter on.

Russell hurried back to the hotel as Ken and Robin collected small chunks of wood, mostly buried under the sand. They made a small pyramid, but it was not enough to start a fire. They snug leaves and empty paper cups in between the creases. They sat on their blankets to wait for Russell. There was no one on the beach. The hotels running along the shore shone their segmental lights against the dark ocean. Russell came back with a plastic container smelling of gasoline.

"We couldn't find much," Ken said. "The beach is pretty clean."

"Yeah, that won't last long. I've got an idea. Here, you pour some gas on them while I go get the kerosene gas lamp from our tent. That should do it."

Ken and Robin looked at each other and nodded in agreement. Ken grabbed the container by the handle and pointed its spout at the small pile. He doused the wood with gasoline then lit it up with the lighter. A small fire began flaring up. They lay on the sheet and covered themselves with the blanket. They were so exhausted that by the time Russell came back, they were fast asleep. He set up the oil lamp near the fire and took the glass chimney off to make the flame more visible. There was no wind tonight so the flame burned steadily. He had brought his sleeping bag along also and he laid it across from Kevin and Robin. He too was tired. He got himself inside the bag face down and was asleep in seconds.

If Margaret and her crew had wanted their vengeance, there was no better moment. For at least four hours, Robin and Ken slept soundly in the sand under the dark of the early morning, their bodies wrapped under the light hotel's blanket, dangerously oblivious as to their surroundings. Together they made a perfect target. Their only protection was the feeble flame of an outdoor gas lamp that could have been blown out with the half breath of any passerby. But weak traits are most palpable in the strong, such as hair in Solomon. The lamp's flame, no matter how frail, presented a threat to the warring Margaret and that seemed to convey a feeling of security to the three people at the beach, letting them sleep peacefully well past dawn until a beach patrol pulled their jeep at their heels while making their rounds in the morning. The passenger officer, dressed in green pants and khaki shirt, got out from his door.

"Here we go again," he said to the driver. "These three might have been so wasted they couldn't even find their rooms."

"Wait," the other officer said. "Don't wake them up too quickly. Let's see if we find any substance on them first. We need an early bust."

They walked around them a few times, looking for any marihuana residue or powder nearby. They examined the burned-out fire, poking the ashes with the tip of their clubs to see if they could turn up any illicit substance—still no reaction from the three sleeping beauties. Finally one of the officers decided it was time to hear their story. He tapped Russell on his forehead with his brown boot. The man had no reaction so the patrolman pushed his body up by clasping his boot under his shoulder and raising him. He turned Russell round so he could face him.

"Time to get up. The sun is out. What are you doing sleeping on the beach anyway?"

Russell sat up, squeezing his eyes.

"Officer, you don't want to know."

"All right everybody up. There's no sleeping at the beach and no loitering. Look at the signs. Where are you staying?"

"Right across," Ken said. He had sat on his sheet and slid his blanket off Robin. He rubbed her face to get her attention.

"Let's go, Robin."

Some bikers were already stopping by the north side of the hotel, facing the beach. The word had gotten out that Ron's caravan from Boston was in town and everyone had at least one acquaintance among the riders. The croaky sound of motorcycle engines, driving slowly or stopping for a peek filled the air. Robin and Ken went back to their rooms and changed. Then they met Russell at the hotel's restaurant for coffee. Ken wanted to get down to business right away.

"Let's get to the van. I want to fix your bike."

"We wanna get going," Robin said.

"Where are you going?"

"We are breaking off the caravan. We want to be as far as possible by nightfall when they return."

"I don't think Ron will go for that, Ken," Russell said. "He is not for abandoning his riders."

"It's not Ron's decision. It's ours. We're only a liability to you guys at this point."

Ken had started walking out of the restaurant, followed by Robin. The large assortment of bikes, parked in straight rows from front to back of the building, looked awesome in the morning sun. The only two four-wheelers were Dave's truck with its van and a Chevy SUV towing a similar van. They both had been parked off the street in back of the hotel. Ken opened the door in Dave's silver van and climbed inside.

"Ken, you're the only mechanic left. I mean, officially. I can tighten bolts and screws but that's about it. We need you."

Russell was standing outside the van's open door. Ken was already busy at work. He was gathering tools from one of Dave's tool boxes and began unbolting the rear axle of the Street Glider.

"You've got an awesome machine, here, Russell," Ken said, ignoring his comments. "I've got to figure what to do with that taillight until we can get to a shop, though. It's really a shame."

"What's going on?" Connolly said from the door.

"Ken wants to leave us," Russell commented.

"Listen, Ron's got enough problems as it is today, dealing with that jerk Gerry and the rest of it. I wouldn't bring that up right now. He's still sleeping."

Ken was not hearing him. Robin helped him lift the rear end of the bike to get the wheel out.

"We're going to need help," Ken said.

Russell jumped on board. Connolly called two other riders who came inside to help. Ken worked fast, removing the chain and cover to get the wheel free.

"It's a total bust," Ken said. "The wheel is damaged. We're going to have to improvise if you want to get this bike running today."

"Darn! I can't believe it." Russell said.

Ken waited as Russell studied the dented wheel wrapped up around the tire threads, the only remnants left of the original tire.

"All right," he finally said. "Do what you can."

Ken had the bike running by noon. It was not an easy fix but Dave had thought of everything. The van was equipped with a large assortment of wheels, tires, fenders, and every conceivable motorcycle part you could think of. Although it was not a perfect match, Russell's bike could run. There was only a slight drop on the bike's rear tire due to a slight difference in size but you could not otherwise tell. Ken found a spot for the Street Glider on the side of the hotel. Some of the riders hanging around came by to admire it and Ken and Robin slipped off unnoticed. They were carrying only the saddle bags that the two had retrieved from their bikes the night before. They left South Atlantic Avenue, walking on foot over the Halifax Bridge, working their way onto Route 1. They had not yet discussed where they were going but the two held hands, not saying a word as Ken's phone kept ringing incessantly. He had not picked it up all day. As they got on Route 1, Robin finally spoke.

"I have some money," she said. "At least they didn't take that. Do you?"

"Yes. I always carry it in my front pocket."

"Most riders leave everything in their bikes. I just lucked out last night when I brought my saddlebag upstairs. How did you get to carrying money in your front pocket?"

"I guess it's an old habit I developed in high school."

They heard the bikes' engines roaring behind them but did not think to turn until they came right alongside of them. It was Russell and another rider in a maroon Night Rod that shined under the sun. Even next to it, Ken thought it was no match for Russell's black Street Glider, even with a mismatched tire on. The machine was outstanding. It had an air of command about it. *Maybe it was the color*, Ken thought. Black was like that.

"Listen, Ken, Ron is calling you. He's ticked off. You shouldn't have left like that," Russell was yelling, moving his bike at walking pace to keep up with Ken and Robin.

"I forgot this," Ken said. He reached out into his vest pocket, retrieved the Nextel and handed it to Russell.

"Ken wait up. This is not right. You can't just walk off." "Russell, if we stay, we'd be putting the whole gang in danger. I don't want that. Let those things chase after us tonight alone. We'll manage."

Traffic was building up behind the two bikes. Some cars were tooting their horns.

"I guess you better get moving," Ken said.

The two bikes zoomed forward but then quickly pulled over onto the shoulder of the road a few feet ahead.

"Listen," Russell said, facing them. He had gotten off his bike and leaned it on its kickstand. He was walking towards them. "I don't know if these things can predict the future, man. I figure that's impossible for any human being to do. Perhaps we're giving them credit they don't deserve. My guess is that if they're really after you, they'll be here tonight looking for you at the hotel. But at least we'll have protection. Ron is dealing with the Florida Highway patrol right now. They've been in touch with the North and South Carolina patrols, and they all know what happened back there. They've agreed to stick around so I'm not worried about us. But I don't want you going on foot. You were pretty darn right to me out there last night. Take my bike. Just drive out of here and we'll meet up with you wherever."

He got on the back of the other bike. He gave Ken the five signs from behind as the bike rattled some dust off the ground and leaped forward on Route 1 and then turned on the first block to go back. Ken and Robin looked at each other. Ken took her hand.

"So where do we go now?" he said.

"Let's go," she replied. "We have to lose her before nightfall."

They both got on the Street Glider, Ken in the front and she in the back of him, holding their saddlebags. He turned the throttle up and got on the road slowly. They went north. At the intersection with Route 40 she told him to turn.

"This is how we came into town last night," she said.

"Any idea where it leads to?"

"It'll take us to 95 but we don't want to go there. Let's just keep driving west."

"I don't really like not knowing where we are if they are coming after us."

"As long as we're heading west, we're all right. We can only end up on the west coast."

He began to speed up as they went farther on the highway. They passed the intersection with Route 95 and kept going west. Route 40 was a two-lane highway in most areas and it was hard to overtake anyone, even for a motorcycle. They followed the stream of traffic and relaxed, enjoying the pleasant scenery of central Florida. It was now late afternoon and the sun was hot. They both were silent for a long time, feeling the wind on their faces and taking pleasure in the sound of their bike, as riders often do. They reached the outskirts of Ocala a few minutes before 5:00.

"We have not eaten a thing. I say we stop." Ken said.

"Keep going. Let's pass the town."

"Do you know where you're going?"

"I have an idea."

Route 40 went right through the heart of town. It was also known as Silver Springs Boulevard and it displayed a large assortment of stores and restaurants on both sides of the highway. It was a weekend and traffic was moderate. They went past the square and the old section of town. They gradually began leaving the city limits and the landscape turned country again. Now the highway was bordered by horse farms as they kept going farther west.

"It is beautiful country out here," Ken said.

"It sure is. It almost does not seem Florida but somewhere out west."

"I agree. It does seem like that."

The highway got narrower in this section. Then suddenly, it ended, and they were facing an intersection. Highway 41 crossed the foot of 40, running north and south. Ken hesitated at the light, not sure where to turn to keep going west.

"Go left," Robin said. "We are bound to find another road that will keep going west."

They went south on Route 41 through what seemed a rural area and then they entered the town of Dunnellon. It was a small town scattered around both sides of 41. They came upon a bridge over the Witchlacoochee River. Flocks of small boats were floating downstream under the bridge. Ken pulled over at the end.

"It's beautiful. I saw a boat ramp on the other side," Robin said.

Ken turned around, going over the breach again, and pulled over on the ramp located on the east side of the river. He parked on a gravel lot. A small store near the bank sold bait and other supplies to the tourists. They went inside to inquire about a place to eat. The young store keeper told them to go across the highway for some fast food, then encouraged them to get a boat. Ken and Robin said they'd be back. They went on the wooden pier to look over the motor boats for rent. There were several outdoor Klamath 11 and 12 footers and some larger boats. There were also a few Osage aluminum canoes roped on dry land.

"If you're gonna go in the river, you might wanna get started soon. The ramp is closed after 6:00," said a thin young man who kept moving back and forth on the small pier, as if in wait. "Here comes someone now."

He started to help a couple bring their motor boat into the pier. Robin and Ken said they would be back. They walked north on the highway and got some fast food at a KFC restaurant. They took the order to go.

"I think it's a good idea," Ken said. "We can go up the river and settle somewhere for the night. I don't see how they could find us there."

Robin remained thoughtful as they headed back to the ramp. She was staring at the ground almost until they were in the supply store.

"You're probably right," she said.

Ken arranged to rent a canoe, and Robin picked up the saddle bags from their bike. The attendant at the pier agreed to cover their bike with a drape.

"Now," he said. "I can't guarantee it. It's quiet at night but a bike's a bike. Someone may decide to grab it in the middle of the night when no one's here. The owner can't be held responsible."

"We understand," Ken said. "We'll take our chances."

"I guess you really want to get to see the moonlight on the river, ah? It's pretty darn beautiful at night. You sure you don't want to get some fishing equipment? Might as well if you're gonna spend the night."

"We are sure," Ken said.

The attendant untied the ropes to one of the canoes and dragged it into the water.

"Two oars inside," he said, pointing. "You got your receipt? Shame you gotta pay for the whole night but those are the rules. Looks like you're all set."

Ken hopped in, followed by Robin. He took the lead at the bow, rowing off the starboard side of the canoe, and Robin rowed from the port side of the stern. As soon as they passed the bridge above them, they got to see how beautiful the river really was. Copious tree branches growing at the banks of the river hung over the water, in some spots almost reaching the surface. Immense cypresses grew daringly deep into the river, their buttressed trunks splintered by the current, but their branches looked alive and robust, and pale green duckweed was shedding on the surface of the water. The misty settings at both shores rendered plenty of shade to wood ducks, wood storks, white ibis, deer and even sporadically, some alligator. They rowed their canoe past a multitude of large homes that gradually faded out as the river narrowed. The water temperature seemed to be in the mid-sixties. Ken pointed to a shady spot on the west bank and they headed towards it. They slid their canoe right underneath a laurel oak that extended its twisting branches over the surface of the water like tentacles. Ken opened their food bags and offered Robin a cardboard plate with fried chicken and mashed potatoes.

"I must admit I'm hungry," she said.

"Me too."

"How long do you think we ought to hang out here?"

"I don't know. Wouldn't you agree this is a pretty good hiding place?"

She smiled vaguely. She seemed unsure. She was petrified of her own reaction to Margaret's influence once night came. Yes, they were hiding, but how would her mind react once night came? She was afraid for Ken, afraid that she would not be able to support him if she fell under Margaret's spell. Ken saw the fear in her eyes.

"Don't worry, Robin. She won't get to you tonight."

She gazed his way but hesitated. She did not dare speak. They did not know exactly how or when, but after they finished their meal, they both lay back at the bottom of the canoe, one at each end, using their leather bags as pillows. They were exhausted and fell asleep almost simultaneously. Ken had tied the tip of their canoe to one overhanging branch to prevent them from floating aimlessly into the river. It was past midnight when they were awoken by a far-away familiar humming.

"People are strange when you're a stranger faces look ugly when you're alone . . . ."

"Ken, they're here!" Robin whispered. "They're here!"

He untied the rope from the tree branch and sat up in the canoe's bow.

"If they spotted us here, Robin, they could spot us anywhere. Let's row back to the ramp."

"Ken, that's where it's coming from! You hear them?"

"I know. Let's row close to the bank. Come on."

Robin was right. The humming kept getting louder as they floated on the river. It seemed they were moving towards them rather than getting away. Robin could not understand, and she began to panic.

"Ken, we're coming towards them! Let's turn back!"

Then she saw them. She saw the two human figures reflected on the moon- silvery surface and instinctively looked up. They were hanging from some branches that swayed down towards the water from their weight. The canoe was going to slip right under them.

"Ken!" she yelled.

She saw them spread their arms, ready to let go. They were going to land right on top of them. Then she felt the quick pull from Ken's oar from the bow as he maneuvered their canoe and took a quick turn to the left, towards the open river. The two creatures threw themselves towards the water spread eagle with a terrible screech that reverberated through the waters, echoing on the shores. They missed the canoe by inches. Ken had evaded them like he had done the previous night on his bike. There was a powerful splash that almost turned their canoe over. But Ken was rowing fast, moving the canoe away from them. Robin looked back. She saw their two heads go under and then float back up for a moment. Then she heard a loud thud coming from underneath them, and she saw the water whirl around them, as if there had been a tornado. She saw their heads being sucked in, deep into the water and inches away from them she saw the long, shell-like tail, sweeping the surface from side to side for a moment and then disappear into the depths of the river. Just as fast as she had seen it happen, it had stopped. She turned quickly towards Ken.

"Ken! What was that?"

He had stopped rowing and turned around. He had caught some of it as he looked past her.

"An alligator got them, Robin. They can be unforgiving."

"Oh, my God! Oh, my God!"

"That was two of them, Robin. There's one left."

"Where is she, Ken? Where is she?"

"I don't know. There's no use in us running away."

He said it and began rowing again. She picked up her oar, not knowing what to do.

"Where are we going? Where are you rowing to?"

"To the ramp."

"Ken, she'll be there. We're better off staying in the water."

He wasn't listening. His shoulders were moving energetically in the bow, sweeping the water from the starboard side in a long stride, and quickly switching to the port side. The canoe was moving rapidly on the river, cutting the current slightly at an angle so as not to go against it.

When it pitched too close to the other shore, Ken turned it, directing it forward but again at an angle that inevitably led them to the other side. He did this several times. Robin watched him in silence from the stern. Reluctantly she slipped her oar into the water and began keeping up with him. The canoe moved faster now, cutting the water smartly, like a dart. They reached the 41 bridge, now ghostly looking, with the occasional sound of a passing car. Ken guided the canoe straight into the wooden dock. He tied the rope quickly around one of the posts and went for Robin.

"Let's go. Come on."

"Where are we going, Ken?"

He did not answer her. He set foot on the wooden deck. The raucous voice came from across them in the dark, but they could not see her.

"That's right, Ken. Where are you going? There's nowhere to go. Don't you see the road ends here?"

Ken turned.

"The lighter. Turn the lighter on."

Robin searched nervously in her breast pocket then her pants pocket. She felt the pockets in her buttocks. The figure standing at the bottom of the stairs stepped towards them.

"It's not gonna matter, Robin. It's not going to make any difference this time. It's time to come home, Robin. Just think, you could be at home right now having your chocolate. We didn't have to be part of this run anyway. It was a bad idea. They can't accept our club, Robin. They try to split us apart. But that's all over now, honey. You're safe. Come back to me."

Ken grabbed her hand.

"Margaret, why are you after us?" Ken said. "What do you want from us?"

"You don't deserve to be alive, Ken. If I let you, it's only because I'm merciful but I don't feel much mercy tonight after what you've done."

"Robin does not want to go back to you, Margaret. She wants to be with me."

"No she doesn't," she said. He could feel her zealous gaze even in the dark. Her posture was the same as the night before, voluptuous and tempting, yet incredibly lethal. Ken noticed the three bikes, parked behind the stairs. Ken tried to descend the steps, but she came towards him and blocked his path. She made a furtive movement, reaching into her chest. She had retrieved an object that she held in her hand. Ken could not see it in the dark, but the reflection from the moonlight on it left him no doubt it was a sharp object.

"Ken! Look out! Look out!" Robin yelled, pulling him towards her. They both missed a step on the stairway and stumbled down.

"My girls never want to be alone, Ken. Not after I show them the way. No man is a match for what I do to them.

They're cured of those earthly cravings."

She was right in front of them now. Ken could see her ashen face with deep black eyes and hair falling over her chest. She kept switching the blade from hand to hand.

"Back off!" a voice thundered behind them. "Back off and face me. I'm your real enemy."

They could not see her, but her voice had a disturbing ring of familiarity. Robin and Ken stood rigidly, trying to find her. The parking lot stretched out with a slight incline next to the goods store. There were no vehicles that they could see anywhere. Yet, they heard her again.

"You made a big mistake, Margaret, when you picked on Robin. You destroyed my family once and I should not have let you live then. It's not going to happen again. This time I will destroy you."

Robin got up from the ground open mouthed. Yes, Helen McManus had made the trip to Daytona. After her daughter fled home that morning, she had finally succumbed to the idea that Margaret McCarter, her old rival, had duped Robin. And she knew what that meant. When you are the subject of affection by the soulless cannibal female, there is no hope for you. She had seen that happen in her youth. She had seen it happen to her husband, the only man she had really loved. She had accepted her defeat after it was over and left as far away as she could, never to return, but she took her vengeance with her. Something she kept close to her heart. She never told anyone, not even her parents or her daughter later. Besides, who would believe it? A body living without a soul? There was no such thing. You are either alive with your soul inside you or you are dead. That is, perpetually dead. That's what people believed. She believed differently. She had seen different and she had spent the rest of her life making sure that such evil would never befall her loved ones or anyone around her. A soul must never leave the body. When it does, the flesh becomes impotent, unscrupulous, or simply dead. Helen McManus had become a child of fear afterwards, living in the shadows, avoiding what she considered the evil in humankind that she had once seen. But it had arrived in her doorstep again. She had refused to believe it at first, that first night when Robin came home and she had felt the premonitions. She was in self-denial, thinking it could not be possible. It could not be happening again. But it was here. Her daughter Robin McManus, the daughter of her John McManus, the fearless rider who had fallen victim to the beautiful, conniving, treacherous, malevolent, soulless Margaret McCarter, had become her captive hostage. What a small world!

"You forget it's my family too, Helen," Margaret said quietly, without a hint of fear. "She's my flesh."

Margaret turned around brusquely, ignoring Ken and Robin, as if they had suddenly become unimportant. She descended the steps and walked over the gravel lot, each footstep yielding a squeaking sound as she moved on.

"Stop," Helen said. "You took John, Margaret, but you can't take Robin. I won't let you."

"You let me take John, Helen. You did not fight for your man. That was your own fault. It's a shame he had to die. We could have been so happy. But you made up for it when you took Robin, Helen. She came out of my entrails. She's my daughter."

"No!" Helen hollered in horror. "Don't say it! Don't say it! You killed John, Margaret, but Robin is mine. You can't have her."

There was a slight snivel in her voice, a quavering that lasted a second.

"Now, now, Helen. John's death was an accident. You know John was an intrepid rider and that was his demise. It's like they say, those who live by the sword, will die by the sword. But even if I had anything to do with his death, I'd say we're even, Helen. You stole my baby. You took Robin from me and never told her. You kept her from me all these years, and now she's coming back. It's daughterly instinct, Helen. She knew how to find me. I did not go looking for her, Helen. I let her be. I could have gone after you a long time ago and got my baby back but I figure, why break up a happy family? You did well by her, Helen. You raised her well. But now she's come to me out of her own accord. That's because she's my blood, Helen, which you aren't. Blood is thicker than water, Helen. She's found her calling, Helen. She's mine."

"You bastard! I should have killed you then."

"Now, Helen. Stop being silly. You can't kill me. You know that. I'm soulless. I'm already dead. As for Robin, she needs me. She's like me. It's nature. Stop fighting us. You can't win. It's you who made a mistake. You should have stayed in your safe little house in beautiful

Cape May, away from the dangerous world of motorcycles that you despise. Instead, what do you do? You come down here, following us, imagine that. You're following a motorcycle caravan, Helen. Like you used to do in the old days when you chased John and me, now it's Robin and Helen. But don't you see that we are one happy family now? You can't have Robin back. And here you are, in this mystifying river so unsafe for the mortals. What a pity."

"Don't move, Margaret, or I'll blow you away."

For the first time, Ken notices the long-barreled Flemington shotgun aiming right at Margaret. Robin had dropped to the ground, her face buried in between her thighs in agony. Ken still could not place Helen's position.

"Helen, if your bullets kill me, you will have to live with the horror of having shot Robin's mother right before her very eyes. You will break Robin's heart. Don't you understand?"

"You will never make Robin a soulless. Never!"

Margaret was standing near the three bikes. She had stopped momentarily, apparently engrossed in the conversation but now began moving again. Ken still could not really see Helen.

The barrel of the shotgun sprang back a bit as it spat a thread of deadly fire. But it wasn't aiming at Margaret. Ken could hear the bullet ricocheting off one of the bikes and he instantly ducked. Robin kept yelling for Helen to stop. Then it happened again as a second shot was fired. And then again. The projectile made a deep, explosive sound as it hit the gas tank, and then a stream of fire mushroomed on top and quickly spread, engulfing the woman standing next to it. It all happened in a second. The flames spread throughout her body as they did on the other two bikes. She slumped forward while walking unsteadily towards the firing gun. It was only now that Robin noticed Helen's figure, moving away from the rear of the wall of the pier house. She was walking towards Margaret, pointing her shotgun at her. It seemed as if the two were going to collide. Margaret flung one blazing arm in the air, still holding her blade. She stumbled and remained in a slouched position for a few seconds, her torso bent forward, and her entire body in flames. Then she fell slowly, sparks and flames sputtering up above her as she hit the ground. Helen was only a few inches from her, still pointing the gun at her. Margaret's body sizzled as the fire ate through her entrails. Robin was getting up, about to run towards Helen, when the gas tank of another bike exploded with a loud bang, tossing metal debris in the air.

"Robin, stay down!" Helen said.

Then, the third bike exploded, and its front tire sprung across the open wharf towards the water. Sparks and small burning metal parts leaped through the air, missing the roof of the pier by inches. The scene resembled a battle zone. Miraculously, none of the structures were hit. Robin ran towards Helen, stepping aside from the burning body on the ground and tightly embracing her.

"Oh, Mom! Oh, Mom!"

Helen had lessened the grip on her gun and let the barrel drop down as she received her.

"I'm sorry Robin. I'm sorry."

"Mom, is it true?"

Helen held Robin in an embrace and stayed still for a few moments.

"Yes, it's true, Robin," she whispered in her ear.

Robin detached from her and turned toward Margaret's remains. Her body was still ablaze. Her left arm had remained in a raised position, holding the blade. Her face was unrecognizable, just a charred mass. Her clothes had burned into the flesh, its remnants showing in streaks of singe buried into what once had been the skin. Smoke was beginning to discharge from her. The strangest thing was that she had not made a sound in her last moment of agony, as if somehow she had embraced death voluntarily and with grace. Robin fell into the ground on her knees, next to the blazing body.

"Oh, God! Oh, no! This can't be!"

She kept staring at her remains, smelling the fumes as if she wanted to feel part of her all of a sudden. Far in the distance, they heard sirens.

Helen reached out to touch her but Robin pulled away. It was only when Ken came around and grabbed her that she walked away from Margaret's burning body.

"The cops will be here in a minute," Ken said, turning to Helen. "It would be best that you go."

"And leave you and Robin in this mess?"

"This is going to hold you up. Leave while you can." "I won't do it. I don't care what happens."

She did not move from her position, holding the shotgun in one hand, watching the three bikes burn near Margaret's body. The white and green patrol entered the parking lot from 41, blasting its siren. It was an awful sound that deafened their ears much more because of the stillness in the area. There was no local police in town and emergency calls were handled by the county sheriff's office. The patrol car stopped half way through the declining path to the pier, apparently after noticing the three persons standing around. Two men with guns drawn jumped out.

"Nobody move!" one of them said with a noticeable southern accent. "Come on! Walk away from each other right now. Disperse."

Ken and Robin retreated a few steps. The officer walked slowly towards Helen, whom they had spotted holding the gun.

"Ma'am, don't move. Drop the gun."

Helen dropped the shotgun onto the ground. The gun clattered on the gravel as it hit and rolled down. One of the officers picked it up with his gloved hand. Another patrol car entered the parking area and two more officers got out with guns in hand. Two officers went straight to Ken and Robin.

"You have any guns on you?"

"No."

He frisked them both, while they held their arms up and spread their legs. The officer felt Ken's keys and cell in his pocket and retrieved them. The grotesque figure of the charred body was still burning in a low fire.

"What happened here?" the officer said to Ken.

Ken gave him a brief account of what had happened as Robin sobbed.

"That's an incredible story, son. What is your name?"

"Kenneth O'Gara."

"Can you show me your bike?"

Ken took him behind the store where he and Robin had left their bike that afternoon. In the back, there was a space reserved for two cars, both of which were empty.

"We left it here," Ken said. "We borrowed it this morning from one of the riders in our caravan after ours were tossed in the ocean in Daytona. I feel that they may have done the same with this bike. I'd like to look in the river."

"The river is a pretty big place to look. You're not going to find it in the middle of the night."

"Can I just look here?"

Ken pointed towards the bank and the officer nodded. He strolled towards the river. The water was too dark to see at night, but on the ground he saw the drag of what could have been only a heavy object. He reached the water with the officer behind him and started going in.

"What are you doing?"

"There it is. I see it."

He bumped into it at knee-deep water. He could see the black frame in the water.

"Can I try to pull it out?" Ken said.

"There is going to be an awful lot of stuff to go over. You better leave it until our team gets here. Anytime there's a death, forensics has to be involved. And from what you're telling me, we may have three here. So let's just leave everything where it is for now. Come back. We have to get back to the others."

The parking area was now surrounded by patrol cars, an odd scene in this small country town. Helen was being questioned inside one of the patrol cars. Another officer took Robin aside. Ken was not allowed to talk to her until her questioning was over. The fire department had arrived at the scene and they had quickly put out the fire that was still burning in the three motorcycles. Then one fireman carefully sprayed Margaret's body with foam. Ken took Robin by the hand and moved her away from the scene. She had been through so much in one night. Ken did not know what to say. They stood near the end of the pier, watching the dark water. There were tears in her eyes as she spoke.

"I can't believe she hid it from me," she finally said. "I can't believe it."

Ken did not answer. He did not think it proper for him to render an opinion.

"Do you realize that rubble of ashes out there is my mother's body? She was my real mother and I did not know it. Who knows? If I had known perhaps I would have tried harder to connect."

Ken was looking down, thinking it over until finally he decided to answer.

"And what exactly would you have done Robin?" he finally said. "Join her club and feast over human bodies?"

It was not a pleasant answer to someone who had just learned such a shocking truth. But he thought it would be best to cut off Robin's doubts early or otherwise she would never come back. Margaret had done enough damage already. Robin was just getting over the shock of discovering a secret that Helen had kept from her. Still, none of that vindicated the evil perpetrated by Margaret McCarter and her gang. And Robin had to be reminded of that. Perhaps she would never recover. Perhaps her relationship with Helen would be spoiled forever. Perhaps Robin could never see past the tragic events of this night and condemn Helen as the insensitive perpetrator of death who took her mother's life away. But deep inside, she had to deal with the truth and understand that Margaret was an evil doer at the last second of her life. And as far as her mother responsibilities, she had never shown any traces of it. It had been only by chance that mother and daughter had met. Margaret knew immediately, but even then, she had not done anything to make up for the time lost. Even then, she was not looking after her daughter's best interests. On the contrary, she had sought to draft her into a barbaric cult with alarming views on life and death that bordered on the insane. In the end, Robin would have to realize that Helen McManus had been her only mother who had saved her from a life of misery.

"No, I don't think so," Robin said, staring at the river thoughtfully. "You know, it's funny. She always said that those who live by the sword will die by the sword," Robin said sadly. "Only I never knew what she meant."

* * *

The next morning, Ken and Robin met Ron Mason and several bikers at an isolated bed and breakfast off westbound Route 40. The sheriff had released Ken and Robin late in the morning, but Helen was kept for further questioning. They did not know for how long or what charges would be lodged against her. The two women had not spoken since the incident.

The local sheriff had sent for Ron and some of his riders. The group booked itself for the next night at the facility. Time was needed to connect all the dots and the sheriff had to hear from the patrols from three other states where the other murders had taken place. Because of the interstate connections, the possibility of federal involvement was very high. Ken's cell rang in mid-afternoon. He had not yet called his parents. He waited until the whole affair was wrapped up to tell them so as not to worry them. He recognized his mother's austere voice on the other end.

"Ken, how are you? It's me."

"How are you Mom?"

"Where are you?"

"I'm in Florida, about an hour from Daytona." "Well, I'm afraid your little rendezvous is going to be interrupted."

"What do you mean?"

"I did not want to open the letter but I saw the name of the Prosecutor's Office on the forwarding address and I had to. You're being subpoenaed to testify before a Grand Jury in Pennsylvania. What's all this about, Ken?"

Ken had to reflect for a moment. So many things had happened since then that the memory of that early morning in Lancaster had almost faded. Then it came to him vividly. He had seen Johnny Kelekes batter a hired Mexican hand at a Pennsylvania farm. It had been a senseless attack, unprovoked and unmerciful. When Ken had left the hospital, the injured man had been in ICU but stable. He now wondered.

"Mom, what does it say?"

"It talks about a murder charge, Ken. That's why I'm so concerned."

"Oh, Mom. That means he died. The worker at the Lancaster farm who was assaulted must have died."

"Ken, I don't know what you are talking about, son. What have you gotten yourself involved in?"

"Of course I'm not involved, Mom. But I saw it happen. I was there. That's why I'm being subpoenaed."

There was silence at the other end. Then her voice took on a normal tone.

"Ken, I wish you stopped floating around. I wish you had stayed in one place and settled down. Most of all, I wish you would stay away from motorcycles. You need to come home, Ken. This can't wait. Forget Daytona."

"Actually, Mom, I was planning to leave already. A lot has happened since I left."

"It's getting kind of cold to drive a bike here now, Ken.

You might want to consider taking a bus or flying."

"I'm not riding a bike back, Mom. I'm going back in an SUV."

"How's that?"

"I'll tell you all about it when I get there."

Ken put his phone away. He was now served with the dreadful task of telling Russell that his bike had been found at the bottom of the Withlacoochee River. He braced himself, but Robin saved him.

"You know, Russell, Ken hasn't told you but we found your bike in the bottom of the river last night."

The young man with the curly black hair had a moment of shock, then he quickly recovered. They were all sitting near the pool of the happy yellow inn, surrounded by rooms that fed into the main building. The fall season in the area was nothing more than a mild summer, but there were some signs of faded colors in the leaves of the trees. They all sat in silence, waiting for Russell to react as they listened to the tapping of a restless woodpecker on the bark of a pine tree and the song of mockingbirds in the nearby woods.

"They did it again? Those creeps did it again?"

"They wanted to make sure we had no wheels when we came back," Robin said. "They wanted us caged with no chance of getting away."

"Russell, I feel like it's my responsibility, such an awesome-looking bike. But I'd like to commit myself to rebuilding it, bringing it back. It would be my first rebuild this winter."

"It's fully insured," Russell said. "My insurance should cover it."

"Whether it does or doesn't, I'd like it to be my job, Russell.

I want to be the one to make it new for you. You know, the river water is less damaging to the bike than salt water. The engine would have to be rebuilt, of course, but some of the parts can be saved."

"Where is the bike now?"

"The patrols have it. I'm sure they'll release it eventually. You can bring it up north on the caravan's return and drop it in New York in my parents' home."

"What do you mean? You're not coming with us?"

"I can't. I have to get back to Lancaster. Don't forget, I have no bike."

"As soon as my mother is released," Robin said, "we can all head back up north together. We all need a rest."

Ken felt a deep relief as she said it. So she had decided to make amends with Helen.

"Ron is not going to like it. You're gonna miss the races at the beach. They've already started."

"Russell, we have no bikes of our own."

"So what? Neither do I."

"No, no," Robin said. "We need a breather. We've been through a nightmare."

The next morning, Robin met Helen McManus at the County Sheriff's detention center. The county had decided to release Helen from custody. The two women met in a room reserved normally for attorneys who interviewed inmates. Helen was sitting in one of the Virco Poly chairs, waiting for her final release. As soon as Robin entered the room, she embraced her, and they both cried.

"I promise never to ask you again if you at least tell me how it happened, Mom," Robin said determinedly.

Helen waved for Robin to sit down. Tears were in her eyes. Robin pulled a chair from the table and sat down. The door behind them was locked, but the room was monitored by a guard who maintained watch through a glass window on top. Helen took hold of Robin's hand and pressed it against the table.

"John was the greatest biker that ever lived," she began with watery eyes. "He was so graceful when he rode and could do things with a bike that nobody else could. It came as second nature to him. He was tall and handsome with long brown hair and those same big hazel eyes that you got from him. We were so happy together. We went everywhere together. I always rode with him, and I left everything I owned just to go with him because I loved him so much. We met her on a ride to New York one time. She had a small bike club that joined ours for the trip to the city. She looked fantastic, more beautiful than any other woman I have ever seen. The men worshipped her because of her beauty, but I knew there was something strange about her, something scary, something to do with death. I didn't like it and I told John about it but he laughed at me. I saw the lust in her eyes. She wanted John from the first moment she saw him and she was going to take him from me no matter what. From that very first day, I had no peace. She looked for him everywhere and he gave in. I think she overpowered him with her beauty. It's true, I could have walked away and left him but John was like a battered child with her. He would always come back to me looking for help, feeling depressed and hunted. He was a changed man after he met her. And then one day I discovered that she was going to have his baby and I confronted her. She laughed in my face. She said I could never have John. She said she had made him lose his soul over her and he could never love me. John kept going away with her on trips, and then coming back to me, but as she got advanced in the pregnancy, she could not ride anymore, so he would stay with her more and more. One day, I went to the McCarter house to look for John, and I was horrified by what I saw. There were people sitting in the room eating human flesh and she was conducting the whole thing like it was some kind of a ceremony. John was sitting there, across from them with a cradle on his lap. You were inside, a newborn baby, crying your head off. I had come determined to kill her and had brought a gun with me. I don't think I would have done it anyway but it was the baby that saved me. When I saw that baby crying so desperately among the whole bunch of them, I didn't think about John or her anymore. I pointed the gun at them and I made him give me the baby. All I could think about was how terrible for a child to be exposed to such evil. And I walked away from them in a daze carrying that baby in my arms like it was mine. I had never before held a baby. It wasn't mine but it did not matter to me at that moment. I only thought about saving her from that tragic scene. I took the baby home not knowing what would happen next. That night or the next day nobody came to look for her. No one called. They all knew where I was, of course, but months went by without a word. It was as if they were relieved I had taken the baby. Eventually, John came back but we never had a relationship after that. He would stop to see the baby once in a blue moon. She never came. She never laid eyes on that baby again, never tried. I had my beauty shop to run and it was hard. I did not have any experience raising a   baby and I had no clue as to what to do, but I went about my business of raising her like mothers always do, as if she was my daughter. That was pretty much it for about five years until one day I heard about the crash. He died supposedly in the highway and his body was obliterated, the papers said. I never knew whether she had anything to do with his death. I suspect she did. It was all too much, too painful after that. So I packed my things and grabbed my child. I moved to Cape May with my parents and never looked back. I never saw her again."

She paused, and Robin remained silent for a long time. Helen had told her the story as truthfully as she had lived it. Robin leaned over the table and took her face with both hands.

"Mom, you'll always be my mother."

Just then one officer walked into the room and interrupted them. He handed Helen some papers. There were no formal charges filed against her but she was being subpoenaed by the County Sheriff of Citrus County. The officer led both women outside the facility. Ken was waiting for them in one of the benches past the main door. Ron and several of his riders were there too. They had come to spend the day interviewing with the County Sheriff. The Sheriff allowed them to take Russell's bike. It was adeptly placed inside Dave's van, as it had been before during the run. Ken, Robin and Helen got inside their black SUV, with Ken behind the wheel, followed by a trail of bikes and the pickup, triggering the curiosity of onlookers along the road who stopped their vehicles to watch them go by. The sound of the Harley's engines left them with an unsettling feeling of joy and anger at the same time. Here was this gang that had temporarily disrupted their lives and now went away as if they did not have a care in the world.

The group turned east on 40. Helen's SUV broke off from them at the intersection with 75, where they went north on that highway. They were looking for Route 10 to connect them to Route 95 for the long trip north. Ken stayed behind the wheel for most of the way while Robin and Helen kept quiet, holding hands and at times crying on each other's shoulders.

"A person without a soul is meaningless," Helen said at one point. "It has no life to speak of. When we lose our souls we lose our conscience and our purpose for living. Human beings are not meant to be that way."

She traded looks with Ken, knowing too well that neither he nor Robin understood any of it. She imagined they would think it was pure superstition.

Robin fell asleep leaning on her shoulder. She dreamed that her father had been a dexterous, skilled young man like Ken.

An adventuresome and restless man who loved to ride and did not compromise freedom for fame or money. Such a man had been married once to Helen McManus and he had made her his rider, his companion. The two had gone far into the sunset, chased rainbows, and found happiness. She chose to stop the dream there. Perhaps she could do that with Ken.

***

Several weeks later, a tall young man with well-defined shoulders, a boyish-looking face, and straight black hair was driving a New York-licensed pickup on the New Jersey State Parkway, heading south. It was now late November, one day before Thanksgiving, and the weather was cold, bottoming on the high thirties. It was too frigid to ride a bike, so he bungeed a blue Harley Sportster in the back of the Chevy pickup he had borrowed from his parents. He had put the bike together himself from scrap pieces that he collected during escapades from his main job of rebuilding Russell's FLHXI Street Glider. Russell had been polite but insistent. His bike was now almost all done except for the new engine that had not yet been delivered because of red tape with the insurance company. If the engine had been available, Ken could have had the bike done by now, but such were the politics with the insurance companies. The day before he had applied the last touches to the blue Sportster. There was no insurance involved in this project so he worked steadily as he collected the parts. And he wasted no time to get an engine that fit the old frame he had himself re-built. The rest came from wrecks he had plundered in various motorcycle shops. He had traveled as far as northern New York for some parts but enjoyed the project. He had tested the engine in the morning, taking it for a ride. He wished he could have ridden the Sportster on the parkway today. It was his favorite road, especially as it went past central Jersey. Only a few days ago, he had driven through it on his way to the Pennsylvania turnpike for his appearance before the Grand Jury in Lancaster. The road was smooth all over, great for motorcycle riding. The traffic was light this afternoon. The scenery was fantastic. The foliage had changed to a brown and tan assortment of leaves that showed fall had unmistakably arrived. He kept thinking about how far he had yet to go. He had never before traveled to the end of the Parkway although he had practically been raised exploring its beginning near the Washington Heights area at the New York boundary line. He had always wondered if there was an end to the road. Today he would see it. His thoughts traveled, and he marveled at the person for whom he had built the Sportster. It was to be a surprise. She was not expecting it. Ken had thought about her much in the past few days, not as a friend or a lover, but as a wife. He imagined how she could change his life. He would cease being what his mother called "the drifter in the family" and become a family man. But he knew it would be different with Robin. She was adventurous like him. She wouldn't mind if he worked on a farm, as he loved to do, or if he decided to open a shop and build bikes. She would support him either way. And when summer came, the two would go on long trips, testing their resoluteness and hunger for discovery. Yeah, it would be nice. With Robin there would not be a dull moment. *The Lord had provided*, he thought. *The Lord always does.*

It was still light out but overcast when he saw the green sign indicating the parkway had ended. It was the notorious exit 0, as referred to by riders. Ken had a funny feeling as if he had reached the end of the world. He laughed at himself for thinking that. He remembered the directions Robin had given him and he got on Lafayette. He spotted the street name he was looking for and turned, moving east, then made several other turns, passing near the historic section of town and heading towards the harbor. He found the street, looking quaint with rows of maple trees in different shades of colors. He slowed the pickup down and checked his directions. He pulled near the driveway of a Victorian-looking house with long black double shutters and colonial white windows. He went to the rear of the pickup and rolled it down over a flat plank he placed against the bed. He rolled the bike to the driveway, behind the black SUV. He released the bike's kickstand and knocked on the back door as he had been instructed to do.

The girl who opened looked stunningly beautiful. Robin's brown hair was unfastened over her shoulders. She was dressed in Chadwick cropped chino pants and a long black silk tunic. Her hazel eyes sparkled as she smiled and kissed him.

"Welcome to Cape May," she said chirpily.

"Glad to be here," he replied. "I brought something for you."

"What?" she said, holding onto his shoulder.

"Come outside. You'll need a coat though. It's cold." She rushed past him at the sight of the shining blue Sportster parked in her driveway.

"Ken, how did you do it? Where did you get it from?"

"I got a mental picture of it from a girl I saw riding it once. I copied it."

"Ken, it's amazing! It looks just like my bike! Mom! Mom! Come outside to see this!"

Helen McManus looked impressively elegant, although she was still wearing a waist-high white beautician's gown under a blue jacket. She smiled when she saw Ken.

"Oh, my!" she exclaimed. "Ken, that looks just like Robin's bike."

"I built it for Robin."

He stood by the door as the two women paced around the bike, admiring it.

"It's marvelous," Helen said. "Ken, it looks exactly like Robin's old bike."

Robin went to stand by him and held his hand.

"Come inside you two. It's cold," Helen said. "I'll make something for you."

They sat at the kitchen table talking about some of the old homes in town. There was a newspaper lying in the middle of the table. What drew Ken's attention to it was the quote under the heading, declaring it Central Jersey's most thorough news. He wondered how a newspaper from that area of the State could have made its way to Cape May, the most southern part of New Jersey. A small article on a narrow left-hand column jumped at him, and he couldn't help but read its heading. "McCarter house burned to the ground. A valuable piece of history is lost forever. Fire blamed on a faulty electric circuit."

He listened attentively as Robin told him about Cape May's bed and breakfast homes, beautiful houses dating back to the American Revolution days that had survived the test of time and still catered to the public. Helen brought two steaming mugs of hot chocolate and laid them on the table.

"Your favorite drink, you kids," she said.

They both smiled at each other as they took a sip.

"I wonder how the old people harvested in this area back then," Ken wondered out loud. "You're so close to the ocean. I can't imagine the land being very fertile here."

"Oh, yes. This was farm country back in the revolution days," Helen said. "The early settlers liked it here because it was close to the ocean but they did their farming nearby too."

"Really? What crops?"

"Oh, I don't know, honey. I'd lie if I said lettuce or cucumbers, although I'd probably be right. Who knows? Maybe you should start a harvest. I heard you're pretty good at that. Would you like to be a Cape May farmer?"

She turned to the stove to pour herself a cup of coffee.

Ken took another sip of his hot chocolate and smiled slyly at Robin. For a second, their thoughts blended together. They both knew there could only be one answer to Helen McManus' question.

www.ingramcontent.com/pod-product-compliance
Lightning Source LLC
LaVergne TN
LVHW021757060526
838201LV00058B/3140